REPRESSION

MORRIGAN ELLIS

REPRESSION

MORRIGAN ELLIS

WICKED INK
PUBLISHING

Repression
Copyright © 2025 by Morrigan Ellis

Published by Wicked Ink Publishing Ltd.
www.wickedinkpublishing.com

Cover and book design © 2025 by Wicked Ink Publishing Ltd.
Editors: Raymond Griffiths & Adam Bamford

First Edition: October 2025
Printed in Canada

Library and Archives Canada Cataloguing in Publication

Title: Repression / Morrigan Ellis.
Names: Ellis, Morrigan, author.
Identifiers: Canadiana (print) 20250259559
Canadiana (ebook) 20250264978
ISBN 9781998278275 (softcover)
ISBN 9781998278282 (EPUB)
Subjects: LCGFT: Horror fiction. | LCGFT: Novels.
Classification: LCC PS8609.L567 R46 2025 | DDC C813/.6—dc23

For Colten: kite and string.

REPRESSION

MORRIGAN ELLIS

We fear what goes bump in the night, but the real monster is what creeps inside.

PROLOGUE
MAY 1999

THE BATTERED DOOR ON THE YELLOW BUS SQUEAKED and slammed shut behind him as it spit him out in front of the high school. He hated getting off here, but it was the closest stop to his house.

The sidewalk was full of kids who were impossibly enormous. He felt so awkward these days, gangly, like his limbs didn't quite fit. His mom thought he was going to be tall one day, but he couldn't imagine his tiny frame bending and stretching into the shapes of these giants that blocked out the bright blue sky.

There was another entire year before he would even go there, and he was already nervous. Pushing his way through the crowd, he kept his eyes pinned firmly on the ground, trying to be as inconspicuous as possible. The hum of excited voices faded behind him, and he could finally relax.

He barely paused on the sidewalk to look both ways, then jogged across the street. He walked past front lawns with sprinklers running, making lazy arcs and raining droplets on colourful toys that were abandoned for the offer of an afternoon snack. The last month of school brought the promise of summer, and he even saw an inflatable pool or two. Sweating under the unusually hot May sun, he fanned his t-shirt to cool himself.

He slowed to a walk as he reached the yawning mouth of the alley. While the street seemed to welcome passersby, the alley narrowed its eyes and told them to mind their own business.

High chain-link fences and tall shrubs sprinkled among wooden slats of varying paint colours stood tall on either side, as if even the houses didn't want to know what might happen right beside them. Many of the fences swelled outward into the alley, the hedges lining the inside of the yards struggling to break free.

Shrugging his backpack onto one shoulder, he slung it forward and dug to the bottom, coming up with a crinkled old paperback. His school's logo was stamped haphazardly over the edge of the pages in faded blue ink. He flicked his head to the side in irritation, tossing his dark, sweat-damp hair out of his brown eyes as he entered.

Dappled sunlight filled the alleyway, but he was disappointed to find the measly shade provided by the tall trees and fences offered little respite from the heat. Ahead of him, sunlight illuminated the curve of the cul-de-sac he lived on.

Cheerful, open front yards sat on either side, the dual carpets of green grass a beacon that lit the way home. The wood and paint changed as he passed each house, and he absently counted as he walked. A peeling red fence was coming up, which he knew from countless passages meant he had five more houses to go before he emerged at the top of his block.

Turning his attention to the last page of the novel in his hands, he sighed in dramatic despair. He put off reading it for English class, and now it was crunch time. Reading was fun, but everyone in his class was saying this one sucked. There was a pile of stuff from the library he actually wanted to read. Plus, his mom just bought a bunch of videos at a garage sale and he was dying to watch them over the weekend. She worked the night shift, and probably wouldn't notice if he left it for just one more day.

Maybe tomorrow, he decided, shoving the book all the way to the bottom of his bag. The end of the school year was for dreaming of vacation, not for thinking about homework.

Before he zipped his bag back up, he pulled out a plastic water bottle, humming as he took a swig of the lukewarm liquid. It dripped from the leaky lid and splattered against his too warm jeans, the flimsy plastic crinkling under his grip. Unsatisfied, he ruffled his shirt once again, focusing on thoughts of the cool basement that awaited him just down the street.

A car rumbled behind him. Without turning around, he moved to the side of the alley, speeding up slightly to bypass one of the trash cans that lined the wooden fences. Everyone was getting ready for garbage day and trash overflowed, escaping from beneath hot metal lids. The sharp tang of rot cut its way through his good mood and he wrinkled his nose as he passed.

As he raised his hand to wave the car by, it smashed into him from behind.

He barely had time to register he was in the air before he crashed back down to the hard ground. A terrible crunching sound drowned out the sudden ringing in his ears. The momentum of the fall carried him back toward the fence and he came to rest on his side.

The world blurred even further as his face pressed against the unforgiving pavement. His eyes roamed wildly, blinking as the blood dripped into them from his hair. The odour of the steaming garbage rolled over him, and he tried to push himself up to move away, but found he couldn't make his body cooperate.

That was when he panicked, blood oozing between his teeth and falling from his lips as he gasped and wheezed.

The car door opened and slow, even footsteps cut through the sudden silence. He thought it was strange he didn't feel relief, just a cold sense of dread as they drew closer, getting louder with every step.

SEPTEMBER 2014
WELCOME HOME

1

Nat swept her wet hair up in a towel and stretched, wincing and rubbing at her shoulder through her flannel pyjamas. The hot shower eased some of the stiffness from a day of unpacking, but a dull ache remained.

She cursed as she caught her toe on a heavy box in the hallway. Grunting, she picked it up and hauled it into the spare room, placing it next to her small desk in the corner. She pushed her hands into the small of her back, twisting to stretch as she stood. Catching movement in the corner of her eye, she stopped.

The curtains rustled, and a furry brown tail peeked out before dipping back behind the hefty beige fabric. She crossed the room, yanking the shiny polyester and making a mental note to add it to her wish list of *"landlord special"* items she would eventually replace.

"There you are!" she said to her tabby, Chaos.

He was fat and old, and she loved him to death. She chuckled as he glared at her in that disdainful way that only cats could, his playground now ruined.

Staring through the cold glass of the French doors to the

porch beyond, she idly thought of some patio furniture she might treat herself to in the spring. The deck was newer than the rest of the house, a simple pine structure overlooking an equally basic but immaculately kept yard. The back yard was massive, a genuine surprise given the small size of the house.

The doors had the look of a cage, constructed with beautiful tiny panels of glass the size of coasters. Despite the cage they formed, the glass left her feeling exposed, the darkness of the yard hiding any threats that could watch her in the well-lit room. Shivering, she pulled the floor length curtain shut again. The stainless-steel rings screeched against the cheap black rod above, but there was another quality to the sound. She paused for a moment, straining to listen.

Something was outside, scraping against the wood of the porch.

She focused on her breathing, her fingers reaching out to spread open a small crack in the fabric to let her peek outside. The cold radiated off the glass, kissing her face as she leaned in. Steeling herself, she flipped the switch to the left of the doors, throwing a spotlight on the pine slats.

The light illuminated a tiny circle, just enough that you could see to the low railing at the edge of the wooden deck. A small patio table, filthy with decades of weather, teetered slightly on its uneven legs in a sudden breeze. The wind stilled, and the night held its breath with her, the silence unbearable as her lungs burned.

She was about to turn off the light when the scraping came again.

Scraaaaaaattttttcccchhhhhhhhhhh.

It was drawn out. A murderer's knife pressed to the porch and pulled in slow, agonizing patience, daring her to ignore it. Heart pounding, she waited for the sound to come again. After a long silence, she finally retreated from the curtains, the old floors creaking beneath her feet.

Shaking her head, she tried to let it go, adding it to the inventory of strange noises she heard today. Rustling, clanging, scratching, it was always brief, over even as she stopped to figure out where it was coming from.

She was used to living in places with neighbours on all sides, yelling and laughing, going about the noisy business of living. Something about these noises unsettled her, intentional and amplified, as if every sound that creaked through this house was a secret meant specifically for her ears.

You're being ridiculous.

A quiet evening in an unfamiliar house could be nerve-wracking. If she wanted a fresh start, she needed to get out of her head and stop treating each step like it was a test she was constantly failing.

It's been so long since you had to get used to a new place alone, she thought, trying to cut herself some slack.

Despite the self-assurance, heat rose in her chest, shame fluttering up and through her body. She felt un-feminist, like she falsified her qualifications as an independent woman.

She thought moving back to her hometown after all this time might feel familiar, more comfortable somehow, but she was on edge. Every little creak and groan was magnified.

In a few weeks time, these would be familiar bedtime sounds that would fade into the white noise soundtrack of her life.

Right now, however, they were the strides of the boogeymen and homicidal maniacs patiently waiting for her to turn out the lights and let the party begin.

Leaving the room without looking back, she flipped off the lights behind her and moved down the short hallway to the kitchen. The hall closet door hung open, overflowing with balled up linens thrown haphazardly inside.

She pressed it firmly shut as she passed, feeling the cheap, hollow door complaining as it bulged. Surveying the boxes still piled in the living room, she dropped her hands to her sides, her body telling her she was at her limit for the day.

Entering the kitchen, she glanced at the clock on the stove, a pang of guilt flashing through her as she realized how late it was. The landlord told her she didn't have to worry about noise on moving day, but she was sure that given he was right below her in the basement suite, he would appreciate her calling it quits. He was shy, and silent, the type to seethe to a boiling point rather than say something about a nuisance. When she first met him, he kept his eyes fixed firmly on the ground.

"Just slide the cheques under the door," he mumbled when she asked how she should pay.

Fine by me, she thought.

The adjoining door in the kitchen was the only thing that separated them, and Nat backed away from it now, as if he could hear her thoughts.

She grabbed the kettle from the electric coil on the stovetop, yawning as she held it under the tap. Water splashed up and over her hand, soaking her sleeve. Flinching at the feel of the wet fabric against her skin, she went in search of a mug, opening and shutting the cupboard doors in quick succession. Her enthusiasm for most things to do with the kitchen and organization was thin at best, so she wasn't shocked to find the location wasn't intuitive.

Regretting her choice to unpack this room as quickly as possible by shoving things into the closest available cabinet, she stood on tiptoes, grunting as she reached behind the other dishes in a high cupboard. She stretched her fingers stiffly ahead, tense, as if attempting to divine the location of her cups. She fell back on her heels and took a deep breath, trying to find a meditative moment in a long and stressful day.

Finally, discovering the mugs in a floor-level cupboard beneath the cutlery drawer, she placed her favourite on the counter and smiled at the happy looking, hand-painted flowers. She moved the rest of the mugs to the first cupboard she had looked in and then stood tapping one hand on a flannel-clad leg as the water spat inside the kettle.

Wandering idly into the living room, she grabbed a handful of books from an open box nearby.

A giant area rug with some padding underneath covered most of the wooden floor, an attempt to keep some noise out of the basement. A wide strip of bare wood remained around the perimeter of the room. The bedrooms, bathroom and kitchen were all small, but the living room was comparatively large and open. During the day, it was filled with an abundance of light from a large front window overlooking the entire cul-de-sac.

The hardwood moaned loudly under her feet as she stood the books on the next empty shelf in the middle of the bookcase. She winced, hoping the smallest of steps wouldn't cause noise complaints from below in the future.

A thud erupted behind her, and she gasped, jumping out of her skin.

She whirled around, only to look right into Chaos' yellow, mischievous eyes. During the day, he was mostly unimpressed with her, but at night he was very welcome company.

Especially tonight.

The shrill whistle of the kettle caused her to startle again, and she rushed to snap off the burner. The sudden silence that followed the scream made her uneasy, and she hummed brokenly to fill the quiet.

She tried to laugh it off as she dropped a tea bag in her mug and drowned it in hot water.

Don't be a wimp, she thought, as her hand hovered in indecision over the living room light switch. *Too many horror novels before bed.*

Since no one was around to see, she casually curled her

hand around the other side of her mug instead of reaching for the switch. Her palm sweat against the ceramic curve as she padded down the hall to the bedroom with the light still glowing behind her.

As she placed her steaming cup on the nightstand, she caught her reflection in the window at the head of her bed. Instead of pretending she had any energy left, she grabbed a paperback from the bag she slung onto an armchair in the corner and turned on her bedside lamp.

Clothes littered the overstuffed seat beside an empty canvas hamper, and she snorted at how quickly her resolution to keep organized and tidy imploded. Giving her hair one last rub, she tossed the towel heavily into the pile of tomorrow's worries.

She crawled into bed, shoving away the creeping self-loathing that filled her as she caught herself sticking to her former side of the mattress. The sheets chilled her through her pajamas.

Determined to remember the move was supposed to be about more than just a change of locale, she pursed her lips and shuffled under the sheets to the middle of the bed. Arms spread like she was getting ready to make a snow angel, she ran her hands along the pillows on either side. She wiggled her toes and stretched, the bulky duvet settling over her feet. The pocked tile ceiling filled her view as she took a deep breath, angrily fighting the tears welling up in her green eyes.

Fuck that.

She punched the pillows aggressively and propped herself up to read, trying to lose herself in the book. The odd little tap came from the hallway or bathroom as the house settled in for the night.

A few pages later, an unmistakable thump sounded down the hall from the living room. She did what people were supposed to do and told herself it was the cat.

Cats are convenient that way, she thought.

A heavier thunk rattled the walls, accompanied by the faint tinkling of glass.

She put the book down, craning her neck toward the door. "Chaos?" she called.

She expected to hear the determined padding of his furry feet moving toward her, excited by the prospect of an ear scratch or two before curling up next to her warm body. She jerked and turned her head as the clothes on the chair rustled, pedalling her feet to push herself up in the bed.

Chaos was curled up precariously on the mountain of laundry. His ears were alert, eyes round and body tense as he concentrated on the bedroom doorway into the hall. She always left her door open at night so he could wander in at his leisure, a decision she was now regretting.

Body suddenly warm with adrenaline, she realized she was holding her breath. Chaos turned his gaze to her, looking for guidance.

The sting of solitude felt acute once more as she realized it was on her to get up and check for serial killers from now on.

The duvet was no longer comforting, its weight pressing heavily down on her as she lifted it, the sound amplified. What was cozy and comforting a moment ago felt oppressive now, as if she was held hostage under the blanket's weight. Every minor movement felt sure to attract whatever made its way into her new residence. She grabbed her phone and swiped at the screen as she moved, somehow unlocking it on the first try despite her shaky hands.

She stood in the doorway for a moment, hearing nothing in the hall. She turned toward the room across from her. The door remained open, darkness spilling out and overpowering the light from the hall that tried to reach inside. She thought of the clawing under the deck, and breathed heavily as the darkness crawled, forming itself into the outline of whatever she imagined might have broken the glass and crept inside.

THUMP.

Her head snapped to the right, toward the living room. Moving into the hallway, she cringed as the old, chilly parquet groaned. The floor seemed to sink slightly under her weight and she hurried on the balls of her feet, overwhelmed by the sudden sensation that it would suck her down into the dark if she rested too long. She leaned forward as she moved, straining to hear. The silence was deafening, rife with nightmares.

Another step and she could see around the corner. Holding her breath, she lunged forward, tightening her grip as her phone threatened to slide across her clammy palm.

The stack of books she propped there earlier rested in a scattered pile, sliding against each other as they fell into a heap. Chaos followed and rubbed at her legs. She heaved as she lifted him and kissed his face in relief, much to his disgust.

"Fashionably late, as always," she muttered into his fur.

She was about to head back to the bedroom when she glimpsed at something shiny on the floor; the light catching it as she moved. A few stray pieces of glass lay scattered across the warm tones of the checkered wood. She followed the trail to a black picture frame laying face down on the ground.

Where did this come from? She didn't unpack her knickknacks or photos yet, and she squatted to reach it over the glass, puzzled.

She flipped it over, and Chris grinned up at her.

She loved this photo. Chris was in the middle, sandwiched between Nat and her best friend, Meg. Their hair was windblown, cheeks rosy with exertion from their hike. Huddled around a disposable camera before cell phones or selfie sticks ruled life, they managed to capture the picture with a single shot. It was nothing short of a miracle that this picture turned out as good as it did.

Chris was the classic little brother with a shit-disturbing grin, his dark curls frozen in a windblown position. His eyes crinkled at the sides, so much like her own it hurt when she smiled. Chris never smiled if he didn't mean it with his whole heart, and this photo was no exception. Capturing him in all his happy glory was special to her all these years later, his freckled face lit from within, proof that her memory of this moment hadn't been tainted by time.

The lake stretched out far behind them with nothing but full trees and a small strip of jagged beach on the other side. It was her favourite view, one of the few spots where the scenery wasn't marred by vacation homes. The rocky beach deterred the tourists and investors with the money to build a mansion just so their kids had somewhere to swim in the summer.

Gathering her broom and dustpan from a corner of the dining room, she swept up the shards of glass, trying to figure out how the photo ended up in the living room.

Nat remembered finding it deep with her closet when she packed, smiling briefly as she wiped dust from the frame with a corner of her t-shirt. If it existed in the age of social media, Meg would have been all over it. Nat could picture the post: *Nat and Meg and Chris conquer the world!* Meg always captioned her posts as if they were children's book titles.

Nat distinctly recalled wrapping it in a little-used blanket, hoping it would be out of sight, out of mind for a little while. She would have to face it eventually, but it wasn't the time to get lost in the memories. Not yet.

Sliding the photo from the frame and placing it on the counter, she turned her attention to aggressively tapping the dust pan against the rim of the trash bin under the kitchen sink.

Clean up completely, she braced herself with both hands against the counter, looking down at the image, the only salvageable piece from the mess. Her fingers reached out to touch a corner of the picture and pulled back as if she was afraid it would burn.

"How did you get here?" she murmured as she gazed at the smiling faces of three kids who had no idea what was still to come.

What makes you think anyone wants you back here?

The now familiar cocktail of guilt and regret bubbled inside her, almost playful, enjoying itself and taking its time as it slowly spread throughout her body. She stiffened, trying not to let it in.

I can't make it the way it was. That ship had sailed, and she wasn't so sure she deserved a second chance.

She studied her own smile in the photograph. There wasn't a hint of the anxiety she knew was there below the surface. Hiding it was an art form for her by now. Even looking back at this memento, she could almost convince herself she'd been completely carefree then.

Less than a year after this was taken, Chris was gone and her already precarious grip on the world vanished. Pretending didn't seem worth it after that, and she cringed at the thought of how she left things with her parents.

Last spring marked fifteen years since it happened. Time stretched, and the anniversary suddenly seemed so enormous, so much harder to ignore than the previous fourteen.

In one swift and decisive movement, she opened her newly designated junk drawer below the picture on the counter and swept it inside. By the time she finished unpacking, the faces in the drawer would be covered with batteries, pens, miscellaneous Allen keys, and various half-used rolls of tape.

Legs shaking, she returned to her bedroom. Sleep wasn't coming anytime soon, so she picked up her paperback again, determined to make the most of the night. The glory of living alone was supposed to be doing what you want, when you want. Walk around naked. Eat peanut butter right from the jar. Read all night.

She grabbed her tea, hoping to warm up. It was freezing in the bedroom at the back of the house. The crisp fall air that she loved so much always betrayed her at night. Taking a sip, she recoiled in surprise as ice cold liquid grazed her lips.

How is that possible? She must have been reading longer than she thought. Chaos jumped up onto the bed, chirping in solidarity.

"Hey, buddy. You nervous, too?"

Weaving back and forth across the bed, he tried to find the perfect spot to settle. His eyes remained huge instead of blinking into relaxation as he curled up to rest at her feet. The wind picked up outside, leaves rustling as if the trees lining the backyard were trying to shake them off.

She twisted her neck toward a tap at the window, chastising herself once she took in the tree branches outside the glass. They needed a trim, and she recalled the hasty promise to get that done when she signed the lease. It was probably a red flag, already a promise to fix something broken, but the rest of the yard was so neatly kept that she didn't push it.

The logical explanation for this latest noise left her feeling somewhat calmer, and she snuggled deeper into the warm, thick blankets. Chaos' head snapped toward her and he rose to his feet, arching his back in a long stretch before moving to her face. She braced herself for a soft, fuzzy head butting firmly into her cheek. Instead, he streaked past her face to stand with his feet against the headboard, trying to get a good look out the window into the yard. He stretched one paw out cautiously to the glass as the branches scratched against it. She turned onto her side, away from him, not wanting to entertain the thought that it sounded like something else tapping.

Something that insisted on being invited in.

Chris was walking ahead of her in the distance, a well-trodden dirt path beneath their feet as they made their way through dense woods. They were wearing the same clothes as in the photo. Turning to look at Nat over his shoulder, he smiled in surprise, but didn't speak. He seemed to be waiting for someone. Footsteps drew his eyes away from hers, and he watched the point ahead of them where the path turned around the mountain.

They watched as a woman approached, jogging up the path with a determined stride. She wore her blonde hair high on her head, dishevelled and sweaty.

She drew closer and closer, rhythmic steps slapping against the packed dirt that Nat could have set a clock to. The world around them fell into unnatural silence, the chirping birds and crackle of pine needles fading as the sound of the woman's running shoes hitting the forest floor took over. Each one pounded into Nat, rattling her chest. She raised her hands to her ears and turned to ask Chris what was happening.

He was gone, the surrounding woods suddenly sinister without his familiar presence.

Darkness descended rapidly as the woman drew closer. Nat took in her bright leggings and sports bra under a baggy, off-the-shoulder sweatshirt. It appeared out of place, with a defunct logo on it she recognized from her high school years. The problem wasn't the logo; it was the vinyl of the image itself. It was pristine, not a single crack or crumble belying its age. A small violet-coloured pack rested over the runner's shoulder, strapped tightly across her chest. The woman raised her hand and pushed foam-covered headphones down from her ears to hang around her neck as she reached Nat.

Jogging in place, she took Nat in appraisingly. Her eyes were bright blue, intense, and Nat felt a violent shock of recognition. There was something between them, something that she couldn't place. Whatever it was, it was powerful.

It was not to be ignored.

The jogger broke eye contact with Nat and moved past her, staring into the distance as if watching for a storm.

Nat followed, and the woman turned to face her again, jerky movements rotating her neck. Horrified, Nat watched as blood bloomed across the woman's chest, spreading languidly across the nostalgic design. It dripped down her arms, soaking through the grey fabric of her sweatshirt to drain in rivulets over her hands, raining softly onto the dirt from her fingertips. Nat backed away, but couldn't turn her head, couldn't tear her gaze away from the intense stare filled with longing and frustration. The bright colour of her clothes faded, dirt obscuring the once pristine design, and Nat looked up to take in her watery eyes and downturned mouth.

What are you trying to tell me?

She gave Nat a welcoming smile, as if she was waiting for her for a long time. Her skin rippled suddenly, flesh pulsing and loosening on her face as the smile faded. The fresh, bright tone of her cheeks paled, and then became ashen.

"Who are you?" Nat asked.

The woman opened her mouth as though to speak, but no sound emerged. A raspy gust of stale breath escaped her lips, followed by a large millipede. Nat recoiled as an endless parade of black, squirming legs tickled its way across the greying flesh of the jogger's cheeks. Those bright, piercing eyes looked at Nat as if they had a secret before they glazed over. The irises rolled backward into her skull, pure white, devoid of humanity, replacing the depth of sadness Nat had seen there.

The runner's face shrank in on itself as the smell of rot mixed with the mildewy fragrance of the damp leaves at their feet. Nat shrieked as a spider made its way from behind one deflating eyeball. She turned to run, but the woman grabbed her face, caked earth from her thumbs spreading across Nat's lips as her fingernails dug painfully into each cheek.

The woman smiled again, her grin widening to a clownish size before Nat realized her lips were melting away, exposing teeth and decaying gums. Her clothing rustled as she deteriorated, becoming baggy on the frame beneath as mud-covered bone emerged.

Wake up, Nat commanded herself in the dream. The earth sucked at Nat's ankles and she stumbled backward to escape. Tree roots climbed her legs tenderly, trying to convince her to stay.

Nat's eyes remained frozen open, unable to shut out the world around her as the smooth tentacles continued their upward climb. Dirt filled her mouth, and she felt herself being lifted, painfully making her way back into wakefulness with lead limbs. The skeleton was flaking apart and crumbling, bits of bone and desiccated skin littered among the pinecones.

The forest floor gave way to the dark green carpet in her bedroom, the moon now cheerful around the stars in the night sky above her new backyard. As Nat kicked her way to the surface, the gaunt and skeletal face peering in her bedroom window finally disintegrated.

On her first night alone, Nat woke up screaming.

2

Hi, Meg. Just wanted to let you know I've moved back to town.

When the message first came in, Meg flipped the phone over, slamming it harder than she intended onto her desk. Doing her best to pretend it didn't exist, she continued checking her schedule for the next week, absently making notes on a yellow legal pad. Her hand was steady, but her breath was shaking, and she watched the phone as if it were an explosive device.

She told herself to relax, that it was probably just a courtesy, something to send her before the parental rumour mill started churning. She pictured Nat's sullen expression as she typed the message, praying it would go no further than that.

Ignore it.

A week later, Meg still hadn't responded, but she went back to the message, over and over, running her hand through her hair as she thought about how she would answer if it was genuine.

Then one day, her opportunity appeared, as if she willed it into being.

I'd really like to see you. The second message glared up at her. *If you're up for it?*

The text on the screen dared her to reply, to unleash it all. Holding the screen between her hands, she thought of the worst of her imagined replies, the ones that would cut as deep as the wound that Nat's absence left.

Sure, I'd like that, was what she typed instead.

Even as she typed, she thought of the million ways this moment would replay in her head. The "should have" possibilities, an endless torture on sleepless nights for years to come.

Great! The response came immediately. *How about Thursday? Coffee or tea?*

It felt like she was being invited for a lunch break with a new co-worker. The clinical exchange made it feel like none of it ever happened, like they never shared a secret, never hopped a fence after curfew, never held each other while Nat cried herself to sleep.

Tea, she said, detached, not wanting to offer Nat more than she was willing to give.

The reply came almost immediately. *610 Pine Drive. See you soon!*

Meg sighed, burdened with the confirmation that they were now strangers. *Is there any way we can come back from this?*

Now parked in Nat's driveway, she still didn't have an answer to the question. Pulling up her messages to make sure she had the right address, Meg tried to summon the willpower to get out of her car. As she lingered over the text on her screen, she wondered for the thousandth time whether coming to see Nat was the best idea.

Slipping her phone into her bag, she took a moment to collect herself, tightening her grip on the steering wheel. Dark hair cascaded over her shoulders as she pulled her ponytail down, examining herself in her visor mirror. Her dark hair, brown eyes and olive skin were the opposite of Nat's fair features, but they were opposites for more than that.

Meg knew the contrast ran deeper than just looks, though. A people-pleaser to her core, Nat wanted her parents to think she was the popular kid. She wanted Chris to think she was happy and wanted Meg to think she was put together.

Meg wondered if Nat figured out who she was after she left. Giving her hair one last shake, she took a deep breath, feeling like she was about to head into a job interview.

A man came into view as she snapped her visor shut, watching her from the side of the house. He caught her eye and moved to adjust the lid on one of the trash cans tucked against the pebbly stucco of the carport. The movements were unnatural, stilted, like he was trying to look like he was taking out the garbage instead of actually doing it.

Nosy roommate?

"Hi," she said, stepping out of her vehicle. "Am I alright to park here, or..."

He nodded. "Yep."

"Thanks."

As she went up the chipped cement steps, she sensed his eyes on her. Music came from inside, a local radio station blaring classic rock on tinny speakers. Suddenly conscious of her clothing, she hastily removed her navy blazer.

The door opened before she could knock. Nat smiled, stepping aside to let her in. Arms dangling awkwardly at their sides, they both tried to figure out the new dynamic, neither sure if they should go in for a hug. Nat still hunched slightly in self-consciousness of her height. Meg's gaze drifted to Nat's hands. The skin around her thumbs was already red and raw, and she continued to pick at them, a nervous habit Meg remembered from their youth. She appeared tired, shadows smudged under her eyes.

"I'll get the tea," Nat said, granting them a reprieve as she moved into the kitchen.

"How do you take it?" she called, cups clattering around the question.

"A little milk, please."

Meg put down her bag and coat, slipping off her shoes on the light blonde flooring before wandering into the living room to inspect the bookshelves lining the far wall. An eclectic book collection filled the bookcases, with knick-knacks and mementos littering the crammed shelves in no particular order. A plastic glow-in-the-dark mouse had a place of honour next to a beautiful antique snow globe. None of this should have worked, but it did.

It was just so...Nat.

A swell of emotion threatened to knock her back, thoughts and memories intertwining to leave her reeling.

Has she changed at all?

The closing of the refrigerator door brought Meg back to herself, conscious of how much time passed without either of them saying a word.

"Your neighbour sure gave me a weird vibe," Meg blurted, needing to break the ice, not to launch right into awkward small talk when Nat came back into the room.

"Who?" The sound of the blinds snapping up drifted in from the kitchen, followed by hasty footsteps outside and the slamming of a door below.

"Oh. Yeah. That's Brian. He's a little strange, but he's quiet. Doesn't hassle me much. He's my landlord, actually. Lives in the basement."

"Does that bother you? I'd feel a little weird if my landlord was living with me, like..." *I was a kid again*.

"I'd have to be really careful what I did all the time," Meg finished, making her way to the couch.

"Nah," Nat came into the room, the word muffled around a bag of cookies she clenched in her teeth. She carried a tray with a teapot and two cups with some milk in the bottom.

"I don't mind," she said nonchalantly as she placed the tray on the coffee table. As she placed the snacks alongside it, she showed a nervous grin.

"He seems harmless enough. Just sort of socially awkward. Besides, I got a great deal on rent." Her mouth twisted uncomfortably. "The old neighbourhood is way too rich for my blood."

Meg pictured all the long bus rides she had taken to school back then. The bagged lunches she brought were soggy and warm well before noon, while Chris and Nat walked to the café down the block to buy a hot meal most days. She peered over her shoulder as Nat settled herself on the sofa, gesturing to the crammed shelves.

"This looks more like the old you."

"What do you mean?" Nat asked.

"It's just so...clean in here."

Nat laughed, and Meg shook her head at a comment that suddenly seemed deeply personal. "I mean, it just doesn't feel lived in yet. All of this...it's more personal, I guess."

Nat busied herself with the sugar, scooping some into her cup.

Meg thought of how this would have gone if they were back before everything went so wrong. The conversation would be lovingly chaotic, seemingly with no start or end, no explicit order, just a stream of consciousness that could only happen without checking what you'll say before you say it.

Total trust.

Instead, there they were, choosing every measured syllable with extreme caution. The room was silent except for their breaths blowing across their steaming cups.

"So, how are you?" Meg asked, making the first move.

"Fine. Busy, you know. With the move."

Meg nodded.

"What about you?" Nat returned.

"Good. Work is busy."

Nat lit up, seizing the opportunity. "Congratulations on the tours, by the way! A local celebrity, right here in my living room."

Meg loved lesser-known history, and a couple of years ago she started up a tour group, giving nightly ghost tours of the downtown area. It took off during the tourist season, and now they did them year-round. In the last year, she branched out into three other nearby towns. One had a corn maze, and they worked in partnership with each other in the fall. Last October was so busy she needed to hire several more guides.

Despite her success, there seemed to be judgement everywhere she went, as if she were claiming to be a psychic, or offering to do exorcisms. She had her beliefs, sure, but she also believed that most people were haunted by their own ghosts.

"Thanks," Meg said curtly, the defensiveness in her voice surprising her. "I'm actually really proud of it."

Nat's features filled with confusion as she floundered for a reply, and Meg flushed. She was comfortable in what she believed, but was so used to having to defend it. Even though Nat said nothing wrong, she found the habit hard to break.

"Sorry. People get weird about it sometimes. Like it's just a new age hobby and not a real job."

Nat nodded. "You should be proud! It's amazing." Leaning forward, Nat grabbed a cookie from the tray and dipped it into her cup methodically.

"I'm kind of jealous, actually." Nat kept her eyes on her

cookie, dropping it into her mouth before it could disintegrate into the hot liquid. "It's really cool you're doing something you love. I don't think that many people get to say that and mean it."

"Thanks," Meg said. "I have a tour group tonight, actually."

"Plus, I hear you're working on a book?" Nat asked.

"Yes," Meg nodded, not elaborating further.

Since Nat messaged last week, Meg was finding it difficult to write. What came out on the page was too personal for her liking.

"You're living the dream!" Nat said, and Meg was surprised to see genuine pride there.

"It's not much, but at least it keeps me out of retail hell." Meg reached for a cookie, needing an excuse to stop talking. "What about you? What are you up to now that you're back?"

Nat snorted. "Retail."

Meg sensed the heat in her cheeks and thought she must be beyond red.

"Oh, God. Sorry. I didn't mean..." she floundered, desperately trying to think of something to say that wouldn't make her sound like a snob.

Nat shrugged, seemingly not offended. "Nothing I haven't thought before. It works for me, for now. Keeps me busy and pays the rent."

God, this is awful, Meg thought, squirming inside.

The fattest tabby she had ever seen meandered into the room, saving the day.

"Oooooh, who's this?"

"Ah, that's Chaos."

Meg laughed. "An ironic name, then."

The animal craned his neck, looking straight up to take in her eyes, and she silently thanked it with everything she had for the welcome diversion. The cat warmed up to her quickly, rubbing his head against her feet. She reached down to scratch his ears, relaxing at the velvety feel under her fingertips.

His fur was a little scruffy around his neck and back, tiny spikes poking up as he arched in a pleasant stretch. *This is an older gentleman.*

"Have you had him long?" Meg asked, trying to sound casual.

Shifting uncomfortably, Nat looked away from Meg. "Twelve years now. Almost thirteen."

Meg leaned back on the couch, ignoring the tabby's pointed look of displeasure at being suddenly abandoned.

You took off and replaced us all with a pet. An old well of hurt she cemented over long ago was leaking, seeping out of her, demanding answers.

"So, what made you move back, Nat?" Meg burst out, ripping off the bandage. "After everything that happened, I never thought I'd see you back here."

Nat picked at her thumb again, a smooth dot of red appearing before she crammed her hand under her thigh.

"Honestly? It's boring. Really cliché. I'm pretty sure my mom told your mom the latest?"

Small-town scrutiny wasn't kind to Nat all those years ago. There was a layer underneath her smile now, an authentic emotion scraped raw. Meg nodded and sat forward in anticipation, not wanting to be the one to ask about the breakup.

"It was...complicated," Nat said, mumbling into her teacup.

"Sorry to hear that."

Nat shook her head. "Honestly, it's for the best."

"Really?" Meg arched her eyebrows. "Are you sure? You look tired." The observation came out blunter than she would have liked.

"Well, not really, really." Their mouths turned up slightly in unison, a shared experience breaking the ice.

"Do you want to…"

"Talk about it?" Nat laughed, effortlessly this time. Meg was relieved it didn't sound bitter.

"You know me. Not my style. Plus…" A pause, and then, in disappointment, "We're not there yet."

Not a question. A cold, hard, ugly fact. Nat was right. Meg didn't know her.

Not anymore.

"I just mean, I didn't bring you over here to talk about me."

Meg set down her cup, waiting. Nat's awkwardness was obvious, and Meg felt a bolt of satisfaction inside. Part of her instantly felt awful for taking joy in Nat's discomfort. The other part of her thought it was justified.

Karma.

The two sides warred with each other as the silence stretched out, and Meg thought they were probably both right.

Nat broke first.

"I just wanted to say I'm sorry."

Meg blinked. An apology was the last thing she expected.

"I shouldn't have pushed you away like I did. You were his friend, too, and I said horrible things to you. Things I can't take back."

Meg hadn't consciously thought of the fight in years, but was going over it in excruciating detail in the days since Nat reached out. She nodded, but didn't trust herself to say anything as everything came flooding back once again.

DURING HER SECOND YEAR OF UNIVERSITY, MEG came home for the holidays. Things were strained between them, and Nat ignored her messages. She knocked on Nat's door one evening after dinner. Mr. and Mrs. Parker were remarried by then, barely back from a second honeymoon.

Nat refused to attend the ceremony.

The atmosphere spilling through the doorway was tense, the perpetual aftermath of an argument staining the air. Nat's parents lit up when they saw Meg. Mrs. Parker embraced her in a firm hug, Mr. Parker scrambling up off of his ancient recliner to say hello.

They asked her animatedly about school, about her classes, about how her mom was doing, and about her plans after graduation. Meg was flattered, but sensed the loss they were feeling of not being able to ask their own daughter about this next step in life. They skirted around the still-sore wounds, but they were trying, and Meg loved them for it.

There was an awkward pause, and they all glanced toward the stairs, hoping for footsteps at any time. Nat used to bound down the steps, usually arriving before the door opened all the way to let Meg in. She would grab Meg's sleeve, yanking her toward the stairs while her parents tried to get a word in edge-wise. Eager energy filled the room, as if the wooden stairs were also waiting for Nat's return.

Go on up, Mrs. Parker sighed, when it became painfully clear that Nat wasn't coming down.

Meg couldn't remember how the fight began that night, but she couldn't forget how it ended. Nat's eyes bulged as they yelled over each other, full of the realization that Meg wasn't going to just sit and take it this time.

...left and ditched me here to rot. You've got a new life now, so you don't have to think about how you...

What would you know about my life, Nat? You never

return my calls, never come to visit, even though you're sitting around here doing jack. I have things I want to do with my life, don't you?

...let me get behind the wheel....

Meg bit her lip, sucked in a breath. Tears came to her eyes at the realization that they were talking about two different things. Nat was so stuck in her grief that she couldn't see outside of herself anymore.

Nat leaned back into her pillow, satisfied at a direct hit, challenging Meg to go on. Meg didn't want to. She didn't want to admit this was it, that it was over between them.

I'm not talking about Chris. Nat's confused face froze, startled by the flat, dead tone of Meg's voice.

*I left you a bunch of messages, Nat. Months ago, about my dad. When he got sick, and then after...*A whisper, now. *You didn't even come to the service.*

Nat's gaze softened. *Oh, Jesus, Meg, I...*

But it was too late. The small cracks between them had become a great divide in the space of a single sentence. *I can't do this anymore, Nat. It's not my job to keep you together.*

Wait....

Meg turned and walked out before Nat could say anything else, knowing if she did it would only make things worse.

Nat's wavering voice cut into her memories, bringing them both back to the present on the couch.

"All I saw when I looked in the mirror was what people thought of me. You were the only one who believed me, who didn't think..."

"It's okay," Meg interrupted, helping Nat out of her struggle for the right words.

Nat shook her head firmly, lips pressed tightly together. "It's not, though, and I'm sorry. I don't expect you to forgive me, but I wanted you to know that."

Meg sat across from her, waiting, not sure how to respond.

"I don't know why I waited so long to tell you this. You deserved to hear it." Uncomfortable laughter bubbled over, interrupting her, and she put her hand to her cheeks. "Oh, my God, I am doing this so wrong. Feel free to tell me to fuck off and die now."

Meg burst into tears, and she laughed. The cause of all that pain sat right here in front of her, and she felt crazed at the feeling of catharsis that flowed through her. She never wanted to let go of Nat, but after that day, she just couldn't see how she could hang on to her anymore.

"I'm sorry, too, Nat. I shouldn't have..."

Nat held up her hand.

"Not needed. Really. I was way out of line. Worse." She paused, testing the waters. "Maybe it's too late, but I really am sorry about your dad. He was a good guy."

"It's never too late to hear that," Meg smiled. "When we were little, he would threaten to trade me for you. Said you were more polite and way cleaner."

That was all it took, and they were off, reminiscing. The flow was stilted as they felt their way through the minefield, still unsure of what was safe. Meg wondered if she was falling into old patterns, letting Nat take the lead as always and going with it. The conversation felt good for now, so she decided not to dissect it too much.

A couple of hours and many cookies flew by, but Meg eventually needed to leave.

"Sorry, I really have to go prep for that tour tonight. Why don't you come sometime? Reacquaint yourself with your old stomping grounds." Meg grinned. "On the house, of course."

Nat stood with her, walking the few steps to the door. "I will. That sounds great. I hope...would you want to do this again sometime?"

Meg nodded. "I would. Very much."

"Oh!" Nat turned. "I almost forgot!" She reached toward the pile of books on the side table and plucked one from the top, handing it to Meg.

Meg accepted the book, its laminated cover dulled by time, its corners weathered, worn soft by her fingers. A scratched library barcode remained at the top right, corners lifting. Bright colours splashed across the cover, a cartoonist's palette. The edges of the stained and yellowing pages look soft, thumbed through many times over the years.

Meg ran her fingers over the cover, tracing the title. *The Doodler's Guide to Becoming an Artist.*

"Hopefully, they're not still chasing you for it." Nat laughed, an uncomfortably forced sound. "I found it at the back of a closet when I was packing. It must have come with me at some point, and I forgot about it."

In truth, Meg never received a notice about not returning this one, because she took it without checking it out.

Stealing, Meg, that's called stealing.

She tried so many times to explain why it meant so much, why she clung to it, but Nat wasn't ready to hear what she had to say. *Jesus,* she recalled Nat snapping. *I said I don't want to look at it. Just leave it alone!*

"Thank you," Meg said, placing her hand on the doorknob. Curiosity got the better of her, and she turned to face Nat again.

"Can I ask...it's been so long, Nat. Why now? I mean, I think it's great, but I'm just curious. Was it just the breakup, or is there something else going on?"

Nat shrugged, "Partly, yeah. We were together for a long time. Nearly ten years. When something like that ends, it makes you look back and really think about your life, you know? You think about all the time you wasted."

Meg got that. Something monumental ends, and you wonder what the point was, what you were supposed to take from it. The lessons never came right away, though. They hit you over the head when you had advice to give a friend, when you did something unapologetically for yourself, or when something great happened in your next relationship that highlighted a gaping hole in the last one.

The epiphanies would scream as the realization dawned. *How could you have been so stupid?*

"I was so sure I wanted to come back here," Nat continued. "I couldn't stop thinking about it. I thought I was done with this place, but I just kept feeling this...pull."

A torn look covered her face, like she had something else to say but was having a hard time figuring out how. Meg chuckled.

"Trust me, I've heard it all. Probably even been in the same spot once or twice. If you want to say it, just go for it."

Nat smiled. "It feels silly to say, but I thought maybe something was trying to tell me to make things right. Once I was here, it felt impossible. I almost chickened out sending you that message."

Meg looked at her curiously. This was classic Nat, an avoider to her core. She didn't like conflict, never had. "Well, I'm glad you did. What changed your mind?"

"There was..." Nat trailed off, laughing nervously, an unexpected response. "I don't want to tell you. You'll get way too excited."

Meg put a hand on her hip. "Okay. Officially intrigued. Spill."

"I don't believe in signs. I hate thinking that if I look hard enough, I can find a way to stop bad things from happening."

Meg nodded, seeing how that line of logic would be dangerous for someone with Nat's past.

"I saw something my first night here, and I don't know how else to explain it."

Meg stared at her, expectant. "What?"

Nat took a deep breath, exhaling through what she said next in a burst of air.

"I think I saw a ghost."

MARCH 2015

SECOND CHANCES

3

Nat had one more day of work before she could be as lazy as she pleased. She was already picturing her evening in front of the television, tucked up on the couch under the quilt her grandma made her, a mountain of candy wrappers growing on her lap.

As she awkwardly hauled her grocery bags inside, she sighed in relief that she was finally back, kicking herself for not being brave enough to face the grocery store closer to home.

The incident in Aisle 5 last month solidified her need for a vacation. She still shrank in embarrassment as she remembered dissolving into inconsolable, overwhelmed tears right there in front of the dry pasta. The empty, gaping hole in the shelf where her favourite brand of sauce was supposed to be mocked her, pushing her over the edge. The teenage shelf stocker stared at her passively, then casually called for a manager as if he was meticulously trained for that exact scenario.

Any future trips to the corner market would require large sunglasses and possibly a fake beard.

She was working non-stop since the move, taking extra

shifts whenever she could. Her coworkers likely thought she was a total suck-up, the new girl trying to get in good with the boss. The extra cash was nice, but she knew that working so often she barely had time to think would never be a long-term solution. When she went to work the next day, she asked for two weeks off. There was no hesitation, and she wondered if there were others looking for more hours. In making conversation, her boss asked if she had any big plans for her time off, and she thought a beat too long before replying.

"Nat?"

"Visiting family," she said slowly. The word rolled uncomfortably over her tongue, her lips forming the word that she hadn't used in so long.

HAULING IN THE LAST BAG, SHE CURSED AS SHE noticed the time. Nat shoved her groceries in the fridge. She ran back and forth between the bathroom and her laundry basket, brushing her teeth as she sniffed at several identical black dress socks to find the least objectionable ones.

So glamorous.

Like most days, she realized after far too long a hunt that she held her phone in her hand. Lifting the bags of assorted junk food on the kitchen counter that was earmarked to get her through her vacation, she found her keys buried in the pile.

She shook her head to avoid spiralling and paused at the front door, glancing around to see if there was anything she missed. Her reflection stared back at her in the antique mirror hanging by the entryway, blame and loss permanently etched into her expression. There was no forgiving herself for what she did, so it seemed only fitting to have it reflected at her for her entire life.

She tore her gaze away from the mirror, letting a deep breath fill her chest until the trembling in her hands stopped. Flexing her fingers, she turned her focus to getting out the door.

She shoved her feet into her shoes and crammed her phone into her bag, ready to fly out the door. As usual, it was a difficult maneuver to hold the cat back with her foot while she wedged herself between the entrance and the pony wall.

When she moved in, she thought she might put a little decorative bowl there, an organized place for her keys, loose change, and other junk living in her pockets when she arrived home.

Not surprisingly, she never got around to it, and now it was a dumping ground, a depository for things her brain marked "DO NOT FORGET" that she always did. The narrow ledge held a pair of sunglasses, a handful of receipts, three lip balms, an overdue library book, and a hair tie.

Chaos stood by the door, his face frozen in an expression of intense focus. He fancied himself a creature of the wild, but he was more a royal at heart than an adventurer. There wasn't time today to dig him out from the shrubs underneath the front window when he decided the wilderness was far too much for him.

Grabbing the hair tie, she slammed the door on his offended face and juggled her messenger bag as she shoved her key in the lock.

"FFFFFFFuuuuuuuuccccccccckkkkkkkkkk!" came the cry from down the block, and Nat smiled as her deadbolt thunked into place, knowing Barb was out in her yard on the corner before she even turned around.

Tying her sweatshirt around her waist, she headed down the street toward Barb's house. The hair tie broke in her hand as she pulled her light brown hair into a ponytail, and she hissed as it snapped against her fingers. Wondering if Chaos wished it on her as she left, she shook out her hair and shoved the broken elastic into her pocket.

"Hey, Barb!" she called out as she made her way down the street.

The houses on Pine Drive were old and rundown, hers included. Overgrown weeds and dead, wilted flowers choked several yards, peppering the gardens beneath the windows. Overnight, a new 'for sale' sign sprouted up in another overgrown yard.

Barb dropped the patio cushions she was wrestling through her front door, the vinyl covers emitting a final squeak of defeat as they hit the sagging wooden deck. She huffed in frustration as she gave an absentminded wave.

"Hey, Nat!"

Tiny flower pots lined the railing of the deck, a box at Barb's feet with more to come. A new bird feeder hung at the top of the steps, ready for the robins that would arrive soon.

"Looking good!"

Barb squinted at the new spring decor, an appraising look, then nodded in agreement.

"You workin' tonight?" Barb mumbled around her cigarette as she hauled the cushions up again, dropping them by the nearby deck chairs.

Nat thought smoking was disgusting, and a nurse should know better. Still, she had to admit, the ability to do such a wide range of activities one-handed while chain-smoking was impressive.

"Yep. Last day before I start that vacation week, though!"

"Ah, that's right! The...*staycation*." Barb forced out the word around the growing ash on the cigarette hanging from her lips.

Barb had a habit of putting air quotes around the 'lingo these days,' as she called it. Nat sensed the movement in the pause, even though Barb's hands were busy tying the cushions to the seats.

"Well, I'll let you get going, hun. Have a good one."

Nat waved one last time as she turned the corner. The blue sky, the birds pecking at the fresh grass in front of houses as she passed, everything was fresh. The brand-new season was out in full force.

Starting over, she thought, smiling a little as she picked up her pace.

4

THE SHOP DOORS CLOSED BEHIND HER AT THE END of her shift. The cool spring night was a welcome change from the stale air conditioning, cleansing her soul of the feeling of a day spent working with the public. Her muscles relaxed as the plastic smile that Meg called her 'retail face' shifted back into genuine humanity. The muffled beeping of the alarm droned on behind the door as the manager locked up behind them.

"See you later!" she called to her co-workers, waving as the herd split up, migrating toward bus stops and vehicles.

It was late, and she thought about following some of them to the bus stop across the street. After a moment, she moved toward the crosswalk instead, zipping up her sweatshirt over the ugly polyester polo shirt that served as a uniform. Walking to work in the in-between weather of spring and fall always appealed to her. She was on her feet all day, so it should be the opposite, but the first blast of cool fresh air on her face never failed to reset her.

Hunching her shoulders against the slight bite in the air, she let her mind wander as she walked. The simple promise of reading in the tub while Chaos drank the bathwater sustained her over the last two hours of her shift.

Drifting into autopilot, she focused on the beat of the music flowing through her earbuds, contemplating what slasher movie she would like to fall asleep to after her bath.

Halfway down the walkway, with the open sports field spreading out to her left, she realized her mistake.

The overpass loomed ahead of her, intimidating in the dark. Abandoned, overgrown train tracks surrounded by a chain-link fence ran underneath it, the reason for the building of the structure above. This side of the path had an urban feel to it, a lack of personality. Beyond the overpass, trees lined the path on either side, winding down along a creek that started near the tracks' end. The route was a dream for any kid with a bike and a taste for freedom. Rides beside the trickling water punctuated the memories of her own childhood summers.

Between the two worlds, a concrete stairwell covered in fading graffiti led to the main road above. The light at the bottom of the stairs was perpetually out, and she surprised someone coming around the corner more than once. She never knew until she got there whether it would be a sheepish smile from a teenager smoking a joint, or a wolfish once-over that would linger on her as she climbed.

The bitch of it was the route was so much faster, cutting about twenty-five minutes off of her time. After a close call where someone had followed partway up the stairs until she met someone at the top, she promised herself she would only take the shortcut in the light of day. When the walkway was filled with dog walkers and baby strollers, its nature changed entirely.

With the bright sun beaming down to illuminate every nook and cranny, it was easy to forget how menacing it could be to step underneath into a darkness deeper than the night.

The dark didn't bother her exactly, and she was used to walking alone. What got to her was the tendency for what was commonplace and harmless during the day to mutate at night, growing in size and shape and intent.

Switching her music off, she tensed as she noticed someone emerging from the shadows beneath the bridge, approaching on the walking path. Inside her sweatshirt pocket, her fingers tightened around her keys, a warm wave of adrenaline pounding down on her. Heart racing, she slowed her stride, head up and alert.

A woman jogged toward her, ponytail bobbing as they gave each other the nod that women universally recognized, the one that said, "thanks for not being a murderer."

They locked eyes as they passed each other, bonded in their instinctual caution.

The footsteps faded behind her, but Nat remained vigilant, her grip still tight on her keys. A sliver of anger and frustration accompanied the automatic response. Watching the runner move toward the main road, she shivered as she thought of the woman from her dream.

It was months, and she still slept with the lights on, unable to consider what she would do the next time she woke up to that face in the dark. Sounds still invaded the darkness of the house outside of her bedroom now and then, but the woman never appeared to her again.

At first, she thought maybe it was her, that something was pushing her to do what she came back to accomplish. After Meg came over the first time, she thought it would be better, that an invisible weight would lift as a feeling of calm permeated her new home. When it didn't happen, she couldn't stop thinking about the dream. The feeling that something was trying to get her attention lingered, a palpable force reaching out from somewhere she didn't understand.

It was just a dream, she tried to convince Meg. Laughing at the skeptical look on her friend's face, she tried to make light of it.

"Look, if something else happens, I'll let you say 'I told you so,' okay? I swear."

In the absence of another ghostly visitation, she was trying to convince herself the noises were just noises. Standing alone beside the overpass, staring into the dark abyss beneath the bridge, it didn't feel like something she invented, but she pushed on ahead with her head up, exuding a confidence she didn't really feel.

She was nearly at the bottom of the stairs, making a wide turn so she could see anyone who might be there. The steps were clear, and she relaxed. A car passed overhead, rattling the foundation above her and humming hollowly.

Hand on the grimy railing, she stepped up onto the first stair, ready to run to the top, when movement farther down the path caught her eye. Some ancient instinct to know what was hunting her forced her to stop, while every cell in her body screamed at her to keep going.

Barely discernible in the shadows of the trees was a shape.

It's NOT a shape, she scolded herself. *It's a person.*

She made out a dark silhouette, but try as she might to convince herself, something inside her knew that this was no human being. She couldn't see any features, the black of the surrounding shadows hiding its identity. It was blurred at the edges, as if it were made of smoke. The leaves of the trees and the concrete at its feet were crisp and sharp in comparison. It didn't move, but she felt it staring at her, drinking her in.

She shook her head, trying to urge common sense back into her brain. Rationality got people home in these situations.

Indecision was a death sentence.

Nat was transfixed, trying to figure out what it would do

next. She resisted the temptation to call out like every halfwit in a scary movie, but she needed reassurance. A human voice that potentially meant her harm was one thing, but what if she got a monster's growl instead?

Stop thinking and run like hell.

She turned as she ran up the stairs, looking over the railing. It rushed down the path toward the steps, blurred limbs jittering in the dark. A high-pitched sound reached her ears—a predatory bird's scream that surrounded her. She ran, every fiber of her being telling her it was no flesh and blood threat, no matter how hard her mind tried to fight it. It stopped underneath the broken light, cocking its head slowly to the side as if it were working out what she was thinking.

An uncontrollable tremor ran through her, and she willed herself to keep going, resisting the urge to stay rooted to the spot to make sense of what she was seeing.

Any sense of control she had left was lost in the void that was rushing her, thoughts spiralling and breaking apart as she fled. *I can't even scream and it's looking at me oh god it's looking and I remember my Grade 8 self-defence class they told us to yell fire because no one will respond if they hear help they won't help a screamer but they'll help put out a fire oh god oh god yell fire!!!!*

She couldn't yell, couldn't scream, her cries catching in her dry throat and shrivelling there. The sweaty polyester shirt under her hoodie clung to her skin. Words like reaper, ghost and demon all flashed through her brain, an endless parade, but she couldn't land on one. Her legs were numb as she flew off the top step, moving onto the sidewalk above.

The screaming ceased, the sudden silence of the street weighing on her. She stopped for a moment, trying to breathe evenly, staring at the top of the stairs where the world dropped into the black hole below. The street lamps stood bright and cheery at her side, a fierce antonym to the pitch-black world that lurked below. Trembling, heart pounding, she waited for something to appear at the top of the stairs. Her breathing gradually slowed, and she walked backward a few steps, her anticipation fading as time stretched on.

It was gone.

She clutched her bag strap and turned, continuing briskly toward home. The tiny corner store appeared, followed by the first houses on the long road, the intersections of populated streets. Darkened windows and closed blinds were all that greeted her as she passed, as if everyone retreated, abandoning her to deal with whatever was chasing her.

Edgerton grew since her childhood, but at its heart it was still a sleepy community, and it would be unusual for her to see much activity on her evening walks home. It never bothered her before, but the feeling that she was completely alone in the world crept over her, and she peeked over her shoulder again to make sure nothing followed.

She reached her street, her brightly lit front door in sight. She always turned it on when she left the house, and it felt like a greeting when she got back at night. With the promise of safety now in her sight, she refused to turn back, focusing on home. Although she had no reason to run, her muscles remained coiled and poised, as if she were at the starting line of a race.

Echoing footsteps surrounded her, and she needed to remind herself they were her own as the streetlights flickered briefly.

A crash behind her made her jump. A plastic trash bin lay tipped over on the road, the wheels circling lazily as a fat raccoon pulled its desired prize onto her next-door neighbour's lawn.

"Shit!"

Laughing at her paranoia, she clutched her now-sweaty keyring to her stomach. The sharp edges dug painfully into her palm, and the throbbing grip became her lifeline, a talisman reminding her she made it this far. She ran her hand across her clammy forehead and back through her hair.

The raccoon was watching her steady herself without empathy, focusing on its dinner. It streaked away from her into the neighbour's garden. She watched its path through the garden gnomes, who stood guard over the still-bare vegetable patch. Fairy doors and wind chimes decorated the large maple tree in the yard. The sight of them calmed her, as if their pure innocence could drive away her fear.

The leaves rustled, and she pulled her arms around herself in anticipation of a cool wind, but the air remained still. The chimes hung unmoving, eerily still and silent.

Unable to process what she was seeing, the understanding that it wasn't the leaves moving at all was slow to come. The dark spaces around them shifted, a slinking blackness that created the illusion of a breeze. A shadow emerged, crawling slowly down the trunk of the tree, pulling itself painfully over the grass toward her.

Nat watched, frozen as the shadow transformed from Peter Pan's lost companion, flat on the lawn, to a three-dimensional figure. Curled fingers ran through the grass as it peeled itself off the ground. It wasn't just a complete absence of colour; it was an absence of everything, threatening to swallow her and take the entire world with it. Nat thought of the darkened windows and wondered if it already happened, if she was the only one left.

One arm stretched toward her, long, thin fingers grasping the air between them as it tried to right itself. The streetlights flickered again before fading completely, plunging the street into blackness.

She ran, focused only on her front door. Even as home grew closer, escape felt futile, and she couldn't stop the thought from entering her mind.

There's no running from this.

She reached her driveway, her feet dead weight as she tried to escape. Running up the steps, she hit the door hard, her numb hands raising the keys. The lock clicked open, and she shoved the door inward, tumbling gratefully into the pitch blackness of her living room. As the door swung shut behind her, she thought she heard a voice calling her name.

Shaking, she swung the deadbolt back into place with a force that comforted her, even if she wasn't sure she believed it would keep the thing out. The bag slung across her chest and shoulder banged against the pony wall, and she yanked the strap over her head to let it drop loudly to the floor.

Willing herself not to breathe and break the silence of the dark room around her, she peered through the peephole.

The front steps were bare, with no sign of the phantom movements in the trees, nothing hiding in plain sight. The streetlamps illuminated the cul-de-sac as if nothing happened. Now that the spectre was gone, the life that was leeched from them returned.

Her breath heaved, and she sagged to the floor, her legs finally giving out on her. Resting her back against the door, she draped her arms over her knees. Tears joined the sweat now that her body could process the chase.

The warm air in her little place came into contact with skin cooled from the chilly night, and she felt more sweat prickle on her forehead in response. She wrenched the smothering warmth of her sweatshirt off and wiped her face with it before tossing it to the floor to join her bag.

The full moon really brought out the weirdos.

Immediate fury rose in her at the instinct to explain it away.

She wouldn't do that this time.

You know what you saw.

A methodical scratching vibrated through the door and

into her back, as she held her breath. Her mind took her back to moving day, to the sounds coming from underneath the deck in the spare room. *Let me in*, the clawing suggested gently. *I'd love to join you.*

When she heard an impatient meow, she shrieked in exasperation. "Goddammit!"

Manic laughter bubbled up in her throat, and she shoved it down. Grabbing the doorknob, she pulled herself off the floor, disengaging the tiny push lock. Holding the furball up to her face seemed like the perfect antidote to this evening's events.

About to reach for the deadbolt, she paused, flashing to that morning, of wrestling to keep him in.

How did you get out?

A large hand clamped around her mouth, and something pressed hard into her back, punching her repeatedly. Held immobile, clamped in a vice grip, her muscles went rigid, but there was no chance to struggle. There wasn't even time for surprise.

As quickly as the hands grabbed her, they let her go. Suddenly weightless, she crashed to the ground. Unable to move her hands in time to stop her fall, she hit the carpet with a heavy thud. She wriggled her fingers into the fibers under her. As her eyes adjusted, she held up her hand, wondering where all the blood on the carpet had come from.

Something pulled itself along the carpet beside her, and she shifted her gaze. A man knelt on the floor next to her, the knees of his grey sweatpants black with blood in the dull streetlight that filtered through the curtains. He was speaking, but she couldn't hear him.

Something lay on the floor behind him, something solid and bulky, but she couldn't make it out in the dark. She dropped her hand to her chest, her fingers tingling. The wetness on her hand soaked into her shirt, dampening the skin underneath.

It's so cold in here.

The living room was blurring, fading into a pinpoint as she watched. The man's face above her swirled, losing all definition.

Fire! she thought, before it all went black.

5

SQUINTING DOWN AT THE GLASS IN HER HAND, BARB had that moment of clarity, the one which warns, *One more sip and you're a goner!*

Fuck it, she thought, raising the glass and emptying it in one large gulp. She gasped in satisfaction, grabbing the bottle and emptying it to fill the glass again.

What's one more hangover? Impulse control was something she gave up on a long time ago.

She poked around at the mess of empty plates and fast-food wrappers on her coffee table. Placing the empty bottle in the middle of the chaos, she adjusted her thick bathrobe and decided it was tomorrow's problem. Footsteps on the street broke through the quiet night—someone in a hurry.

The base of the glass missed the coaster as she put it down, sloshing red wine on the table. Cursing, she barely caught her balance as she moved to peer out her bay windows.

Even from afar, Barb saw the twisted hysteria on Nat's face, as if she was trying to convince herself there was nothing to worry about. She passed Barb's house, legs rigid and knees locked, a second away from breaking into a run. Barb ran to her door and hurried out onto her deck in the dark, prepared to wave Nat over.

Nat glanced around wildly, neck taut, a gazelle watching cautiously for a lion. She paused, staring into the yard next door to hers.

Barb's eyes widened as Nat bolted in a flat-out desperate life or death run to her driveway.

"Nat!" she called, but she didn't respond.

Barb moved to get a better look, and her breath caught in her throat. There was someone in the shadows, crawling toward Nat and reaching for her, imploring her to come closer as they struggled to their knees.

Barb's brain was fuzzy; the wine sour in her stomach. It sloshed around as sobering concern competed with the effects of the alcohol.

"Nat!" she tried again, louder this time, but Nat wasn't stopping for anything or anyone.

Barb's call echoed down the street as Nat made it up the stairs and through the door. The door slammed behind her, but the lights inside didn't come on. The street fell silent again, charged with a heavy anticipation that covered everything like a snowfall.

Barb turned her head back to the meticulously tidy yard next to Nat's, but it was empty, leaving no trace of the figure. Crossing her arms, she rubbed them and lowered her chin to her chest, pulling the sides of her robe closer to guard against the cold.

Crisis averted.

He's back, she thought, as she went back inside, wondering what he wanted with Nat.

6

Nat turned in a circle, disoriented. Her limbs tingled, and she was jittery, vision slowly returning. She was standing in the middle of the road, facing her house at the end of the street. The king at the head of the table, it loomed over all the other houses. The streetlights were out again, casting everything in sinister shadows. A strange buzzing filled the air as the bulb above her flickered and then burned brightly, casting her in a spotlight. Exposed and on display, she shrank from it, stepping out of the circle into the cover of night.

How did I get here? A fresh wave of panic crested, and she choked it down, knowing it would knock her over if she let it.

The shape crawling across the grass felt like forever and just a moment ago, all at once. The neighbour's off-duty garden gnomes' white eyes appeared to glow in the exaggerated darkness. She focused on their faces, trying to decide if the gnomes were facing the same way or if they had shifted their tiny bodies to observe her.

Am I asleep?

She wondered if this was what sleepwalking felt like, existing but not real, all at once. If it were, she didn't know how people lived with it. All the possibilities that could inhabit the hole in time flooded her mind, and she struggled to clear them away, sifting through her memories to focus on the last thing she remembered.

A large, rough hand pressed firmly over her mouth, squeezing hard as she was helpless to do anything but inhale. A musty scent overwhelmed her, and the hand didn't feel right as she grabbed it. The skin felt fake, like rubber, or...

Latex, she realized as she placed the scent. Latex gloves.

What happened to me?

Prodding at her body, she felt for injuries, but there was nothing amiss.

Am I in shock?

She walked down the street, searching for any houses with a light on. Hoping to feel the comforting weight of her cell phone, she reached into the back pocket of her jeans. Even as her hand grasped only scratchy denim, she pictured it on the floor beside her bag where she dropped it.

The air surrounding her dark windows seemed to stand still, holding its breath and daring her to go back in.

Nope.

In the absence of any signs of life, she knocked on Barb's door.

As she reached Barb's lawn, a flash of white gleamed in the middle of the street, out of reach of the single functioning light's glow. A boy stood watching her with curiosity in his eyes. Something about him was familiar, but she couldn't put her finger on it. There was a baby-faced appearance to him, lanky limbs ready to sprout, and she guessed he was about fourteen.

The brightness that drew her eye was his t-shirt, which was the too-clean white of bleached teeth. The way it glowed in the dark reminded her of a predatory fish in the deep sea, dangling a light to attract prey. Approaching him slowly, she found herself cautious, ready to bolt. A touch of silliness washed over her. He didn't exactly strike her as a hardened criminal.

"Hey!" she called. "Hey, can I use your phone?"

The boy didn't move. The middle part of his dark hair fell to his ears, a style she hadn't seen in years.

Is that cut back in style?

Given a strange woman was demanding to use his phone in the middle of the night, he seemed oddly comfortable standing alone in the dark. There were no friends around that she saw. Memories of adolescent defiance came to her, of staying out late and secretly hoping to get caught outside after curfew.

His arms were bare, and she thought he must be freezing. He closed his eyes as if he wished he were anywhere but here.

"Hello?" she tried again. "Do you have a phone? It's kind of an emergency."

As she got closer, his features came into focus. The skin on his face was smooth and completely unblemished. It wasn't the result of a great skincare routine, but rather he looked like a sculpted doll, too perfect to be real. Until he opened his dark brown eyes and answered her, she thought it might be a mask.

"I don't have a phone," he said in reply, watching her inquisitively.

Inhuman. The word bubbled up from somewhere within herself. Despite the strange look to him, she was certain she recognized him from somewhere.

"Oh. Look, someone attacked me in my house, the one at the end of the street? I'm going to my neighbour's place." She gestured behind her to Barb's house. "There. You should go home if it's close. It might not be safe out here. I don't..."

Taking a few cautious steps back, she suddenly wondered if this could be her attacker. It seemed ridiculous that a hundred pounds soaking wet kid could have taken her with the level of violence she remembered, but trusting strangers right now felt like a terrible idea. "I don't know where they went."

Behind her, Barb's porch light flicked on, shining like a lighthouse in a stormy sea.

The boy gazed at Nat, staring a little too long to be comfortable. This time, his calmness triggered something in her, something from earlier that night. Backing toward Barb's, she held eye contact, afraid to look away from him even for a second.

"It was you," she said, taking another step back. "You were following me tonight."

His chin jerked down, eyes narrowing. "What?"

"I think...I think something's wrong with me."

"Yes," he said, simply.

The matter-of-fact tone threw her off; his easy agreement worried her even more. To put her at ease, he smiled. Hands out in a placating gesture, he moved toward her.

Am I high? Maybe some kind of drug accounted for the missing time.

His sad, desperate eyes seemed to be willing her to figure something out, as if he had something to tell her but didn't know how to say it.

She had seen that look before, and it never ended well.

The air in front of him seemed to bend, distorting his smooth, flawless features into blurry strips. At first, she thought it was smoke rising in waves to obscure him as if he was standing behind a campfire. Flowing upward, it gained heft and weight, becoming something tangible and messy, like runny paint. The boy's perfect features slid in and out of focus as he disappeared behind it, his gaze a spear through her chest, pinning her to the spot.

The strange curtain rustled, and for a moment she thought it was going to open and something would emerge. Rippling and rolling over on itself, it moved forward, closing the gap between them. Muscular striations appeared as she stepped back. It moved toward her and enveloped the road where she stood just a moment before. The air became sultry and oppressive, sour as it burnt her lungs. The experience felt surreal—a hallucination.

It's not real; it can't be.

The cloak pulsed, picking up speed and moving closer. A dark, gaping hole opened in its center, ready to pull her into its crushing weight.

Behind her, Barb's front door swung open, and she stepped out, swaying slightly in a cotton candy coloured robe and slippers.

Nat was so relieved to see her, this harried angel, that she practically wept. A strong sense of déjà vu overcame her as she darted through an open door, seeking refuge for the second time that night.

Except this time, it wasn't just the door she tumbled through. This time, she shot straight through Barb as well.

THE DAY NAT MET BARB, SHE COMMENTED ON THE rusty fleur-de-lis pattern on the prickly, extra short carpet, the same one her grandma used to have. Without touching it, she sensed its scratchy nubbiness, bringing her back to sorting plastic shapes while after-school shows played on above her.

The carpet she landed on tonight shattered that nostalgic cocoon. The memory of the rug dispersed as she sank into it. The floor was spongy beneath her palms as she pushed herself to her feet. She thought of a movie set, an imitation of her reality.

Nat stood facing the back of Barb's head as she remained at the front door, transfixed by something outside.

"Barb?" she whispered, reaching for her, willing her to turn around.

She raised her hand, trembling fingers lingering above Barb's shoulder for a moment before she let them fall carefully. Instead of the reassuring warmth of human contact, Nat's fingers encountered no resistance as they slipped through Barb's body. Mouth open, Nat held her hand up to examine it for what felt like an eternity.

Have I disappeared?

"Please, help," she croaked, pleading for Barb's answer to bring her back to reality, to tell her this was all just a terrible dream.

Barb turned around stiffly, eyes enormous as she gazed right at Nat.

"Oh, thank God." Nat braced her hands on her knees, feeling out of breath as the pressure inside her dissipated. Allowing herself to drop her guard, she smiled at the floor.

I made it.

Barb's face twisted into a scream as she propelled herself backward, running away from Nat and out onto the porch, tripping over her own feet.

"Barb, stop!" Nat cried as she followed her. "Come back!"

The enormous shroud was waiting for them, and as Nat followed Barb into the night, it expanded. Before it was a full clothesline, stretching from one side of the street to the other. It grew outwards and bent towards them. The fuzzy outline of the boy was still behind it, motionless, waiting. Barb kept running as it closed in on them, and before Nat could warn her, she hit the wall.

"Barb!" she screamed, running after her, half expecting a bloody mess, an electrocution of some kind, like a security fence.

However, Barb moved through it as if it weren't there. One moment she was there with Nat, and the next, she was gone. Nat was surrounded, and she craned her neck to glance up at the towering height of it. The edges there reached for each other, as if a giant beast was folding its hands together to hold her in its palm.

Gnawing and crunching filled the air, and she looked up in time to see the entire thing collapse, raining down on her and absorbing her into its mass. Drowning in the viscous heat of the substance surrounding her, she kicked and opened her mouth in a muffled, watery shout.

The grinding built, vibrating through her bones until she knew nothing other than the sound. She tried to cover her ears but couldn't move, couldn't breathe, couldn't curl in on herself for comfort.

The pressure grew as the entity gripped and caressed her, claiming her as its own as it squeezed. The inevitable crush took her over. Her ears popped and sinuses burned until she stopped trying to struggle. Sharp teeth surrounded her as she screamed, hands gripping her legs to pull her further into the abyss.

The grinding stopped, and the entity let go, exploding out from under her and dropping her onto the concrete. Eyes pressed shut, she didn't dare move, counting every second she escaped the crippling heat a blessing. A storm wind battered her, dirt from the sidewalk stinging her skin as it bit into her face.

The wind stopped, and everything went quiet. A door slammed, blocking the noise behind it and making the world quiet again. Bracing herself for some sort of nuclear wasteland, she cracked her eyes open carefully.

Not a single blade of grass was out of place; everything looked exactly as it had before. Despite its comforting appearance, everything *felt* wrong. The sidewalk was soft under her, molding to her body like a quality mattress.

Footsteps made their way to her, and a pair of running shoes came into her vision.

"You okay?"

The boy stood over her, hand raised in a shy, hesitant wave. The wave was strangely friendly, but she wasn't going to take any chances.

She rolled onto her knees, legs shaking, wondering if he would lunge at her at any moment. Unfolding to stand tall, she saw he was shorter than she initially thought, surprising her. There was a pre-adulthood, fragile leanness to him, an innocence in his gangly awkwardness.

"Do you know what's happening here?" she asked.

"Yes."

"Were you following me earlier?"

Confusion once again creased his porcelain exterior. "No. I don't know what you're talking about."

She watched his eyes, trying to gauge whether he was telling the truth. He shifted his weight back and forth, fidgeting.

She extended her hand in front of her as far as it could go until her fingertips brushed something solid. Tendrils of silvery air followed her movements playfully and highlighted the obstacle in front of her as she moved her hand along it. It was slimy and dry, sliding through her fingers easily while stiffening at her touch, pulsating rhythmically like a heartbeat.

The barrier was solid, and she couldn't push through. When she pulled her arm away, the tendrils disappeared, evaporating. The tips of her fingers were red, irritated, like she touched a harsh chemical. As she watched, the redness faded, the new, unmarred quality of her skin returning.

"Don't worry, you'll get used to it," he said. "Unless you try to touch it, you'll forget it's even there."

The calm night sky twinkled above them, and she tried to ignore that she was in an invisible jail cell. "Am I dreaming?"

"You're dead." Their eyes met so abruptly that she took an involuntary step back. "Look, I'm sorry. There's no easy way to do this. Might as well rip off the bandage."

"Dead?"

She used the word a million times before, but now it felt so strange on her tongue. The battery of the remote was dead. Her phone was dead. That bird the cat dragged in was *really* dead.

It's not a word I thought I would apply to myself.

Although she expected to be more surprised, it strangely made sense to her. Just because she didn't want it to be true didn't mean it wasn't. The words had the ring of a deep and life-altering truth, one that you could never take back once it was in front of you. A sense of calm drifted over her, and she wondered if it was a good thing she accepted this so easily.

"Oh."

He laughed, but caught himself and tried to hide his smile. "Sorry. I didn't expect you to react like that."

"Like what?"

"Like you're fine with it."

Am I fine with this? Masking her emotions came naturally to her even after death, and she was grateful for it. She still wasn't sure whether she could trust him. Monsters could smile and laugh, too, and when they did, it was probably already too late.

If she were dead, there wasn't any fixing it.

"No offense," she continued, "but is this your first day on the job or something? Aren't you a little *young*? Isn't Death supposed to be older than, like, twelve?"

He seemed somewhat offended.

"Okay, I've never even met the Grim Reaper, dude. And for the record, I died when I was fourteen." Seeing that she remained unimpressed, he hastily added, "Almost fifteen."

Standing straight, he pulled his shoulders back, pure peacock.

A giggle bubbled up, and she held it in her mouth, determined not to set it free. It was the dangerous, hysterical kind that wouldn't stop once it started. A tiny puff of air breached her lips, betraying her.

His mouth puckered at the perceived insult. "Why? How old are you?"

"Older than you," she snapped back.

"Oh," he said, in the adolescent way that suggests in as few syllables as possible that he couldn't give less of a shit what her answer was.

"Forget it," she said, shrugging it off.

She had been through worse things than being stuck in her thirties for eternity. Besides, there were clearly bigger fish to fry at the moment.

"How did you die?" she asked, curiosity getting the better of her. He was in pretty good shape for a dead kid.

Surprise flitted across his face. "You can't see it?"

"See what?"

"Look harder," he said, watching her for a reaction.

As she blinked, she saw his body as it last was. The moment of his death stretched on, everything appearing in slow motion. His face was a mess of blood, and fluid leaked from his ears. One eye was swollen shut, and blood leaked from the other, its pupil hugely dilated. The immaculate white shirt he wore was now torn and streaked with dirt, as were his jeans. He was missing a shoe, and his clothes were in tatters, road rashed flesh peeking out through the rips. Dark scales stretched up his arm, neck and cheek on one side, and as she leaned closer in sick fascination, she saw it was gravel.

The blink ended, and he stood before her in his blinding t-shirt once more, completely unscarred.

"What happened to you?"

"Car accident," he said shyly, glancing at the ground as if he was trying not to brag.

She pictured a party full of undead people trying to decide who had the best end-of-life story. *Hey, Joe! Come on over and meet Nat and tell us about how you fell into a concrete mixer!*

"Hit and run," he elaborated, looking away quickly.

The fact that someone left him there made it infinitely worse. *Could they have saved him?* She wondered if he was torturing himself with similar thoughts.

There were so many questions that needed answering, but changing the subject now felt disrespectful. "Sorry."

Squirming at the attention, he shuffled his feet.

"It was a long time ago," he said. "How did you die? Do you remember?" He lit up at the prospect of some hot gossip.

She shook her head. "No. Is that normal?"

What a joke. There is nothing normal about this.

He shrugged. "Who knows? Sometimes I wish I didn't. Maybe you're lucky?"

Lucky. The idea of gratitude of any kind in this situation made her stomach turn.

He switched gears quickly, as if he was worried that she would suddenly remember and he would have to deal with the fallout.

"Hey, did we know each other? I mean, I don't recognize you, but I've been here for a long time. Do you know me?"

The question took her off guard. He was so familiar to her, but she still couldn't place him.

"I don't know. I feel like I recognize you, but I'm not sure where I know you from. Why?"

"Nothing. It's just, well, I've never had to show people my car accident self before. I don't see myself that way. I always kind of thought maybe it's because I can remember what I looked like before. Since we don't know each other, I thought for sure you'd see...well, dead me, I guess."

The way he was glancing at her suggested he wasn't seeing her best self. She didn't want to know what she looked like to him. If gloves were involved, her death probably wasn't clean and pretty. Human brains did all kinds of crazy things for self-preservation.

"I'm Nat." She offered her hand, hoping his name in return would ring a bell.

He stared down at it as if it were an ancient relic from another time. He didn't reach for it and didn't seem at all fazed when she pulled away. *This kid's social skills are a little rusty.*

She glanced down as she brought her arm back to her side. Her skin had the same waxy tone as his. Her birthmark remained, but the minor imperfections disappeared. Freckles, sunspots, even the little scar on her wrist from falling off her bike when she was seven years old—her history was wiped away.

A clean slate.

An opportunity to start fresh was exactly what she hoped for, and now it was here. What did that look like exactly?

This wasn't how she imagined it. She didn't get to hug her parents one last time, to say goodbye to Meg, to let go. As far as she was concerned, she was still stuck, still leaving everyone behind without a word, without telling them how she felt.

The time for second chances was gone.

A checklist formed in her mind, all the things she failed to prepare before this unexpected trip glaring at her from the page.

She lived alone and was a quiet tenant. This month's rent was already paid, and her landlord told her he was working out of town for a while. She was supposed to be working up the courage to talk to her parents this week, but she hadn't called them yet. She pushed Meg away yet again when she offered to come by for moral support, telling her she would want to be alone.

Coward. The next anniversary of the accident was looming, sweet sixteen. The dark voice rose in her, the one that told her she was nothing, worthless.

Tears welled in her eyes as she thought of Chaos and how he loved to believe he was a hardened hunter. It was killing her that no one would be around to let him in.

No one will even notice that you're gone.

She hoped Barb would stop by. Barb was pushy, and would likely notice something was wrong if they didn't visit like they planned. Her relief faded at the thought of Barb finding her like...however she was. She didn't deserve that.

The kid cocked his head to the side. "Hello? Earth to Nat!"

"Sorry," she said, trying desperately to get back into the present, to put aside the things she couldn't control. "What did you say?"

"My name's Gavin."

A shock went through her body as she realized where she recognized him from. *Holy shit.*

"Wait. *Barb's* Gavin?" Nat recalled the photos on the mantel in Barb's living room, the brown-eyed kid with the goofy smile, frozen in time, never older than this.

He appeared taken aback. "You know my mom?"

"Yeah."

Who knew dying wouldn't be the biggest surprise of her night?

THE ROAD LESS TRAVELLED

7

Inside her living room, Barb paced back and forth, considering how Nat would react when she explained the shadowy figure. She flipped the porch light on in anticipation of the return trip.

Nat's number was in her phone, saved to her contacts when she kept an eye on the cat once. Swaying slightly, she rested on the couch for a moment and tried twice before she selected the number. She hesitated, trying to prepare something to say before she dialled. It all seemed so crazy, and she didn't think she would ever need to explain this. She struggled to temper her excitement at something she gave up on.

When the Edwards' advertised for renters last July, it was months since Barb last saw the figure who came to visit.

Barb stayed close to her living room window, which is usually where she saw him from. While she waited, she watched the people coming and going, wondering which one would be her new neighbour. It was the end of summer, her spot on the sofa just a little too warm.

The front door slammed open, heavy footsteps clomping

in. If it were anyone else, barging in without knocking would be intrusive, but Sherry was a friend who didn't need to knock, the closest friend Barb had. Sherry still loved to talk about the unusual way they met, through their mutual ex-husband, flouting the story as if it was a script for the next big rom-com. Barb knew the circumstances were a little darker than Sherry made them seem, that she didn't reveal all, but even she had to admit it made a hell of a dinner party ice breaker.

Sherry kicked off her shoes haphazardly and crossed over to the couch, fanning her hair away from her red, sweaty face.

"It's hot as hell out there!" she panted, groaning in gratitude at the air conditioning, torpedoing herself onto the cushions and making herself comfortable.

Peering out the window beside Barb, Sherry readied herself for gossip.

"Who are we spying on?"

"I prefer to call it people-watching." Barb didn't look away from the street as Sherry sat down. It wasn't technically a lie; she just neglected to say who she was watching for.

Sherry raised an eyebrow. "What people?"

Barb looked indignant and leaned over to point to the Edwards' house.

"Brian and Darryl, down the street? They're looking for renters. There have been cars coming and going all afternoon."

"Really?" Sherry twisted her head back, moving the curtains so she could see better. "I didn't think that old bird would let that house out of her grip. Mrs. Edwards, right? The one you go check on now and then?"

Barb thought it sounded strange when grown adults addressed each other by formal titles in social situations. With Mrs. Edwards, however, informality didn't fit. There was a sort of regalness about her, and calling her by her first name, Eileen, didn't seem right.

Barb recalled the way the old woman's white hair fell neatly around her face in a sleek bob, pinned back behind her ears, perfectly styled even after she declined.

Sitting straight and tall in her chair by the window, Mrs. Edwards would purse her lips together as if she were judging the world. Her stare would intimidate anyone walking by, but if you were lucky enough to be let in, she was the sweetest, making cookies for Gavin and bragging about her own boys.

Barb shrugged at Sherry's observation. "She died a couple of months ago. Didn't I tell you?"

It was a rhetorical question; she knew she had. Barb loved Sherry, but sometimes the unpleasant bits of reality fell on deaf ears. Sherry's face reddened further, her foot firmly planted in her mouth.

"Oh, that's right. That's too bad. She always seemed nice. From what you told me, anyway."

Mrs. Edwards may have been nice, but she was the stubbornest person Barb ever met. Brian came over, frantic because she wouldn't let her son pull her out of the tub and the nurse wasn't due until morning.

After that, Barb went over to help sometimes if she was home when Brian worked. She didn't do much, just watered some plants, made the odd lunch. Brian asked nothing of Barb, but he refused nothing either. He just stood aside to let her in, and she was glad for the arrangement. It was nice to be taking care of someone else without the expectation of a paycheque.

"She was a sweet lady," Barb agreed. "She hung on for a long time. It was sad to watch, really. I think the boys are probably trying to make the best of it. I've seen them with paint and stuff. Darryl's been out working in the yard, helping make it look nice, I guess."

The sound of the mower revving up got Sherry's attention. As she pulled herself onto her knees to get a better view, Barb smiled at how much her friend was enjoying the novelty of being a nosy neighbour. Spying wasn't really an option from the fifth floor of Sherry's apartment building, but at least she heard plenty of dirt through the walls.

"Who's that one giving him the stink eye next door?" Sherry asked, pointing her chin to a neighbouring yard.

Barb leaned back in time to see a curtain pull slightly, a sour scowl practically pulsing through the glass and over to Darryl.

"Oh, that's Dora. There's been sort of an ongoing feud around there."

Sherry leaned forward. "Do tell! My kids are teenagers. *Adult* gossip, please!"

Barb chuckled.

"Trust me, in this case, I guarantee the teenage gossip is way more interesting. Noise complaints, mostly. Nothing ever comes of it because her definition of what is late compared to the bylaw doesn't exactly agree."

Sherry snorted. "Really?"

Barb laughed.

"Thinks the fact that she's a light sleeper means she gets to dictate the activities schedule around here. She's just a nosy old biddy."

Sherry raised an eyebrow at the statement.

Barb pretended to appear offended. "What?"

"People in glass houses..."

Barb laughed and kicked Sherry playfully in the shin as she flopped back on the couch. Their feet joined in the centre cushion, toes brushing lightly. Sherry let her legs fall against the back of the couch, and she leaned her head back, fanning herself as she cooled off.

A young woman walked past Barb's window down the cul-de-sac, heading straight for the Edwards' house, head held high like she lived on the street her entire life. She consulted the scrap of paper in her hand, confirming the address. Her long hair was tied up in a ponytail, the light brown her mother would have called dishwater blonde. She appeared vaguely familiar. Barb thought she was probably about the age that Gavin would be now, and she wondered if they went to school together.

Jogging up the steps, the woman raised her hand to knock, but Darryl opened the door before she could, shaking her hand enthusiastically. Sherry called him "The Politician" after they met in passing one day, saying he would be right at home kissing babies and lying through his teeth.

"Always the charmer, that one. Makes sense they have him meeting people. Do you think they're renting out the whole thing, or if the brother is going to keep living in the suite?" Sherry plowed on without waiting for an answer. "I wouldn't live with that guy if you paid me. There's something off about him."

Barb considered. "Brian's alright. Wounded, maybe, but harmless. He was the one who moved in when his mom got sick, remember?"

Sherry shrugged.

"If you say so. He gives me the creeps." She shifted her watchful eyes away from the house down the street to look at Barb. "The quiet ones are always the ones to watch for."

Barb grunted in acknowledgement, only half-listening.

"Hey!" Sherry waved her hand at Barb. "Where'd you go?"

"What do you mean?"

"You want to tell me what's kept you stuck to this couch the last couple of weeks?"

"Oh, come on. You're exaggerating."

Sherry sat up, armed with receipts.

"Barb. Please. I've been here five times in the last two weeks and you haven't moved."

Barb didn't want to see the pity spread across her friend's

face if she told the truth. The couch was the best vantage point to watch for him, to make sure she didn't miss him if he appeared. It was so long since she had seen him; what if he needed her and she wasn't there? Just like last time.

Maybe he moved on. The thought cut into her like an ice-cold blade in her gut, and guilt spread through her bones. She should be happy about that, overjoyed.

In truth, she was gutted he didn't need her anymore, but she couldn't tell Sherry any of that without admitting she was seeing him.

It was the last secret they would ever share.

Instead, she said, "I'm thinking it's time to clean out his room. Maybe a garage sale in the spring?"

Sherry was enthusiastically on board, and they spent the rest of the afternoon making a plan of attack for going through the house.

After that day, Barb gave up on ever seeing him again, and now that he was back, her heart surged. It was selfish, but she felt better, less alone.

Nat's house remained dark, and Barb decided she should explain. The poor thing must have been terrified. Lingering at the window, she kept her eyes fixed on Dora's yard, hoping to get one more glimpse now that she knew he was still here.

She wasn't going anywhere.

Don't worry, she thought, hoping he heard her. *I can't move on either.*

DESPITE HERSELF, SHE SNORTED AT THE ridiculousness of the situation. It wasn't as if Gavin accidentally threw a ball through Nat's window.

Seeing it only once would have inclined her to blame the alcohol, but it kept returning sporadically over the years, loitering near her front lawn. Most often it appeared after dark, and she learned what to look for, its edges darker than the night as it watched her from afar. The figure never approached, always frozen to the spot as if considering whether it should.

She wasn't sure when the figure changed to Gavin in her mind. There was no pattern to his appearances, and never on the anniversary of his death. The face never revealed itself to her, but she accepted it was him, checking in on her.

These types of stories were never her cup of tea, but she couldn't think of anything else it could be. Her former therapist, her well-meaning sister's idea, wasn't able to hide the pity when she told him how comforting it was when she first saw it.

"So, you believe that this is Gavin coming to visit you?" The words were chosen carefully, as if he was already considering side effects and calculating dosages of whatever pill would make the figure disappear.

Condescending prick. Even now, she balled her fists, recalling the conversation.

She never saw it before Gavin died, so what else was she supposed to think? It would be a hell of a coincidence.

Of course I fucking do, she thought.

The office door shut behind her, and she strode to the receptionist's desk to cancel all her appointments. It sounded crazy then, and it didn't sound any less crazy now. She couldn't bear the thought of Nat thinking that way about her, but she needed to reassure her.

Guilt flashed through her as she replayed the terror in Nat's eyes, in her jerky movements, as she fled across the sidewalk to the safety of her home. She couldn't leave it this way. Barb had to tell her, but didn't know where she would even start.

After the shrink's reaction, she told no one else, for obvious reasons.

Comfort wrapped around her when she saw him, so after a few sightings, she decided there wasn't any harm in letting herself hold on to this one thing. She stopped questioning it and just let it be.

After all these years, this was the first time she ever needed to justify herself to anyone. Apologies were needed, and she had to be the one to clean up a mess she didn't make. Gutted, she relished, for the first time in a long time, that she felt like a mom, even a bad one.

Nat will understand. Barb wasn't sure how she knew that, but there was something in the way Barb did not put her off that made it true. Before she could change her mind, she dialled the number.

The ringtone sounded hollow, like it did when you knew no one would answer.

Her front door moaned as it swung open, and Barb stepped into the cool air outside. The curtains in Nat's living room were still, and if Barb didn't know any better, she would think no one was home. Staring up at Barb, he stood in the middle of the street, frozen as usual, his longing permeating the air between them.

"Gavin?" she whispered.

This was the longest he ever stayed, and she held her breath, willing him to show himself, to say something, anything. The shadowy head swivelled to the right, shifting its viewpoint to look over Barb's shoulder. Skin crawling, she turned, twisting her neck inch by slow inch.

Another figure stood behind her in the open doorway, reaching out its arms. Gavin looked like he was behind tinted glass, but this one looked like it was freshly drawn in thin air, defined lines surrounding the outline of a human body. Every colour, every sound, every memory Barb ever had was contained in that person-shaped crack in the universe.

Barb turned and ran down the steps, spilling out onto the street. Gavin was barely visible now. She barrelled toward him. Was he here to protect her, or was he here to take her with him?

A sudden silence engulfed her, vacuuming up every sound and then spitting it back out. Something shifted, and she knew before she turned around that the beings that had visited her would be gone. The street was quiet, back to normal.

A phlegmy cough escaped her lungs, and she peered down the road to Nat's, trying to catch her breath. Barb waited, watching, expecting a light to come on any second, for Nat to poke her head out and ask her what was the matter. The minutes drew out, and Barb became uneasy, pacing on the deck.

Something is definitely wrong.

Taking a deep breath, she made her way down the street, keeping her eyes glued to that front door that seemed to grin at her, daring her to enter. Halfway there, a speck of embarrassment crept in as she realized she still wore her robe before she snuffed it out, knowing that attire didn't matter in an emergency.

Placing her hand on the railing for balance, she climbed Nat's front steps. As she got closer, she realized the door wasn't latched, the tiniest sliver of darkness from inside escaping through the crack.

"Nat?" she whispered, reaching out a hand slowly toward the door.

She pushed, and the door felt heavy as the weight of her anticipation pushing back.

She shrieked as Chaos launched himself out of the darkness inside, shooting past her legs.

"Shit!"

His round, green eyes shone in the dark, body coiled to spring as he crouched at the bottom of the steps, taking a moment to decide if Barb was friend or foe before diving into the dense leaves of the bushes that peppered the shadows under the windows.

She leaned down, attempting to coax him out with her hand.

"C'mon, you little monster!" He rubbed against her palm, then nonchalantly moved farther back into the garden bed before bolting out across the lawn. Barb sighed, pulling herself out of the shrubs.

She stood up, rubbing her hands on her pants. They were wet.

Wait. Examining her fingertips, she frowned as she rotated her wrist for a better look.

Dark spots smudged across her fingers and down her palm.

"Nat!" she shouted as she realized what the wetness meant.

All further pretense of politeness gone, she hurtled into the house and fumbled along the wall for the switch.

On the few times she was here for a visit, Nat was welcoming. She wasn't the neatest, but had never hesitated to clear a space for Barb, to offer her a drink, to have a chat. Barb didn't talk to many people, and marvelled at the speed at which she and Nat became comfortable. Nat seemed equally surprised.

She was a bit of a lone wolf, and Barb saw her trying to navigate to common ground. Despite the gap in their ages, the pieces clicked into place without effort, just like with Sherry all those years ago.

That warmth was gone; the thick, dark air was now charged with the weight of fear and pain. A lump formed in her throat. Sluggish with dread and drink, she tried to force her dry mouth to swallow.

A wave of nausea rose in her as a coppery smell invaded her nostrils, acrid and stale. As a nurse, she knew that smell, encountered it so many times a day she was used to it. In a friend's home, it made little sense, and she pushed herself forward into the dark.

"Nat?" She realized she was holding her breath, the name on her lips forced out in a rush.

The sound was barely a whisper, yet it seemed to take immense effort. She licked her lips, cleared her throat to call more forcefully, to hope it wasn't true.

"Nat."

Her voice was unnaturally loud in the dark, filled with certainty.

The empty dining room snapped into view in front of her as her fingers finally found the switch. A mug rested on the heavy wood table along with a messy pile of opened mail.

Barb turned around, eyes huge as she took in the source of the blood on her hands.

In the middle of the living room floor lay a man. At least, she thought it was a man. She certainly couldn't tell by his face, which lay in pieces on Nat's throw rug. Blood and bits of brain matter and crushed teeth crawled sluggishly down the leaden base of Nat's standing lamp, which lay across the man's chest.

A pale hand peeked out from beyond the low wall at the entrance, fingers crooked upward above a second pool of blood. Barb moved into the living room, and the rest of the body revealed itself.

It was Nat. Her right arm was stretched across her body, as if she had been attempting to roll over, or to reach for something. The blue polo shirt she was wearing when she saw her in the morning looked black with the blood that coated it. Her eyes stared vacantly up.

Barb thought of all those murder mysteries she loved so

much, where the victims appeared surprised or afraid, an exaggerated expression forever etching their last moments on their faces.

It was all horseshit. This wasn't Nat, not anymore. The lively green of her eyes Barb admired so much was faded now that Nat wasn't behind them.

Barb clasped her hand to her mouth, the blood from her hand squelching as it squeezed between her fingers to smear across her face. The lovely Merlot burned up her throat, and she lurched outside just in time to vomit into the bushes.

Bloody fingerprints trailed across the keypad as her shaking fingers dialled 911. The cold concrete steps dug into her as she sank down to wait for the police.

Barb fumbled in her robe pocket for a cigarette, popping it in the corner of her trembling lips, numbness overtaking her. Chaos trotted toward her, bloody smudges trailing him on the cement walkway by the bushes. He rubbed against her hand briefly, then sat stoically by her side. Sirens wailed in the distance, growing louder by the minute, and lights in neighbouring houses switched on as red and blue lights washed over her.

She stooped to pick up the cat, holding him close as a blanket was placed on her shoulders and uniforms swarmed past them into the house.

8

"How do you know my mom?"

Gavin's eyes were enormous with wonder. The promise of having a connection with someone who had so recently been in the world that left him behind was written painfully across his features. Nat thought back to that first day and wondered how much she should tell him.

In the first month Nat moved in, she saw every other neighbour in the cul-de-sac puttering around their yard, preparing for fall. The street was alarmingly empty, the houses long abandoned and the yards unkempt. Empty nesters and retirees at least twenty years older than her inhabited the remaining homes.

The prospect of a young renter who might be loud and obnoxious was a hot topic in conversations she assumed happened over hedges and mailboxes. Flattery aside, she was well past her loud party years, so she kept her head down and went about her days as usual.

When it became apparent the squirrels hanging around on her fence had a more active social life than Nat, the neighbours chatted with her. She smiled and nodded through conversations about the weather, or how Christmas used to be called Christmas because that's what it is, and none of this 'holiday' crap.

When most of them discovered she didn't have kids or a partner, they weren't sure what to say to her beyond that. Mostly, they didn't bother her anymore, and she didn't bother them. The unspoken arrangement suited her fine.

As fall turned into winter, she watched the neighbours walking past the house on the corner, whispering to each other as they passed. The car in the driveway would periodically disappear or return like magic, but she saw no one in it. Once or twice, she observed a hand snaking out the front door to reach into the mailbox, digging through the flyers accumulating there before the door slammed shut behind it.

Sometimes she imagined it as a house from a fairy tale. There was a feeling of fog around it, unwelcoming and dark. Whenever she walked by, she tried to work out if it was intentional, or just sad.

In winter, she finally got the chance to find out. It was following a series of good ol' West Coast Canadian winter days. Snow fell and melted on an endless cycle, creating a crust atop the fresh snow. Every resident became an archaeologist, beginning the slow and painful process of chiseling themselves out, one tiny piece of ice at a time.

While Nat was out shovelling on those days, she saw just about every grandkid out on the cul-de-sac, keeping the driveways clear. She didn't see anyone out at the house on the corner the entire weekend. Snow piled high on the driveway, trapping the car under the attached carport as the storm continued over the next few days. The house's dark windows and drawn curtains suggested it was empty, abandoned to the elements.

When the snow finally stopped, a shout from down the street got Nat's attention, rising over the sound of water as it splashed over her dirty dishes in the sink. If the language she heard coming from the driveway at the end of the street was any indicator, the occupant was paying the procrastinator's price.

Nat soon came to understand that swearing like a trucker was pretty much Barb's natural state of being, but it never failed to make her smile. Talking to her neighbours and customers at work was all pretend, engineered interactions designed to pass the time. Barb's heated tirade was the first completely genuine stream of words Nat heard since she arrived back home.

She picked up her shovel and made her way down the street, noting the curtains that parted open to reveal disapproving gazes as the cursing got louder.

Nat neared the snowed-in vehicle, her breath puffing in front of her and her cheeks tingling as the cold kissed them. Barb was leaning against her car, resigned, lighting a cigarette. She possessed an air of extreme confidence about her. The cigarette fell limply in such a regal way after each deep drag. Thin auburn hair floated around her head in an outdated puff. Light blue pajamas peeked out from under her unzipped maroon parka.

Barb was not a woman who cared what people thought, and that endeared Nat to her immediately. She was everything Nat wanted to be when she grew up.

In that moment, Nat guessed Barb to be in her early sixties, nearly ready to retire, but she found out later that some hard years threw her estimate off by over a decade. Experience dulled the once mischievous sparkle in her friendly eyes.

"Need a hand?"

Barb tilted her head up at Nat, and she hunched slightly in defense, feeling enormous next to her neighbour's tiny frame. Barb's mouth pursed in a good-natured way as she twisted her neck and blew smoke over her shoulder, away from Nat. "Was it that obvious?"

Nat was drawn to Barb's hardness that day. It was fascinating, like wondering idly on certain birthdays how much she had become like her mother. She wondered how Barb had gotten that way, not yet realizing how much they had in common.

Once the car was free, Nat turned to head home, but Barb stopped her.

"I was going to run errands," Barb said. "But now I'm wiped."

Nat grinned, and Barb insisted she come in for something to drink for her trouble. Nat followed her through the living room, snaking their way around the maze of boxes that lay everywhere.

"Sorry for the mess," Barb said as they went. "Watch your step."

Nat laughed as they passed a faded couch covered in a print of roses. "I don't mind. It's not like I'm the tidiest person."

"Spring cleaning," Barb said.

Nat glanced at the mantle, the only place that seemed not to have been touched yet. It was full of family photos, a younger Barb with a dark-haired boy, happy and smiling. From left to right, the photos painted a timeline, from infant to toddler to junior high. Birthday parties, bowling, hockey.

The last photo was of Barb with her arm around him on the floral sofa, the upholstery shiny and bright. The boy rolled his eyes and squirmed while Barb tried to plant a kiss on his cheek, the tiny dimple giving him away. Warm longing ran through Nat at some toys and clothes in the pictures, many of them familiar from her own childhood, and she wondered what this boy was doing now.

Sitting in the kitchen, they chatted about random things. What they both did for a living, cats versus dogs (*cats, obviously*), and, of course, books.

Barb was also an avid reader, and it turned out they had similar tastes. She was jealous of the fact that Nat worked in a bookstore, and Nat had to convince her that the retail life wasn't all glitz and glamour, no matter what store you were in.

"Being surrounded by books would be fun though, I think! You must have great conversations." Barb leaned over, elbows on the table, waiting for all the literary gossip that was sure to come her way.

"I do!" Nat laughed. "But it's also a really busy location. It's hard to finish a thought sometimes, let alone an entire discussion about your favourite summer read."

"You must have a lot of books, though."

"Too many! The staff discount sure doesn't help that problem."

"I have some I'm getting rid of," Barb said, examining Nat with the eye of an antiques dealer, looking for the right home for a priceless treasure.

She gestured to the high piles of overflowing boxes, stacked high along the hallway until their fate was decided. Tinted borders of nicotine surrounded bare patches on the wall where pictures once hung.

"The thing with cleaning is sometimes it has to get worse before it gets better." Barb wasn't apologizing for the mess, simply stating a fact. "I thought a garage sale in the spring might be a good idea, and now my hyper-organized friend won't let me off the hook. Would you like to take some?"

"Oh no, that's alright. I can wait for spring and put a little money in your pocket."

Barb leapt into action, as if it was just what she was

waiting to hear. "I insist. My treat! You were so nice to me today, I really should return the favour."

"You don't have to..."

"Thank you," Barb cut her off, a no-nonsense look settling on her features.

"But I really would like you to have them. I want them to go to someone who will appreciate them. They belong... belonged," she swallowed, jaw clenched, "to my son, Gavin. He passed away."

"I'm sorry," Nat said. The wound seemed painful, but old and deep, not fresh.

"Thank you. It was a long time ago. A car accident. They've been sitting for a while, and I think it might be time. Come on," Barb said abruptly, clear she wanted to change the subject. "They're in the basement."

Nat crammed her hands in her pockets as she followed, hoping she could hide the fact that they were shaking.

Wooden steps bowed under her feet as she made her way down. As a child, Nat's cellar had steps like this, with a space between the stairs where anything could reach out to grab her ankles and drag her into the abyss below. One slow step at a time, Nat followed Barb, letting out a breath she didn't know she was holding when they reached the bottom and entered a warm but slightly damp rec room.

Cinderblock walls plastered with faded movie posters surrounded one window high on the adjacent wall that let in a single narrow shaft of light. Barb made her way to the middle of the room and reached overhead to find the pull chain on a dangling bare bulb. A click pierced the room, and the bulb came to life, its arc shortening with each swing until it stood still, a dull halo of light casting a sickly pall over everything it touched.

An old TV sat in the corner, propped up on a battered-looking nightstand with a VCR on top. Magazines and VHS tapes cluttered the top of a nearby bookcase. A thick line of dust remained on the outer edge of each shelf, the ghost of the books that had previously called them home.

A complicated board game with tiny game pieces lay scattered across a small, round coffee table. Pens and paper with copious notes were in an oddly neat pile right in the middle of it all, as if someone picked them up off the floor to vacuum, but forgot to throw them away afterwards.

A stiff square of shag carpeting was tossed over the concrete floor. Nat remembered a musty, chocolate brown rug just like this in her childhood home, refusing to get clean no matter how often her mom tried. Every wayward crumb and dust mite burrowed as deep as it could get, its invisible carcass lining the hard shell far below the top of the carpet.

A pair of vinyl beanbag chairs splashed with a tie-dyed pattern sat across from the TV. A console controller of some kind lay abandoned in one. Fondness upturned her lips as she imagined peeling herself out of it, the material clinging to her thighs as someone from above called that dinner was ready.

"Gavin loved fantasy, horror, all kinds of stuff like that." Barb moved to the bookcase, and Nat followed to help adjust the pile of boxes that was shoved up against it.

"This is great, thank you," Nat said, wrestling the first box off the stack.

A framed photograph of a much younger Barb and her son sat on top. A mini-golf course was in the background. Barb's arm pulled him tight to her side as they laughed, both squinting in the sun. Unsure of how much of herself Barb wanted to reveal, Nat averted her eyes.

Barb was giving her a strange look as they hauled the box upstairs, and Nat wondered how much damage she recognized in her.

"You took my books?" Gavin asked, a look of supreme offense in his eyes.

The memory of that snowy day melted away as Gavin interrupted her, bringing her back to this strange place that was now apparently home.

"Seriously?" Nat snorted. "*That's* your takeaway from this story?"

Hands on hips, his chin jutted defiantly, trying to mark his turf.

"Yes, okay? What can I say? You have good taste."

Gavin's eyes were huge with wonder, the promise of having a connection with someone who had so recently been in the world that left him behind written painfully across his face. He was buzzing with excitement.

"Did she talk about me a lot?"

The tense of his question sliced into her, and she realized that everyone she knew now existed only in her past. "Just the once."

The excitement leaked out of his body like a punctured balloon, his entire body deflating. "Oh."

"I'm sure she thinks about you all the time," Nat added hastily, trying to course correct. "Plus, I haven't known her for very long. I only moved down the street about six months ago."

Some things just hurt too much to talk about. The fracture in her own family hung over her, and regret overcame her once more.

"I still can't believe you took my books," he grunted, pain sitting behind his pout, like he was expecting Barb to hang on to them forever.

The painful narcissism of her teenage years long forgotten, she reminded herself to be compassionate.

"I never unpacked them, though. Just in case."

He looked confused. "In case of what?"

"In case your mom changed her mind." Nat paused, finally identifying the feeling that permeated her when she carried the box home. "They never really felt like they were mine."

Nat spent the rest of the night alternating between smiling and nodding and wishing Gavin would just shut the hell up already. After peppering her with questions about his mom, he settled into spewing random anecdotes about his friends, his school, the dog he always wanted.

They strolled side by side, in no particular hurry. Gavin droned on as her mind catalogued the events of the day, trying to figure out exactly what she learned.

How Gavin died ate at her. It couldn't be a coincidence, not after what she did. Clutching her arms across her ribs, her skin scratched against the polyester of her shirt. She couldn't believe she was stuck in the hideous short-sleeved polo for all eternity.

Am I being punished?

If she were, it was far less than she deserved. A small smile flicked across the corners of her mouth as she remembered conversations like this with Chris, one or the other of them relaying a stream of unrelated items about their day.

As annoying as it was, Gavin's excitement was contagious, somehow pure, and she decided to just enjoy the ride.

The joke's on the punisher.

What if it wasn't a reckoning? Gavin was so young, snuffed out before he had time to become who he was meant to be. If this wasn't supposed to be some kind of personal hell, or a way to make her regret what she lost, then why was she here with him?

The sun peaked over the ridge of the mountains in the distance, soft pink lighting spreading across the concrete toward their feet. Despite her exposed arms, it occurred to her she didn't feel cold during her walk home. As the sunlight climbed up their legs to kiss their arms and face, no warmth accompanied it, no comfort.

Looking around at all the empty homes, the apocalyptic sense of desolation and abandonment grew deeper and more pronounced than the night before. They met no one since Barb disappeared, dead or alive. Loneliness crushed down on her, and she wondered if she and Gavin were the only two people on the face of this new earth.

Face reddening, she was feeling more and more out of control. She was missing so many pieces of the puzzle. What happened to her that night was there, pushing on the edges of her memory, just out of reach, buried in the place where Chris was.

In the background, Gavin's voice buzzed on in time with her whirring thoughts.

"So, my friend totally snuck out and thought he was all hot shit, but he forgot his dad would take his baby sister out in the car to get her to go back to sleep and she was crying all night and his dad drove up behind him at like two in the morning and he was *soooooooooo* busted and…"

"Hey, Gavin?"

Annoyed at the interruption, he ducked his head when she didn't immediately speak.

"Yeah?"

"What do you remember about the day you died?"

With the prospect of a willing audience too good to pass up, he brightened immediately.

"Dude. I remember *everything.*"

9

Flattery had Gavin standing straighter, proud that Nat wanted to hear his story. There was a park nearby that had three huge rocks in the middle of a stretch of grass, just beyond a sandy area with ancient playground equipment. They each chose a rock, clambering up to sit across from each other, legs crossed.

"Tell me," she said, her enormous eyes pleading with him.

Even though it was years since his death, it wasn't something that was easily forgotten. As he cleared his throat to speak, the details came rushing back.

"It was almost summer vacation," he leaned forward, setting the scene. "I was going to go to Math Camp soon. Trust me, the chicks *loved* me at Math Camp."

Nat's face was pinched as if she had a terrible headache. "Okay, okay, take a pill already."

"I was walking home from school when I heard this car behind me, and then suddenly I was in the air."

There was an instant, long and drawn out, where everything was fine, like he possessed a superpower which must have kicked in under stress. He believed it with all his heart until he slammed into the ground, rolling into the trash cans before coming to a stop against a fence.

He held his hands in front of him, as if he had a crystal ball she could see into. "That was the worst part, you know? The *sound*, sort of like a tomato dropping off a balcony."

Nat winced, and he took it as his cue to keep going. The story was gross, but he could tell she was totally hooked.

"Do you know what happens to an eyeball when…"

Green spread across her face, a cartoonish shade that wouldn't have existed when they were alive.

What is her problem? Raising a hand to his eye, he could feel the swelling there, the blood that was leaking down his cheek. The death mask was intruding, creeping across his face. The story was creating a visual. Not wanting to lose her attention, he skipped ahead and tried to temper his enthusiasm.

"Sorry. Anyway, I'm lying there blinking cuz there's blood in my eyes and thinking about how lucky I am that my mom's a nurse, that when she got home, she would fix it. That's when I saw these runners walking up to me, with these really white running shoes. They must have been brand new."

The rubber tread in the scorching sun stung his nostrils and burned into his lungs as he struggled to breathe. A weird gurgling noise surrounded him, and he vividly remembered his terror as he realized it was coming from him. The shoes were approaching him so slowly, and he wondered why they were taking their time in what was clearly an emergency.

Letting his waving hands drop to his lap, the showman's mask slipped. Showing the hurt and anger underneath was something he wanted to avoid, even only for a second. Clearing his throat again for the finale, he carried on.

"I was lying there for a while, or at least it felt like it. I tried to get up, but it got too hard."

"So, I quit trying to move, and then I felt someone

grabbing my face, like this." He placed his hands on either side of his cheeks to rest on top of the phantom fingers that still lingered there. "I thought someone was helping me, trying to talk to me. At first, I was relieved, but then it felt different. It hurt, and there was this weird pressure, like I was shrinking."

The excitement over getting a chance to tell his story diminished as he remembered exactly how it felt as his lungs burned as he gasped for air. Hot liquid filled his mouth, eyes, and ears.

"The whole time, I swear there were people there, watching me die. There were voices around me, arguing. It was really creepy. What kind of person just stands around and doesn't help?"

Anger seeped into his voice, and it pulled him out of his memory.

"Like, 'Oh, don't mind the dead kid on the side of the road. Nothing to see here. Just a bag full of this week's trash.'" Lowering his voice a little, he continued, choosing his words carefully to reign in his emotions.

"Don't," she whispered with a ferocity that surprised him. "Don't think that about yourself, okay? People miss you, Gavin. You..." He was surprised as her voice cracked and she looked away. "You mattered."

Why does she care so much? He couldn't figure her out, but that didn't mean he was stupid. He could tell when someone was hiding something from him. No one ever thought that kids could figure it out.

Maybe they just didn't want them to.

He thought of his dad, of the last time he saw him. His mom was a terrible liar, too.

Don't shoot the messenger, he thought. Taking in how upset she was, he thought better of it before he spoke, something he hadn't had to worry about in so long.

"Sorry."

"It's fine," She said curtly, waving off the apology.

"It's nothing you said; it's just…I don't know. This whole thing is just going to take some getting used to." She sighed. "It's just all so fucked up."

A thrill ran through him as the f-bomb rang through the air. He hadn't heard one in forever.

"That's it?"

"Yeah."

"You just died, and then what? Got swallowed up by that goo thing like I did and that's it?"

He shrugged, his patented "No shit" gesture.

Nat hopped off the rock. Gavin didn't want to be a dick; he really didn't. On the other hand, pushing her buttons was really fun, and he couldn't pass up the opportunity.

"Okay, okay, don't get your panties in a bunch already. Yeah, it was there, sort of all over me. Then I blinked, and when I turned around, my body was gone. Everyone else, too."

"Everyone? There was no one else here when you came through? No other dead people just living their lives?"

Smiling at the unintentional pun, he shook his head. "Nope. Just me."

"Alone?"

The sharpness of the word made him flinch, but he nodded.

"Yup."

"For how long?"

Irritation came off him in a palpable wave as he rolled his eyes. "I don't know! Do you even know how long it's been since I even looked at a calendar? What's the point? I don't even think it works that way."

"What way?" She touched a nerve, and she knew it.

Oh, shit. He wasn't careful enough, and now she was suspicious.

"Time is weird down here, man. Sometimes it feels like it's

daytime forever. If I want it to be sunny, it's sunny. If I feel like I want to have a nap, it gets dark."

To illustrate his point, he closed his eyes. Cracking them open, he flapped his hand impatiently, forgetting for a moment that he had to show her what to do.

"Close your eyes. Think about December."

Despite her skepticism, she did the same. She twitched as something wet hit her face. Opening her eyes, she saw a dense blanket of snow covering the ground, already past their ankles. Fluffy snowflakes made their way lazily from the sky, and he watched them cling to her hair and eyelashes playfully.

"Holy shit!"

"Yeah." He shrugged. *No big deal. Just another day.*

Once upon a time, this was all so exciting, but he figured out so many other cool tricks since this one. It was at the bottom of his stack now. The wonder in her eyes at the instant white universe brought a pang of jealousy. He used to be like that, convinced he was powerful, that this was magic. It was only a matter of time before she noticed she wasn't wet or cold, that her breath didn't fog the air in front of her.

It's all pretend.

"Hey, what year was it when you died?"

Gavin frowned. He wasn't sure he liked where this was going. "1999. Why? How long ago was that?"

"Sixteen years," she whispered, the green colour returning to her cheeks and down her neck, an unsettling match to her eyes.

The surrounding snow melted away, and the spring weather returning as their concentration shifted to the topic at hand.

I've been dead longer than I've been alive, he thought, trying to detach himself from that fact as if he were reading it in a textbook. Was the world like all the science fiction books he read by now? Were there hovercrafts? What kinds of video games did people play? What was the human to robot ratio?

All that could wait. Right now, there was only one thing he needed to know.

"So did Y2K happen, or what?!"

10

"Sixteen years." Nat stated, as if saying the words out loud gave her control over them. "You've been alone. This whole time."

The weight of the facts tumbling from her lips crushed any hope of figuring out what she was supposed to be doing here. Gavin opened his mouth to reply, but she rambled on.

"Are you stuck here? Why didn't you ever move on? Isn't that what we're supposed to be trying to do? You saw your mom when I died, right? Does she know about you? Have you ever tried to talk to her?"

Gavin stared at her, a look of profound contemplation on his face. After a beat, he burst out laughing, a bitter, old laugh that chilled her to her core. Kids his age were way too young to have a laugh like that.

"You're kidding, right? I didn't even know how long I've been dead! I'll be wandering around minding my own business and then just randomly pop up in front of my house for no reason. Nope...it never occurred to me to talk to my mom. Thanks for the tip," he spat through quivering lips, the words filled with venom.

Irritation gripped her insides, twisting and writhing as it threatened to explode out of her in an angry rush. This little brat was too self-absorbed to notice she was only trying to help.

"Ghosts are supposed to have some sort of unfinished business, aren't they?"

The words forced themselves through her clenched teeth as she tried to keep herself from screaming. Determined not to fight with the only other person on her planet, she dug her fingers into her palms.

"What are we even doing here? What's the point? There has to be a point, right?"

"Dunno," he shrugged, maddeningly indifferent about the philosophical questions governing where they were.

"Aren't we supposed to be here to *do* something, or learn something?" Unsure if she was asking for answers from Gavin or the universe, she was yelling now, as if that would make herself heard. Feverish sweat beaded on her hairline. "I want...I don't know. Someone killed me. I want it to mean something!"

"How do you know someone killed you if you can't remember anything?" he challenged, unfazed by her outburst.

The scraps she remembered played in rapid succession, over and over. Being grabbed from behind, her surprised mouth worked frantically to bite his hand, get some air, make a sound, anything. The dry, powdery latex coated her tongue and teeth, and the sickening scent invading her nose. The sudden pressure in her back left her helpless on the carpet. The man watched coldness drown her until numbness consumed her completely.

Was it senseless? Was it random?

"I remember enough."

Exasperation with the new kid filled Gavin's eyes.

"Well, I do too, okay? What exactly do you think I've been

doing this entire time? Do you think I *want* to be stuck in this hellhole? I *tried*. Nothing. Ever. Changes." Full of truth and acceptance, his wide, clear eyes drilled into hers.

Crouching down, she placed her head between her knees as television static greyed her vision. *Can ghosts have panic attacks?*

Done with feeling exposed, she tried to hold herself back. She might be stuck with him, but she could still keep this one thing to herself.

"Stop crying."

The words hung in the air, waiting for a reaction, and for a moment, she thought she said them out loud. Gavin's voice cut through her foggy, muddled thoughts. She thought it might be the precursor to an apology, but when she glanced up, it wasn't remorse that she saw, but undisguised disgust at her tears.

Heat rose to her cheeks, and anger rose in the back of her throat. *Who does he think he is?*

"Screw you, kid! I'm a person, too! Was, at least. I don't know what I am now, but would it be so bad to let me figure it out without being a fucking asshole?!"

"That's not it." His condescending mouth turned up at the corners, only serving to further fuel her rage.

"Oh, yeah? Then what is your goddamn problem?"

His fingers traced a lazy circle around his own face with pointed fingers, the universal "wipe your face, asshole" gesture. Tears wet her cheeks, escaping in her rage. As she brushed them away, upset with her own loss of control, she recoiled as thick and sticky mucous slid through her fingers instead.

A disgusted wail escaped her throat as she pulled her hand away. Sludge covered her hand. There was no other way to describe it. It was bright red of a cheap crayon, with an orange tint underlying the cartoonish hue.

A memory hit her like a ton of bricks. She remembered the mood ring Chris bought for her when she turned fifteen.

After the accident, she pulled it out of her jewellery box to wear it again, trying to feel close to him. It was such an unusual colour, and people couldn't stop asking her about it.

"What does it mean?" they asked, grabbing her finger for a closer look.

After she looked it up, she wrenched at the cheap band and shoved it into the bottom of her jewelry box.

Fear. Anger.

The muck began crawling down her face to caress her neck and shoulder. She shivered as she realized she was literally wearing her emotions on her sleeve.

The mucus oozing from her eyes was a dark, cold jelly, and she wiped at it again, more frantically this time. Steam came off the remnants that stuck to her palms, surrounding her in a humid plume. She clawed at her face wildly to dislodge whatever droplets remained there.

The substance reeked—a bouquet of raw sewage and pig guts, splattering back at her as she flapped her hands to get it off. The blobs hit the ground with a sizzling sound. She expected it to eat through the pavement at her feet. Instead, she backed up as the hot mess crawled its way back to her, drawn to its source.

Gagging, she took a step back from the growing pile of festering garbage juice collecting at her feet. Touching her sneaker experimentally, it lovingly stroked the laces before making its way up her leg. She was paralyzed as it continued its ascent. It reached her thigh, and she choked as the mass leaned off her leg to reach for her dangling hand. Ice cold on her skin, it sucked on her palm to give her a terrible kiss hello. Thin tentacles of residue slithered over her knuckles before reaching for her fingertips, molding itself to her.

A metallic taste rose in the back of her throat, coating her tongue. For better or worse, she was home to this stinking yet oddly tender life form. Her arm tingled with an icy burn and pulled downward, the skin stretching as if trying to escape it.

The flesh on her forearm parted, exposing the butcher shop that made up her muscles and bone. She clambered to grab the dark pool, but her fingers simply parted the mess as it crawled inside, injecting itself into her exposed veins.

Gavin's face was infuriating, pure delight at hazing the newbie in the supernatural life skills knowledge department.

The flesh closed behind it with a slurp, and her arm shook as it fell back to her side. More of the substance appeared on her skin, and the cycle repeated itself. She kept her head still, unsure where to look as it crawled over her face, blurring her vision once again. Unable to move, she sensed herself going to that place, that sweet relief of just shutting down to make it all go away. Gavin's voice slowly emerged from somewhere deep underwater.

"Hey, you just have to calm down, okay? Take a deep breath."

I'm beyond a deep fucking breath, she thought, seriously hyperventilating now.

"Okay, how about a trick? Let me show you a trick."

He was talking to her as if she were a rabid dog. A magic show was not what she needed right now.

"Think of a place. Anywhere you want."

"Anywhere?" Her breath was jagged, a rough wheeze that fought its way up her constricted throat and through the viscous slime that covered her lips. It coaxed itself between her teeth, opening her gums to reabsorb.

"Yep! Just make sure it's somewhere you've been before." He frowned, considering what would work best. "Think of your *favourite* place, somewhere that always makes you feel better. Once you think of it, you'll be there. Just be ready. It happens fast, okay?"

Nodding, she closed her eyes.

"Wait!"

A familiar chill crept across her skin, prickling the nape of her neck. Nat forced herself to keep her hands at her side, resisting the temptation to wipe it away, knowing it would only prolong the process as it crawled back to her.

"Don't forget you get back the same way. Just think of here. Duh."

"Back?" She assumed he was speaking metaphorically.

"Just do it."

Taking a deep breath, she built the image in her mind, brick by brick.

My favourite place.

SHE WAS SITTING IN A CHAIR, THE CLAMMINESS ON her skin drying as her breathing evened out. She opened her eyes to a dark room, a soft, worn seat underneath her, hard armrests on either side. Springs squeaked as she shifted to look at the large blank screen in front of her.

Whirring filled the small space, and a light flashed behind her, highlighting the faded maroon seatbacks and curtains that always looked like they needed a good vacuum. A candy wrapper crunched underneath one foot, and a pile of stale popcorn spilled on the floor surrounding the other.

An old-school coming attractions commercial populated the screen, one that she and Meg always giggled about because there was no way that the hot dog wasn't suggestive.

It actually worked.

A scratchy, booming voice encouraged her to get up and get a snack as a snappy jingle filled the room. Tempted to stay and see what was playing, she let the cool air settle over her and put her feet up on the seat in front of her. Hiding out and rolling herself up in other people's stories for hours seemed like a great idea right now.

Something moved in the dark, coiling and ducking between the rows in front of her. She shrunk back into her chair, trying to identify where it had gone. Behind her, the swinging door to the theatre opened, and she got up from her seat, following the movement to the exit. The door swung back, and something slithered through, blocking the door for a moment before it wobbled shut.

The unexpected summer sun beyond the door took her off guard, and she raised her hand to her eyes. The lobby looked as it always did, with the tiny concession counter in the corner and a carpeted entryway too vast for the number of patrons that usually inhabited it.

"Hello?" she called.

The old hits of the 50s that were piped in over the crackling loudspeaker echoed against the absolute emptiness. Static crackled through the air, her hair rising slightly. Something skittered along the floor, shying away from her footsteps.

Her heart quickened, and she squeezed her eyes shut, not about to let whatever was lurking ruin one of the last places she felt truly safe.

THE EXCURSIONS TO THE MOVIES WERE MEG'S IDEA. Meg sat with her for days in her room after her world shattered. She didn't know what either of them was supposed to say, but decided it didn't matter.

All people saw when they looked at Nat was someone who did something so terrible and still got to roam freely, the rich girl whose parents must have pulled some strings. Everywhere she looked, she saw accusation, and she was doing enough of that when she saw herself in the mirror.

Meg said it wasn't true, that no one even knew who she was. Unfortunately, they both knew it was bullshit. In small towns, you become your sins.

After a few weeks, Meg decided enough was enough, and told her they were going to get out of the house.

"No way, Meg. I can't. Everyone knows."

Meg hit her with a pillow, shocking her a little. People treated her like a piece of glass since it happened. "No one's looking at you. Get over yourself."

Nat was about to yell at her, but stopped herself when she saw Meg's face.

Meg peered down at the bedspread to avoid looking at her. "Not everything is about you, Nat."

She blinked, not used to hearing Meg talk to her like that.

"Okay. Fine. Nowhere really busy or anything. I don't want anyone from school to see me. It feels weird to have fun, like I'm doing something wrong. I just need to..."

"Turn off your brain?"

"Yes!" she perked up, pleased to be understood.

Maybe I'm not crazy.

"I have an idea," Meg said. "We'll go somewhere where no one will look at you."

After that, they went down to The Station every weekend, rain or shine, no matter what was playing. The new multiplex down the highway had all the big-name blockbusters, so most of their classmates went there instead. If they saw anyone they knew, Nat would go to the bathroom until Meg let her know the coast was clear. If anyone she knew saw her, they always whispered, scampering off as soon as they made eye contact.

When that happened, Meg pretended not to notice, and Nat loved her for it.

They would sit side by side at the very back of the room,

Meg always on her right. Sometimes she would catch Meg looking at the screen with a wistful expression on her face.

"What?" Nat whispered in the dark the first time she noticed.

Meg looked startled, lost in thought. "Nothing," she whispered back. "It's a good movie."

"You sure? We don't have to keep coming every weekend."

Meg had looked at her and forced a sad smile. She squeezed Nat's arm a little, trying to reassure her.

"It's fine. I zoned out for a bit, that's all."

The odd awkward moment aside, those weekends reassured her of their ride or die status. No matter what.

Until I went and fucked everything up.

Behind her closed eyes, she pictured the park, the playground equipment, the green of the grass against the yellow curb, the boulders in the middle of the square.

When she opened them again, her skin was dry, with no trace of the vivid horror remaining. The cluster of large rocks loomed beside her, Gavin sitting on the biggest one, legs dangling. He held a book, looking up from the pages as she returned.

Where did he get that?

"So?" he asked, his eyes glinting with conspiratorial glee. "Where'd you go?"

"The movie theatre downtown." She didn't feel like explaining why it qualified as a place to calm her down. Luckily, Gavin didn't question it. "The one that used to be an old fire station."

"No way!" Gavin cried happily, jumping down from the rock to meet her. "I *love* that place! Wanna go sometime?"

He was practically vibrating at the prospect of an outing

with another human being, and she thought of all the times she wished for just a minute to herself.

"Oh man, we should go see my favourite..."

Trying to get back on track, she cut in. "So, I guess I can't cry anymore?"

He looked offended that his distraction technique hadn't completely pulled her away from their earlier conversation.

"Well, you *can*. Like, there's nothing stopping you. I just look at it more like leaking, not crying. Try not to get all worked up. That's like poltergeist time."

"How do you know?"

"Long story," he said, evading the answer.

"So...what? I can't get mad, or sad, or glad?" *God, I sound like 'The Dead Person's Big Book of Feelings,'* she cringed.

She became a pro at masking her feelings quite some time ago. *I've been prepping my whole life for this,* she thought bitterly.

Gavin smirked. That sense of superiority in the upturned corners of his mouth pissed her off so much. He was snatched from life before he could have a proper rebellious phase, and now he was compensating. Feeling terrible, she begrudgingly let it go.

On the other hand, it's not like a punch to the face will kill him.

"Yeah," Gavin said, nodding sagely. "The dead are like that. I've totally seen it before. Like no one else has problems? They act as if the world revolves around them."

Nat rolled her eyes at the irony. This all sounded very personal, and she wondered what beef two ghosts could have. It was obvious Gavin's reaction came from personal experience.

"Wait." The implication of what he said dawned on her, and she raised her hand, pointing at him.

Gotcha.

Realizing his mistake, he turned away from her. "Just drop it, okay?" he snapped, but it was too late.

What he said when he was telling her about how he died came to her, the contradiction obvious to her now.

I've never had to show people my car-accident self before.

"There have been other people here with you before, haven't there?" she asked, eyes narrowing.

Caught in the lie, his eyes brimmed, but he held his ground, jutting his chin forward and locking his stare. He looked like he was expecting to be told he was a stupid child.

Patience. More flies with honey, her reasonable inside voice reminded her. Lowering her volume, she calmly forced herself to ask nicely.

"What happened to them, Gavin?"

He shrugged, eyebrows raised, stretching his lips as a forced smile split on his face.

"Gavin?" she snapped.

Inhaling sharply, he turned away from her and walked down the street.

"Hey! We're not done!"

Trotting after him, she grabbed his arm at the elbow to spin him around. A sweet relief coursed through her at still being able to feel a touch of any kind at all.

A familiar silence took hold of them as a jolt rocked her body. From the look on Gavin's face, he sensed it, too. It was like licking a battery, or touching an electric fly swatter. In life, this sensation would have been unpleasant but fleeting. The trauma would soon fade from recent memory, but instinct would remember the sensation, forever stopping her from touching a hot stove.

Nat braced to pull her hand back reflexively, away from the sparking sensation, but it didn't move. She tried again, with more force this time, but it was no use. Something glued her to him, creating a grotesque statue of the two of them.

Shifting foot to foot and flexing the fingers on her other hand, she was relieved to find she could still move. A leaf fell in the air near Gavin's ear and stopped, hovering just above his shoulder. She reached up to pluck it from the air, but it was stuck there, an invisible force beneath it pushing up against her fingers.

They were suddenly living things trapped in a painting.

"What...?"

The air shifted around them, a cyclone building from their feet. The wind picked up speed, sucking the floating leaf into the cyclone and twirling it faster and faster as a light grew between them.

"Let *go!*" Gavin yelled at her through the growing howl as her hair whipped across her face. Trying again to wrench herself away from him, it was no use; her fingers were locked to his arm, her muscles completely frozen.

What if this was it, the proverbial light?

As it grew, she hoped not. It was dull and depressing, like a garage bulb, not welcoming or comforting like you would expect the other side to be.

Increasing in intensity, the light washed away what little colour remained in her vision. The light brightened, and it enveloped Gavin, his arm disappearing against her palm. Growing and spreading, the brightness relentlessly swallowed up the rest of her arm. The force of it finally overcame the rest of the world around them, and she squinted to shield her eyes.

A sensation of weightlessness fell over them, and she kicked her feet, no longer feeling the reassurance of the pavement beneath them. An explosion boomed as the brightness peaked, and the blast wrenched them apart, carrying them up into what was now a full-blown tornado.

11

THE WIND DIED, LEAVING THEM SUSPENDED IN MID-air before they fell, like characters in a Saturday morning cartoon. Bracing herself for the fall, she hit the ground hard, coughing as the force of the fall knocked the wind out of her.

Flexing her fingers, she felt dirt sifting through them, pine needles lodging themselves under her nails. The scent of damp earth surrounded her as she rolled onto her back. Tall trees and a blue sky above greeted her as she opened her eyes, the gentle movement of branches swooping in the breeze caressing her ears.

Heavy shuffling came from across the path—the sound of something dragging itself along the forest floor. A pair of hands gripped the low wooden barrier that was propped up, reminding people to follow the path. She breathed a sigh of relief as Gavin's face came into view and he pulled himself up to lie on his back next to her, gasping for air.

"Holy SHIT! Gavin, what the hell was that?"

His eyes were saucers, and he was shaking. This was unexpected in a world where he thought he knew all the rules.

"I have no idea. I've never touched another dead person before."

Did he do this?

If ever someone needed an excuse to change the subject, this was it, and she couldn't help but be suspicious that maybe he manufactured this distraction.

"Where are we anyway?" she asked.

He shrugged, unconcerned.

"I don't know. Don't you?"

Looking around, she scoured the area for any landmarks that might help. The mountainside ran up on a steep incline to her left, sparser than the side Gavin came from. It was rockier, covered in scrub as opposed to the thick trees that ran nearly to the base of the mountain.

Taking a tentative step and peering down, she saw the lake far below, choppy and angry in the chilly air. Wet leaves completely covered the forest floor, a slippery carpet protecting many tiny critters.

Frowning, she glanced up at the sky. When she confronted Gavin, it had been late morning, grey and overcast. Now it was cloudless and blue, and the sun wasn't nearly as high, much later in the day. There was a crisp bite to the atmosphere, everything coming down from a summer of being lush and green.

The leaves in the trees closest to them were that autumnal orange she loved so much, becoming patchy green and yellow toward the bottom, where the weather was warmer. The skin on her arms prickled with goosebumps as the cool air around them ran over it. Blowing onto her hand, she felt the warmth of her breath on her fingers. Steam plumed in front of her, and she shivered at the bite in the air.

I feel this.

Gavin's voice brought her back to the matter at hand. "Nat?"

Big picture, Nat.

"How should I know?" she asked exasperated.

He sighed, explaining it to her as if she were a toddler asking why five came after four.

"You have to be thinking of a place before you move. If I don't know, you have to. Plus, we both must have been here before."

"How do you know that?"

Happy to fall back into the role of spirit guide, full of wise-sounding answers with extremely vague details, he spoke confidently.

"It doesn't work. If you try to go somewhere you've never been, you just get stopped. It's like you're locked out. You can't get in, and you can feel it, too, like you don't belong."

It sounded like the equivalent of a vampire not being able to enter uninvited. While she could accept that she was dead, she wasn't quite ready to ponder the philosophy around the fact that she was no longer human.

"What, like a supernatural passport?"

Indifferent to the travel barrier, he shrugged.

"That sucks," she said, wondering if he just didn't think about it that hard, or if he just accepted it by now.

"Yeah," he agreed, a wistful expression tugging at her heart.

She hoped she hadn't opened a can of worms. "I didn't really go anywhere before I died. We didn't have a lot of money, you know? The farthest I've been was my uncle's farm in Alberta. I hated it. All the other kids would go on these cool vacations, to hot places, tropical places. FUN places."

He sighed, reminiscing. "The most excitement I ever had was the water park an hour away. When I figured out I could go where I wanted, I tried to go to California. I always wanted to go to Hollywood. Didn't work."

What kind of afterlife has an income bracket? She thought. Before she got into that one, he continued.

"I tried a few other places where I wasn't allowed before, too. Some..." he stopped in his tracks and somewhat impressively steered into the skid.

"...clubs and stuff that I always thought would be cool. I tried a few places, but when I opened the door, there was nothing there. Just a black hole."

Trying to make him feel better, she downplayed her frustration with the system.

"Don't feel bad. I was the same." It wasn't quite true.

There were a few big family trips before the divorce, but she wasn't going to mention them. A painful reminder of a time when things were good, she would rather not risk Chris coming up in conversation. There was no way to explain what happened without it bringing up painful memories for both of them.

"I didn't go on a proper trip until I was thirty. To Paris."

He stared at her as if she grew a second head. "Geez. At least my mom was saving up to take me on a trip before I graduated."

"Smartass." Turning her focus to the surrounding woods, she concentrated on figuring out where they were. "Okay, so, what were you thinking about before we got here?"

"Me?" he scoffed. "It's never like that when I do it. You're the one who's new at this. You must have screwed it up somehow!"

"I didn't do anything! I was too busy chasing your lying ass."

Gavin rolled his eyes.

"You're not off the hook," she warned him. "Don't think I've forgotten about that. We'll deal with it later."

"Wait!" Gavin gratefully changed the subject, his grin expanding into a triumphant smile.

"I know where we are. I used to come here on field trips. Overlook Park?" he insisted, frustrated as she still looked puzzled. "Listen."

The sound of rushing water was faint in the light breeze, and he gestured toward it.

"See where it gets all narrow there? The waterfall is around the point."

He was right. Peering down the path until it turned and disappeared, a vivid memory surfaced. The view of the lake, and the mountain beyond, how it all opened when you came trekking around that corner, like nature was unlocking a door for those willing to visit. Meg told her they should hike it together.

"A rite of passage to re-instate your local status," she grinned. "Let's go soon, while it's not too hot and the tourists aren't around."

Like so many things in her life that went undone or unsaid, they never got to it. There were people she would never see again. There was something about the finality of that which seemed so much worse than when she was young. At least back then, there was a tiny sliver of youthful hope that things would get better with her parents. As she got older, the sliver narrowed until the wound healed over with all the crap stuck inside.

She pushed her hair out of her face and looked down at the ground, packed from thousands of feet passing over it. The earth was damp, the deep brown colour so unique to autumn. Taking a deep breath, she inhaled the dusky scent of damp pine in the quiet. The odd chirp of a bird rang out, making the silence so much more natural, putting her at ease.

As she listened to the meditative sounds of the woods, something else made its way in. Something that was definitely out of place in their two-person snow globe.

Steady footsteps approached, a beat that swelled and grew louder as someone ran toward them.

Gavin jumped, looking at Nat as if he expected her to disappear. Whatever was here was unexpected; that much was clear, and she didn't want to be in its line of sight whenever it arrived.

Moving up the hillside to her right, Nat pulled herself awkwardly along, using roots and prickly branches as a makeshift rope, crouching low among the scrub and wildflowers there. Dry branches and stems cut into her hands, but she held tight.

Steady puffs of air accompanied the footsteps now, growing as someone got closer and closer to the corner. Gavin nervously stepped over the low railing at the side and aimed for the nearby treeline, trying to work his way down the steep slope enough to hide.

A woman turned the corner, her sudden presence jarring them both. She was moving briskly toward them, her eyes trained straight ahead on the trail. The music pumping through her headphones distracted her, and she didn't slow down.

She doesn't see us.

Still, Nat held her breath.

A large square lump protruded from the jogger's leggings, and a burst of bittersweet nostalgia hit when Nat realized it was a portable CD player.

She used to walk to school listening to her own bright yellow one after Christmas break when she was a teen. The struggle to clip it to her sweatpants in the right spot to avoid skipping the disc as she walked was very real. Nat would constantly jerk the cotton pants up because of the weight. The leggings seemed to hold it tight to the woman's skin, at least, but it must have been sweaty.

Who listens to CDs anymore?

"Eva!" Gavin called, stumbling as he climbed out of the bushes to catch the woman.

This revelation briefly interrupted Nat's attempt to reconcile the outdated tech. She made her way back down the hillside, calling to Gavin as she went.

"You know her?!" Nat called down from her perch.

Hyperfocused on the woman called Eva as if she was a long-lost friend he was picking up at the airport, Gavin forgot about keeping secrets.

"EVA!!!" he shouted, running toward her wildly, arms waving like an air traffic controller trying to assist a landing.

Although Gavin was jumping up and down like a maniac, Eva continued to barrel toward them. The sharp edge of a branch caught Nat's shirt and scraped her arm. Hissing at the burning it left behind, she put pressure on it with the flat of her hand, bright blood smearing across her palm.

Stumbling as she took the last few steps to return to the path, she kicked a stone from the soil, sending it spinning with a few other pebbles. It careened down the hillside toward the path before lazily rolling to a stop in front of Eva's feet.

Eva stopped, jogging in place as she checked her surroundings for the source of the movement. She picked up the rock in the path, muttering something about rabbits. Nat's mouth went dry, recognition bolting through her as Eva turned to toss it back to the side of the trail. Nat circled her, not sure how this was possible.

The last time Nat saw the woman, she watched her skin deteriorate and peel from her skull, blood and dirt dulling and then obliterating her icy blue eyes. Now, her purple pack and clothes were clean, unmarred by dirt and blood. A blonde ponytail bobbed behind her, high on her head but wilting at the repetitive motion. Sweat covered her face, but she looked content, unbothered.

Alive!

Nat was looking at the rotting woman from her dream.

Through her confusion, one thought rose above the rest, a promise she could never fulfill.

I guess Meg owes me an 'I told you so.'

12

Nat heard Eva's steady puffs of breath as she tried to regulate her breathing. Was this another nightmare? Was she real? If she was, Nat needed to follow.

I have to know.

Eva ran right through Gavin, who was still on the path. The distance between them increased, and he yelled at her back. Nat joined him on the path, and they ran to catch up.

"EVA!" he tried one last time, as they lost sight of her around the bend.

"She can't hear you," Nat said, feeling instantly useless as she stated the obvious.

Gavin's arms dropped to his side in defeat.

"Duh," he muttered crankily.

"How do you know her?" she pressed.

"I met her a long time ago, okay? I don't really know her."

"Did you meet her here? You know, after..."

"Can we forget it already? It doesn't matter!" He erupted, turning away from her to walk in the other direction.

Where there's smoke...

"Look, I know her, too!" she shouted.

The revelation stopped him in his tracks, and he turned slowly to meet her eyes. "What?"

"Kind of. I had this vision the night I moved into my new place, and she was there. I think she wanted to tell me something."

"A vision? Like, you're a psychic or something?"

"Well...no. I don't know. It was a nightmare."

He scoffed, rolling his eyes. "Are you serious? You had a bad dream?"

After everything that happened, he found the dream about a ghost unbelievable. A pointed insult made its way up the back of her throat, which she stifled with a cough.

"Look, we'll get into it later. Believe it or not, we're not getting anywhere just standing here. We need to catch up with her."

"I'm not going."

Shrugging, Nat moved down the trail in the direction Eva disappeared. A few more paces and he sighed and followed, dragging his feet like a toddler she threatened to leave behind.

The sun was going down, dark shadows stretching over the ground. They came around the corner to emptiness, as if the woods had devoured Eva whole.

The only place the trail led to was the falls, a dead end. Even if she got that far ahead of them, they should have encountered her by now.

Gavin caught up with her and turned in a circle, puzzled.

"Where did she go?"

"Why don't you go ahead to the falls, see if you can see her doubling back?"

He nodded and moved further up the path, leaving her to think. Standing at the railing, her foot knocked into something. A water bottle toppled and rolled onto the path.

Curious, she glanced underneath the wooden beam, a flash of colour catching her attention. Resting on the edge, almost obscured by a tree root, lay a small purple bag with a single strap.

Nat grabbed the railing with both hands and leaned further over to glance down the mountainside. It was steep, but walkable if you were careful. Toes on the edge, she leaned forward to get a better look.

Someone stood with their back to Nat in the growing darkness, a hood up over their head. One hand rested straight at their side, weighed down by something heavy in their hand.

At their feet, Nat made out Eva squatting on the ground, unaware of the person hovering behind her. The hood bent down as the figure lowered their head, staring down at Eva's ponytail. Taking aim, the hand slowly lifted, waiting for the right moment to strike.

"Get away from her!" Nat screamed.

The rock came down, and Eva fell into a heap on the moist forest floor.

Without thinking, Nat barreled down the hill. She tripped and fell, sliding the rest of the way down to where Eva lay sprawled across the damp leaves.

Startled, the assailant ran, the thick trees enveloping them. As they disappeared, the woods fell silent again, keeping their secret.

Nat turned her attention to Eva. She lay still, her mouth ajar, but her eyelids fluttered as she struggled to remain conscious. Leaves around her lips moved gently as she breathed in and out.

"Gavin!" Nat called, but he was nowhere to be seen.

The earth where Nat slid down the hill was disturbed, and the last of the dirt sounded like rain as it meandered through the leaf bed covering the ground before slowing to a trickle.

"Wake up, come on!" Reaching for Eva's face, she tried to slap her.

That's what they do on TV, right? Nat rocked back on her

ankles in frustration after her hands went through Eva's pale face.

"Gavin!" she shouted again.

The woods cackled behind her at the treeline, the killer ready to return, self-assured in the silence as the darkness fell.

13

As soon as he was out of Nat's sight, Gavin stopped to really take in his surroundings. There was something off since he and Nat arrived in the woods, but he couldn't put his finger on it.

The wet odour of earth was around him, the air full of the expectation of colder weather. The smell of cedar filled his nostrils, and he realized what was different.

I can smell it.

It was crisp, and damp, and mossy. Sticks and pinecones crunched under his feet, the stiff pressure under his shoes, the sound of crackling in his ears. The spongy, pretend feeling that defined his life for so many years was gone.

It felt like it was...*alive*.

Gavin tilted his head up to the sky, hoping it would rain, just so he could feel it on his skin. A squirrel chattered high above him on an unseen limb. Stopping at a tree, he placed both hands on the trunk, feeling the rough texture of the bark. He rubbed it until his fingertip felt raw, hoping the sensation would linger for a while.

He closed his eyes, concentrating on the nature that

surrounded him, breathing it in, soaking it up for as long as it would last.

"Gavin!" A panicked cry made its way through the air, crackling through the sounds of nature.

Nat.

Jogging back toward the edge where he left Nat, he scanned the path for his partner in crime.

"Gavin!" the call came again, closer, and he strained his eyes in the darkness over the low wooden barrier.

Eva lay on the ground, Nat kneeling next to her, trying in vain to wake her up.

Surprising himself in his calmness, he made his way carefully down the hillside, knowing this was the end before he even got there.

"She's still breathing," Nat said.

Puzzled, he glanced down to examine her body. The blood was there, dripping down her face, but her clothes were fairly clean, unmarred with the blood that was there when he first met her.

It hasn't happened yet.

"C'mon," he said, as the sound of something shuffling through the trees got louder. "We should go."

She stared at him blankly. "Where?"

There would be no answer that would make this better, so he stuck with the simplest.

"Away."

Standing behind her, he pulled on her shoulder gently, trying to get her to stand. The spark rose between them again, the fuzzy hair on his arms standing straight up.

"I want to go home," she whispered.

As he breathed out, something shifted. The sounds of the forest stopped; the dark of night completely covering the woods. A complete and unnatural stillness surrounded him, the sounds he enjoyed disappearing into some unknown realm. There were no crickets, no owls, not even the gentle swaying of the trees. It was like a movie skipping a frame or two, stuck until you got up and fast-forwarded over the kink in the tape.

A strange whoosh built, the ocean in a seashell, and everything blurred, the whirlwind returning. Leaves and dirt scratched against his face as the wind picked up speed.

"Nat? NAT?!" Gavin's cries grew fainter. Her mouth was moving, but no sound came out.

Before he wondered what it meant, Nat and Eva were gone, and it all went black.

14

A strange weight built low in Nat's belly, her arms and legs falling backward as the force pushed her to the ground. Gavin was wrenched away from her in the wind, yelling and gesturing, but she couldn't hear anything. She was in a vacuum, completely isolated from everything. The ground beneath her feet disappeared, and her body pinwheeled into inky blackness, like a doll tossed into the air.

A pinpoint of red light appeared and grew. Completely helpless as she screamed into the void, she spiralled faster and faster toward it, unable to shut her eyes against what was coming for her.

The tunnel suddenly spat her out, and she slammed into something hard, her vision still red as the eye on her in the darkness. Nat rolled over in a coughing fit, trying to catch her breath. Experimentally, she relaxed her face, cracking her eyelids in the tiniest increments.

It was still dark, and she shivered in the chilly night air. She was in a structure, some kind of shed. The ground beneath her was hard-packed dirt, and her muscles shrieked as she tried to roll over some errant pebbles digging into her back.

A groan filled the small space from somewhere across from her, and she froze, waiting for it to come again so she could pinpoint it.

"Gavin?" she whispered.

As her eyes adjusted in the dark, Eva's ponytail came into focus, her brightly coloured runners smeared with dirt. Eva moaned again, hands pulling against the ropes holding them behind her back.

April 2015
Aftermath

15

The knock on the door startled Barb out of her fitful afternoon nap. Chaos heaved himself off her chest, forcing a grunt from her. He careened down the hallway, shedding fur in a cloud as he went.

Forcing her eyes open, she scrubbed a hand across her face. Makeup smeared onto her fingers, gummy bits lodging in the corners of her eyes, but she decided that was the least of her worries. The knock came again, loudly and more persistent this time, and she cleared her throat as she clambered to her feet.

"Coming!" she barked, her phlegmy cough cutting off the word. Her oversized tee had drifted off one shoulder, and she hoisted it up as she yawned. "Whatever you're selling had better be good!"

The only people who came to her door these days were solicitors, and now, because of obvious recent events, cops. The police saw her a few times, asking her questions about that night. She saw them taking in the dark stains on her lips, the way she stumbled slightly. The questions were the same, over and over, as if they expected her to slip up.

"If there's anything you can remember," they said each time, handing her a card as if they hoped she would remember something when she was sober.

They were already there once today, early this morning, and here she was, still in the same clothes, teeth and hair unbrushed. When the police talked to her about Gavin, their questions oozed with judgement. Her shame grew as they questioned her whereabouts and why she didn't notice earlier that he hadn't come home.

Ripping the door open, she had enough. She didn't kill Nat, and she sure as hell didn't kill her own son.

"What now?" she growled, surprised to find not a police officer, but a very startled woman instead.

Rather than a salesperson's smile, she looked to see how Barb felt. Her rumpled clothes and hastily done hair showed it. Dark circles sat below her reddened eyes, and Barb considered whether she should invite her in for a nap as well.

"Sorry," the woman said timidly. "I'm not totally sure this is the right house. Are you Barb?"

"Yes?"

"I'm Meg. I'm...I was..." She was struggling to hold it together. "Damn, sorry."

Fishing a tissue out of her pocket, she pressed it against her eyes as they threatened to overflow.

"Nat's friend," Barb finished, spying the cat carrier at her feet. She wiped her hands on her baggy shirt as if it would magically make her presentable. "The cat bolted, but I'm sure he'll come out in a minute."

A pang of sadness washed through her, and she realized how much was going to miss the little jerk. Standing back against the door to make room, she gestured for Meg to join her.

"Sit," she said, leading her into the living room and hastily clearing off a pile of junk mail that had amassed on one side of the couch. "Let me put on some tea."

Placing the carrier on the floor, Meg settled gingerly into the cushions as Barb went to the kitchen.

She banked a ton of sick time and was taking full advantage. When Gavin died, she buried herself in work. Someone needed her to take a shift because their kid had a birthday party? Thanksgiving and Christmas? Sick?

No problem.

Keeping away from her empty house always stopped her from getting lost in her own head. This time, she was just so *tired*. There were always ghosts waiting for her when she got back, so why fight it?

Normally, it was a relief to have Gavin's spirit around, but right now she wasn't so sure. Barb wondered how many times he was trying to deliver a warning that she wasn't willing to hear, and she hoped whenever he returned that his presence wouldn't feel ominous.

The kettle whistled, snapping her out of her thoughts and back to reality. The silence out there was palpable by now, and it occurred to her what a poor hostess she was being.

"Chamomile okay, Meg?" she called.

"Yes, please, that sounds great."

Placing two cups on a tray, she turned the handle of the chipped one toward her, making a mental note to take it for herself. Barb poured the water into her teapot, giving Meg a moment to herself while it steeped.

Meg took a cup from her gratefully, sagging into the cushions as she took a tentative sip. *Ah, tea, the universal healer.*

"Sorry I'm late," Meg said. "I've been helping her family with the arrangements."

Barb waved her hand dismissively, watching her guest through the rising steam as she blew across the surface of her own cup. "No problem. Not like I had any plans. Besides, I love having him as a houseguest." As if on cue, Chaos appeared in the living room, jumping up on the couch and curling up against Meg's thigh.

Traitor, Barb thought affectionately.

"You sure you don't need me to keep him longer? With everything going on, I'm sure things are hectic."

Meg shook her head. "No, thank you. I've been looking forward to it, actually."

Barb nodded. "I get it. He's good company."

Putting her cup down, Meg examined Barb, debating whether the conversation would be personal or all business.

"Nat really enjoyed your company, you know. She said that she finally met someone on the street who talked to her like a human being and not a weird, unmarried cat lady." Meg squirmed awkwardly as the words tumbled out, scanning the dishevelled living room behind Barb rather than make eye contact. A laugh erupted from her as some memory of Nat filled her.

"Although if she were here, she'd remind us that's exactly what she was."

Barb smiled, moving her eyes up and down the street, out the window behind Meg before leaning in to whisper conspiratorially.

"Don't worry. That's how the neighbours talk to me, too, and I don't even have a cat."

"I can see why Nat liked you," Meg smiled.

A silence hung in the room between them. Barb knew better than to fill it. Meg seemed to toy with what to say next.

"I didn't really know Nat that well anymore. We were sort of recently reconnecting, you know? High school soulmates. We didn't stay in touch after she moved away."

Barb nodded. "It happens sometimes, and we don't always mean it to. For me, it was my sister. She's about five years older than me. When we were little, we were super close. After she moved out, there was a period that we didn't speak much. She doesn't live here, so we still don't see each other that often. For the genuine relationships, that don't matter. Those are the ones that six months in, a year in, ten years in, you can just pick up where you left off and keep going. Like you were never apart, you know?"

Meg's lips pressed tightly together as she composed herself before she spoke. There was something more there, something that Barb couldn't see yet.

"We were getting there, I think." Meg squared her shoulders, focusing on the subject at hand. "She really liked you. I doubt she ever told you that, but visiting you meant a lot. She said you get it."

"Get what?"

A fight between her loyalty to Nat and the knowledge that she was dead and that it didn't matter anymore played across Meg's features. She was holding on to something she couldn't take back once she said it out loud.

"I should go," Meg said, bending over abruptly to unlock the carrier and plop the meatball of a cat inside in one fluid motion.

Shocked that she tricked him, he pressed his face against the bars, glaring at her in his defeat. The carrier tilted oddly with his weight as she lifted it.

"Thank you for the tea."

She rushed back to the door, putting on her shoes awkwardly before running out. Barb stood on the porch, watching her go, wondering if she would ever make peace with this.

Closing the door softly behind her and turning to take in her cold house, dust motes floating in the dim light that peeked through her curtains, she thought she already had her answer.

16

IN THE DAYS FOLLOWING NAT'S DEATH, MEG stopped by to see the Parkers and offer her condolences. As bad as she thought it might be, it was so much worse. They were both an unhealthy grey colour, sinking in on themselves. The air in the house was stale and dark, and the curtains were drawn to avoid prying eyes. Reporters still lurked, vultures circling a vulnerable kill.

"If there's anything you need, let me know." It was just something you said, but Nat's parents grabbed onto the offer like a lifeline.

While she wasn't sure that any of this should fall to her, Meg also knew they had no one else to do it. It started out small, picking up groceries, making a few phone calls, ordering some flowers for the funeral. She dutifully went through old family photos to find the best ones, and before she could linger on the memories they unlocked, she was on to the next task on the list. Having something to keep her mind off of processing everything wasn't healthy, and she knew it, but for now it felt good.

The turnout at the service was decent, and she was initially relieved, hoping that if they heard a bit more about Nat's life, it would offer them all a bit of closure. As she worked the room, that hope faded.

Mostly, Meg was reminded of just how far apart they grew. Aside from Barb, the bulk of the people there were co-workers from her current job. A lot of the others were rubberneckers, flustered when she asked how they knew her friend and leaving shortly after.

Nat's ex was there, and Meg pulled him aside, hoping to get some information about their relationship. He seemed unwilling to talk about it, refusing her offer to come over and take anything sentimental he might want. He spent the afternoon with his hands on his new girlfriend's hips, avoiding the family like the plague.

It became apparent the girlfriend fell into the rubbernecker category, glancing around and asking questions like she was at a celebrity wedding. When Meg brought over Nat's parents, there was an awkward moment of blushing and mumbling as she realized too late that they didn't know who he was.

After the service, everything went quiet once she had the space to think beyond the immediate tasks at hand. She went back to work, and everyone's sympathy surrounded her, the support there if she needed it. Meg smiled, nodded, thanked everyone for their offers, but she wouldn't be taking them up on it. The horrible truth was Meg lost Nat a long time ago.

At the end of another long day, she kicked off her heels, a footwear choice she regretted as the day went on. Peeling off her nylons, she lay down on the bed, pulling Chaos close and petting him until they both fell asleep.

Meg dreamed of the before, a typical day after school.

Two girls chased each other up the stone steps on a sunny day.

"Not the library again. Let's go to the park this time."

Nat said nothing, face scrunched, and they continued up the stairs. Meg used to like Nat's decisiveness, but lately, it was getting under her skin.

Why can't we do what I want?

Meg didn't enjoy coming here all the time. She didn't take out a lot of books like Nat did. She was embarrassed, actually. On most visits she grabbed a few books she would check out but never read, just so she wouldn't feel so dumb.

Nat was just so freaking smart, reading whatever she walked by when they went to the library. She was always keeping up with what was new, and had a million things on hold.

Nat always seemed totally lost wherever she was when she had a yellowed spine cracked open across her lap. Sometimes it took her a minute to even notice that Meg was there. Meg was kind of jealous of that.

Nat tripped on the top step, and they both giggled, Meg distracted once again from fighting about it.

While Nat went on her usual hunt for her next favourite, Meg decided not to tag along. It would have been an act of rebellion, but Nat wouldn't even notice if she went her own way. Moving deeper into the stacks, she headed to the dustiest and darkest aisles in the back corner, where she could have some privacy.

There was a sheet of paper crammed in the inside pocket of her jacket, hastily folded into a tiny square. She opened it up and laughed at the dorky cartoon inside. Chris liked to doodle, and she thought he would be great one day.

Today's scrawls showed two figures, hand in hand, a boy and a girl at the movies. It wasn't the new theatre way up on the hill, either. She hated that one. It was weird to call a brand-new building creepy, but it was. Bright, gaudy and crowded, it always seemed to try too hard, pretending.

Soulless.

Instead, the cartoon depicted her favourite, The Station. She could tell because some of Chris' sketches showed the pole in the lobby.

The couple in the drawing went to the counter and got popcorn before walking past posters with funny made-up titles lit with huge white bulbs on the walls. Flipping the paper over, she found the last piece of the story. The pair stopped, looking at each other in front of a poster for one she told him last week she really wanted to see. A question mark hovered in a bubble over the boy's head.

"Want to come with me?" was scrawled out in boxy letters at the bottom.

Without Nat.

The thought came to her even though it wasn't spelled out on the page. The implication loomed large, and her heartbeat quickened at how the doodle people were looking at each other, the dizzy symbols over the boy's head. Her palm itched where the phantom feeling of the note being shoved into her palm between classes remained.

Two boxes at the bottom of the page reminded her she couldn't get out of answering this one. One for Yes, one for No.

It couldn't be both.

Was it her imagination, or was the No box so much smaller than the Yes one?

Digging through her bag for a pen; she lowered the tip to the paper, lingering over Yes. She pressed the pen to the centre of the square, and as it touched the paper, she thought how easy it would be to make that sweeping motion. With a simple flick of the wrist and the enthusiastic checkmark would practically write itself once she moved her hand.

Instead, the fountain pen moved lower, below her two options. A weight crushed down on her chest as she wrote below the boxes, "Sorry. Can't."

She felt silly writing it, but she couldn't bring herself to check the box beside No.

Sitting with her head leaned back against the wall, the sun set and rose over and over against her eyelids. The library grew darker, colder, the light and airy feel of *before* now tinted with the feel of *after*. The feeling of being watched covering her, dragging her into an even darker place.

She opened her eyes again to find she was in different clothes, surrounded by art books. After what happened to Chris, this became the aisle she waited for Nat. Being around something he'd been so passionate about made it feel like he was still here.

The note was still in her hands, but the cartoon had lost the stiffness of paper recently ripped from a sketchpad. It was soft; the creases worn white over the pen marks from a million unfoldings. She clutched the note in her hands, wrists resting on her thighs.

As she sat staring at the question, tears rolling down her cheeks, it was tugged out of her hand. Meg's face reddened, and she looked up guiltily, almost relieved to be caught, the decision to tell Nat the truth out of her hands.

No one stood above her, the aisle still empty except for her. As she peered down at the paper on the floor, the hairs on the back of her neck stiffened and stood tall. *What the hell?*

"Chris?" she whispered.

The word crept out of her mouth before it crossed her

mind, and she bit her lip, allowing herself to entertain the possibility.

"What did you say?"

Nat stood at the end of the aisle, holding a pile of books. She looked tired, her mouth pinched at the corners, cracked at the effort of speaking. She was dressed in an oversized hoodie and faded pajama pants with cheery-looking sundaes all over them. It was the trend, and no one batted an eye when she left the house like this.

Depression chic hit just in time.

Nat was cutting class way too often. The normalcy her parents insisted on angered Nat, but she soon learned that if she made an appearance and then said she wasn't up for it, nobody called her on it. Her mom went back to work in the fall, and Nat would make sure she ended up downtown for the usual pickup to avoid questions.

Meg would meet her here, day after day, riding home in the backseat behind Nat and her mom, the silence a physical pressure that threatened to crush them all.

No one ever asked Nat how school was; school never asked how home was. One hand washed the other without either realizing it. Nat would coast until graduation, and no one would bat an eye.

"Meg?" Nat asked again, snapping her out of her thoughts.

"Sorry, nothing. Just talking to myself."

Nat nodded and walked robotically toward the checkout desk.

The meekness of her tone killed her. She realized she never really stood up for herself with Nat, never really argued. They always did whatever Nat said, even applying for colleges together. The ones Nat said looked good, of course.

Meg received two offers, Nat received one. There was

never any question of which she would pick. Whispered promises to be roommates, pick the same classes, go to parties together were the foundation of their future, had formed a contract. The two of them laughing on a warm fall day, textbooks scattered on bright green grass, was a foregone conclusion.

After the accident, Meg's excitement was all conditional on Nat's. With everything that happened, she didn't think there was any way Nat was going.

Nat couldn't even brush her hair some days. She needed time, and Meg couldn't wait.

She was trying to build up the courage to tell Nat she accepted her first choice offer instead. There was a weight to it, her first real grown-up decision, with nobody's help. She could crash and burn, and she had no one to blame but herself. A terrified thrill ran through her at the prospect that anything could happen, and she wasn't sure why it felt so good.

The cranky-looking man at the desk was about halfway through checking out Nat's enormous pile of books. Hauling her messenger bag onto her shoulder, Meg moved down the aisle.

The bar of fluorescent lights above her swung, slightly at first and then in a wider arc, casting shadows over the tall shelves surrounding her. Stillness took over for a moment, the flickering shadows punctuated only by the faint squeak of the bare bulbs rocking above her.

A low vibration ripped through the floor, rattling her chest as it climbed her body and the shelves at her sides. Something rammed into the metallic shelving hard enough that it swayed. A pile of books fell off the top shelf and landed on the floor in front of her.

Jumping over the mess, she rushed to the other side, half expecting Nat to be there, trying to scare her. A few people working at some nearby desks were staring at her in mild annoyance, attention drawn to the noise. Nat was still at the counter, oblivious, shoving her sizable pile by the handful into her canvas tote bag.

The librarian, however, was giving Meg the stink eye that said that whatever she was doing, she should stop. Nat stood like a zombie, transfixed by the methodic beeping of the scanner and its sharp red light, completely unfazed by the noise.

Meg piled the scattered books on the shelf. Her hands were shaking, and it was a mess, her only goal being to get them off of the floor before the guy behind the counter came back to the aisle.

There was one that rested slightly away from the pile, its new, unblemished cover standing out from the rest. It landed spine up, its pages rumpled under its own weight. The fluorescent tubes still swung gently, catching the sheen of the cover as they slowed.

Running her hand gently over the title, the clamminess of her fingers left four streaks across the front cover. She watched as they faded across the title.

The Doodler's Guide to Becoming an Artist.

"Chris?" Meg whispered, staring at the lights in awe.

"Come on, quit screwing around," Nat said in an irritated but flat tone, bringing Meg crashing back to reality.

She was on a short fuse these days, and Meg could never be certain when she would snap. The fire in her eyes, combined with the low, emotionless pitch, told Meg that she needed to tread lightly.

"My mom is going to be pissed if we're late again."

"Sorry, I'll be right there."

Nat sighed. "I'll be at the front door," she said, stomping away from Meg.

Meg stared at the cover, unable to move. The librarian was

coming over, laser-focused and ready to yell at some misbehaving kids. Cramming the book into her bag, she ran to meet Nat.

Chris? She thought again as she touched the square weight of the book through the canvas resting against her leg.

This time, she didn't dare say it out loud.

OCTOBER 2000
WITNESSES

17

Eva heard the unconvincing smile plastered on her mother's face loud and clear over the phone, and she wondered if the roast she planned for dinner would live up to her mom's standards.

"Can't wait to give you the tour," she said as she examined her nails and tried to force cheerfulness into her tone.

"Don't forget about the *trick 'r treaters*," her mom interjected, as if Eva had said nothing. "Do you need me to bring the candy?"

Eva rolled her eyes. As if she forgot it was Halloween.

"No, thanks. I've got it."

A loaded pause crackled over the phone line, and Eva waited for the question that always came.

"Are you sure you two can't work things out?"

She still couldn't believe that the divorce hadn't killed her mother.

An uncomfortable silence came through the line to fill Eva's tiny apartment, but she would not cave. The question was asked and answered repeatedly; the answer just wasn't what her mom wanted to hear.

"Eva? Are you there, honey?" the voice cut back into her thoughts. "I asked about John. It's just..."

"I've got to go, Mom," Eva cut in. "I'll see you tonight."

Hanging up quickly to avoid more conversation, she turned her attention to preparing the meal. Once everything was ready, she set the timer for two hours. Still on edge from the phone call, she decided she had time for her usual run.

She pulled into the lower parking area on the mountainside, hoping the cleansing outdoor air would help put her in a meditative state to deal with tonight's visit. Her father would sit like a statue, staring at a point in between them, his mouth conveniently full whenever her mother railed on as if being a divorcee were tantamount to being a serial murderer.

This time, however, Eva vowed to remain calm. If she didn't react, maybe her mother would eventually stop.

Ironically, it was the advice that her mom had given her when she was little, when the boy that sat behind her would pull her hair hard enough to snap her head back.

Picking up her pace, she came around the corner of the path and felt herself relax; the tension leaving her body as she took in the landscape below. The trees below went on forever, rolling out in front of her like a vast carpet, as if welcoming observers to the lake beyond. There was no one else on the usually popular route that night, but she thought nothing of it.

It was Halloween, after all, and she supposed people were busy or hunkering down for a night of handing out candy. She didn't mind. She always felt the most like herself when she was completely alone, no one around to placate or please. As she gazed across the treeline, the mountains creating a bowl that cradled the lake beyond, she couldn't believe her good luck at living in a place like this.

A rock skittered down the embankment onto the path,

rolling to a stop ahead of her. As she slowed, she caught the rustle of leaves out of the corner of her eye.

She pulled her headphones down to dangle around her neck, watching for any more movement. The sun was low, shadows growing along the mountainside. The realization that winter was on its way struck her, and she glanced at her watch. It was early, but it would be dark soon.

Just a while longer, she thought, telling herself she would turn around when she hit the footpath that led to the falls.

"Rabbits," she muttered, as she continued her run.

An uncomfortable prickle spread across her neck as the tiny hairs there stood on end, and she chastised herself for fearing a little rock.

Five minutes later, she encountered a man standing on the path. After just settling into the solitude of the path again, it felt odd to have that bubble abruptly popped. Eva eyed him cautiously, debating whether this was her sign to turn back.

The man was pacing back and forth, his sad eyes looking distressed. She thought he was only in his late 20s maybe, not much younger than her, but a profound exhaustion lingered behind his features, aging him. Bags lined the thin skin below his deep brown eyes, and wrinkles lined his brow from frowning in worry. Leaning over the ridge, he moved his mouth as if he were calling out to someone below, his words muffled by her music.

She removed her headphones as she slowed, and his voice became clear.

"Come on, boy!" he called.

"Hey! Everything okay?" she panted.

She remained in motion, running on the spot to discourage an unwanted conversation.

"I...I...my dog," he babbled, holding up a red leash in his hand.

"I know I'm not supposed to let him off the leash here. He

just loves the run and there's not usually many people this time of year, especially with it being Halloween and he always stays on the path but he chased a squirrel down there and I heard him whimpering and I think he's stuck and..."

His head bobbed in all directions as he avoided eye contact with her, focused on scouring the hillside for his dog. There was a secret struggle just under the surface, the dam close to breaking.

"Did you try stepping down the bank a bit, or is it too slippery?"

"I tried, but I have a bad knee." He bit his lip, distracted, still averting his eyes. "It's not too bad down there, but I'm worried it'll give out and then I'll be stuck, too."

The bank was steep here, and she looked around for movement in the growing dark, but there was nothing.

"Do you think you could go down a little way and call him?"

The vegetation appeared damp and slick, and she considered she might slip and fall herself. As if reading her mind, the sun dipped lower, kissing the treetops.

"I really should get back."

"Please? It's going to be dark soon, and I don't want to leave him. Jinx!" he called.

There was a shuffling, a shifting of leaves, but no dog emerged from the underbrush.

Not far down there was a fallen tree, an enormous trunk left to rot, overgrown with moss. She thought maybe if she could reach it, it would support her while she called for the dog.

"Jinx is a cute name. What kind of dog is he?"

"He's brown. A Lab." A hiccup punctuated the sentence, and she was reminded of her friend's little boy, who did the same thing after bawling through a dramatic and life-altering moment.

The last time it happened, it was because the poor kid dropped a cookie.

"Okay, look," she said, smiling to put him at ease. "I'm going to crawl down there a bit and see if I can spot him."

She pulled off the small pack she carried and dug around inside. She took out a water bottle and took a swig. Placing the bottle on the ground, she rummaged in the bag some more and pulled out a small baggie with a few large pieces of jerky inside. She was paranoid about twisting an ankle or something and being stuck alone for a while, so she always had some kind of snack with her when she ran.

"Let's see if we can get him to come for a treat."

"Thank you! I really appreciate it. Thank you so much!" He smiled at her, a smile that showed a genuine reaction to a kind act, and she felt herself relaxing.

She lifted her leg to climb over the creaky, low wooden rail. Crouching, she found her footing and began a shuffling crab walk down the embankment. Trees were scattered sparsely near the top, leading into dense woods a little further down.

Messy piles of debris were piled, trees deemed to be past saving waiting for removal before the snow fell. The trees that stood alone in front of the pack leaned toward the mountain above, battered into position by years of winter windstorms.

Her running shoe slid forward, and she leaned back to fall onto her backside. Bracing for impact, she was relieved to find that the thick layer of crunchy leaves coating the ground went a long way to cushioning the fall. With the bag of jerky pressed between her lips, she moved excruciatingly slowly so as not to slip until she was closer to the fallen tree. She scooted toward the long trunk and wedged herself against it. Dry leaves and pine needles poked into her palms as she steadied herself.

"Jinx!" she called, clapping her hands to encourage the pup.

"Hey!" she called over her shoulder toward the top of the

slope. "Can you try calling him? Maybe if he hears you, he'll come."

The forest had fallen still, and the man on the path didn't respond.

"Hey..."

A stick snapped behind her, loud as a gunshot in the falling darkness, and she turned, expecting to laugh at a slobbering, smiling chocolate Lab.

Eva didn't even have time to wince before a large rock collided with the side of her face.

18

Eva pried her eyes open slowly, wincing at a tearing sensation as her blood-sticky eyelashes ripped away from her face.

The world around her was blurry and muffled as she blinked away tears. She could have sworn she heard someone's hushed voice whispering to her through the confused haze that was her brain, but it wasn't her name they were calling. What was it? Allen? Alvin?

Gavin.

The skin on her forehead felt stretched, tingling as something dried there, and she longed to scratch it but couldn't reach. Itchy ropes secured her wrists tightly behind her back. Her legs throbbed as she tried to roll, and she glanced down to find her ankles tied just as securely.

Moving only made the ropes scrape against her already raw, burning skin. The memory of the rock came back to her, of a blinding light as it collided with her forehead.

Dirt pressed into her sweaty cheek, and she tried to sit up, but it only made her dizzy. Head throbbing in time with her heart, her stomach clenched, threatening to bring up her lunch.

It was so dark, and she wondered how long she had been here.

Is anyone worried yet?

She pictured her mom barging into the apartment with her spare key, pulling the roast out of the oven, clicking her tongue and going on about manners and responsibility. The banging of plates and cutlery would join her droning voice, floating to her father sitting quietly on the sofa, unaware that precious minutes were ticking away. How long would it take for them to call the police?

You don't have control over that. Focus.

Her dry mouth tried to swallow, cotton coming with it as the gag in her mouth was drawn inward. She stopped moving and tried to figure out where she was.

It was a kind of storage shed. There was a tiny window high on the wall, but it was more a small vent than anything, far too small to fit through even if she could reach it. Rippled metal, coloured military green, made up the walls. Wind whipped against the structure from outside, the walls whining and pleading for a respite from standing guard.

Tipping her head back, she spotted the door on the wall behind her. Rolling onto her stomach, dirt mixing with saliva on her cheeks, she wormed her way toward it, painstaking and slow. Head down, knees up, contract, release. There was no way for her to reach the handle, but the door didn't look all that sturdy. *Maybe I can shove it open?*

The door rattled when she pushed her back against it. Vibrations lingered and moved through it from the force of her weight, but it didn't give. Twisting her neck upward, she pushed back into the door again and saw it was stuck at the midpoint, locked from the outside. *Maybe a padlock?*

Repositioning herself, she kicked against the lower corner of the door. It gave outwards slightly, but the space would barely fit her toes through. There was no way that she could bend it enough to make a space for her to escape.

What are you going to do even if you get out of here? You don't even know what's outside. You could be in the middle of nowhere with no one around to help you. Tears now flowed and soaked the dirty rag in her mouth as she sobbed.

After a moment, she abruptly slammed her head into the dirt.

Figure. Something. Out.

She closed her eyes, willing herself to calm down. A solid-looking worktable sat in the middle of the structure. A vast assortment of empty burlap sacks, used for collecting leaves, covered a few large bags of fertilizer stored underneath the worktable. There were no tools that she could see on the bare walls.

Her eyes travelled up to the dark stains near the top of the table legs. She didn't want to think about what they were. The roof was flat, seams visible where it was nailed to the top. This box was handmade, and it wasn't meant to keep anything for a long time. A shudder ran through her body at the implication.

You're running out of time.

Eva's resolve hardened as she worked on the corner of the door once again, pushing at it with her foot. Rather than kick it, she applied regular pressure, slowly bending the thin metal at the bottom of the door outward to create a gap.

Reaching down, Eva stretched her fingers through the hole. Cold grass poked her skin, the evening dampness making her fingers slick. Frantically curling her nails against the ground, she tried to loosen the soil.

Once she displaced a couple of handfuls of dirt, she jammed her fingers into the hole again. She grabbed the edge of the door and pulled it down, bringing the sharp corner in toward her.

It was cheap material, and the already bent, thin metal yielded under the steady pressure. The sharp metal dug into her, blood smearing her fingertips. Eva twisted her hands, rocking as she worked the rope against her makeshift blade.

19

THERE WAS NO GETTING RID OF THE ANGER THAT boiled up in Nat as Eva kicked at the door. Tinged with the rancid flavour of hopelessness, the potent combination ran through her veins, a mutant heroin that twisted her insides irreparably.

Swiping her palm across her face, she wondered morbidly if this anger was the same mood ring red, or if there were different shades for different layers of emotions. When she glanced down at her hand, she frowned as she saw only cold sweat glistening there.

There was no colour to it, no sludgy quality. The spot on her arm that caught on the bush burned, a scab forming over a bloody, puffy line, regular blood coagulating there. Turning her wrist, she frowned at the freckles reappearing and ran her fingers over the small, raised scar that disappeared after she died.

Something's different, she thought, contemplating the aches and pains she was feeling, so different from the numbness she was experiencing before the woods.

A heavy thud interrupted her thoughts as Eva fell backward, bursting into loud, heaving sobs. Her face crumpled in on itself, her eyes tightly shut against her surroundings. Just as quickly as she lost control, she took a deep rattling breath, pulling herself back to take in the room.

Watching Eva compose herself made Nat think of all those times she locked herself in her bedroom, workplace bathrooms, restaurant restrooms. Nat had a long and well-documented history of letting her anger out at inappropriate times. It wasn't about saying that everything was going to be okay; it was about acknowledging everything was shit. The control of allowing herself a set amount of time to cry about it before she got her ass up was empowering.

Watching Eva navigating every woman's nightmare felt like the ultimate intrusion. She always thought that when she died, she would understand everything. The meaning of the universe. Why are bad things happening to good people? Exactly what part of the chicken was the nugget?

She imagined when she walked through that door that there would be someone on the other side, comforting her, strapping on a pair of wings and maybe a halo, or at least greeting her with a welcoming smile and open arms.

Instead, she got Gavin.

Where is he?

It was tempting to hold on to her hope that Gavin was a figment of her imagination brought on by seeing Barb earlier and having too much junk food tonight. Maybe she was asleep on the couch in her chilly living room, a blanket from the chair across the room draped over her as she sweated under a large, purring cat.

Even though she hung onto the wish to keep herself sane, she couldn't ignore Eva. Realizing what she was doing with the corner of the door, Nat was impressed.

The thin yellow cord was fraying, and Nat leaned closer in excitement. It was the cheap kind you could buy at the hardware store, good for strapping something to your car, but not much else.

This could work.

A tiny piece of the cord snapped, and Eva leaned forward, spurred on by progress, working her hands quickly.

He was coming back eventually, whether they were ready or not.

The bright yellow cording was smeared with blood, the slippery strands shifting slightly as Eva moved her wrists over the metal. The knot could easily slide apart now if Eva reached it at the right angle. Instinctively, Nat reached to still Eva's hands, determined to help.

She moved through Eva's arm, as predicted, and helplessness crept back to her. *What did you think would happen?*

Nat moved to stand, and as her fingers travelled up between Eva's pale wrists, the itchy cord brushed against her and she closed her hand around it. Eyes wide, she fell to the ground and pulled. Eva shrieked as the rope hauled her backward, her legs kicking ineffectually.

Nat released her grip on the rope, and Eva rolled clumsily toward the opposite corner of the room. Cheek pressed to the ground, Eva spat gritty dirt from her mouth as she pulled her hands free. Pushing herself up, she peered wildly in Nat's direction, stretching her stiff fingers and rubbing her wrists.

Prickly goosebumps invaded Nat's sweat-slicked skin. For a moment, she thought Eva could see her. However, she shoved herself into the corner, head weaving in all directions as she tried to find out who touched her.

Nat looked down at her hands in awe and admiration, as if she had developed a superpower.

Holy shit!

"It's okay," Nat tried, but Eva didn't hear her. She shoved at the loosened coils around her ankles, freeing her legs.

A sound from outside pierced their odd meeting, and Eva scurried along the wall, trying to shove herself as far from the door as she could get.

Footsteps were approaching the shed.

20

THE SOUND OF LEAVES BEING CRUSHED UNDERFOOT came closer and closer to the shed. Eva looked around frantically for something, anything, that she could use. The blood was rushing back to her extremities, her hands and feet still tingling as she stretched.

The steps outside stopped.

Eva inhaled, holding a sharp breath. A set of fingers, wide and calloused, wormed its way into the hole she dug in the dirt. They felt their way upward and almost lovingly caressed the sharp corner, her blood smearing across it.

The fingers disappeared, pulled out slowly through the gap, in no rush. Every movement seemed amplified, every grain of dirt that shifted under her sneakers as loud as a dinner bell.

Adrenaline and survival instinct coursed through her veins, a cocktail that made her feel invincible even as her heart raced in terror.

The padlock scraped against the latch as the door creaked open, whispering against the grass as it was pulled outward. A man made his way through the door, work boots stomping on

"

the dirt floor. His tall shadow fluttered over her face, bending into the darkness of her hiding space.

The rage poured off him, and she couldn't reconcile that palpable desire to hurt her with the gentleman on the hillside, looking for his dog.

He moved into the shed, bending down to pick up the discarded rope. Moving behind the worktable, he peered into the corner, his back to her as he strained to see in the darkness. He slammed his hand into the wall, then moved away from the table, leaving the doorway clear.

The cocoon of yard sacks scattered as she burst from underneath. As she slammed the door shut, she took in the empty hook by the latch and scanned the ground at her feet.

He has the padlock.

The door burst out against her as he shoved his body weight into it, and she pushed back with all her might.

With nothing sturdy enough to shove in there, she couldn't keep him in.

She turned and ran, barely able to take in her surroundings as he came rushing through the door behind her. His hot breath kissed her neck, his fingers brushing her sweatshirt as he barrelled out of the shed.

Huge cedar shrubs stood high and thick around a large yard, boxed in by a high wooden fence, too high and smooth to climb without being a sitting duck. A small house sat on the opposite side, and she made a beeline for it across the dry, unmowed grass. At the last minute, she veered away, toward the corner of the building. Trapping herself in a house he knew was not a risk she wanted to take.

There has to be a way out.

Rounding the corner, she plunged into the blackness cast by the side of the house, praying there would be a way out.

21

Nat saw Eva's panic-stricken eyes gleaming in the dark for a split second as she let go of the door. They teetered through the door into the night, and Nat pushed off on her toes to grab the back of the man's shirt.

Tangling together, they hit the dirt facedown just outside the shed; the wind knocked out of him in a surprised grunt. Nat scanned the yard to find Eva as he kicked at the air.

Eva was streaking across a lawn toward a wall of fence. Puffs of white fogged the air as Eva ran, and Nat became conscious of the cold air biting at her bare arms.

"Not today, motherf..."

She trailed off as he kicked her off, the long barrel of a rifle visible over his shoulder as he stalked toward Eva.

22

EVA SLAMMED INTO A HIGH WOODEN GATE, PEELING paint and cracked slivers digging into her hands. The handle rattled as she stretched to reach an old metal hook. It was tight, and she grunted as she pushed it up, the force finally getting it to budge.

Blind relief washed over her as it moved upward, and she pushed the gate open. Not even twenty feet away, a friendly house came into view, its front porch lit by the streetlights lining the road. The street seemed untouched by the evil of the dark in the yard, and for a moment she felt that the devil chasing her wouldn't be able to follow once she left the shadows.

Wind chimes sounded merrily in the night, the slight breeze that moved them kissing her face as she opened her mouth to scream. The gate creaked as she swung it wide, positioned on the balls of her feet as she lifted a foot to run.

"HEL..."

The world lit up with a cracking sound, choking the rest of the word from her throat, and then she was on the ground, face down in the grass. The dry blades prickled against her face, dry leaves embedding themselves in her hair. She tilted her chin up, willing someone, *anyone*, to walk by.

No footsteps rang out, no one was on their way to see what the noise was, no *trick 'r treaters* cried for help. The silence following the crack was absolute, highlighting her complete abandonment at the end of this empty street. Her hands were like ice, her body not co-operating as she desperately told her brain that she needed to move. A whistle and boom filled her ears, drowning her as colourful lights above her cast shadows across the grass below her.

Something rattled inside her as she breathed in and out, the function she had taken for granted getting harder and harder as something pressed down on her chest. The view of the picture-perfect safety of the neighbourhood shrank; the tall trees above welcoming her back as she was dragged into the yard by her ankles.

A hand above her grabbed the gate and swung it shut, plunging her back into darkness, as the bright and cheery street disappeared completely. The wood trembled, the metallic click of the latch reminding her that this was a jail cell and she was a prisoner. A boot nudged her ribs painfully, pushing her over to face the sky.

Her focus was going, but she saw the rifle in his hands. Blood dripped down her throat, her lips now slick with it.

Two tiny glinting spheres hovered in the air where he stood, his eyes staring directly into hers. She didn't know him, didn't know why. All she knew with certainty was that begging wouldn't work. There was no remorse in his stance.

He held the rifle ready, both of them waiting.

A short distance away, someone walked toward them on the grass. A woman, about her age. Eva tried to reach for her, to get her attention.

Someone was seeing this. Someone would tell her story.

She set her jaw, her eyes hardening as she panted and sweated. She looked right into the dark mask that was his face.

She would *not* give him the satisfaction.

Fuck you.

In the distance, another boom, and the sky exploded behind him, cheerful fireworks bursting with orange and white, crackling in the sky. She tried to focus on childhood Halloweens spent down at the beach after trick or treating, watching the fireworks reflecting off the water. That memory was hers.

He can't have that.

The fireworks' cheerful light starkly contrasted with his shadowed face.

The gun bucked upward, the flash of the barrel consuming her before it all went dark.

23

THE MAN STOOD OVER EVA. HE HAD BROAD shoulders and a large frame. He was tall, confident in his stance, as if he was born for this. A light caught her eye, and Nat gasped as Eva's body glowed. Her killer stood over her, breathing deeply as if to contain her spirit. Saliva crawled from the hood to drool onto Eva's chest. As Nat watched, the rest of the scenery melted into the same wet, viscous boundary that trapped her here, surrounding Eva and pulling her under. Before she could move, the storm returned, taking Eva's corpse and her killer with it.

The breeze moved inward, and debris from the unkempt yard whipped against her skin, forcing her to shut her eyes. She didn't struggle this time, cartwheeling through the air with no semblance of control.

Unlike the emptiness she experienced earlier, a blur of colour surrounded her, scenery from a speeding train. The landscape blended together, but she saw outlines of trees, buildings, cars, people, all streaking past her in a collective high-pitched wail.

She plummeted and braced herself for impact. The

concrete was spongy, not solid like the ground on the mountain or in the shed. She glanced at her palms, detached, as she picked off tiny pebbles that she couldn't feel digging into the skin there.

The flesh rippled as the pits left behind by the gravel filled themselves in. The flawlessness returned, and she shuddered at a perfection she didn't feel.

24

Gavin slammed face first into hard concrete, the air still dark around him. Muscles aching, he stood shakily, feeling uneasy. He recognized this feeling, as if he'd just run full speed into a wall.

Taking in the surrounding street, he saw he was back home, standing in the middle of the street. A bang vibrated through the night sky, moving from the house at the end of the street and exploding into the quiet neighbourhood.

"Nat?" he called again, hoping she could hear him over the noise.

There was a thud to his left, the heavy wooden gate slamming shut, the latch rattling against the wood. He turned, walking to the side of the house. The tall door stood shut as it always did, blocking the yard from prying eyes on the street. Something breathed on the other side, the sound fading as the soft hiss of something being dragged across the ground overcame it.

Reaching up and over the top, he felt a rusty metal latch. The hook screeched, stuttering unevenly through the latch as he pulled upward. More pops surrounded him, fireworks lighting up the sky above in bright orange and white explosions.

Wrenching open the gate, he saw nothing but blackness, the unknown of a yard he'd never been invited over to visit. It wasn't the shadowy expanse of a yard in the moonlight, but a black hole ready to enfold him into its orbit.

"Nat?" he whispered.

Taking an experimental step through the gate, his foot disappeared into the abyss. He explored further, pushing his foot down. Instead of the soft grass he expected, his foot dangled into nothing, a pit with an unknown ending.

Forcing himself to walk through, the dark consumed him. Glancing over his shoulder, he found nothing but darkness there; the light shining from the street through the gate completely smothered by the expanse of black.

Sound was nonexistent in this place, and his mouth hung open, the scream he tried to summon vacuumed into the void. Intense pain spread through his limbs, and he was ejected into the air, landing hard to find himself on the front lawn.

The landing was soft, and the rattling latch on the gate was still. The sky was empty of fireworks, his street quiet and lonely once more, as if nothing ever happened.

April 2015

A New Day

25

When the Parkers called asking for help with one last task, Meg hesitated, not sure it was the best idea. She was exhausted, finding herself stuck lately. Sleep was eluding her, but she was afraid to close her eyes for fear of reliving that last day, the day she lost them both.

Now, parked in Nat's driveway, she wondered if it was too late to back out.

Meg leaned over the steering wheel and looked at the front windows, preparing herself for what she would see when she went inside. The locks were changed, and the house was clean, sterilized, scrubbed of Nat's presence. The roof of the car closed in on her, and she ripped her seatbelt off, breathing deeply.

The cleaning crew put anything that was knocked over aside, promising not to throw anything away. Luckily, there wasn't much damage. The entire struggle that ended Nat's life amounted to one not very full box.

At first, the police thought Brian might have heard the robbery in progress upstairs and gone up to investigate. His brother said the key that Brian usually left under the mat was gone, which explained the lack of forced entry.

Nat must have walked in not long after. It all happened quickly, before she even turned on the light. All of this made a sad kind of sense; shit sometimes just happened. That it was simply the wrong place and the wrong time was something Meg could eventually accept.

But then the police started digging the holes.

Thinking the perpetrator couldn't have left long ago, they brought in dogs, hoping to catch the trail. The dogs whimpered and whined, none of them wanting to leave the backyard.

In the early days, it was Nat's face plastered everywhere. The violent crime fascinated everyone, the senselessness of it, a genuine mystery, right here in their sleepy town. As more and more holes were dug and the bones came out, an endless parade, the collages on the news stories grew and grew until Nat was just a smudge at the center. Meg watched the emerging story with horror, a new patch in the yard stripped of its lush grass with every updated shot.

The comments on social media became more about those holes and less about the human lives that they contained. *Sucks the girl came home when she did, but that guy had it coming. Whoever took him out did society a favour.*

Noting with a frustrated sigh that there was no other vehicle in the driveway, Meg got out of her car and slammed the door. She rested her cup of coffee on the roof of her car, a paper bag containing a muffin clenched in her teeth while she grabbed a stack of flattened boxes from the hatchback.

The sweet smell of blueberries wafted into her nose, and her stomach twisted. Given the circumstances, she wasn't hungry, but it was going to be a long day and she would need something to get her through.

The stack of boxes swung in a wide arc as she turned, and

she was startled to find a man standing in the walkway that led up to the door. Gasping, she dropped the armful of cardboard at her feet, the saliva-covered bag in her mouth falling with a thud into the disorderly heap.

Where did he come from?

"Can I help you?" he asked, arms folded across his broad chest.

His voice was deep, assertive and smooth, and she recognized it from their phone conversation.

"Sorry, you startled me. I didn't see a car," she said, her face reddening at his disapproving eyes. "Are you Darryl?"

The stony expression on his face softened.

"Meg? Sorry. There were some reporters hanging around, so I parked on the side street down the alley. I thought they finally gave up, but then I found one digging around in the trash last week. I think they're gone now, though."

"Sorry," she said. "That's..."

He nodded. "Yeah."

An awkward pause fell over the conversation, and she knelt and busied herself, pulling the scattered boxes into a pile on the concrete.

"Shit, I'm an ass. Here, let me help." He bent down and picked up the bag containing her breakfast.

Meg shook her head as she rose, balancing the bundle under her arm and against her hip as she accepted the bag.

"I'm fine. Really."

"At least let me get the door." Darryl hustled up the porch steps, unlocking the door and stepping inside to get out of her way.

"Thanks," she said, following him in and dropping the boxes to scatter in the entryway.

The noise echoed inside, as if the house already considered itself empty.

"You said you're helping her parents pack everything up?"

She nodded. *Close enough.*

Meg was the scout, sent ahead to be sure that there was no visible evidence of the horror that had happened here.

"I think this is going to be harder than we think."

He nodded.

"I know. Take all the time you need. I don't mind if you need to take the next week or so," he said, wandering into the kitchen and absently running his finger along Nat's dining room table.

"She seemed like such a nice girl. So pretty when she smiled." Meg felt rage building in her and wanted to scream at the platitude she heard so often these days, the life of her friend being boiled down to good dental hygiene.

Darryl picked up the mug that was washed and placed in the center and ran his fingers around the rim thoughtfully. The way he looked at it, as if he owned it, sent a wave of distaste through her.

Don't touch her things.

"I heard she had an accident years ago?" Darryl asked, with the slight upturn of his lips telling her he was looking for some good gossip.

The local news mentioned the accident again when Nat's death was first reported. It didn't come up again, and Meg hoped it was because someone at that tiny station had a soul. What she suspected was probably closer to the truth; that a sixteen-year-old tragedy was less exciting than a fresh series of murders.

Nat's past and her murder would be the only things this town would hold on to about her. Meg balled her hands into fists and maintained eye contact with Darryl, making sure he understood she would not be discussing it.

Nat wasn't perfect. If anyone knew that, Meg did.

She also knew that Nat deserved to be remembered for more than those damn holes.

"I'd better get to it," she said, a little more sharply than she'd intended, her mouth suddenly dry.

He turned his head in surprise at the shift in her tone. Resentment bubbled up in her as she smiled at him through gritted teeth.

She needed him gone, and a pretty smile was going to accomplish that.

"Sure thing," Darryl said, setting the mug down. His expression remained the same, but a spark seemed to leave his eyes, something darker lurking behind them.

Relaxing as he agreed, Meg felt a twinge of guilt. He was probably going out of his mind, grieving the brother he thought he knew and trying not to see every memory through a tainted lens.

"Look, I'm sorry. It's just…"

"I know," he said again and headed toward the basement door, head lowered.

"Hey, I'm sorry about your brother," she said as he put his hand on the doorknob.

Darryl turned to study her face, the intensity of his gaze making her feel as if she were under a microscope. Given the circumstances, people probably didn't say that to him much, so she could see why he would be suspicious.

"Thanks," he nodded, deciding that she meant it. "If you need anything, I'll be just downstairs. Take your time."

Shutting the door softly behind him, his steps faded as he retreated down to the basement. After a moment, she heard the shuffle of boxes being assembled and the screech of packing tape as he prepared to box up his brother's life, like she was getting ready to do with Nat's.

Finally alone, she picked up a large reusable bag from her supply, flattening the cardboard bottom into a cube. Opening and closing cupboards, she looked around for pet supplies for Chaos, placing a mostly full bag of dry food and his dishes in there. She finally located some catnip toys and a bag of cat treats in a drawer beside the sink.

As she tossed them into the bag on the counter, she caught sight of a smile peeking out from the bottom of the drawer. Clearing away the usual clutter of bag clips, batteries and matches that was piled overtop of the picture, Meg's eyes welled up. The thick bangs that Nat cut herself stuck up around a sweaty headband. She marvelled at how young they were, how quickly it all went wrong. Tragedy struck and destroyed their little family in a single moment.

Meg hadn't seen the picture in years, though she thought she had a copy tucked away in a dusty album. Periodically, she would pull out old photos, looking for memories of her dad. The albums all had bare patches now, photos of her, Nat and Chris all relegated to their own book for when she was ready. Looking at Chris' smile here brought it back in a crushing wave, and she slammed the drawer shut.

She left her bag on the counter and wandered over to the dining room table, shaking her hands in front of her and breathing deeply. Nat's mug on the dining room table was smudged with Darryl's fingerprints. Meg hated the idea of a stranger's hands on it.

Grabbing the cheerful cup, she brought it over to the kitchen sink, rinsing it under the hottest water she could stand. She scrubbed obsessively until the normally caffeine-stained ceramic was clean. The water ran, reddening her hands as she composed herself. Drying the mug gently on her shirt, she tucked it carefully into the bag with the cat supplies.

She would not do what she and Nat did for years and not acknowledge Chris. Meg eased open the drawer again, pulling out the photo and walking toward the fridge. It was emptied and cleaned—one less thing to worry about.

Meg slid the photo under a magnet in the shape of a cat's face. After stepping back, she noticed someone arranged the magnets in a neat, tidy row. She dragged them around, mixing them around in a slow circle. The haphazardness of the placement was comforting. Her eyes wandered across the gleaming, freshly cleaned countertop to the knife block resting near the sink, the largest slot ominously empty.

She was over to see Nat less than a week before it happened. They passed a lovely afternoon breaking down the minutiae of one of their favourite television series in excruciating detail. The conversation still lived there, a part of the fabric of this place now.

People always said they would remember a person's generosity, their personality, their sense of humour, all the broad strokes.

With Nat, Meg would remember how her face would light up when talking about a fictional character, how passionate she would get about a random article she came across. She would think about how fascinated she was with trivial facts, or how she showed off when she found a dress with pockets.

She would hang onto that last day, the sun reflecting off of her hair, steaming cups on the table, laughter ringing through the small house. Whenever she pet Chaos' silky fur, she would remember how Nat would scoop him up and kiss his furrowed forehead.

Moving away from the knife block and into the living room, Meg stared at the floor. The carpet was new, replaced when the old cream-coloured one was declared a lost cause by the cleaners. There was no sign that a life faded away where her feet rested on the rug, a life she was just starting to know again.

She rushed down the hall, trying to escape the feel of the carpet under her feet. There was a small closet on either side of her, bedrooms to the right and left, and the bathroom in front of her. She turned left into Nat's bedroom. Approaching the nightstand, she touched a book lying spine up, a pile of bills waiting to be paid, a notebook.

The blinds were open above the bed, looking out over what was left of the yard. The house was modest, but the yard was enormous. Nat loved it, and Meg felt a pang that she never got to enjoy the spring back there in full bloom. There was a giant pit surrounded by posts under the deck, with smaller holes scattered around the backyard where all the remains were removed.

Almost no grass was left, and the scale and enormity of the killing field they found hit her hard. The single gigantic tree in the corner still stood, its branches bare and sickly. The clawlike limbs made her shudder. It was as if it sustained itself by feeding off the horrors buried around its roots. Now that the contents of the yard were gone, the tree was fading away.

Crossing the hallway, Meg wandered into the second bedroom. It was a smaller room than the master, but there was a lovely set of French doors and a raised deck outside. Nat told her the renovation was a gift from Brian and Darryl for their mother when she got sick.

Meg thought of the scratching Nat described coming from the deck when she first moved in. Nat tried to shrug it off later, but Meg caught her listening intently in moments of silence, waiting for the sounds to return.

Belief in anything like this was so unlike practical Nat; it was always Meg's wheelhouse. Meg offered to do some research on the house for her, but Nat declined.

Nat laughed, stilted and forced, also accustomed to it being the other way around. *"I got carried away, that's all."*

Skepticism flashed across Meg's face, but she stayed quiet. She was tempted to do it anyway, but didn't want to overstep.

Standing in this room now, Meg listened, too. No sounds, nothing creeping along the edges of her vision, just a room brimming with stuff that never felt so empty. Nat had made this room a little library with assorted storage. It was still too cold to spend evenings out on the deck, but Nat was excited about a summer full of visits, including a refreshing cocktail or two.

A stadium blanket was abandoned there, tossed forgetfully over the back of the single folding chair. Stepping outside, Meg grabbed it and shook it out, folding it sloppily against her stomach.

She returned the blanket to the linen closet and stood leaning against the closet door, letting her mind wander as she faced the living room again. It was lit with spring light, cheerful, like nothing had ever happened.

It's just so...clean, Meg recalled saying when Nat first moved in. Nat's laughter echoed through the room.

The faint smell of sanitizing agents wafted toward her, and she breathed through her mouth to avoid becoming nauseous. She sidestepped the middle of the rug and moved toward the front window, fumbling with the latch. Leaning against the screen, she breathed deeply, drinking in the air outside.

She wandered over to the bookshelves along the far wall, stepping quietly, suddenly very conscious of Darryl's presence below her. The spines were hard against her fingers as she ran her hand along the rows. Besides the books, the shelves seemed barren. She picked up the snow globe that remained and shook it, remembering the day they graduated high school. Nat didn't come to the ceremony, but her parents tried to maintain some normalcy afterward. Their families got together, had cake and some gifts, nothing fancy.

"A gift for your dorm room. To remind you of home," Mrs. Parker said as Nat ripped the paper off the snow globe. It was beautiful, a scene of a lake in winter, surrounded by thick green trees.

Setting it down on the coffee table, Nat marched back upstairs without a word.

"They can't wait to get rid of me," Nat confided to Meg

that night, eyes welling with tears. *"I don't blame them. They can't stand the sight of me."*

They wanted you to be happy. The words were on the tip of her tongue, but she couldn't bring herself to offer the reassurance now.

The box from the cleaner rested on the floor near the bookcases, its logo splashed discreetly across the sides. Meg squatted beside it, pulling the tape off the top.

A fresh wave of the bleach smell hit Meg as she pulled off the lid, wrinkling her nose. Inside the box, the missing knick-knacks from the shelves lay nestled together, a sentimental treasure trove to explore. They were all items that didn't have enough weight to withstand the vibrations of a body hitting the floor must have caused.

Meg imagined them falling, the cheap particle board of the shelves swaying slightly at the disturbance. She pulled these items that were so precious to Nat at random, finding places for them on the shelves as she went.

Pausing as she picked up a small figurine of a cat, she ran her thumb over the calico spots. She could see now that it was tacky dollar store trash, but when she bought it with her own pocket money for Nat's eighth birthday, it was the height of elegance. She slipped it into the pocket of her sweatshirt, giving it one last squeeze before returning to the box. There were a few that were broken, but maybe not irreparably. They might be good as new with a little crazy glue and a steady hand.

She moved the box into Nat's little library, deciding the broken ones were best hidden for now. As she gently placed it on the floor near the closet, she noticed another box peeking out from underneath Nat's desk. Crawling over, she sat on her butt to provide some leverage to pull the cumbersome box out. The box was sun faded, and dusty. *Maybe something left from the move?*

A note was attached, and she peeled it off to read it.

A timid knock interrupted her thoughts, a strained voice calling "Meg?" as the front door cracked open.

"Coming," she called.

Pocketing the note, Meg dragged the box out, placing it near the door so she wouldn't forget to return it to its rightful owner.

26

THE AFTERNOON WITH NAT'S PARENTS WAS EVEN more awful than Meg thought it would be. Even after everything Nat told her, Meg underestimated the extent to which Nat cut ties with them. Interactions were restricted to the odd, strained phone call, walking on eggshells when someone passed away, a card at the holidays, the obligatory 'Happy Birthday!' text messages.

The last time they saw Nat was before she left. Nat had with her own parents essentially what she had with Meg, and that was just so fucking sad.

Meg thought back to the fall after the accident. The fork in the road in their relationship.

Meg told Nat not to worry, that people moved on over the summer. There would be something new for everyone to talk about. She could barely convince Nat, let alone herself, and they both knew she would just be fresh chum for the gossip machine.

Nat's parents were different; everyone looked at them with special pity. Losing their son was bad enough. How could they live in the same house as the person who ruined their lives?

How could they look at the child that lived and bring themselves to be grateful?

Meg got the feeling that Mrs. Parker's silence over the years wasn't to avoid her daughter; it was so she didn't say something she would regret.

Before the accident, Nat and her father never really talked much, not about anything real. Afterward, it seemed like they were always picking a fight, relating to each other through their anger without ever addressing why they were mad.

When Nat left town, she burned the bridge behind her, flicking the cigarette into the gasoline of her identity. The only thing Meg had to comfort them with was the knowledge that Nat was working herself up to making amends with them. It seemed to make her dad feel better, but her mom left shortly after that revelation.

Mr. Parker sighed. "I think she regrets not having made a genuine effort sooner. You tell yourself there's time, but..."

Nat's words came back to her, an unwanted mantra pounding away in her head the rest of the day, reverberating from the walls, forever trapped in this house.

You think of all the wasted time.

Meg and Mr. Parker started small, emptying all the loose figurines and picture frames from the bookcases before packing up Nat's novels. It should have been simple, an icebreaker, really, but to Meg it was painfully clear they had no clue about Nat's friendships, who she might have been in touch with since coming back.

There were some items Mr. Parker smiled at, some secret story playing behind his eyes. An old, well-loved teddy bear. An inscription in a battered children's book. A scratched plastic dinosaur. Those things he held tight before placing gently in a box, surrounding the bubble-wrapped snow globe.

There were ten items he hadn't ever seen for each one he kept, and Meg felt herself wilting with each question.

"This is nice. Do you know who gave this to her? They should have it."

After the first few, she took pity on him.

"Sure," she said. "Let's put it in a box and organize it for some of her friends later."

Meg didn't have the heart to tell him she had no clue either. The few names she gathered didn't respond to her messages since the funeral. There was no one to claim anything, but Mr. Parker didn't need to know that, and he certainly didn't need to feel worse than he did now. The box would come home with her, Mr. Parker none the wiser.

They made quick work of the kitchen, the most impersonal room in any home. A pot is a pot; a pan is a pan. Meg covertly removed the photo and the fridge magnets shaped like cat butts, the magnetic poetry, the promotional images from publishers, dumping them into his box to find later. They were only working on the bedroom for a short time when he hit his limit.

"Sorry, Meg, I thought maybe doing this fast was the way to go, but..." he trailed off, exhausted.

"Of course," she nodded. "Darryl doesn't need everything out for a week. We have time."

"Thank you," he nodded gratefully.

"Anytime, Mr. Parker."

What am I still doing here? The depth of how pathetic she felt, still trying to fix things for Nat all these years later, pulled her down.

"Please, Meg. We're all adults. Call me Mike, okay?" There was a twinkle in his eye, the ghost of a smile, and Meg nodded. They both knew she never would.

"Maybe we'll tackle the clothes tomorrow? I don't know if anything is to your taste, but you're more than welcome to any of it."

"Sure. I'll stay behind, take a quick look."

He bent over to pick up the box of items at his feet, knees buckling slightly as he realized that this was all he had to take with him.

He looked ready to crumple, and she crouched to pick up the box for him. "I'll give you a hand."

"Thanks," he said gratefully.

They walked down the steps together, and he unlocked his car so she could slide the box across the backseat. The four flaps were folded inward, and tufts of the teddy bear's fur escaped from the top, rustling slightly like the feathers of a trapped bird as a breeze picked up.

Mr. Parker slammed the door and paused as he buckled his seatbelt. Meg lifted her hand in farewell, and as she turned back to the house, he rolled his window down.

"I don't think it's any secret that we didn't have the best relationship with her. That much was clear when we talked to the police. Not knowing who her friends were, what she liked to do, even where she worked..." His breath hitched, the embarrassment and shame a palpable force coming off him. "I sensed how wrong everyone knew that was, and I'm sad I've only just realized it."

Meg opened her mouth to comfort him, some sort of platitude about it being a two-way street ready to comfort him.

He held up a hand to stop her.

"I know she had a part in that, in how we all were with each other. All that matters, all these years...was she happy, Meg? In her way, at least?"

Meg blinked, taken aback at the ridiculousness of the question. Nat and Meg were just getting started, and there was so much lost time to make up for. They weren't *themselves* yet, not really.

His eyes were pleading, hoping for the best, but expecting the worst. Meg considered how closed-mouth Nat was with her about the extent of the damage done in her family, about the hasty message to tell her she was back in town, and it was at that moment she realized their falling out hadn't made the list of approved conversations.

Sudden anger flared in her as she thought of how easy it had been for Nat to let herself off the hook, and she cracked her knuckles to avoid saying anything in haste.

The weight of regret was still there when she died, lingering and poisonous. "She had a hard time," Meg said carefully. "But yes. She was."

A little white lie hurts no one. Nat was trying to be.

Doubt clouded his eyes, but he nodded, relieved. One less thing to feel guilty about. People see what they want to see, hear what they want to hear.

The fading rumble of his car fell away behind her as Meg walked back into the house. Kicking her shoes off in the hallway, she walked into Nat's bedroom, intending to jam as many clothes as she could into garbage bags and get the hell out of there. She pulled the boring clothes off of hangers, the multiple copies of the same shirt that Nat wore for work.

As she moved deeper into the closet, she discovered more personal items. An ancient hand-knit wool sweater. The sundress she bought for a recent blind date who stood her up in the end. A pilled old robe. With each item that went into the bag, she sensed Nat disappearing a little bit more. She slid hangers meant for keeping, leaving them hanging for a final decision. Her hand touched a garment bag, and she unzipped it, expecting maybe an old bridesmaid dress, or the dress that went unworn to her graduation.

White tulle exploded from the bag as it opened.

A wedding dress.

Meg pulled it out, frowning. He was already with someone else at the funeral. How serious was the relationship?

They needed time, Meg knew that, but this? How could Nat not tell her about this?

It was...complicated; she had said, brushing it off and hiding it away within herself.

Nat didn't trust me.

Grunting, Meg wrenched the wedding dress from the rod and shoved it deep into the donation bag. Red-faced, she dislodged the clothes by the handful, hangers flying as she tossed them aggressively in a heap behind her. The last of it was some winter wear, a heavy coat and snow pants that heavily weighed down on the bar.

Wrapping her arms around the whole bundle, she lifted them up and dumped the clothing in the now massive pile. Kneeling, Meg pulled the garbage bag toward herself and shoved things in by the fistful. The bag burst, and she screamed in rage, standing to kick it into the vanity.

The mirror on top wobbled, and a small dish filled with earrings fell off the side, metal pieces scattering across the carpet. Her arms went limp at her sides, and she bent to pick up the mess, panting and cursing as a tiny stud dug into her knee.

Meg placed the bowl back on the wooden tabletop, resting it among a jumble of items tossed there at the end of each day. A row of jewelry boxes lined the mirror. The one on the end, a beat-up wooden one with a cheap clasp, caught her attention. It was a popular design back then, a girl on a swing.

Clutching the box in both hands, she sat down in the middle of Nat's bed. Half expecting an angelic glow, some kind of revelation when she opened it, it was almost a letdown when all she got was the tinkling of the music box. The plastic ballerina in a highly flammable white tutu turned slowly, whirring as the ancient parts inside came to life. It was a mess in there, dirty old keychains tangled with brooches and watches unworn for decades.

Meg was pulling apart a plastic beaded necklace from some costume clip-on earrings when something fell into her lap. She reached down and retrieved it from between the duvet folds—something cold and smooth.

It was a mood ring. She remembered Nat wearing this all the time, a gift from Chris. She rubbed at it, but it remained the same gaudy red. Placing it on her pinkie so she wouldn't lose track of it, she would add it to her own jewellery box later.

As she continued to pull things out, she found a clump of threads rolled in a ball at the bottom. It seemed to be scraps, the detritus of some long-ago sewing kit.

Pulling it apart to make sure there was nothing caught inside the mess, she dropped it to the bedspread, hand over her mouth. Moving more gently, she began the slow operation of detangling the threads to reveal friendship bracelets, soft from so much wear. Making them for each other was a summer tradition of theirs. Meg could tell from the braiding how old each one was, the sloppy loops and short strings for their tiny wrists of the first years graduating to more intricate patterns. She lined them up in a row, an even dozen.

Nat kept every single one.

Surrounded by all that remained of the friend that she barely knew anymore, Meg crawled under the duvet to shut it all out. The warmth inside filled her to her core, armour against the rush of air conditioning. Images and memories flooded her as she clutched the oldest bracelet, and she let herself float away into sleep.

Unsurprisingly, she dreamed of the past.

WHEN THEY GOT TO THE BEACH, THE CROWD WAS immense. It was supposed to be a small group, but word of the plan spread, and there were now a ton of their classmates invading the park, joined by some people from the school across town. Apparently, word spread, and a beach rager was in progress.

So much for inconspicuous. Meg shook her head, but grinned, thinking she could use a little fun with exams coming up. It was so close to the end of the year; she doubted anyone would really make a fuss. Taking in the surrounding faces, she realized her afternoon calculus class would be virtually empty.

Nat and Meg chattered endlessly, raising their voices to be heard over the blaring of someone's boom box.

"I can't believe your dad finally caved and let you wear that," Meg gestured to Nat's new top, tiny straps exposing bare shoulders.

Nat laughed. "Yeah, that's not happening. I wore it under a sweatshirt when I left the house."

"I don't get it; like shoulders are soooooo scandalous." Meg rolled her eyes. "Why guys are sooo scared of bra straps?"

"I think he's worried something will happen," Nat said, suddenly quiet.

Meg winced, remembering the fight Nat told her about last week, where the phrase *asking for it* had come up more than once.

"Sorry, I didn't mean..." Meg said.

"It's cool. I'm staying at mom's this week anyway," Nat said, brushing it off. "Hey, do you want to g..."

The bottle of water she was bringing to her lips fell to the grass, cutting off her question.

Meg laughed, bending to pick up the bottle.

"Way to go, klutz." Nat's brand-new runners were soaked with the water that escaped.

When she tried to hand her the bottle, Nat's fingers twitched, her entire body stiffening. Meg watched in horror as a tremor moved through Nat's body and her eyes lost focus.

"Nat? What's wrong?" Meg grabbed her shoulders, shaking her.

Nat opened her mouth as if trying to speak. She inhaled, wheezing like air being sucked through the world's tiniest straw. Her eyes were saucers, screaming for help.

Meg turned, ready to call the nearest person for help. As she looked away, she felt the muscles she held under her hands relax. There was awareness in Nat's pupils again, but she looked confused.

"What?" She seemed shaken and tried to shove Meg's hands away. Meg loosened her grip slightly but didn't let go.

"Nat. What happened? Are you okay?"

"Yeah, I'm fine."

Nat's hand rubbed absently across the back of her neck, pain evident in the way she held herself, the way she looked down to shield her eyes. Meg sometimes got migraines, and Nat's eyes reminded her of how she sometimes got really sensitive to light a couple of days before.

"Are you sure? Maybe we should go." Chris was wandering nearby, and Meg waved him over.

An oblivious puppy, he bounded over happily, holding a plastic cup that sloshed over on his hands. Whenever he got to tag along, he looked like he won some kind of cool kid lottery even though he was only a year younger than them.

"Whassssuuuuuppppppppppppppppp?"

Meg rolled her eyes, doing her best to act sufficiently annoyed.

Chris stared at her, searching her face. They hadn't spoken since she gave him the note back last week. Throughout the entire car ride, Meg talked more than usual, trying to make sure there was no room for him to cut in. Normally, he would be full of annoying interruptions, but he stayed suspiciously quiet in the backseat.

Meg watched Nat out of the corner of her eye, but she

didn't seem to notice anything was up. The seed of annoyance grew in Meg on the ride over. Nat's continued obliviousness angered her in a way she didn't really understand.

Maybe she doesn't know me.

Meg punched his shoulder as he reached them. "Hey, dummy, your sister's not feeling good."

Concern filled his features in an instant, his head snapping over to look at Nat's face. Nat smiled, but it wavered slightly. The skin where Meg's hands still rested on her shoulders felt clammy, and she appeared paler than before. She still didn't trust Nat's balance.

Nat winced and brought her hand up to cup the back of her neck. Fresh sweat beaded on her forehead, knuckles whitening as she gripped the flesh there.

"Nat?" Chris asked gently. "You look like you're about to hurl."

Meg didn't have any brothers or sisters, but she'd been friends with them long enough to speak sibling. What he meant was, *"Are you alright? Do you need help?"*

"Yeah, I'm okay. Really. Probably just too hot out here, or something." Her eyes remained trained on the ground, her voice barely a mumble, so they needed to lean in to catch what she was saying.

"Do you wanna go home?"

She seemed to take inventory, trying to decide how sick she really felt.

Nat tried to smile again, but this time it was merely stretching her mouth.

"Nah. I think I'm just going to go sit in the car for a few minutes. Crank the A/C, Cool?". The glazed, unfocused look returned to her eyes.

He searched her face. "Okay. How about I come meet you in about ten minutes? If you're still not feeling good, we'll go."

Nat opened her mouth to argue, but seemed to consider

that would only delay her moving to the car. Nodding wearily, she stumbled a little as she took a step.

"Whoa! I'm coming with you," Meg said, grabbing Nat's elbow to steady her.

What the hell is this? Meg was with her since they arrived. All she had to drink was water.

Didn't she? The grain of doubt wasn't there back then, implanted only after what happened.

"I'm fine," Nat grumbled, ripping her arm away.

They watched her go. Once she reached the parking lot, she looked around, getting her bearings, then headed toward the car.

Satisfied she was going the right way, Chris jammed his hands into his pockets and turned toward Meg.

"What the hell was that?" Chris asks. "Did you tell her?"

Meg shook her head, frowning as she watched Nat's bobbing head until she lost sight of it in the tangle of hot metal roofs jamming the parking area.

Something's wrong.

"Is she okay to drive?" he asked.

"I don't know," Meg said honestly. "She hasn't had anything, though."

As he wiped his hand on his shorts, she examined him more closely.

"Have you had a few?"

"Yeah," he laughed. "That was the plan. Nat's the DD, remember? If she doesn't seem right when I get to the car, I'll come get you to drive."

Meg avoided his eyes, the hope that she would see him again today making her heart beat a little faster. "Hope she's okay."

"Are you like, ignoring me?" Chris burst out, seizing the opportunity now that they were alone. The alcohol emboldened him, and he seemed to think it was now or never. "Did I do something wrong?"

Meg flushed. All she wanted was to pretend none of this ever happened. She wished he never asked her on that date.

Liar.

"Do you like me?"

Heart racing against her ribs, she tried to keep her hands from trembling as she pictured them clamped in his.

She imagined them happy, laughing and joking. Making out in the car's backseat, or in her dorm room next September, they would talk all night, *really* talk. There was nothing she wouldn't say to him, and for some reason, that scared her. She pictured herself guiding his hand up her shirt, his happy intake of breath as his wonder melted into clunky but fiery scrabbling as they removed each other's clothes.

Jesus, I have to lay off the fan fiction.

Searching the hopeful expression on his face, she reached for the courage to say yes. The word would topple from her lips easily if she let it, but she couldn't. Deep down, she knew how this would really go.

After she left town for university, it would be too hard to be away from each other. She imagined the mounting frustration of only phone calls, only emails, maybe some cards or letters in the mail. The guilt of not coming home enough and missing him would grow to a head until inevitably, everything would implode.

All possible, but could be overcome. Breakups were hard, but if it didn't work out, she would be okay eventually. Chris was worth it.

What she was really worried about was what would happen when Nat was forced into picking sides. This was where she always fumbled in deciding what to do about Chris. Nat would hear them both out, try for a while to stick by both their sides. In the end, though, Meg knew for a hard and solid fact that if Nat needed to choose, it wouldn't even be a question of who would win.

Meg didn't stand a chance in that contest, and she would lose them both. In the end, she decided that the best answer was the honest one.

"It would just be too hard, Chris."

His gaze didn't waver.

Her eyes filled with tears, which she hastily wiped away. Lifting her chin, he leaned in and kissed her softly, sweetly, a bold gesture likely fuelled by the alcohol they'd been sipping.

She eased into it, reciprocating, smiling at his surprise as she kissed him back. When they drew apart, he was flushed, unsure of what to do or say.

She leaned her forehead against his, then stepped away, frustrated.

"You know I'll be going away after graduation, Chris. That's always been the plan."

"So? Long distance is a thing. It can't be that hard."

"Are you serious?" she snorted. "Literally *every* movie with a long-distance relationship says it is."

He scoffed. "Yeah, but they always get back together at the end."

"That's not how it works, and you know it."

"Come on, Meg. You haven't even applied anywhere yet. It's still a year and a half away."

The temptation of a wonderful year pulled at her, but she couldn't take the bait.

The mutual understanding that this was the turning point hung heavily between them, and they were no further than they were before. Whatever was said now, there was no coming back. She felt like she was letting go of Nat's hand, and she wasn't sure yet how it felt.

"How about this?" Meg spoke experimentally, her tongue thick in her mouth.

He glanced at her with trepidation written across his face, trying to decide if this was good or bad.

"We have the summer. How about if we just take things slow, okay? See what happens?" She cut off his joyful expression with a caveat.

"Let's not tell her. I mean it," she said hastily, seeing the excitement in his eyes, the tell the world energy in his tapping heels. "Not until we know for sure that there's something to tell, okay? If it doesn't work, she never even has to know."

I don't want to ruin everything.

Pulling her to him again, he put his arms around her. The relief of a decision made and the excitement of a secret twisted together inside of her, and she vibrated with joy.

Ohhhhh, I am in sooooo much trouble.

They parted, and he jerked his thumb awkwardly toward the parking lot.

"Maybe I should go check on her."

Meg's heart sank, partly because he was leaving, and partly because she completely forgot how they found this moment alone.

I'm a terrible person.

"Could you call me later?" She asked, more breathless than she wanted to let on.

He grinned, and she backtracked. "To let me know if she's okay."

"Sure." He smiled, that lopsided, genuine smile spreading across his face.

Chris walked toward the parking lot. As he reached the first row of cars, he turned to Meg one last time, grinning and waving as he went to find his sister.

The memory played out exactly as she remembered it until the dream crept in.

"Come back," she yelled.

But he didn't turn around, because she never told him to stay.

27

"Nat?!"

She turned to find Gavin standing across from her in her front yard. With the dark night sky having snapped back to a cloudless blue, a spring sun high in the sky. Through the window, she saw the top of her sofa, her mosaic of bookshelves holding the living room together.

She stood up, wiping dirt off her pants with her hands, noticing her knees were scraped. Instead of a little skim of blood across the joints, they shone, reflecting the surrounding light, a silvery grey.

She thought back to her mood ring and remembered the stormy cloud of colour signifying sadness. *Like a rainy day,* Chris said, looking at the tiny folded paper which had the wheel of emotions printed on it. *That's easy to remember.*

It didn't feel like sadness. It was deeper than that, more dire.

Hopeless.

Her arm stung, and she glanced down to see the bloody scratch from the forest healing over, a few flecks of leafy debris being forcibly ejected from her skin.

As it disappeared, she looked down, frowning at her knees. There was no blood, just the liquid rain clouds crawling lazily around her thighs before making their way back into the cuts. The denim of her jeans knit back together, closing courteously over the healing skin.

"What the hell, Nat? What was that? Where were you? Are you okay?"

All things considered.

Back on solid ground, the intertwining memories of Eva's corpse, of how she rotted away, remained burned in her brain.

"What happened? Where did you go?"

His questions were all wrong. One question consumed her, the only one that mattered.

Why, why, why, why, why, why, why?

"You okay?" he paused his rambling, taking a step back.

The calm finally slipped.

"One minute," she croaked, turning away from Gavin's concerned face to throw up as politely as possible into the flower bed under her living room window.

28

NAT WIPED HER MOUTH AND TURNED ON SHAKY LEGS to find Gavin sitting on the curb with his back to her, wisely giving her a bit of space.

In what sick world is this kid my fucking welcome wagon into the afterlife?

The sight of him elicited laughter, the cosmic joke of it all overwhelming her.

"What?"

"Nothing, man. No offence, but I'm supposed to be...I don't know. Drinking margaritas on a beach for eternity or something. Not stuck with a teenager who's been dead for sixteen years but somehow knows next to nothing helpful."

The words were out of her mouth before she had the chance to even realize she was saying them. Eyes brimming, he turned away from her, bringing up a hand to chew on his fingernails.

"Fuck," she whispered, looking up in the distance toward the mountain.

She grew up with it in her world, its majesty forgotten until her return. In this place, it seemed to loom over them, a reminder of how vast the emptiness here was. As if it heard her, the wind picked up, clouds covering the sun to cast the mountains in shadow.

"What happened, Nat?" Gavin stood in front of her, cheeks red, but ready to talk. She shook her head and tore her eyes away from him to look at the houses on the street.

I can't.

He approached her slowly, as if she were a wounded animal and he were trying to avoid having her face scratched off in a flurry of angry claws and teeth. She wrenched her body away before he could touch her, the only comfort he offered her.

"Don't touch me!" she yelled.

Hands in front of him in a non-threatening stance, he took a step back. She immediately felt like shit, turning away too late to avoid the hurt look on his face.

His expression brought back all the people she pushed away, all the times she yelled at friends, at family, when she couldn't hold in her rage anymore. She would watch herself from somewhere else, powerless to stop herself from getting out of control. When they refused to yell back, she only got angrier. When someone yells at a person, they yell back, and on and on until someone can't yell any louder.

Those were the rules. She didn't make them; she just made sure she was the loudest one yelling. *Easier to push people away before they get hurt. Better to hurt them a little, so they leave before the damage is irreparable.*

Like Chris.

All I do is hurt people.

"I just...I'm sorry, okay? What I saw with Eva, it happened after we touched. I'm not ready for more."

Dropping his hands to his sides, Gavin nodded, seeming to take it as an explanation, if not an apology.

"I get it. This wasn't supposed to happen to me, either."

She was shaking, and his compassionate eyes stayed trained on her. "Look," he said, his voice imploring her to listen.

Sheets of gunmetal grey, tinged with red and orange, were pouring off her, like she was sweating after a marathon. It completely obscured her vision, and she blinked as it dripped into her eyes. The emotions were literally pouring out of her, too big to be contained.

Did I hide it this terribly when I was alive?

Overpowering shame washed through her as she thought of the casualties of the pointless show, of her parents and Meg. She told herself for years she was protecting everyone, that she was only punishing herself.

What would Chris think of me?

The enormity of the wave crashed over her, overcoming her now that it had freed itself. Gavin was completely obscured by the shroud she found herself in, creating her own little world. It was excruciating, but she couldn't scream. Somewhere deep and comfortable where she didn't have to think about things anymore pulled at her. The promise washed over her, freedom from worries.

"Don't go there." Gavin's voice remained slow and soothing, like a hypnotist. "Please. Come back."

Gavin was so far away his voice barely found her. "Let it all go."

I can't. It's who I am.

Gavin's voice reached her in the place she'd given in to.

"It is, but it's not all of you. It's only part."

Slowly and methodically, she exhaled. Skin crawling, pushing aside the pain to concentrate on the slithering sensation, focusing on making it stop. The last time she saw Chris, Meg, and her parents all came flooding back to her at once.

A genuine conversation could have happened between her and them. But she didn't, and this was where she was now. She couldn't go back and finish what she started, but that wasn't her fault.

Let it go.

When she opened them again, it was all but gone. A shred of sanity came back to her, and she held it tightly, willing it to grow as the last of it curled up inside her.

I'm sorry, she gasped inside herself.

"There," Gavin smiled. "You did it."

Maybe the kid's not such a bad spirit guide after all.

Nat sank to her knees, suddenly exhausted, wondering how she managed the weight for so long.

29

Deciding a change of scenery was in order for a serious talk, Nat took Gavin to her latest favourite lunch spot, a little café that had been there for ages. The desserts were amazing, somehow rich and light at the same time. A tiny round table waited for them on the red brick patio, with surprisingly comfortable high-back chairs on either side. The restaurant inside remained dark, but Nat's standard order appeared in front of them. Gavin squirmed in his chair, looking at the brick under his feet in awe.

"What?" Nat asked.

"I never tried this place when I was alive." Gavin's face fell as he looked at Nat's mousse, unable to order the dessert he was hoping for.

"What do you want?" Nat asked, reading out options for him from the menu he couldn't see. She suspected it wasn't so much about eating a dessert they couldn't taste, and more about not being left out.

After this much time, being able to have a fresh experience was probably just what the doctor ordered.

Three layers of heavily iced chocolate cake appeared in

front of him. A smile lit up his face, and she was pleased she could repay a kindness to him. Maybe they were here together to beat this place.

The food sat untouched between them. Devoid of smell or taste, it was strictly symbolic, but that didn't matter. Nat let him chatter, let him feel normal for a little while. She found her hands curling around the cup of coffee on the table, leaning forward to engage with him.

When he was done hours later, she dove back in.

"Tell me about Eva," she said, taking a habitual sip from the cup. The dark, steaming liquid inside turned to vapour, dissipating on her tongue.

"You said you saw her in a dream," he said in reply, a non-answer.

Fine, kid. I'll show you mine if you show me yours.

"Yeah, I did. Scariest one I ever had. Believe me, I remember it. It was when I moved in on the street, the first night. To be honest, I haven't stopped thinking about it since."

Fear flickered across his eyes. "What happened when we got separated? What did you see?"

"I saw...everything that happened to Eva."

"So, did you know her when she was alive? You looked totally freaked out when you saw her." Gavin frowned.

Nat remained deep in thought, distracted. "Like I'd seen a ghost."

"Not funny, dude."

"I think...I think she *was* a ghost. In my dream, I mean. It was like she was trying to warn me." She was rambling, talking out loud to make sense of things. Part of her was talking to Gavin, but the other part was just her trying to put everything in some semblance of a reasonable order. They had more pieces now, so maybe she saw the complete puzzle.

This was the first hint that there was a bigger picture here, and she was going to grab it. She finally felt like she was supposed to do something other than this endless wandering.

"What do we all have in common?" Nat asked rhetorically.

Gavin snorted. "Definitely not taste in clothes."

Nat ignored him, concentrating, feeling a sense of purpose that she had been searching for since she'd arrived in this hellhole.

We were all murdered.

She finally understood.

"I think I know why we're here."

30

NAT'S HEAD SPUN WITH THE IMPLICATION OF IT ALL. "Eva was trying to warn me what would happen before he could kill me, too!"

That ship sailed, but maybe they could figure out how to stop him.

"So, you're saying if the same guy killed you and Eva, and I'm here, too..."

Nat nodded, happy he had gotten there on his own and she didn't have to be the one to tell him.

"What if the same person killed all of us, Gavin?"

"Are you serious?" Gavin scoffed. "That's crazy."

"Right now, it's the only thing that makes sense. How else would we all be connected?"

"Eva and I died so long ago, though," Gavin reasoned. "Would this guy even still be killing people?"

"Maybe he's not that old," Nat smiled, remembering the hubris of youth. Even a few years older than you, was ancient. "If he was only in his twenties or thirties then, he could be maybe mid-forties or fifties now."

Hardly geriatric.

Another piece clicked into place, and her eyes flashed with understanding.

"What?" Gavin asked.

"I moved the rock," she yelled, laughing up at the sky.

"Yeah, so?" Gavin kicked at a pebble on the ground between them. "Big deal, I can do that, too."

"No, not like that! When we saw Eva, I slipped and knocked a rock down the hill. It's why she stopped on the path."

"What do you mean?" he asked. "Are you okay? You're freaking me out."

Ignoring him, she shook her head, ignoring a few deep red droplets that splattered onto the table. "The thing that happened when I grabbed your arm. You felt that, right?"

Grimacing at the reminder of being a human bug zapper, he nodded.

"She couldn't see us. She was jogging, so she was sweaty. Like, regular sweaty, not covered in whatever this is." Nat gestured to the last droplets that were slowly reincorporating themselves into her body.

The colour was different from fear, less jarring. It more closely resembled how she thought of blood, excitement coursing through her veins. She hated the sensation would eventually become her new normal.

"Plus, she had a pre-MP3 player jammed down her workout gear."

Nat thought this would seal the deal, but he still looked confused. "You've seen a cell phone, right?"

"Yeah," he said, rolling his eyes. "My friend Jamal had one. It held *three* ringtones."

"Not anymore," she grinned, happy to be the one imparting wisdom now. "Now, they're like a tiny handheld computer that you can carry in your pocket. Pictures, calendars, the internet...we use them for everything." *Except as a phone,* she thought.

The kid looked awestruck, and she remembered how she felt thinking about the future in the time before everyone carried advanced technology around in their pockets.

"Anyway, trust me. No one in their right mind wants to carry around a portable CD player while they're running anymore. I think we saw her in the past."

"What, like time travel? Without the time machine?"

Nat nodded, once again glad that he was filling in the gaps. Her rationality sounded completely irrational. "When we touched, whatever energy that was...I think we *are* the time machine."

Gavin laughed. "Are you nuts? It was just a rock! How do you know it didn't just fall on its own? Maybe you just thought you kicked it."

Eva's body falling on the ground, full of determination that wasn't enough, flashed through her mind.

"When you were gone, I was with her. She was tied up, and I wasn't even thinking, just trying to get her ropes untied before he came back. Out of nowhere, I could just *feel* the ropes in my hand. I grabbed them, yanked her across the ground, and got her loose." Nat paused, trying to figure out the difference. "Maybe, we can't touch living things?"

"Wait, really? That's so cool! Did you save her?"

"No," Nat said, lowering her head in frustration. "She still...she's gone. I tried, but it didn't help."

You can't change this.

The moment of clarity rose in her again, and she tried to shove it down, tried to take Eva's warning as a sign they could figure this out.

Eva's face was defiant when she died, ignoring her impending death to look toward Nat. Maybe Eva was a little less scared in her last moment, or felt a little less alone.

Perhaps it was all she was able to do.

At least it was something.

Something seemed very wrong here. In every ghost story, the whole point of ghosts haunting people was to help them, to get them to find something out, or to find their killer. Ghosts were supposed to interact with people, or make them see some truth.

Were she and Gavin haunting each other?

Or is Eva haunting us?

Maybe Nat had it all wrong, and this wasn't a ghost story. All she knew for sure was that Gavin knew more than he was telling.

"Okay. That's all I know. Really. Your turn. How did you know her?"

"It doesn't matter." He glanced down at the table, folding his hands over each other.

Sitting back in her chair, she crossed her arms over her chest.

"So, what you're saying is, we just *happened* to run into the dead lady who showed up in a traumatizing dream of mine? Oh, and you have a special psychic ghost ability or something. Otherwise, how would you know her name? Who is she, Gavin? Spit it out already."

Fidgeting with the cutlery on the table, he dismantled his fluffy piece of cake into crumbs.

"Look, I promise I won't judge," she whispered, trying to put him at ease. "What happens in Purgatory, stays in Purgatory."

Weariness took him, causing him to slump over in his chair.

"Eva was already dead when I met her," he whispered, giving up.

Nat leaned forward, giving him her full attention.

"Do you know where she is now? How come I haven't seen her?"

Gavin was stuck, lost in thought. She was feeling like a dick for making him tell her about it, but she needed to know.

"Gavin?"

He peered up at her, his brown eyes rimmed with sludge, the beginnings of grief threatening to spill out as his terror built to extremes, unlocking a place in his mind he boarded up a long time ago.

"I know it's hard for you to talk about, but maybe if it's easier, you can show me, instead."

He remained silent, lips thin and white as he kept them squeezed tightly together. Nat thought for a moment, then held out her hand.

"This whole time-travel thing? There's only one way to find out if I'm right."

Gavin sighed, placing his hand tentatively in her offered palm as if she held every one of his worst fears there.

OCTOBER 2000

FIREWORKS

31

Eva arrived soon after Gavin figured out if he wanted something badly enough, he could get it.

With no one to talk to, he hated to admit he was getting lonely. He always considered himself a bit of a loner, used to spending time by himself while his mom was at work. The realization that he needed other people around was difficult, like he was learning who he really was.

Boredom set in with unsettling speed. Travelling to some of his favourite spots was fun for a while, but there were only so many times he could go to the arcade, bowling, and to the movies. Aware that he was complaining about not having to do homework ever again, he begrudgingly turned his thoughts to the library. He thought about the book he was about halfway through when he died, wishing he could finish it. It was getting good.

The school had its panties in a bunch about it and said the school library wouldn't carry it. His mom wasn't happy. She was pissed, actually, and freaked out about it at the next PTA meeting.

"Are you serious? They were losing their minds about that one when *I* was in high school!"

The school was pretty uptight, and she didn't change their minds, but she still let Gavin read it. The used bookstore had a copy in pretty good shape, and she handed it to him with a smile. He wasn't really sure what to say, since he didn't care about all the stuff the PTA said.

He just heard it was really scary.

"I'm really proud of you," she said, giving him the book as if he won an award. He blushed, eyes on the ground. Mom said stuff like that all the time.

Not like his dad.

Forget it, he thought, trying not to cry.

The book had a dark cover, with slightly upturned corners. He'd left it on his nightstand, and imagined touching the glossy cover, feeling the weight of it in his hand. Turning his thoughts to home, he was surprised to find the book in his hands before he could move. The book dropped to the floor of the arcade as he let go in surprise.

Afraid to touch it, he squatted down to inspect it and noticed the flaws on the gently used cover, his bookmark poking out precisely where he stopped. Deciding he had nothing to lose, he picked it up gingerly between two fingers.

This is my copy.

Tearing open the pages, his smile faded as he realized it was more like a publisher defect. At the end of Chapter Four was where he stopped. The large bold "5" glared at him from the blank white of the page, torturing him with the fact he never knew how it ended.

Wandering around the empty shell of his community, Gavin tried book after book. Library books that he never got around to reading. Books from the top of his dresser. Devoid of people anywhere, with the cash register abandoned and empty, Gavin flipped through title after title at the local bookstore and tossed them aside in a heap.

In desperation, he even fished the book he didn't read yet for English class out of the bottom of his backpack, cover bent backwards where he accidentally closed it in a binder ring. The pages inside the cover contained no words, and he threw it into a nearby trash can with a frustrated grunt.

Determined to make the trick work to his advantage, he tried something bigger.

His cousin bought a junker a few years ago that he slowly rebuilt. The hunk of junk had turned into the coolest car Gavin ever saw. Taking a deep breath, he closed his eyes, recreating every detail he could remember in his mind.

When he opened them again, the car was sitting in front of him, parked on a diagonal as if someone hopped out and left it for him. Shiny red paint gleamed on the hood, with a stark white stripe running up to the squeaky-clean windshield. Green fuzzy dice hung on the rearview mirror, just like the ones Gavin saw in a store once and thought he would like in his own car one day.

Afraid it would disappear at any moment, he walked toward it slowly, as if a car could be scared away. Probing the hard plastic cover of the headlight with his hand, he half expected it to disappear underneath his touch, another trick this place might play on him. He walked the length of the vehicle, dragging his hand along the shiny paint to the handle. Easing the door open, he winced as it squeaked.

Gavin sank into the immaculate leather of the driver's seat. Keys dangled from the ignition, swaying slightly as if someone just turned the car off.

Twitching with excitement, he turned it.

The car remained silent, a simple click when he cranked the keys, not even a choking gasp as it tried to start.

Are you serious?

He got out of the car and lifted the hood. He wasn't sure what he would do under there, but it was what people did in the movies.

The inside of the car was an empty space. The car was a gutless shell, all fancy outside and none of the inside stuff it needed to run.

Will I ever learn anything new?

He never thought he would miss homework.

Time passed, and he did what he could to entertain himself. He re-read his magazines and rewatched movies, whichever ones he wanted at the theatre downtown. Accepting his fate when it came to literature, he read everything he could and made-up endings to the ones he didn't finish.

Perpetual sun existed if he wanted it, and he went swimming in the lake, floating idly on his back for hours. The dark water was never warm, never cold, and he never felt wet.

The quiet was deafening, so he went for a walk. Passing empty coffee shops, he tried to ignore the restaurants with patios all set for brunch but no one to eat it. The tiny little tables for two appeared as if they belonged in some of those romantic movies his mom used to watch.

It was so unfair that he'd never get to go on a date.

The sky cleared up, puffy white clouds parting to release a high summer sun. Music blared through a shop door that was propped open, the first notes of his favourite song travelling through the air. Maybe it would be fun to play some mini-golf?

His mom used to take him every few weeks, and he was getting pretty good. He thought of the feel of turf under his feet, the smell of the hot dogs you could buy inside. Expecting his next step to land on the sticky floor in front of the counter where he would get a putter, he was confused when long, crunchy grass materialized underfoot instead. In the blink of an eye, the sun vanished, plunging the world around him into darkness. His eyes adjusted, and his house came into view in front of him.

A cloud rolled away from the full moon above, illuminating the street he lived on. The streetlights flickered on the sidewalk, sending scattered light bouncing off the empty cars parked in driveways. The alley where the road ended remained shrouded in gloom, a place he never wanted to see again.

Being here, seeing the place he took his last breath, made it feel like it happened yesterday. Something moved in the corner of his eye, and he turned in time to see the gate at the Edwards house slam shut before the street returned to stillness again.

The front windows of his house were lit, and shadows moved behind the curtains. The sight of other people, the first he encountered in a long while, made him inhale sharply. Unsure if he should run, he stayed frozen on the lawn.

The door swung wide open, bashing against the side of the house and making him jump. He grinned as his mom stepped outside and yelled something about there not being any candy left. Light lit up the sky, but he barely heard the fireworks. They illuminated her pale face, the wrinkles along her mouth and eyes.

How many Halloweens has it been? He thought as he took in the weedy front yard, the grass dry and brown. The normally cheerful street looked different, sucked dry as if it were poisoned.

"Mom?" he asked, not even caring it sounded more like a plea.

Moving toward her, the surrounding air shimmered, and he walked into it. Struggling to breathe as it filled his mouth, he spat frantically as the barrier hemmed him in and covered the rest of his body. The house behind was fading, getting harder and harder to make out, and he panicked as she faded along with it.

"MOM!" he bellowed, hoping against desperate hope she would hear him.

As the last of his street faded away, a sound surrounded him, crunching and grinding, so loud he thought the ground under his feet would crack wide open. Ridiculously, he thought of the crunchy cereal he used to like and couldn't shake the thought that something was chewing. Bracing for the accompanying swallow, he crouched behind a bush, hoping whatever it was wouldn't see him.

The barrier backed away from him, as if it belatedly realized he was already part of this and it didn't need to spend the effort. Retreating into the surrounding neighbourhood, he watched as it gathered like a storm over the house at the end of the street. He lifted a hand to shield his eyes from the dirt and leaves that were kicked up in its wake.

Peering over his shoulder, he saw his mom was gone, the windows of his house dark and empty once again. The streetlight flickered one last time before plunging him into darkness. Gavin stood in the quiet, absorbing it, trying to wrap his head around the fact that his world was lonely again.

"Hello?"

Turning his head slowly toward the sound, he wondered if he snapped in isolation, if he was imagining things.

A woman appeared on the street in front of him.

Where did she come from?

He should be happy over the moon, but all he could manage was suspicion. Was she real, or did he conjure her like the car in his desire to see people again? Fear buzzed through him, worry that this couldn't be what it seemed.

"Hello?" he asked quietly as she got closer, not ready to trust his eyes.

As soon as she turned around, he knew he couldn't have brought her here.

Dirt covered her, and blood was everywhere. Her shirt resembled one of those inkblot tests he read about for a project in his science class. An enormous bruise covered most of one side of her face, peeking out from under even more blood dried in her hair.

The woman walked toward him, calling as she came. "Who the hell are you and where the hell am I?"

As she got closer, her eyes grew enormous, and she ran toward him.

"Are you okay? Jesus!"

Despite himself, he backed away from her.

"What happened to you?" he asked.

A stream of alarmed words followed, as if she was trying to keep him talking.

"What are you talking about, kid? What the hell happened to *you*? Why don't you sit down, and I'll get some help, okay? We'll get you to a hospital. Can you tell me your name?"

The woman took his arm at the elbow, putting her other arm on his back.

What the hell is she talking about?

At that point, he decided it didn't matter, and he begged his mind to stop questioning this. He didn't care what she looked like or what was wrong with her.

Gavin let her ramble, taking a moment to savour the sound of another human being.

"I'm Gavin," he said. "Are you a...ghost?"

It sounded so stupid, even to him. He knew he was dead, but he didn't really think of himself as a ghost.

"A ghost?" She was looking increasingly worried, like he was losing it on her.

"Are you sure you're okay?" he persisted.

"Me? Kid, you're the one who looks like they got hit by a truck."

He glanced down at himself and saw what she did.

"A car, actually," he sighed, realizing he was going to have to break the news to her.

Anger filled her features, her eyes darkening, terrifying but impressive. He hoped she was on his side.

The ooze appeared, glistening in the wound on her forehead and through the bloody hole in her sweatshirt, and his delight faded.

"Where did the person who hit you go?" she asked in a low voice. "Did you see? Has anyone called an ambulance?"

He had driven himself crazy for a long time. It was all he could think about, and he didn't want to go back down that road.

Gavin held up a hand, trying to stop the endless stream of questions he didn't have an answer for.

"That's nice of you, but I don't think an ambulance is gonna help."

"What do you mean?"

Her blue eyes were blank, her tone soothing, trying to placate him while her brow furrowed in confusion.

"What's the last thing you remember? Before you got here?" he asked, pulling away from her.

"I...I was jogging. I helped someone find his dog. After that..." She frowned and reached for her forehead, touching the dried blood there. "I don't know."

Sometimes he wished he didn't, and jealousy pulsed through him. Specks of envious green seeped through his shirt as memories of his death, of someone leaving him there to die, overwhelmed him.

Stop it.

It didn't matter anymore; the point was he was stuck here.

The green slunk back into him, retreating into whatever dusty corner it went to wait for the next time he lost control.

"You okay?"

He shook his head. "No. Not really."

Gavin recounted what happened to him, the things he discovered since. Hours later, when his wounds didn't look any different, and he was still upright despite several obviously broken bones, she finally believed him.

32

A FULL BOWL OF CANDY SAT INSIDE THE DOOR, NOT A single *trick 'r treater* in sight. There were kids shambling along the sidewalk outside of Barb's house, the sound of laughter and toddling footsteps passing her by.

For the first time since Gavin died, she let herself really consider what her house looked like, acknowledging what a mess she let it become. Laundry and dirty dishes covered every available space. The porch light was out, her lawn overgrown, and she wondered if anyone even thought she was home.

Idly picking up some mail that was piled by the door, she sifted through the unattended pile of flyers and miscellaneous newspapers. Surprised by the number of envelopes addressed to Gavin in the pile, she sorted them into a stack and sat down on the couch to read them. The most recent letter was a card dated just last week, a Halloween greeting.

Ripping and tearing at the colourful envelopes, she put them in chronological order. A birthday card with a little cash, Christmas wishes with a gift certificate, a Valentine's postcard with a photo of his siblings. The cards were all signed in sprawling loops, a mixture of the kids' blocky scrawls in crayon, and Sherry's in pen with a heart underneath. Derek's name was there at first, omitting her ex-husband's name beginning on Gavin's last birthday.

The last time Gavin saw his father was about a year before he died. When she picked him up from his weekend visit, he climbed into the car without saying a word.

"Everything okay?"

"Fine," he said, staring straight ahead as he buckled his seatbelt.

The car pulled away, and he didn't look back. When she called later and asked what happened, Derek was defensive, as usual.

"I don't know, Barb. Teenagers are moody as shit. Maybe it's you. Do you ever think of that? Maybe you've been spouting off to him about me."

With teeth clenched, she quietly put the phone down, cutting him off mid-rant. The phone stayed silent, the sound of Gavin being ignored louder than its ring.

Gavin never told her what happened, but he never went back. Not wanting to push it, she told him he could talk about it with her when he was ready, and left it at that.

The following weekend, she called to say Gavin didn't want to come, and hung up before Derek replied. She didn't hear from Derek again until the funeral, where he pulled her aside to a private room.

"Where were you?" he screamed. "How did you not know he didn't make it home on time? I'll tell you why, Barb. You are a *shit* mother."

The yelling continued, climbing up the walls and spilling out into the gathering that had hushed uncomfortably outside. Trembling, she sank slowly to sit, avoiding her ex-husband's gaze while he berated her. She took it because she was tearing herself to pieces worse than this and couldn't summon the energy to tell him he was wrong. Part of her wasn't sure he was.

His screams faded, and he stilled, panting, red-faced, a toddler having a tantrum. She glanced up at him through her tears, his own face dry. Her hands shook as she rubbed her face, makeup smearing, the hair from her neat bun already teasing itself out around her face.

"You're right," she said. "I wasn't there. And where have you been exactly?"

"Bitch," he spat.

"It wasn't my mess to clean," she whispered, flinching as he stormed out.

The hush outside the room turned to a murmur as the outer door screeched open, the buzz of gossip making its way to her. This was who he always was, and she would not make the day about him. Mouth pinched, she smoothed her skirt as she stood. She held her head high as she joined the crowd. A few colleagues came to comfort her, but she waved them off. She knew she would never hear from Derek again, and she wasn't wrong.

Small blessings, she thought, instantly regretting it. If she had to listen to his bullshit every day until she died just to have Gavin here again, she would.

Turning her attention to the bottom of the cards, she took in the phone number scrawled across the bottom.

"Call me if you ever want to visit!" the cheery handwriting invited. Barb took a deep breath and dialled. Sherry answered on the first ring, sounding puzzled but eager. "Hi! Gavin?"

The picture became clear as they talked. Marriage Number Two met the same fate as theirs. Sherry caught him cheating and kicked him out not long after the blowup with Gavin. He didn't bother to tell Sherry what happened, let alone about the funeral. Gavin's siblings didn't even know he was gone.

Rage brewed in Barb's heart at the thought of two small

children being left to believe they had an older brother who didn't want to know them.

"Oh, my God, Barb. I am so sorry. He was so sweet, the nicest kid. I knew his relationship with his dad was complicated, but I wanted him to know we were still here. The kids still ask about him sometimes. They love him. I did too." A sob made its way through the phone. "This...this must be torture for you. I can't even imagine. I am so, so sorry."

"His death was no one's fault, Sherry. There's only one person to blame for what happened after," Barb said quietly, her anger growing as the diplomacy she was so accustomed to applying to Derek melted away. Gavin already made up his own mind that his father was a piece of shit, and she was done protecting Derek from that. "And it's not you."

Barb tried Derek's number after they hung up, prepared to tear him a new one, but it was disconnected.

Good riddance.

Later that night, a knock at the door surprised her as it reverberated through the house. The sound boomed and echoed loudly, as if the walls became unfamiliar with the sound over the last two years.

Barb peered out the window to see Sherry on her porch, pacing in a slow circle, focusing on the bottle of wine that she carried in her hand. Glancing up as Barb opened the door, she took a step back, waiting for Barb to tell her to leave.

"He always used to show me pictures. You know...those costumes you would make for him. I was thinking of those after we talked, how special it seemed to both of you. My mom has the kids." Sherry rambled in a rush, holding out the bottle of wine as an offering. "I don't know if this is out of line, but I just thought maybe you could use some company?"

Until then, Barb didn't realize how much she wanted someone to care. Not try to understand, or try to fix things. Just *care.*

The silence dragged on. "Sorry. I just...I'll go. If you ever want to talk, though, just call me, okay?"

Without another word, Barb embraced her, tears rolling down to soak into the shoulder of Sherry's soft blouse. Behind them, the first *trick 'r treater* of the night arrived, as if there was a beacon signalling there was life within these four walls again.

That year became the first of Sherry and Barb's annual wine and candy Halloween tradition. The evening was spent reminiscing and ranting, how comfortable they were together surprising them both. Barb thought of what it took to get them here, and she busied herself with throwing the remains of their snacks into the empty bowl so Sherry wouldn't see her eyes brimming again.

"Don't start again!" Sherry said, fanning her hands over her own eyes.

"Sorry, sorry!" Barb laughed and shook her head, straightening up to take the trash to the kitchen.

Eyes level with the window, she saw it standing on the sidewalk, staring at the house, unmoving.

Waving from the dark porch, she called out. "Sorry, no candy left, kid!"

There was something off about its featureless form, and as she examined the shape more closely, she realized it was just that. It was only a *shape*. There was no dimension to it, simply a cookie cutter in the shape of a human imprinted on the world. The shadow moved then, its head-area turning as if it were looking over its shoulder. *Who, me?*

A loud crack pierced the charged air, making her jump. The empty bowl and a handful of wrappers clattered to the porch. Fireworks lit up the sky, an annual Halloween tradition that usually emptied the streets as families went to the beach to watch.

"Who are you talking to?" Sherry came up behind her,

peering into the street now illuminated in bursts of unnatural colour.

"Right there, that creep just staring!" Turning to gesture at the spot, the shadow had disappeared.

The hair on her arms stood as her eyes swept the street, desperately searching for proof.

"Woooooo okay," Sherry giggled, reaching to snag the glass from Barb's shaking hand. "Maybe we'd better put the wine away."

Teetering slightly on her way back inside, she mumbled something about calling a cab, leaving Barb shivering on the front porch.

Consumption

33

People weren't always as they seemed; it was a life lesson Eva was intimately familiar with. The man's face hung in her memory, his watery eyes so sweet and so lost. Hunched over the railing, calling to a dog that might not have even existed, he played right into her pity for him.

Some days she was angry at herself for being so stupid. She beat herself up, replaying their conversation, trying to think of any hints. Every single detail ran through her head over and over—what she was wearing, how she spoke to him—anything to figure out where she fucked up.

Eva tortured herself for days, weeks, before her anger shifted, becoming more and more focused on laying the blame where it belonged.

"Do you remember who killed you?" Gavin asked her when they first met. It seemed like a weird conversation to be having, let alone with a stranger.

"I do." She couldn't get his face out of her head.

"Did you know them?"

She shook her head. "No." Look at her, defying statistical odds. One for the books.

Lucky me.

Why did he pick her? Why was she so important to him?

Why, why, why, why, why?

The question was all she thought about, and she was powerless to stop it as it burrowed under her skin, becoming a part of her.

Eva couldn't talk to Gavin about this, couldn't make him understand. Someone snuffed him out, sure, but a hit and run was different. Maybe it was an accident. Maybe it was plain old fear that gripped the driver. Driving away was a shitty reaction, but it was human.

The person who killed her was a straight-up monster. It was cold, calculating, evil. Someone lured her down the hill to hit her with a rock.

Gavin could eventually find his way to forgiveness, but she didn't think she ever would.

Brightly coloured slime gathered at her hairline, mingling with the dried blood there.

"What?" she snapped, catching Gavin watching her closely.

"Nothing," he said, averting his gaze.

"Do you ever think about the person who hit you?" she asked.

He appeared taken aback. "Not in a long time, but sure, sometimes, I guess. It's kind of hard not to."

She nodded.

"I do," she answered the question, even though he hadn't asked it. "A lot."

She swiped at her cheek as she felt something crawling across it. Unhinged words came out of her mouth without thought.

"I think about what I'd do if I ever found him. About other people he might have hurt. I wonder where they are sometimes. I wish I could talk to them. I wish..."

Gavin's mouth was open, jaw slack. "Eva..."

The sludge was covering her arms now, her legs. It flowed freely, unstoppable, a fountain. At first, a single colour would appear and disappear throughout the day, reflecting her fluctuating emotions. Now, it was all colours, as if every emotion she ever held in was pouring out of her. There was no reason to hold it back anymore. No one to think less of her.

"I wish I could kill him."

The burning desire to hurt her murderer was everything now. It was all she thought about. She wanted to make him feel how she did, to make *him* ask why. She knew this should concern her, but it didn't. For the first time in a long time, she felt free.

"You don't really mean that, do you?" She could hear the edge in Gavin's voice and wondered if she should try to reassure him, but she couldn't find the words.

Remembering where she was and how she got there grew more difficult with each passing day. She started talking to herself. All the time, her mutterings centred on revenge and escape.

Gavin was with her sometimes, but she let herself travel, flitting wherever her mind wandered. When she was with him, he didn't talk to her much anymore. He could usually tell with a simple hello whether it was going to be a good day or a bad day.

The emotions were everywhere now. A trail followed behind her like a slug when she walked. She ought to be disgusted with herself. The sidewalk burned wherever she went. Steam came off her and wafted the noxious odour up to her nostrils. The fact she couldn't recognize herself anymore should have been enough to pull her back, but part of her knew it was too late. The endless, agonizing cycle of destruction and regeneration tore her apart and then sewed her up again. Eva was consumed with the need for revenge, to know the *why*.

Most of the time, she could barely remember her own name, but vivid memories, the one that made her angry, that hurt her to watch tortured her.

She remembered her marriage, and how it had ended. They planned a nice day together—a brief excursion to a bookstore, followed by a pleasant drive and a picnic.

The night before, he went out with his work buddies. She eventually fell asleep waiting for him, but she didn't mind. She wasn't about to begrudge him a little fun.

The next morning, John slept in, and she debated waking him at noon so that he could get up and they could leave as planned. The alarm went off, and she thought it would all be fine. He would get out of bed sheepish but prepared to enjoy the day. She felt a surge of love for him, how he was such a great guy to take one for the team. She gathered a few things to make him a smoothie to chase down a few painkillers. Breakfast of champions, a hangover cure-all.

Looking back, she wondered why she constantly rewarded him for doing the bare minimum. The hurt at all of her expended effort rolled off her, the rage in her feeding off this new source memory like a parasite.

The alarm went off again, and again, the flat of his hand slapped into the clock, a tremor running through her body each time it repeated. The sound stabbed through her in eight-minute increments, the memory of each shriek of the snooze alarm piercing the air and driving ice through her veins.

Asshole. Asshole. Asshole. Her heart screamed in time with each aggressive jab at the alarm, simmering in fury each time the springs of the mattress followed, the sound settling as he rolled over to go back to sleep.

She remembered her mother, her happy childhood memories burning away as she focused on the predictable diatribe of children and when would be a good time to have them and the chorus of "you're not getting any younger, you know."

"Why you got married if you didn't want babies is beyond me," her mother frowned.

She remembered the final straw when a supervisor position came up at the bank. In the interview, her boss hit on her, grabbing her ass when she turned to leave the room. It wasn't as though she didn't know he was an old-school creep. This time, the way he looked her up and down was so much more. A predatory glint in the small sliver of teeth showed through his suggestive smile. Eating her alive was simply the natural order, and the ass grab wasn't where this stopped.

It was merely the opening negotiations.

"Smile!" he mouthed as he walked by her later, pointing to his lips as they broke open into a grin.

She remembered her friend Nancy, also a teller, coming in, heels clicking cheerily on the marble floor.

"Eva? Are you okay?"

Eva burst out of the stall at the first hint of friendliness. Nancy embraced her as she relayed what had happened.

As soon as she felt safe in being vulnerable, Nancy peered into Eva's eyes and told her if the job was important to her, she should have just slept with him.

She relayed the story of her quitting when she got home, and when she took a breath and waited for John to be appalled, to hold her, to threaten to go down there.

"Are you sure they wouldn't take you back?"

She blinked at him, not comprehending what he just said.

"It's just, you know, things have been slow at the site. We could really use the money."

All the signs she failed to recognize showered over her. When she picked him up from work, his construction buddies would make lewd comments while John guffawed, "Good one!" and gave them a pat on the back. When she didn't laugh, he repeated the joke as if the problem was that she didn't get it the first time. With a thin-lipped smile, she told herself she should be flattered and pretended she wasn't bothered by being the punchline.

Was her blouse cut too low? Were her heels too high? Did she flirt or wear too much makeup?

It wasn't good enough.

The happy memories were slowly sinking, harder and harder to retrieve.

Was this all there was?

Once in a while, Eva came to herself for a moment, screaming at the white-hot pain before falling into the tumultuous seas again.

No one heard her as she fell.

34

When the spinning stopped, Nat glanced around to see the four walls of Gavin's basement surrounding them. The objects in it hadn't changed, the same chocolate shag carpet on the floor, the same grey cinderblocks, the same bare bulb, almost as Barb kept it, preserved in a time capsule. The room had a quality to it that wasn't there the day Nat took home the box of books. Gavin's version was sunnier, brighter, as if Barb's grief and time combined to make it a tomb.

Underneath the single tall window, Gavin was sitting on the ancient sofa, staring at the television.

"Holy shit," came a whisper from behind her.

The Gavin on the couch didn't move, his lips still despite the voice at her shoulder. Nat turned slowly, eyes widening as she took in Gavin standing behind her, staring at his past self.

Part of her couldn't believe it actually worked.

As she stood there, wondering what she was supposed to be watching, something appeared in front of them, standing before the Gavin on the couch.

It was a blob. She couldn't think of any other way to

describe it. The stench was unbearable, and she clasped her hands to her nose and mouth to seal it out. The colourful streaming tar slowly reshaped itself to reveal its host underneath.

"Eva?" the Gavin on the couch asked, looking shocked. "How did you get in here?"

When Nat glanced over at her travel companion, she found his eyes were firmly shut to prepare for what would come next.

Not a great sign.

The woman-shaped blob vibrated, tiny droplets shaking onto the basement floor. Behind Eva, the cinderblock changed, gradually fading out of view like a desert mirage. The shimmering colour keeping them there replaced it, dripping as it hovered, waiting to be told which direction to go.

The goo on Eva retracted, sucking itself back into her body in one quick gulp. From what Nat saw, it was usually languid, relishing the feeling when it came back to you, the most fucked up game of lazy afternoon fetch.

This wasn't that. The messy mucous looked like it was fleeing, crawling back into its host to hide from whatever was coming.

When the last drop re-entered her, Eva appeared as she did when she was alive. She looked around in wonderment as she took in her surroundings.

"Gavin?" she asked in confusion.

He smiled and jumped up off the couch, so happy to see a long-lost friend.

Before he said anything in reply, a bomb went off, reverberating through the basement like a giant belch. The barrier crawled down the cinderblock and rushed toward Eva in a giant wave. Just before it hit her, her entire body exploded outward, painting the entire room with her insides.

35

NAT'S MOUTH HUNG OPEN, GORE DRIPPING ALL OVER her, horrified as the sunny lazy Sunday of the basement was soaked in red. She raised her hand, reaching out to touch the runny, blood-soaked wall that remained.

The opaque, filmy veil pulsed beneath her touch, with a slight glow emanating from the other side in the shape of a person. It was as if Eva's shadow was separated from the body they were now wading in. As quickly as Nat saw it, Eva's form disappeared, and the barrier glitched out of focus. Blood rained down in a fine mist, as if it was shaken from a giant wet dog.

Gavin never sat down with her and detailed how Eva's intestines looping over the rec room looked like streamers at a party, or that her eyeball landed and perched on his shoulder like some sort of nightmare baby parrot. Chunky liquid slid down the slate-coloured blocks of the basement wall, dripping slowly over a calendar hanging there, plopping onto the floor, dyeing it to match the rest along the way.

He didn't tell her any of these things, but she saw it all anyway.

All the regular blood and guts you would expect to find in a body were mixed with the sludgy stuff—a bullshit cosmic joke considering they didn't have bodies anymore. The colourful slime was fading, frantically swimming around the mess, searching for its lost host.

As Nat watched, it slowed and finally stopped, floating lifelessly on the surface of the pools of blood. Separated from the person who created it, from their emotions, it had nowhere to go. It was the last way for this realm to say "Fuck you!" and cruelly remind them she was human. If it were just the goopy emotions, they could have pretended it wasn't Gavin's friend they were standing in.

Eva was here.

It was a strange feeling, living someone else's trauma. You don't have a sibling die as a teenager without getting forced into a lot of support groups. But seeing it, living it with him? This was a whole different level of empathy. Nat gazed around the room and couldn't stop herself from gagging.

The Gavin by the sofa looked as shell-shocked as Nat felt. He wailed as the rogue eyeball slipped from his shoulder and hit the floor with an audible plop.

The room was a total disaster. Viscera dripped from the wicker-panelled ceiling fan above his head; bits of something resembling brain matter rained down and stuck to his shirt. Past Gavin reached for the quilt that was spread haphazardly over the back of the couch. The blanket was already soaked through, and all it did was spread the gore across his face. The cloth that was squeezed in his palms dribbled through his fingers, over his hands. He flung it to the floor, spitting frantically.

Rubbing downward on his arms, the chunky mess oozed through his fingers, dripping onto the floor. His gaze was drawn to something behind them, his mouth twitching as if to scream. He disappeared, leaving only bloody imprints from his shoes behind.

Nat couldn't say she blamed him.

"I'm so sorry, Gavin," Nat whispered. She didn't know what else to say.

Gavin opened his eyes, resigned.

"What were you looking at?"

"That," he said, pointing.

Two silhouettes remained clean on the wall behind them. Blood seeped down the cold cement, slowly obscuring the evidence that they were there. She glanced down at her arms, her clothes completely covered, shuddering as she felt it drip down her shirt to coat her back and stomach.

I want it gone.

The memory obliged, and they were clean as quickly as she had registered that they were covered in the stuff.

A methodical ticking broke through her thoughts. She glanced at the clock on the wall, but the hands weren't moving, cemented at the last time Gavin looked at it.

Tick tick tick.

No, her brain registered. Not *tick tick tick.*

Drip. Drip. DRIP.

"Let's go," Gavin said. "Please?"

Wait.

Most of the carnage settled in pools by now, the surfaces still and quiet. Still, the dripping continued. Nat moved toward the calendar taped up on the wall, sitting in the bare concrete of her outline, not yet entirely distorted by the remnants of Eva.

The blood was being diverted by the crease where it was stapled together and dripped off the pages in a thin, steady rivulet. It looked like a giveaway calendar, the kind businesses handed out for free with pictures of local scenery.

Moving closer to it, she read the dates. *May 1999.*

Through the lines of red and silver streaking across the grid, she saw Gavin was counting down to something, crossing out the days in thick, black marker.

Big black Xs crossed out the days, all the way to May 14.

The calendar blurred as Gavin pulled them out of the basement.

She didn't move, mouth dry, staring steadily at the calendar as they were ripped from the past. The blood beneath their feet settled as they were lifted, pooling in on itself to cover their footprints. As the wind battered them, she kept her focus on the wall, training her eyes on a specific point to avoid getting sick like she was in a speeding car.

The carnage disappeared, but the dates remained as they returned to Gavin's current version of the basement, the one existing for them coming into focus. No longer looking at it through a screen of crimson mucus, the image above the grid of dates was clear.

The shot was a landscape of the lookout point at the cliffs, their town's claim to fame and notoriety. It was a hot spot for weddings, photographers and daredevils alike. In the photo, the entire park stretched out in front of the drop above the calm blue water, inviting the leap, with the implied promise of safety and serenity. Picnic benches sat quietly at the top of the perch, a romantic spot for any couple.

Nothing bad would ever happen on a sunny day like that.

After what happened to Chris, the images documenting the cliffs changed. They were all shots of the lake looking up, or the lake spread out below the cliffs, camera held high over the fence. The tall chain-link barrier was erected after the school board, led by her own mother, launched a successful petition. There was some grumbling, but now families could have a lovely Sunday picnic without fear of a toddler wandering too close to the side.

Money means you get to lay the blame anywhere except

where it belongs, she recalled some PTA members whispering outside after the meeting.

Nat's hands were shaking as she ran a finger over the last stark X marked on the bright white page.

"Hey, Gavin?" she asked, without turning around.

A shaky inhale and exhale behind her was the only response as he tried to re-bury what she forced him to dig up.

"What happened on the 15th?"

She gestured at the squares in front of her. The big black X's leered at her aggressively, like a child's drawing of dead eyes on stick figures. She was sure why she bothered asking. She already knew the answer.

"I died."

Gavin and Chris. Living in the same town, in car accidents on the same day.

What. The. Fuck???

She wasn't so sure this wasn't hell.

36

After Eva had...whatever it was, Gavin was in shock.

He didn't remember concentrating on escaping. One second, he was in the basement, screaming as Eva dripped around him, into his mouth and eyes. Next, he was out on the quiet street outside. He hoped he did it without thinking, that he wasn't losing his grip, that he wasn't becoming her.

Cut yourself some slack.

It wasn't every day that he saw someone splattered all over his walls. Even if she gave up and ditched him a while ago, Eva was a friend.

"H...h....h...hello?"

A timid voice rang out behind him, and he turned to find a young man, older than him, with a football player's build. Gavin stiffened, remembering his first meeting with Eva, how he found himself in this exact spot with her.

"Who are you?"

"My name's Thomas. I don't...how did I get here?"

Thomas didn't look too bad, knuckles a little bruised like maybe he was in a fight. Then he raised his arm, and Gavin registered the screwdriver peeking out from under his denim jacket, jammed low into his side.

"Well, I hate to break it to you, Thomas, but you're dead."

Thomas laughed. He *laughed.* Gavin didn't find it so freaking funny given pieces of Eva were still dripping down his legs. The sludge was circling him, trying to reach for him, but knowing he wasn't quite right. Long tendrils of it slowly flattened, smudging the sidewalk like long, fat worms on a rainy day. There was something sad about it, the personality of it gone now that it didn't have Eva.

Gavin turned away from Thomas, racing in the other direction.

"Wait..." Thomas didn't sound anxious, more curious, as if he was trying to figure out what trick someone was trying to play on him.

But Gavin couldn't wait. Stepping into his house, he walked across the kitchen and down the basement stairs. Everything was the same as when he left it; the remnants of his friend stained every surface of what was his sanctuary.

Try as he might, he couldn't erase the mess that was down there. The horror of the scene burned in his imagination, overriding every memory no matter how hard he tried to think of a time that his fortress wasn't decorated with someone he knew. Turning his back on the basement, he silently retrieved a mop and a bucket from the upstairs closet. Soapy water sloshed all over the stairs as he made his way back down.

The light in the room was red. He reached up and wiped off the bare bulb hanging from the ceiling. The brightness replacing it was almost worse, highlighting all the details in every shadowy nook and cranny. A random long white tooth gleamed on the carpet under the cheerful light.

He rinsed the rag and cleaned, literally scrubbing it from his brain, inch by inch. Bloody water dripped down to his elbows as he reached up to clean. Working on the wall where his calendar hung, he thought of the eerie shadow people he saw.

They were gone, not a trace of them anywhere. As he washed and rinsed and squeezed the blood from the towel down the drain in the adjacent laundry room, it became more and more a thing he must have made up.

He heard Thomas yelling outside for a while, beating on the door. Gavin wasn't worried. He'd never been in there, and couldn't come in.

He felt bad for Thomas, but it was better this way. Wherever he was, it wasn't a place to make new friends.

37

Eva was hot, expanding, busting at the seams. The film coated her vision so long ago that she forgot when it abruptly cleared. Her body bucked as it returned to her in one swift movement, her former self slingshotting back.

A couch came into focus, the boy sitting on it leaping to his feet to greet her. She recognized him, and his name was right on the tip of her tongue.

"Gavin?" she asked, hoping that he might have some answers that she was looking for.

She glanced down at her hands, her arms, as if they were accessories, something newly gained.

Before he answered, she was just gone. Whatever held her loosened its clutches and spat her out back to a world full of sounds and smells.

This time, the why didn't matter. All she knew was that she was free.

No longer in limbo.

She should be excited about this, but she felt herself fading, losing energy. Everywhere she moved was one painful step at a time, each one growing more agonizing by the day.

There was so much to worry about, but she was numb; all the things she should do were of no consequence. She didn't know who she was without *should*, but she felt like it might be too late to find out.

When the light hit just right, she saw herself now and then, in fleeting moments in windows or in puddles. She thought about how Gavin looked at her when she found him and wondered if she looked this bad back to him. Bits and pieces were going, going, gone; his name was getting harder to remember.

She sensed herself shrinking, becoming less. One day, she thought hard about it and realized that she didn't entirely remember who she was. She wasn't disappearing; she was *rotting*. Light slapping sounds trailed her as she walked, and she turned to see bits of herself plop to the ground, a horrific trail of breadcrumbs marking her path.

Deep down, lost in the darkness, a tiny piece screamed that this wasn't right, wasn't *normal*. She should care about this loss of self; she should fight it. Watching her decline from outside of herself, she was still unable to muster the strength. A vague idea from another time in her life, a funny word.

Zombie.

She didn't know what it meant, but she felt like it fit somehow.

Day after day, Eva wandered. She didn't feel much of anything, trapped inside herself as her body moved about, driven by some kind of muscle memory.

Her sense of boundaries dissipated as she discovered she wasn't limited anymore, could go wherever she wanted. She shuffled aimlessly all over town, stumbling into strangers' homes. There were so many *people*. Even though they couldn't see her, she felt like she was a part of things again.

Sometimes she rode the bus, her fascination with other people's lives growing as her memories slipped away. She didn't look like them anymore, her clothes hanging off her in decaying strips. Some dressed professionally, uncomfortable-looking shoes peeking out from underneath dress pants. She remembered clothes like that, a concept which seemed old-fashioned to her now.

Working. Jobs.

A man sat next to her, navy tie hanging down between his knees as he leaned over the pages of a book.

"Where are you going?" she tried to ask, several of her teeth spilling onto the floor of the bus as she opened her mouth.

Hearing the clatter, he glanced around for the source of the sound, assuming someone lost a handful of loose change. Not spotting anything, he shrugged and went back to his book. These people all seemed to have a purpose, and Eva didn't understand how she fit, or what she was doing.

So, she just kept going.

With every blink, her control over where she visited decreased, her sluggish mind recognizing she was at the bank, or her old house, or her mother's. With no recollection of travelling staying with her, she went from nothingness to finding herself at the university campus, the home of a childhood friend, a construction site where a man passed her, carrying a ladder.

Something about him sent a surge of anger through her, and she swatted at the ladder as it bobbed by her face. He cursed, stumbling as it sent him off balance. An odd sense of satisfaction washed over her before she moved on to the next location.

Every once in a while, she would wake up on the hiking trail.

That trail caused the remnants of her skin to crawl like nothing else could, the only place left that gave her any feeling. A beautiful self-torture, she returned, over and over.

The time between lucid moments was getting longer all the time. Once, she was on the trail in the morning. The sky was blue and clear, as it always was in summer by the lake.

Peaceful, she thought, taking it in.

The monstrosity of her remaining mouth twisted into a smile. Maybe she was meant to appreciate this. Every time she saw something, it could be her last chance to say goodbye to it.

She hoped that when the time came, she would give a shit.

April 2015

Revelations

38

NAT COULDN'T TEAR HER EYES AWAY FROM THE empty space on the calendar. The day her life changed forever was infinitely bigger than the tiny white square; her entire being formed around that one afternoon.

She spent so much of her life listening to what others said must have happened. Memories built from her dreams interspersed with snippets of what felt true, what *had* to be true based on what the police assumed.

But what if it wasn't that way at all?

Maybe her being here had nothing to do with helping Gavin, and everything to do with exposing her, showing her the truth of that day? It was a terrifying prospect, and she wasn't sure she was ready.

"Nat?"

She kept this piece just for her, for now. Given the circumstances, she couldn't bring herself to tell him what she did. Once people found out, she hated how they looked at her, their shocked eyes wondering how they looked past this monster for so long. She decided long ago that keeping the secret was the lesser of two evils. It was so much easier to keep people at arm's length than to hurt them when they learned the truth.

"Yeah. I'm just thinking. Did anyone arrive after Eva?"

Gavin appeared thrown by the question, the unexpectedness rocking him on his feet.

What am I dredging up this time?

"I didn't really know him," he whispered.

She nodded.

"Okay. That doesn't matter. Maybe if we can figure out how to help them, we can get the hell out of here." Not bothering to ask this time, she held out her hand impatiently. "Are you ready?"

Nat already sensed the spark as the energy they were harnessing crackled between them.

Gavin took the plunge and squeezed her hand.

The shock travelled through them; her elbow grew numb as they transferred it to each other. Body straining as the building wind whipped her face, Nat braced herself for the storm. The wind died, and as she cracked her eyes open, they were thrown apart, Nat landing on the couch and Gavin on the beanbag chair. Some papers around Gavin's room that were picked up in the sudden breeze fluttered as they floated to the ground, evidence that the connection was made.

"Gavin?"

"Yeah?"

"Why didn't that work?" she asked, letting go of his hand.

"Like I have a manual hidden somewhere?" he asked sarcastically, throwing up his hands. "How should I know?"

There was still a charge in the air. A sharp smell circled around them, the burnt, acrid aroma of an electrical wire. It reminded her of being a kid, dragging her socked feet across the carpet with deranged glee, seeking a victim to zap, the flash in the air making her laugh maniacally.

"Is this like when you tried all those fun places when you first got here?"

"Yeah, it's no big deal. He must have died somewhere we can't go. Guess we've never been before." He looked at her, hopeful they could stop now. "Do you want to try someone else, or...?"

Nat considered their strategy. What were they supposed to do? Work their way through the lineup of who knew how many until they could get somewhere?

"How many others have there been besides Eva?"

"I lost track." There was no trace of deception here, just a cold, hard fact.

"How many of the others...exploded?" She asked, peeling herself up off the sofa.

The word was sticky on Nat's tongue. It seemed like the wrong word when applied to a human being's actual body.

When his eyes came to rest on her, he saw the pain there, the thing he was avoiding all this time. He peered up at her, considering whether he should say anything.

Not good.

"How many?" she whispered.

"All of them."

39

"That...that can't be true," Nat said, even as her mind whirled, putting together why Gavin didn't want to tell her.

It's going to happen to me.

"I don't get why they keep showing up right by my house," he said, interrupting her thoughts.

"What do you mean?"

"I'll just be minding my business, doing whatever, and then I end up on the street in front of my house," he paused, trying to figure out a way to describe what they saw happen to Eva. "You know. After."

"Every time?" she asked.

Gavin nodded, and the last thought before she was picked up and deposited beside Eva on the cold ground inside the shed came back to her.

The morning after she dreamed of Eva, the earthy aroma of the forest lingered in her room when she awoke, though she rarely remembered dreams in much detail. Those piercing blue eyes kept her up the rest of the night, burrowing their way into her mind every time she was about to drift off again.

As she unlatched the squeaky wooden gate, the rising sun glimmered off the outdated pink flecks of stucco siding on the house.

In her slippers, she crossed the dewy morning grass and stood under her bedroom window next to the lattice below the balcony. The garden beds below were undisturbed, with no crushed plants or marks in the damp soil. She wasn't sure what she was searching for, but there was nothing unusual. A millipede crawled its way across the dirt, and she shuddered.

"Nat? Everything okay?"

Brian's ground-floor window was sliding open at her feet. She backed up a bit to look down at his puzzled expression, foggy with sleep, through the dirty screen.

A few days' worth of stubble lined his cheeks, and he scrubbed a hand through his dishevelled hair. Sunlight hadn't reached the dark basement behind him, but he squinted, trying to make sense of what she was doing there so early.

"Sorry, just um...enjoying the sunrise. It's beautiful back here."

He peered at her strangely, and she felt his eyes boring holes in her back as she went crimson and turned to go back inside. Now that she was safe in the bright sunlight, she felt childish, not quite able to believe she was out at the crack of dawn looking for footprints in the dirt like an adolescent detective story.

In the dark, when Eva died, the house had looked so different. The grass was poorly kept, dry and brown patches trampled down in spots in the damp ground. Around her, the green border of the property was gone, a simple, unfriendly fence surrounding them instead.

There were no signs of the French doors and balcony she loved so much. The tree consuming the entire corner of the yard wasn't there, the awful shed in its place. The back of the house was completely bare; the friendly trees and flowers climbing the sides of it were not yet planted.

Nat's mind went back to what she said to Gavin before they were separated, the words coming from a place of longing that was getting closer to the surface all the time.

I want to go home.

What the fuck?

Soft green grass, damp in the cool spring evening, fluttered across her hands as she imagined the backyard. The promise of the summer to come was in its colour, picture-perfect and uniform. The nostalgic, peaceful 1950s glow of the yard she remembered was now overshadowed in her mind by what happened there.

"I don't think it's *your* house they have in common."

40

Gavin couldn't shake Nat's stare, and he couldn't say he blamed her. Avoiding the truth was second nature by now.

Gavin knew what he said about the others sounded like a lie, but it was true. When they arrived, he didn't have any warning; he would be pulled back to the street, and they were just there, in front of him. He never knew how long they had before they would show up next to him, looking completely healed for one peaceful second before BLAM!

He learned to shut his eyes and mouth at the right times. He saw from across the street. One second they were waving at him; the next they were nothing but a puddle of yuck. At least he didn't have to clean all of them up. After a while, he got used to it and was able to block out the imagery, to remember how it looked before.

He wasn't sure it was a good thing he could so easily pretend it never happened.

Gavin didn't see a point in telling her about the ones he wasn't sure about. He couldn't save them now, and he couldn't help Nat either. The sound was always there, even if he didn't see it happen. The pop and splatter of a large water balloon behind him would interrupt a song he was listening to, or puncture the sound of water lapping at the beach. *It's nothing,* he would tell himself, not believing it for a minute. A second later, he would be back in front of his house, looking at a newcomer down the street, trying to get away before they spotted him.

In the early days, he would see elderly people wandering around, confused. They would appear briefly, then disappear to places unknown. Usually when it happened, they came in batches, very close together.

Recently, an old woman came by. Thin, sunken skin covered her, a walking skeleton. On catching sight of him, she reprimanded him for standing in the middle of the street. He was shocked to realize this old, frail woman, who used to bake him cookies, was Mrs. Edwards.

Mrs. Edwards never seemed young, exactly, but she seemed like something beyond age. Grandmas were old, but this Mrs. Edwards wasn't just old, she was ancient, like something out of a dark fairy tale.

Haunting.

Gavin shivered as she gave him one last glare and went back inside her house. He let her go and never saw her again after that.

Deflated, Nat perched on a corner of the coffee table.

No one wanted to know they were on borrowed time.

"What causes it?" she asked.

"I don't know. It's almost like maybe there isn't room."

"What do you mean?"

Gavin sighed. The thought that had seemed so genius to him even a year ago suddenly sounding silly now that he had someone to voice it to.

"It's like I'm here to let people in, and then once someone new dies, they get kicked out of the house, you know?"

Nat seemed to take it in.

"There was no one here when you showed up, right?"

How many times do I have to say it? His carefully placed grown-up mask slipped slightly, and the petulant teen emerged.

"Yeah, so?"

"So, what if you were the first one to be murdered?" It was strange to think of his death as a murder and not an accident.

An accident was one thing. That someone could leave him alone to die made him angry, sure, but murder? Murder seemed so *personal*. Who would want to kill him?

"Maybe it has something to do with why you never..."

"Blew up?" he inserted helpfully.

"Yeah, that. Hey, Gavin?"

"Yeah?" He didn't like her tone. It sounded like she was about to ask him for a favour.

"Why do you think we're here?"

He blinked, not expecting an existential question.

"What do you mean? Like, the meaning of life?"

"Yeah, maybe. Or the meaning of death, I guess."

He never really thought about it. When he considered his death, it was mostly about how it wasn't fair rather than why he might be here. When he was alive, there were things he wanted to do. Maybe they weren't realistic, but they were his to wish for.

When he arrived here, those thoughts, those wishes, they all stopped. Why think about what you wanted to be when you grew up if you didn't have a future?

"I don't know," Gavin answered simply, his thoughts too big to escape his mouth.

"I don't either," she agreed. "But I don't think it was an accident that we saw Eva, Gavin. It felt *good* to help her. I know it didn't make a difference, but I think it showed us something."

"Oh, yeah? Like what?"

"Like maybe we can help *someone*." Nat looked determined now, a look he was growing wary of. Standing straight, she paced in front of him as she formulated a plan. "Maybe we can stop him, you know?"

Gavin didn't like where this was going, but Nat didn't really seem to care.

"Who was the last person you saw before me?" He couldn't help rolling his eyes. She sounded like a detective on TV.

"Before you? That would be Ricky." Gavin snorted, amused.

"Something funny?"

Definitely the bad cop, he thought, picturing her in an interrogation room, slamming her hands down on a table. Gavin smiled even wider.

"If you'd met Ricky, you would know."

"Okay, might be on a timer here, remember?" she snapped.

The corners of Gavin's mouth turned down as he became serious again.

"Ricky was drunk."

It sounded so stupid. *This place...*

"Ghosts can get drunk?"

Gavin shook his head.

"Believe me, I've tried. I think Ricky was hammered when he died. So, when he got here..."

Nat thought of the stab wounds on her back and the rifle blast to Eva's chest, suddenly reminded of how thankful she was that she didn't have to see Gavin that way.

"...he stayed drunk," she finished.

"Okay, so maybe we should try him."

Gavin rolled his eyes again.

"Trust me, the guy was a mess. He barely knew his own name."

She arched her eyebrows.

He sighed. "Okay, but it's gonna be a waste of time. The only time I ever saw him was when he would show up on the street and piss in people's flowers. He used to wave at me while he did it."

Gavin tried not to laugh as the image of it came back. He didn't want her to think he was just a kid. He wasn't sure if they were past that yet.

"It was hilarious. I mean, it *was* for the first few times, but after about fifty, it just got old. The guy was *so* annoying. Why do you want to help him?"

Nat shrugged, her eyes like steel. "Why not?"

Gavin could see she wasn't screwing around anymore, and replied, chastened.

"What if we can't?"

"We're already dead," she shrugged. "What do we have to lose?"

Gavin turned away so he wouldn't see her flinch when they were carried away.

July 2014

Travellers

41

Nat's vision went white as she smashed into something hard. The shattering of glass broke through the storm, and something wet splashed over her pants.

"Fuck!" she cried, her surrounding slowly coming into focus as she rubbed at her side.

A chair scraped across a floor, accompanied by a squeal of annoyed surprise.

Music blasted, classic rock growing louder as the storm faded, the sticky floor beneath her shoes vibrating to the beat. The cacophony of travelling gave way to a familiar buzz of sound. Despite the pain in her hip, she grinned at the treat.

People.

The crowded room was full of people enjoying themselves, maybe after a game. It felt like a Friday, with the promise of the weekend running amok. The dark green stained glass of the windows and the cozy dark wood panels on the wall were instantly recognizable, and she smiled at the familiarity of the place.

Flanagan's was a pub that felt like it had existed there since the dawn of time. The hum of conversation filled the cozy space, the chattering clientele somehow evenly balanced between college kids and local curmudgeons. The walls were covered in...well, just about everything. It didn't have a theme, just whatever struck the owner's fancy.

Old, wrinkled movie posters were taped up alongside professionally framed art prints. Shelves of old paperbacks sat near the front door, perfect for when you wanted to hunker down with a plate of the city's best fries and not be bothered. A scattering of stained armchairs sat near the shelves, somehow managing both to encourage cozy conversation with a drink and to provide a place where no one would bother you if you were reading.

Nat used to occasionally see people there, drink in hand, but Nat herself never sat there. There were no tables, and the best reason to come to Flanagan's was for the fries.

Seriously, greatest fries ever. She breathed deeply, taking advantage of the momentary break from their nightmare to inhale the smell of pub food. The sauce on the ribs was the daily special, tangy in her nostrils.

Damn, I miss food.

The hard thing that she connected with was a sticky and wobbly table. A surprised-looking couple was frantically mopping ineffectually at the round, wooden top, their tiny cocktail napkins an ineffectual sopping mess. A server hustled over and swiped the ice off the table into a shallow plastic tray.

"Everyone okay? No broken glass?"

The young woman rolled her eyes, angling her thumb aggressively toward her companion.

"No, no. We're fine. Genius here kneed the table."

"No way!" he huffed, indignant. "Don't lay that on me! I was just sitting here. You were the one getting up to use the bathroom."

She glared back, swaying a little as she stood. "Screw you."

"Oh, what? You're storming out?! Real mature."

The server's pupils mimicked a tennis match as he weighed his options in picking a side and possibly a new career.

"How about an order of nachos, guys? On the house. We've got an empty table here. I'll move you over and get this cleaned up."

The fading throb in Nat's hip reminded her of every public embarrassment over the years, and for a moment she was happy to be invisible.

Maybe there's an upside to this after all.

Spotting Gavin by the front door, she waved him over as she pulled at her jeans. The denim stuck to her uncomfortably, cold and wet, courtesy of the drinks that sloshed on her.

The smell of whiskey wafted up to her, making her instantly uneasy. She always hated when people pressed her about why she wasn't drinking. It was an odd societal sticking point, a rare situation where peer pressure as an adult was deemed okay. Their faces twitched when she told them honestly that her family history always made her anxious around the smell.

It was enough that they never bothered her about it again. They didn't have to know the history was hers.

Nat forced a smile as Gavin came closer.

"You've been here before?" She asked, raising her voice to be heard above the crowd.

"Yeah. My mom took me here for lunch a couple of times." He inhaled deeply. "Best fries ever!"

"Right?!" she chuckled, happy to have something good in common.

Her good mood didn't last long as she surveyed the pub.

"What?" Gavin followed her gaze to a booth in the back corner. The seats were covered in cracked green leather, well-loved by day but seedy and ominous by night, providing dark corners for villains to plot in. Red glass lamps hung above, swinging slightly as haggard waitstaff hurried by.

Two men sat across from each other; one was facing away from Gavin and Nat, talking a mile a minute. His hair was dyed so black it was almost blue under the tinted pub lights. It was slicked back, hair product soaking into the collar of his shirt. From here, the talking man seemed to fit in this atmosphere. He was friendly, animated, and pleasantly drunk.

His booth mate's eyes were somber, the smile plastered on his face as if he'd forgotten how. His eyes were downcast, lethargically running a now soggy fry through a large blob of ketchup as they talked. A pause in the conversation forced him to respond. As he glanced up, she saw his warm brown eyes appeared calmer than they were a moment ago, as if Brian came to a decision.

Gavin ran into her as she stopped short.

"What the hell, Nat?" he asked, rubbing his shoulder dramatically.

"Is this Ricky?" Nat asked, flicking her chin at the chatterbox.

"Yeah," Gavin nodded.

"For sure. Still not as drunk as when I last saw him, but close. I think I've seen that dude before," he said, head cocked to the side as he considered the sad-looking creature Nat was focused on.

She nodded, wondering how the hell Ricky knew her landlord, Brian Edwards.

42

Nat evaluated Brian, trying to figure out where in time they were. He looked the same as she remembered him, but maybe a little lighter, as if some hidden stressor wasn't there yet.

"Let's have one last round. On me, okay?" Brian asked, smiling as he put down his empty in the sea of bottles already at the table.

Ricky nodded, and as he answered in the affirmative, she heard the slurring in his voice. He barely had one more round in him.

Ricky must not have died that long before me.

Brian had that look that was all too familiar to her, the one which said he just agreed to a demand. She thought back to the branches tapping against her bedroom window when she moved in. They scraped every night, and she was on edge about it since the first night. After a month, she approached him about it when she handed him the next month's cheque.

"I thought I told you to slip it under the door," he said, taking the piece of paper roughly.

"Sorry, I'm just wondering about those branches? You

mentioned you were going to trim them? It's been getting windier, and I'm worried if it's not done before winter, I'll be listening to them tapping on my window until spring." She smiled, hoping to take the sharpness out of her voice.

"Ah, sorry, sorry, sorry," he stammered, softening. "I'll get right on that. Sorry, sorry."

***

Nat stepped back as Brian got up from the table and pulled Gavin to the side. Brian said something to Ricky. Squinting through his drunken haze, he tried to take it in as Brian squeezed his shoulder.

"Stay here. Keep an eye on Ricky. I'm going to see what he does," she said, not taking her eyes off him as she spoke to Gavin.

"What do you mean? Who...?"

She wasn't listening, already focused only on the slump of Brian's shoulders as she followed him as he made his way through the crowd to the bar.

She sidled up next to him at the dark wood. His sleeve accidentally brushed against her, and he jumped. He scratched his arm absently, as if he experienced a bug bite.

Does he know I'm here?

The bartender approached. "What can I get you?"

Brian held up his fingers in a peace sign as he downed the last of the beer in his hand. *Two more.* He slammed the bottle down on the bar, more forcefully than she was expecting.

Startled, her elbow caught a tray with a paid check resting on top, sending cash and stray coins flying to Brian's feet. He stooped to pick it up, putting the money back onto the tray and sliding it across the counter. The bartender nodded his relieved thanks as he concentrated on multiple orders, whisking away the empty bottle in front of Brian and reaching under the bar for two fresh ones.

Brian rummaged around in a worn brown wallet. Throwing several bills onto the bar, he gestured to their table.

"I'd like to settle up."

The bartender printed up the bill and shoved the cash into the black apron tied around his waist.

"Sure thing. I'll just grab your change."

Brian waved his hand dismissively, not even looking at the cheque.

"Don't worry about it. Keep it."

"Thanks, man!"

Brian watched him move to the register at the opposite end of the bar and reached into his pocket, pulling out a tiny envelope made of folded paper. He snapped it open, tucking it into his palm.

Nat's eyes widened, memories of catching someone doing this to a friend years ago coming back to her. Brian had the same look now, darting his eyes around him, making sure no one was watching an old, shy barfly.

Nothing to see here, just a nice guy getting one last round.

"What are you doing?" Nat asked, to no avail.

He placed his cupped hand around the neck of one of the beer bottles and tipped the contents of the envelope in. Picking up the bottle, he swirled it, the white powder disappearing into the tint of the brown glass.

Nat acted on instinct. Brian let go of the bottle to put away his wallet, and her hand shot out in a sweeping motion. Her palm slapped into the bottle with a satisfying thud, and they both sailed off the edge of the bar.

A nearby server looked up at the sound of the glass as it hit the floor. A hoot followed by a smattering of good-natured applause rang out around the pub, and a rowdy twenty-something guffawed from a table packed with a group in jerseys intensely overjoyed about some win.

"Damn, second time tonight! Shoulda made this a drinking game!"

Brian looked around helplessly, hunching over the bar, his face nearly purple.

Tough shit, asshole.

A server walked over, looking vaguely annoyed.

"I...I'm sorry," Brian stammered.

She plastered a smile on her face, an expression that Nat herself had worn that said accidents happen, but she was off in five minutes, and cleaning this up was the last thing that she needed.

"Not a problem."

The bartender noticed the ruckus now, too. The expression he wore was a little friendlier than his co-worker's as he remembered his tip and the rescued cash.

Reaching under the bar with a wink, his hand emerged wrapped around two fresh bottles.

"On me, alright?" he said, placing them on the bar in front of Brian. "Enjoy your night."

Brian looked like a fish out of water, brow furrowed and gears grinding as he took the drinks. Both Ricky and Gavin turned toward the bar.

Ricky held his hands up in a gesture, curiously signalling an offer of help. Brian gave his friend a forced grin and a reassuring salute with the bottle. *Whoops! My bad!*

Brian turned to thank the bartender again, collecting himself before he turned back. Gavin gestured at Nat from the booth, with impatient confusion in his wave.

Nat watched Brian, and as he stood next to her to chart the best path back to Ricky, she caught something in his expression, something she couldn't place.

Wait...

The lost memories slammed into her like a truck, paralyzing her as they played on a loop. The sensation of something sliding, the feeling of being punched in the back, over and over.

She saw herself lying on the carpet in her living room, not sure how she got there. The floor under her was wet and warm, the slowing pulse of her blood soaking into the rug. She felt like she was deflating, all energy sapped from her body, unable to move.

A man hovered above her as he kneeled beside her body, the soft wetness of the carpet sopping with her own pumping blood. Brown eyes watched with a pale, curious expression as he watched her fade from existence.

Brian's eyes.

Eyes shut tightly, mouth open as she breathed heavily, she tried to make her thoughts be quiet. Logically, she knew he was now no more of a threat than the monster under her bed.

He couldn't hurt her anymore. He already did his worst.

It didn't stop her from whimpering, and she hated herself for it. "Stop."

"Nat?" Gavin called from somewhere nearby, his voice cutting its way through the noises in her head as he made his way across the room to her.

"He did it," she whispered.

"What?" Gavin asked, striving to be heard above the din.

"Brian. He killed me. He killed Eva." Gavin whipped his head back to take in the booth.

"Wait. Brian *Edwards*? He lived on my street. He looks so...old," he observed.

Nat took in Brian's watery brown eyes, his thinning hair, and she knew what Gavin meant. If she hadn't seen it, she would have doubted this man's capacity for evil herself.

He kept to himself, did the yard work with his head down, avoiding looking toward her windows. He mumbled his responses and went to bed early. She never even heard his TV on at night.

Old was code for "harmless."

People change.

She saw him now for what he was—a true-crime doc cookie-cutter cutout. Never made trouble, never made noise.

Never got caught.

I'm so stupid.

43

THE IDEA OF HER KILLER WAS ABSTRACT, BUT remembering Brian's face hovering there, watching her go, made it suddenly real in a way she wasn't able to accept until now. Everything that happened that night coursed through her all at once. The burn of the rug against her elbows as he dropped her while coldness spread from her heart through her bones. The memory seared itself into her, already scarring wherever it touched.

Gavin frowned a little, processing, trying to reconcile these two versions of Brian.

"Whenever I talked to Mrs. Edwards, she would tell me stories about how Brian would come over to take her to do her shopping and stuff. My mom always said it was nice that he took care of her."

"Well, times change. It was him. I saw him. It's the only thing that makes sense." Nat paused, unsure how much of Eva's last night she wanted to share. "He murdered Eva right there is his backyard. *My* backyard. That fucking bastard *lived below me.*"

She couldn't believe she was this stupid, that she didn't

piece it together as soon as she recognized the house, as soon as Gavin recognized him. Of course, he still lived there after all this time, keeping the secret safe.

Lost in the disturbing realization, she re-evaluated all their interactions from the last six months. Sometimes he stared a little too long outside of her door when she bumped into him getting the mail. Other times it was passive-aggressive ways of showing he was monitoring her, like the fire extinguisher that silently made its way into her kitchen the day after she burned something on the stove.

When he came home, it would go quiet on the other side of the adjoining door after he took his boots off on the basement landing, an abrupt and prolonged pause before the stairs gave under his weight as he made his way back down. The first time it happened, she imagined his ear to the door, listening to her breathing.

Weird but harmless, she always thought.

Her mind was reeling, picturing the true-crime serial killer documentary series of her life that would get made. *Living Above the Killer: The Nat Parker Story.* The waxy flesh of her arms crawled; the sensation travelled to her neck like a million ants.

"How do you know he killed you?" Gavin asked, guiding them backwards to be heard above the din.

Nat realized their invisibility once more as they shouted about murder amidst the sounds of people having a great time.

She recounted the pieces Gavin missed. The memories of her death. Brian's impassive face above her as she slipped away. Eva's murder.

"I *saw* him, Gavin."

She repeated it, feeling more and more sure as she spoke.

He nodded. Nat expected him to be a bit more skeptical, but maybe with all this time spent here, he was used to unconventional reasoning.

"Just like that? You don't think I'm crazy?"

He shot her a lopsided grin.

"Are you kidding? You're like, majorly batshit! But I think you probably remember your own murder accurately, so I believe you."

She stared at him blankly, so he elaborated. He lifted his thumb, pointing it downwards between his shoulder blades.

"You're back."

"What?"

"You said it felt like you got punched in the back, right? Your back is...let's just say it's a mess. Like a disaster. It looks like..."

"Okay, moving on," she said hastily. She didn't want to know.

Movement at the booth signalled that Ricky and Brian were finished their last round and getting ready to leave. They stood and shrugged on their coats, heading for the door. Ricky was wobbly on his feet, and Brian had to direct him through the doorway.

"Come on," Nat said, and she and Gavin moved to go outside, cutting off their path.

She was lost in the flame of her rage when Brian walked right through her. Her skin crawled at the violation, tingling and throbbing in the aftermath like a bad sunburn.

Cold night air hit their faces as they exited the pub, Brian and Ricky rosy-cheeked beside them. As Ricky gestured into the alley, the ground beneath their feet shook, a large crack appearing and crumbling the pavement all the way down the block.

The patrons spilling out of the bar after last call went about their business as she cried out, oblivious to the destruction being wrought around them. A hole opened up, chattering patrons being sucked inside, conversations still going as they spiralled and disappeared.

What is this? She thought, her feet lifting off the ground, legs and arms dangling and frozen. Gavin rose next to her, his neck bent at an odd angle, eyes roaming furiously as he tried to see what was happening.

The brick building slid past their field of vision, and it happened so quickly it wasn't until the roof appeared beneath her feet that she realized they were being pulled up into the night air.

Her shoulder connected with the ragged corner of the rain gutter, tearing apart as easily as paper. She fell onto the cement below and was momentarily freed as the fall jostled her. She looked up to see Gavin dangling against the side of the building. A raindrop hit her forehead, and then another, picking up speed and rolling into her eyes.

The sound of a car trunk opening echoed off the high cement walls below the starry night. A body lay facedown in the dark, paved alleyway, dyed and slick black hair visible within the ring of blood growing around it. Parked in front of a nearby dumpster, the car's taillights glared at her like two eyes in the dark. The raindrops continued their gentle patter, gently pinging off his faux leather coat.

Ricky.

She screamed as she was pulled backward, and her fingernails scraped on the dirty pavement until someone ripped her from the ground once more.

As she flew rapidly upward, the events of Ricky's death got smaller and smaller, featureless action figures playing out the scene. A man came around the side of the car, holding a tire iron as he approached the body. It came down over and over, a maniacal glee to the motions as the flying blood misted with the rain. After he was long gone, the blows continued to rain down, driven by pure hatred that radiated from the assailant in waves.

Eventually, she couldn't see the alley anymore. The city

lights grew smaller and smaller, tiny pinpricks in the darkness. Mountains became pebbles before disappearing completely.

They sat suspended in complete darkness. Nat couldn't move, couldn't speak. She didn't know if she could breathe, because she wasn't sure that she still did.

A pressure grew inside her skull, and she tried to twist away from it, but she couldn't, couldn't even close her eyes against what was coming.

A ringing built in her skull to accompany the crushing heaviness until she was being pulled apart, wiped from existence. A light enveloped them, obscenely tinted like a cloud of mustard gas surrounding and choking them.

LIGHT RETURNED ABRUPTLY, SHOOTING THROUGH Nat's brain in a painful spike. She clamped her eyes shut against it, and the sensation of reversing came to her, reaching the apex of an amusement park ride, that moment of stillness right before the fall. Plummeting once more, she tried to will herself to relax instead of tightening every muscle she had.

I'm so over this.

Concrete rushed up to meet her, and she braced herself, waiting for the crunch of gravel digging into her skin. It never came. Instead, it was a slight pressure on numb flesh, like she was watching a video explaining what scraping your wrists would feel like.

She ignored the shining rivulets as they crawled across her arm, almost happy to be back where things made a kind of twisted sense. Her cuts and bruises from the bar, from the real world, were already healed and forgotten by her body. Standing on wobbly legs, she tried to figure out what fresh hell they were in now.

Gavin was lying on his back, gasping like a fish on land,

rolling onto his side to catch his breath again. His eyelids drooped as he flailed, his remaining sneaker flopping spastically on the ground.

Apparently, this was a new one to him, too.

"Get up, Gavin. We've got to *go*. In case...*whatever* that was comes back!" she stood, not bothering to wipe at the streaks of slime covering her, trusting they would clean themselves up as her adrenaline faded.

"*Nat!* Just stop, just for a minute! Geez!" Gavin gasped for air again, fumbling with a pocket.

His hand stilled and came out empty. Nat wondered if he was asthmatic in life, still trying to find his inhaler out of habit when he hyperventilated. He shook his head, hands on his hips as he leaned forward to catch his breath. Her lack of sympathy momentarily stopped her, but he was already healing, his breath evening out. Whatever happened to them, it was over. They were back where they started.

The sky darkened above them. It moved slowly at first, a dense swatch of fog rolling to cover the sun. More and more clouds gathered. Thunder clapped loudly, making them both jump.

The clouds gathered together and funnelled downward. She thought of an elementary school project, taking a jar of dyed water and swirling it until a tumultuous tornado formed inside. At this distance, it was calm outside of the whirlwind, but they could hear clawing and shrieking coming from the eye.

Something was coming, and from the sound of it, it wasn't exactly pleased.

What the fuck is that?

A figure hit the ground inside the whirlwind. It appeared tiny, but she shuddered at the fact they could even see it from here. Whatever it was, it was enormous. As the tornado drew closer, it pulled the surrounding air into its folds. The figure was oddly aloof, completely indifferent to the storm, floating down through the funnel until one foot touched the earth, and then it simply stepped out, a celebrity emerging from an airplane. It was confident at home. There was none of the chaotic flailing of limbs they experienced. A face emerged from the storm, parting the tornado as easily as a stage curtain.

There were no eyes in the face, and sniffing at the air, it tried to determine where it should go. The slash of a mouth full of long, pointed teeth broke the smooth skin on the enormous head. It looked toward them, knowing exactly where they stood even though it was sightless.

It had to be close to eight feet tall, disarmingly skinny, all knobby joints and bones. There was desperation in the stilted movements of its scrawny limbs. A sharp rib cage protruded from its sides, lungs inflating the shiny, thin skin in sharp bursts.

It's starving, Nat thought.

This thing could crush Nat's head like a grape under one of its knuckles. If it was hungry, it was hunting.

This was no ordinary, run of the mill dead thing. They were just appetizers.

Stale, foul-smelling breath reached them even this far away. Steam emanated from its mouth, moving into the fog and joining the clouds.

"Gavin, go!" she shouted, and they ran down the street.

The creature was making giant strides, easily one for every ten of theirs.

We'll never outrun it.

"Nat!" Gavin yelled as the surrounding air grew stronger, sucking to gather them along with everything in its path

"If we split up, it can only chase one of us! I'll meet you at The Station!" she yelled back.

Understanding, Gavin blinked out of sight to parts

unknown. Her feet dragged backward as the force of the storm overcame her, and she was painfully pulled back toward it.

An ungodly roar came from everywhere as it galloped. Unable to force her feet forward in the surrounding storm, she glanced back over her shoulder, regretting it almost immediately.

Its skin was translucent, almost shimmering. Something about it was familiar, and she realized it looked like the stuff that drowned her in front of Barb's, the mysterious wave that she rode here on.

Close enough for her to take in the details, she saw it was the basic structure of a human face: space for eyes, nose and a mouth, but it was dripping, half-formed. It looked like it was seeking to shift into something, but couldn't quite latch on. The eyeless face set its sights on her, and the not-quite mouth opened wide, roaring and revealing teeth just as monstrous and sharp as she'd been expecting.

Feet dragging below her, with the unstoppable force of it taking her, she closed her eyes and concentrated. The roar became less confident, enraged, as it figured out what she was up to. The beach appeared under her feet, and the monster followed.

She tried location after location, using every space in her memory. She was at the beach, at her old house, at a diner, in Paris, under an old leather loveseat she used to hide under when she was three years old.

Teleporting was not as easy and effortless as she thought it would be, and she was tiring. The time between jumps was getting longer and longer as she lagged. Her muscles burned, her breath coming in short panting gasps under her fear-soaked clothing, the substance dripping off the tip of her nose as she exerted herself. Teeth snapped just behind her whenever she landed. The herculean effort for her was only a mild irritation for the creature.

Nat reached a farmer's market. Fruit and vegetables were laid out pleasingly for sale on checkered tablecloths. She would come here every Sunday on her bike when she was twelve, buying honey sticks before riding downtown to read at the park. The creek was roaring across the road, her constant. She loved it when it was high, all wildness and anger underneath the calm surface.

Like everywhere else, it was eerily abandoned, the high stacks of garden wares put out for an audience that didn't exist. As she tried to move to the next location, a spark lit the air in front of her face and fizzled in a puff of smoke. She tried again, but the market wouldn't fade into her elementary school.

A display of enormous crisp apples resting on crates was in front of her, and she crouched behind it to rest. The skin of the fruit was impossibly red, the deep primary crimson she remembered them as, and not the red they were. Clamping a hand over her mouth, Nat's sweaty breath wheezed against her fingers, barely suppressed as the crates rattled above her.

The creature's snout gulped at the air above her, tongue dipping out to touch the market's offerings. Fruit fell around her as the giant's footsteps retreated. As the apples rolled to her feet, the bright red skins started to shrivel. The sharp scent of overripe fruit permeated the air, and a crowd of fruit flies materialized and entered her nostrils. She sniffed in surprise, pinching her nose out of reflex, freezing as the retreating steps stopped.

Something inside her tugged, as if enticing her to follow. Her knees ached, trying to propel herself to her feet. She gripped the slats of the crate hard, refusing to let it take hold of her and make her a puppet.

A few breaths later, the sensation was gone. Nat crept out into a peaceful and serene atmosphere, a perfect spring day. The lot where the market was set up remained empty, not even a bird trying to steal a piece of the perfectly uniform pastries. As the grey fog chased her, it parted, giving way to a cheerful sky. The fluffy white clouds were perfectly uniform and completely still, a child's rendition of a perfect spring day. Still rotting, the fruit's bruising and discolouration spread in a perfect circle. The decay progressed until she was standing in the middle of a compost heap, the ground beneath her feet spongy and sunken.

Nat waited, impatient, until she felt her strength gradually return to her. She pictured the blinking marquee outside, the single ticket seller at the front entrance. She willed the pavement at her feet to become the threadbare carpet in the entryway, lovingly trampled by so many moviegoers. This time, she felt the shift, the promised security of the Station making it seem much more vivid. The walls seemed shiny and new, the chandelier lighting shimmering off the waxy surface of the floor in front of the concession counter.

"Gavin?" she called. Her voice sounded hollow in the empty space.

Hot breath huffed behind her, accompanied by a muffled cry. She turned excruciatingly slowly, already knowing what she would see on the shiny floor of the theatre lobby.

Gavin was trapped between its long, tapered fingers, wrapped in a loose fist. The claws formed a makeshift cage; the thumb creating a lid that made it impossible for him to climb over. Between the monstrous digits, his eyes gleamed, and he reached one arm out through the gap.

Crouched as low as it could, it met her at eye level. It chased them with a more or less human gait, but right now, it looked like a diabolical hybrid between a dog and a spider. Its knees were high, the joint bent just above its lowered head, ready to pounce. She somehow knew that it was smirking *(Caught you!)*, its head cocked to the side in victory. The absence of a face faded in and out of focus, as if it was perpetually standing in front of a green screen.

"Let him go," she said, refusing to look away this time.

To her surprise, it sat up, tipping its hand as if getting ready to roll dice. Gavin was pushed aside as its fingers unclenched and it lifted its palms upwards. The boy recovered with a surprisingly graceful somersault and ran toward the concession area. His sneakers squeaked noisily on the floor, the low staff door banging loudly as he crashed through it to duck below the glass countertop.

Drool dripped onto the ground as the creature stirred and adjusted its freakish limbs to stand at its full height. It rose toward the lobby ceiling, exposing its torso to her as it did. A grumble erupted from its stomach, and it squirmed against the hunger pangs. A prism of light shone out from beneath its oily skin, dappled spots reflecting hypnotically on the floor at her feet. As the colourful lights inside it swirled, she realized in horror what she was looking at.

Faces rotated slowly underneath the flesh, covering its stomach, frozen in fear and pain. A low whistle emanated from the creature, and the skin on its stomach vibrated, nearly imperceptibly. A man's face went by, his mouth was a gaping black hole. The beast remained silent, the muffled cries of the souls trapped inside it begging for release.

Eva's face was there, one of the few that was screaming in rage rather than sheer terror. Her angry mouth made Nat remember all those times when she had been told to be good, to be quiet, to behave. To smile. Nat swore she saw the flash of the rifle light up her face as she moved out of her view.

Ricky joined the rotation after a few more faces, looking surprised but unfocused, a permanent glaze of confusion covering his features. So many faces, ages, ethnicities, there was no reasoning to it all. A young man Nat guessed to be about twenty, calling out to people only he could see.

"Help me!" she heard, muffled as he went by. "I don't know where I am!"

They wove in and out of her view, moving along the inside of its intestines. A screwdriver glinted in his eyes as he moved by.

The faces inside its stomach quivered beneath the opaqueness of its skin. The closest thing she could think of in nature was the belly of a fish, cold as it shimmered and cut through the water.

This place is keeping us still.

Unable to process the endless rotation of faces, she turned away at the realization that there hadn't been a repeating face yet. As she turned, a familiar face caught her eye. A teenage boy, green eyes so like her own, hair flopping over his forehead to his eyes. He was in pain, screaming for someone to let him out, for it to be over.

Chris.

She watched him in horror, helpless until he passed, other faces replacing him in the endless line. Struggling to keep him in her eyeline, the stillness at the centre of it all caught her attention. There were two faces at the center of it all, eyes closed, their troubled slumber undisturbed by the surrounding wails. They were on a pedestal of their own, coveted and sheltered.

She backed away as she recognized herself and Gavin. Its stomach pulsed, and the faces collectively cried out. The skin of the beast glowed brightly for a moment before fading again, the faces cast in shadow like the lights in a house flickering in a storm.

We're all being digested.

With her fists clenched at her sides, she faced the abyss of the beast, face after face drifting by in a seemingly endless parade. Above her, it grumbled, shifting its feet as it screeched, its rank breath blasting through the room. Lights rattled, the ceiling fans swaying slightly.

Fuck you, she thought, even as she shook at its power.

It seemed angry that she wouldn't look up, wouldn't show it how much it terrified her.

It stood taller than she thought possible, showing off, exposing all its teeth to her before crouching down again, licking its hot tongue across her chest and up her face. Nat spit and wiped her face as a reflex, but there was no need. The slime crawled down her and back to it. Its own mess of emotions. It was dusty pink, the colour of candy hearts on Valentine's Day.

Mine, she heard inside her head, a temptation coming over her like none she'd ever heard. The disembodied heads inside the monster moaned, tortured as it became frustrated.

Moving back toward the concession stand, she did not know what to do. The effort to hide seemed ridiculously futile. This thing could kill them with no more effort than swiping at a mosquito.

So why didn't it?

It shuffled forward almost comically to follow her, snuffling at her trail, swatting at obstacles as it went, metal garbage pails cracking underfoot as easily as twigs. The stench became overwhelming as it drew closer, as if all things dead and rotting in the world were seeping from its pores.

Her lower back hit the counter. As she looked around for something, anything, that could help, she spotted the purple velvet-roped stanchions shoved into the corner, ready for a busy evening. They weren't needed for a quiet matinee.

Nat was all flight until now, and the desire to wield one of the heavy posts against the monster surprised her. Warm pride filled her at the drive she needed to fight, but she had the feeling she would only piss it off. Hitting it with one of the stanchions seemed like the equivalent of tossing a toothpick into a bonfire.

Chocolate bars and licorice displayed by the cash registers went flying as she slid around the case of candy to join Gavin behind the glass. Fresh popcorn was sitting in the machine; the heat was fogging up the glass. Panting, the absence of the distinct buttery aroma, such a big part of her happy place, made her inexpressibly sad. Gavin sat on the floor with his knees pulled up to his chin, trying to make himself as small as possible.

Rubbing the back of her hand across her clammy forehead, she glanced at Gavin, seeing what must have been reflected on her face. A light sheen of the mood ring red dotted his face like a pox as it seeped up through his pores. She sat down slowly, joining him on the floor.

"Where do we go now, Nat? Name it and we'll go." Gavin was shaking, desperate for someone who would know what to do, who would tell him it would be fine.

Fighting was pointless, and they both knew it. "We can't get away. Don't you see? We're *inside* it."

"What are you...?"

Nat cut him off, knowing they were running out of time. "This isn't the afterlife, Gavin. Not like you think. We were some monster's dinner."

He stayed silent. Not a word of objection or denial struck her, and she knew in that instant that he'd seen the faces inside it, too.

She drew in a breath as she voiced the thought that she hadn't wanted to, but was now a certainty. "It's a dead end."

"What does it want? It's never come after me before. Why has it waited so long?"

"I don't know." She thought of the fact that they were still alive, of their faces anchoring the others.

It's keeping us safe.

"Whatever it wants, I think it's after me. You were bait; it grabbed you to make me stop."

The metal slats between the panes of the glass candy counter bowed alarmingly as the creature crashed against it. They lifted their arms over their heads as glass fell and shattered around them. The insistent sniffing as it tried to pinpoint them intensified, yellowing claws tapping at the remains of the display case. The lights in the lobby dimmed, and the sign to their right glowed more brightly, as if on cue.

EXIT.

"You can get out," she whispered, pushing her shoulder into Gavin's. "It wants me."

The side door creaked open, reinforcing her unspoken order.

Sudden silence filled the air, and she resisted the urge to peek over the bar. Slobber from sharp and ancient teeth splattered down on them, and they glanced at each other, two dead people ready to die.

"GO!"

Nat shoved Gavin again, gesturing toward the exit, but he grabbed her hand, holding it tight.

Twisted, knobby fingers shot downward, grabbing her arm. An icy burn travelled to her core, and she shrieked as the world fell apart.

44

The monster's grip was strong and unrelenting, and Nat tipped her head back, howling at the pain of it.

She twisted and wrenched her wrist, but the ironclad hold didn't give. The knuckles below its enormous talons creaked and cracked like old tree limbs as the fingers rolled in on themselves, seeking to squeeze further.

The tips of the claws dug into her arm, the skin inflamed and glowing red. Her veins lit from within, and she screamed, convinced the flesh was melting away from the bone. She tried again to pull away, and her tendons stretched and popped in the immovable, monstrous vice grip.

If it hurts, I'm still here.

She clung to it like a lifeline.

The light within her intensified, burning hotter, hotter, then white hot at its peak, skin searing as if it was holding her to a hot grill.

STOP! The word reverberated through every molecule of her, the desire all-encompassing, the only thing she ever wanted.

Just as she thought she couldn't take any more, her arm was relinquished. The brightness of a summer day wormed its way behind her closed eyelids, cheerful sunshine on her face. The toxic smell of exhaust filled her mouth, a car engine rumbling nearby as she coughed.

Awareness of her individual body parts slowly spread, and she wiggled her fingers experimentally, unsure if her arm was even still there. Her thumb twitched, and she realized Gavin's fingers were still gripping her other hand.

Peeling her fingers away from his, she let go of his hand to grab her injured arm, moving it at the elbow, cringing as she straightened it, trying to get the feeling back. There were bruises the width of sausages circling her entire arm.

Pins and needles ran through her wrist, the ugly purple stains fading as she watched. The marks burned away, flaking off her arm like ash until her skin was clean again. She opened her eyes uneasily, not trusting where it took them, half expecting it to come at her again, a little game of hide and seek.

Trying to erase the feeling that she was tainted now, she continued to hold her arm across her chest, claiming it as her own. There was a heavy feeling holding her down, the feeling this wasn't over, that she was branded underneath her flawless skin.

Marked.

Hot asphalt was beneath her, and she pushed herself off the ground. She kept her head down while she gathered her bearings, stumbling forward as she stood.

Fences swirled on either side of her, tall trees closing them in. The day was bright and sunny, but a shadow stretched behind a car idling in the alley. Nat glanced up to see dark storm clouds gathering, getting ready to ruin the perfect weather. The cheery cul-de-sac waited behind them, so close yet so far.

Gavin was already standing, staring at the car, the

passengers obscured by the spidery legs of the cracked windshield.

Nat recognized it as the old beater her dad bought for her to share with Chris. The hood was massive, with cracking navy paint and rust spots visible through a large dent.

The driver's door opened, and shiny new white sneakers swung onto the pavement. A teenage girl got out of the car. Her straight hair was styled in a bob haircut with bangs cut straight across her forehead. She was wearing baggy grey sweats and a tight, blue-striped tank top with spaghetti straps. A pendant nestled on her collarbone, a hemp choker. The classic teardrop alien head dangling from it was such a product of the nineties it hurt.

Nat absentmindedly scratched her collarbone, remembering how much that necklace itched.

She stopped herself, moving her hand to her shoulder as the girl pulled up a strap that fell to her bicep. The tank top was brand new, a present for a recent birthday. It caused an argument with her father, who claimed it showed too much skin. She remembered this was the first day she wore it, how by the evening, it would be in an evidence bag, covered in mud and dirt and blood from her brother's broken body.

I don't remember this.

She begged for anything that might listen as she watched herself in a memory she buried.

Anywhere, anytime but here.

Left Behind

April 2015

45

MEG JOLTED AWAKE, SWEAT COATING HER SKIN AS she baked under the duvet. Her nails had left half-moon imprints in her palm, the bracelets still tightly gripped in her hand. Drool had soaked into the sleeve of her sweatshirt, and the cheery red cotton darkened to crimson.

The room was cast in the low light of evening as the sun descended behind the mountain. Chastising herself for falling asleep, she swung her feet to the floor and crammed the bracelets in her pocket. She stripped the sheets from the bed as she got off, determined to make it look like she did something after everyone else left.

Packing was Meg's kryptonite. The chaos it caused always putting her on edge. Surveying the mess of clothes on the floor, she lost all faith that this would be a mess that could be cleaned up nicely. Each minor task that was tackled seemed to reveal a mess on top of a mess, impossible to fix, a can of worms exploding everywhere. Piles of clothes, piles of linens, piles for the food bank, piles of dishes, all of it stacked up to the point she couldn't look at it anymore.

She dragged a bag of blankets from the bedroom to rest

just outside of the linen closet in the hallway, shivering at the change in temperature in the house. The gauzy curtains in the living room were blowing slightly in the breeze. She slammed the window shut and was surprised to see it was almost dark.

The digital display on the oven hadn't moved, was stuck at 10:31. Nat's clock, the classic big-eyed cat, was still mounted above the dining room table.

Six o'clock. She was asleep for hours.

Jesus, how did that happen?

Moving back into the bedroom to make sure she hadn't forgotten anything, she glimpsed herself in the vanity mirror. She looked exhausted, her right cheek rosy and wrinkled with the imprint of the sheets. She rubbed her face and pulled her hair back. As she slid her hands back to tie it up, loose hair attached itself to her fingers, floating down on the floor as she pulled a clump loose.

Meg frowned as she ran her fingers through the ponytail again, pinching loose another small segment, longer hairs coming up between her fingers. She gathered them up and tossed them into the small wastebasket in the corner, wondering if she'd caught it on something, hoping it wasn't stress.

Purse slung over her shoulder, she pulled on her shoes, cursing as she tripped over the box that she had left in the foyer earlier.

Barb's books, the note on it glared at her, her reminder to take the box down the street to its rightful owner.

She crouched to pick up the box, hefting it onto her hip as she cracked the door open. The kitchen floor creaked, and she turned to find Darryl standing in the dining area behind her.

The box narrowly missed her foot as it slammed to the floor. The sound filled the room, the scuffed wooden floor protesting at the sudden burden.

"I'm sorry. I thought you'd left so long ago, and then I

heard noises. I just came to check it out." He held up his hands, a placating gesture she hated so much.

Don't get hysterical, his hands said smoothly. *This isn't what it looks like; you're being crazy.* Darryl's condescending demeanour was on full display, and her skin crawled at his thoughts as if he'd said them aloud.

Don't be afraid, little girl.

"Sorry," she huffed, straining to reach any tiny shred of patience she could find. "Long day. I fell asleep, but I'm heading out now. We'll be back tomorrow."

The "we" was unconscious, a part of her wanting to remind him there were people who would notice if she disappeared.

Darryl blinked, and something behind his eyes shifted; the focus was gone. He suddenly appeared thirty years older, pale and drawn. Sagging against the doorframe, his suddenly brittle frame crumpled under the simple weight of his clothes.

Meg took a step closer to him, ready to catch him if he fell. Déjà vu washed over her, her last day with Chris, of worrying that Nat couldn't stand, flashing through her mind.

"Are you alright?" She kept her voice calm and even.

Smiling, he looked into her eyes and slid his hand uncomfortably from her elbow to her shoulder to rest near her collarbone. It had happened to her on the bus before, some creep falling into her and using the opportunity to grab her. "What? It wasn't my fault."

The man on the bus raised his hands in the same gesture Darryl used now, the one that said, "Don't be crazy, don't read into this, what you think couldn't possibly be true."

Darryl's wizened face displayed the same accompanying leer. The implied forced intimacy of it made her skin crawl, and she flinched, shaking his arm off before he could grip it harder, before something happened that he could tell everyone she'd invited because she didn't say no.

"How did you get in here?" Darryl squinted at her, taking a step back. "Who are you? What do you want? I don't know who you work for, but you're trespassing."

He thinks I'm a reporter.

"I'm Meg. We met earlier? I'm helping clean up Nat's things?" She frowned, alarmed at the sudden lapse in memory. "Do you need me to call someone?"

Darryl shook his head. "No. Thanks, Meg. I'm just exhausted. I feel so..."

"What?"

He seemed to search inside himself, seeking the right descriptor. "Empty."

Something about the way he said the word was just so brutally honest and raw. Meg gestured to the table, pulling out a chair.

"Why don't you sit down? Just for a minute."

He might be a creep, but he was still a human being who looked like he was having some kind of medical emergency.

"No! I..." he trailed off, and suddenly his features smoothed again.

A deep, rattling breath filled his chest, and he stood up straight, rolling his head and shoulders. Suddenly all charm, he levelled her with a confident smile.

"I'm fine, really. Back to my old self. I'll just go lie down for a minute." He reached for her arm again, less lecherous and more controlling, and she wrenched herself away, moving back toward the door.

Meg picked up the box, never taking her eyes off him as she fumbled for the keys that she had dumped on the pony wall.

"I'll be back tomorrow, okay? Get some rest." That instinctual feeling, the one she had listened to her whole life without any regrets, was telling her to get the hell out. That voice got her this far, and she wasn't about to ignore it now.

"Okay," he said, his steely eyes staying trained on hers. "There's a key in the mailbox for you folks."

Without returning a farewell, Meg turned and ran down the steps, leaving the door wide open behind her.

The car door slammed behind her, swinging harder than she intended. Staring at the doorway from the safety of her vehicle, she still felt so exposed, her skin crawling as his touch lingered on her. The front door remained open, a dark mouth against the faded pink siding.

She picked up her phone, checking the single message on her voicemail while keeping her eyes on the open door.

"Hi, Meg. It's Mike. Listen, I don't think it's going to happen tomorrow. We're trying, but it's...I think we need a day. How about you call us in the morning? We'll try to sort out a good time."

Dropping her phone onto the passenger seat, she let her eyes travel to the kitchen window. Darryl stood staring at her, his icy eyes drilling into her without apology.

Don't give him a reaction.

Craning her neck over her shoulder, Meg backed out of the driveway, turning swiftly. The dusty cardboard box of books shifted as she accelerated, and she stopped the car short as the box bumped into the door.

Dammit.

Glancing in the rearview mirror, she saw the kitchen window at the end of the road was now empty, the front door closed. The lights remained off.

She pulled over, parking at the curb beside Barb's house. As she wrangled the box from the car, she caught sight of something sticking out from underneath the seat.

It was her stolen library book, the one Nat returned to her back in the fall. She had a vague memory of her bag falling off the seat as she took a hard left on her way to work after leaving Nat's.

The book and Nat had been out of her life for so long, were so intertwined in her memories of how it all fell apart. It felt strange to have one back but not the other. A glint of silver on her hand caught her attention as she tossed the book onto the backseat.

The mood ring she jammed onto her pinky was still that god-awful red. Wiggling it off her finger, Meg held it up to her mouth, breathing on it, trying to warm it up, but the colour didn't budge even a shade.

Chalking it up to age and the cheap material, she tossed it into the empty cup holder between the front seats. She moved to the backseat, hauling the box with a curse and slamming the door shut with her hip.

The ring rattled against the hard plastic, the garish red a mockery of blood.

46

As Barb pulled her dinner out of the microwave, something hit the porch with a thud. Startled, she stood in the kitchen, listening intently.

Something heavy shuffled on the porch, followed by a light knocking at the door.

"Hello?" she called, hand on the doorknob.

"Barb? Sorry to bother you so late. It's Meg. Nat's friend?"

"Meg?" Barb said in surprise, unlocking the door and pulling it open. "What are you doing here?"

After Meg left the other day, she had zero expectations she would see her again. Meg's face looked drained from the effort of this small conversation. Recent sleep glinted bright in her eyes; her ponytail was loose, her hair a dishevelled halo around her face.

"I'm sorry to bother you." Meg stammered again. "I just... I have something for you."

A box sat at her feet. Barb drew in a breath at the sight of the cardboard box, the flaps open to show the book covers she debated for so long about parting with. Getting them back

296

this way felt even worse than giving them away in the first place.

"Don't be sorry. Please. Come in."

Meg leaned down to pick up the box, but Barb shook her head, pushing on Meg's shoulder a little more harshly than she intended to get her attention.

"Leave it. We'll get it later."

The door shut gently behind them. Pollen from the neighbours' cottonwood trees blew across Barb's front deck, peppering the faded black "G" hastily scrawled on the side.

MEG WAS BACK ON THE SOFA, SAME SHIT, DIFFERENT day, fresh cup of tea. Barb left her cup on the coffee table to cool, cringing as she saw Meg had the chipped cup this time. Suddenly self-conscious, she glanced down at herself and realized she lost track of how many days she was wearing the same outfit. She did laundry this week, though.

Didn't I?

"Are you alright, Meg?"

Meg sank into the cushions. "Sorry. I just...Darryl, he really freaked me out. He grabbed me and..."

Barb narrowed her eyes. "What do you mean?"

Meg waved her hand, clearly feeling silly now that she had some distance from the situation.

"I think he's just not doing well."

"It's not an excuse for being a creep. He's always been a bit like that. Charming, so I always got the impression he thought he could have whatever he wanted. A bit spoiled, I guess. Are you sure you don't..."

Meg cut her off, clearly not wanting to bring any more attention to the incident.

"No, no. I've dealt with worse. Look, Barb, I'm really sorry for running out of here like that the other day," Meg said. "It was really rude."

"Not at all," Barb said. "I get it. I'm glad you're here."

They sat in silence for a moment, letting the cups of tea cool. After a few moments, Barb broke the silence.

"Can I ask...how did you know those books were mine?"

Meg's hands shook slightly.

"Nat had a horrible memory. Maybe even worse than her sense of direction. When things were important, she wrote them down. There were sticky notes *everywhere* in her house."

Picking her bag up from the worn carpet, she rummaged around inside and fished out a bright orange sticky note.

Barb's Books were scrawled across it in red marker.

"This was on the box. She hadn't unpacked them." Meg gave a wry smile. "Nat didn't really own anything, wasn't married, no kids. I don't think she even considered a will."

Meg leaned back, her exhaustion clear, bags under her eyes.

"I'm glad I'm getting at least this one thing right by giving these back to you."

Barb couldn't bear to contradict her. The box itself seemed cursed, and Barb wasn't sure she wanted it back.

"Nat's always been...always *was*," the word came out bitterly, the past tense still unfamiliar regarding a friend.

The tea steamed on the table between them, and they watched it spiral lazily as she tried to find the words she was looking for. Nat could never be anything new. Meg licked her lips and cleared her throat to start again.

"She mentioned you had a son. He passed away?"

Barb nodded, the pain like a dormant volcano. Over time, it solidified from a bad dream into fact, but it was still there, bubbling beneath the surface.

She never knew when it might explode.

Barb nodded, unsure what Meg wanted her to say.

"I take it she never mentioned her brother?" Meg asked.

Barb shook her head.

Meg sighed.

"Nat was always guarded about sharing that part of her past. She had a rough time when we were younger. In high school, there was an accident. Her brother, he..." She trailed off, dabbing her face with a nearly shredded tissue she pulled out of her pocket. The soft square left bits of dandruff across her cheeks.

"It happened when he was sixteen. Nat was seventeen." Meg gazed at Barb hard, willing her to see.

"It was a car accident."

Barb felt like all the air was being sucked out of the room. "Like Gavin."

Meg nodded. "Like Gavin."

"So, you think she felt some sort of connection with me?" Barb asked, not sure where this was going.

"I do, but I think it was more than that."

"Well, she certainly never said anything to me. What do you mean?" Barb asked, trying to absorb the glimpse into the life of a woman she never got to know otherwise.

She sensed that there was something there, and now she knew just how much they had in common.

"Nat mentioned you were packing some things up, getting ready to let some things go? I think she really believed that if you could eventually be okay, that maybe it meant that things would be okay for her. Like maybe she could see a way that her parents might forgive her one day, down the road."

Barb frowned, unsure how Nat thought she was at all okay. "I don't understand."

"We were all friends. We were so close in age, and our dads worked together since we were born. We knew each other our whole lives." Meg considered, then blurted, "Sometimes I think that maybe I never fully forgave her, either."

As soon as the words emerged, Meg brought her trembling hand to her lips, almost startled that they had come from her mouth.

"I'm sorry. How could I say that? I loved her, I did. But I loved him, too. I missed him too. A lot. I still miss him sometimes."

Unburdened by the confession, she babbled on, encouraged because Barb was a relative stranger. Unloading on her was safe.

"No one could miss him more than her."

Barb wanted to tell her that whatever she had to say, that Nat had known, that it was okay. All the well-meaning things people said to her after Gavin died were on the tip of her tongue.

Meaningless phrases washed over her every time she thought, "If only I'd come home sooner," "If only I'd picked him up from school," "If only I hadn't been working night shifts that week."

If only.

The platitudes meant nothing. They were reassurances for other people, so that they could tell themselves it would never happen to them. Maybe her tragedy would inspire them to make good on a forgotten promise, or call a friend they argued with.

The truth sank in a long time ago, digging its claws deep into Barb, but maybe Meg would come to the truth on her own. Nat would never know. Gavin would never know.

They were gone, and it was too late.

Barb realized now why Nat seemed so familiar. She gripped Meg's hand, trying to steer her back to something she said at the start of her ramble.

"Forgive her for what, Meg?"

Before Meg opened her mouth, Barb knew what she would say. The girl and her brother, in an accident the same day as Gavin. The couple was from a respectable part of town, their remaining child traumatized.

Punished enough.

Barb, on the other hand, lived...well, here. She worked nights and was a single mom. No one was shocked it could happen here, and so it wasn't covered, a tiny brief mention in Gavin's obituary, the only thing pointing to a wrongdoing.

Barb twisted her shirt between her hands, remembering talking to the officer at the station. Weeks later, they hadn't figured out who left her son to die. The storm that night wiped away most evidence, and not a single neighbour saw anything.

The next time she stopped in asking for updates, she saw it in the detective's eyes; he wanted her to go away.

Barb was furious at everything and everyone for a long time, but she came to understand that gone was gone. Gavin wasn't coming back, and no one was going to help her. All she hoped was that karma would provide.

This wasn't what I wanted.

Taking in the look on her face, Meg hesitated.

"Sorry, do you know about this? It was all over the news."

Barb shook her head. She was talking to the police, so whenever the news came on, she looked away. She knew too much already.

Meg grabbed another tissue as she forced the words out.

"We'd been to a party. Nat left early with Chris. She said she wasn't feeling well and went to wait in the car. Chris went to find her in case he needed to drive her home." Meg stopped here, and Barb realized the moment she was holding onto playing behind her eyes once again.

"When she said she wasn't drinking, I believed her," Meg whispered.

Barb recognized the look on the younger woman's face, the same way she felt when she told her sister that she was going back to her cheating husband time and time again. Her tone was that of someone who told themselves they weren't letting someone get away with bad behaviour, but deep down they knew they were lying to themselves.

The tea finally cooled. Meg picked up her cup and took a sip to steady herself, her eyes surprised as she set the cup back down, coughing. She breathed in roughly, her eyes watering.

"You alright?" Barb asked.

"What..."

"Sorry, I should have told you," Barb said. "From the look on your face, I thought we could use something a little stronger this time."

Meg laughed. "Oh, my God. I mean, thank you. I think I needed that."

Meg collected herself and took more delicate sips from her steaming cup, appreciating the distraction.

Barb leaned forward. "Nat was driving, wasn't she? She blamed herself when he died?"

Meg brought her eyes up to meet Barb's, realizing she didn't understand.

"Sometimes I wish he had," Meg whispered, eyes brimming with shame.

MAY 1999

Origins

47

NAT WATCHED AS HER YOUNGER SELF EXAMINED THE outside of the car. Concentration permeated her features as if she were stopping to check the tires, but something about the way her body was moving made Nat's skin crawl.

The teenager was flexing her fingers and staring down at her hand, examining her yellow fingernails with curiosity. Nat remembered the polish was scented, the smell of chemical-laced pineapple carrying to her nose whenever she scratched her face or laid her head on her desk to do her math homework.

This Nat didn't look how she remembered herself. Unnaturally confident, she exhibited none of the hallmark awkwardness she associated with her high school years. She rolled her head from side to side as if she were settling into a warm bath. The world was hers for the taking; she had things under control.

Nat filled in the blanks of that day so many times over the years, but she wasn't sure she was ready to see them re-enacted. Could she trust these memories? These lost pieces of time were something she was simultaneously hoping for and dreading all of her life.

Let me out, out, out, out, out, out, out, out, out, out!!!!

The pavement stayed under her feet; the car was still running, and the younger version of her was still in front of her. Whatever brought them here, whatever it had done, things had changed, and she was simply playing in a make-believe world, placed where it wanted her.

It wants me to see.

Lowering her hands to her sides, teenage Nat gazed past where she stood, out to the street beyond. A dark shadow clung to her young self's shoulders, copying her movements, a perfect mimic apart from a slight delay. This obscene doppelgänger reached back in through the door, shutting off the car.

The sudden silence was expectant, waiting for her next move. Moving toward the front bumper, she was still acting as if she were waking up from a nap. A streak of red splashed across the broken blinker, another higher on the now dented hood. She stopped, bending to inspect it. Reaching out slowly, enjoying the moment, she touched the crimson stain, an unnatural smile curling her lips as she rubbed it between her thumb and forefinger, bringing it closer to her face as the blood became tacky on her skin. Dabbing it on her tongue, she smiled.

Simon says, "Taste the blood."

She was watching a movie with dubbing, actors' lips moving out of time with the words. The mass fluttered now and then, a dark and nervous butterfly trying to rest on a windshield. Slowly, it morphed, building itself into the shape of the girl it was following. Walking past her ghost self toward the street, the assured set of those shoulders frightened Nat more than her interest in the blood. The thing on her body moved them jerkily to the end of the alley, near where Gavin stood.

What is this?

Nat turned to the car, heart pounding, blood rushing to her ears and cheeks. She didn't know if she could trust her eyes, but she didn't care.

Sitting in the passenger seat, gripping his seatbelt with both hands, was Chris.

He was exactly as she remembered, green eyes mirroring hers so perfectly, the horrified expression in them something she often dreamed about but wished she would never see. His hair was damp; the heat of the day and the stress of the situation coated his skin with sweat. He was shaking, and she wondered if he was in shock.

The last pieces of the day that were clear to her flooded back. Their little trio cut the last class of the day, heading to a party at the beach. She invited Chris along, mostly so she would be sure he wouldn't snitch. They were close, but they still had those teenage secrets and bribes.

What siblings didn't?

In no way did she want him to keep this one for a rainy day. They were only a year apart, so it wasn't really weird that he was there. He knew people; she didn't have to entertain him or anything.

She remembered not feeling well and leaving early. After that, it was hazy. The drive home was fragmented, pieces emerging from nothingness without context. Chris smiled and cranked the radio, singing along to the song of the day, enthusiastic as always, arm out the passenger side window. In slow motion, her hair whipped around her face as the refreshing air blasted through the windows.

There was nothing after that, a black hole in her memory until the awful moment she woke up, her entire life forever changed. Even when they told her what they found after, a piece of her had always hung on to the hope that it wasn't her, it couldn't have been. That scrap of hope was all that held her together for so many years. If it was gone, she didn't know who she would be.

Stomach flipping, she drew in a sharp breath as she watched this unfeeling version of herself.

What if I was wrong?

A strangled noise behind her got her attention, pulling her away from the brink of panic. Gavin had followed young Nat toward the alley's opening, facing his home that was so close and yet so far from safety on the last day of his life. He was looking at something on the ground, something he couldn't tear his eyes from.

"Gavin?" she called. "What is it?"

He didn't answer.

From the car behind her, she heard Chris' voice, sounding impossibly tiny.

"Is...is he...?"

"Shut. Up."

The clipped and heartless monotone coming from the thing's throat chilled Nat to her core. Between the words her mouth was slack, a talking doll without the batteries included. The shadow on her back clung to her, the outline of arms snaking down over her shoulders and chest, a loving embrace she watched herself lean into.

Revulsion wracked her, a memory surfacing of unwanted hands sliding around her while she was somewhere dark, trapped inside herself, unable to scream or move. Eyes aching with unshed tears, the violation released itself from the rubble, buried all this time in anxiety. The battle cry escaping her was a catharsis for all the times her story didn't matter, and she charged herself, grabbing in vain at the monster that presumed to own her body. Behind her, her little brother cried in the car.

Her heart hardened as the darkness slipped through her

fingers, as elusive as smoke. Sliding through the fabric of her once coveted shirt, her hand flopped uselessly back at her side. It wasn't like before with Eva, where inanimate objects could be manipulated.

"Fuck you!" she screamed.

The darkness turned toward her, a slight smile on its lips. She tripped on something and glanced down out of reflex, panting through her unsatisfied rage. There was a dark-brown skate shoe lying on the ground. Darkly, she thought of a cartoon, some animated creature running away so fast that it left its smoking footwear behind.

Her youthful body was moving slowly, walking with knees locked, a newborn foal finding its footing. Gavin wouldn't look at her, eyes fixed on her demon self. As she reached him, he grabbed her arm, his fingers cold.

Nothing happened.

Reality didn't shift; their touch sparked nothing. It brought them here, and it was going to keep them here until it got what it wanted from them.

Ears ringing, she saw Gavin talking to her, lips moving. He was pointing at the ground, his mouth moving slowly, underwater to her.

It wants us to see. She followed his pointing finger, turning her head to look down at the garbage cans scattered over the road.

A boy was lying on the ground, his back to them, white t-shirt moving up and down as he gasped for air. Flicking an ankle, her teenage self flipped the body over with a kick as if it weighed nothing. Confused, Nat felt her world turn upside down.

Gavin lay on the hard ground, panting and wheezing, covered in cuts and bruises. Movements slowing incrementally with every breath, his gaze shifted toward the white sneakers on her past self's feet.

"I said, *take us out, Nat!*" Gavin's voice beside her became clear, breaking through her anger.

"I can't! I don't know how to control this!" She flailed, not sure what to say. "How did we get here? I don't understand."

That got his attention, and she crumpled inside as he snapped.

"Don't *understand?* You killed me, Nat! You *lied* to me! How could you not know we were connected all this time?"

"I didn't! I swear! Gavin, if this is real, it wasn't me. It was that...thing! It had to..."

"Shut up!" His voice slapped her, and she knew it was useless to argue.

His anger triggered something. The scene froze, and they were standing amid a tableau, waiting for someone to show them their cue cards.

"Gavin, I..." Gripping his shoulders, she stooped to lock his eyes with hers, needing to make him see she was telling the truth, to see that this couldn't possibly be her.

"All this time, you were trying to throw me off track." The hurt in his eyes cut to her center, lodging there like a splinter. "I trusted you!"

"Gavin, no. Listen. Please. Just listen. Something isn't right here! It wasn't me. It was that monster!" She pointed at her young self. "Don't you see it, holding onto me?"

A strength fed by his anger coursed through him, and he easily shook her off. It was soaking the blankness of his t-shirt, soaking with the now familiar red and something new, a moody purple. She didn't know for sure what it meant, but she could guess. Confusion. Despair. Betrayal.

Take your pick.

"There's nothing there, Nat."

"Please, just..."

The look in his eyes was all-encompassing, so hateful she needed to look away.

"It's a big afterlife, Nat. Just *leave me alone.*"

The pause button came off, and Gavin was gone. Chris blubbered faintly back at the car. She wanted so badly to tell him that everything would be okay, but the demon-her didn't care, and the real her knew it was a lie.

Nat watched as the dark fog used her body to peer down at Gavin as he slowly stopped thrashing. The mist faded slightly, seeping into her flesh, her youthful body's movements growing smoother as she watched.

Crouching down beside him, she desperately reached for his hand only to disappear through it again and again. He stopped moving, his breaths shorter and further apart.

"This one," came the unfamiliar voice from the body standing above them, hers and not hers all at the same time. The voice lilted, pausing as if to make sure the words were exactly right. *"This one has so much potential."*

The thing in her body grabbed his face roughly, pulling him closer, out of sight from the street between the trash bins. Gavin moaned as he was yanked upward, yellow nails woven through his sweaty hair. Barely aware and clearly in pain, he seemed to relax slightly, convinced help arrived. The bone under his ruined eye shifted beneath his skin as she snapped his head backward.

"Shhhhhhh," it whispered, and Gavin's face appeared to wither, skin loosening and wrinkling.

Ribs were visible at his sides, his shirt now a loose tent over his torso. It breathed deeply, inhaling him.

As his breath rattled and hitched, Gavin's skin glowed. The aura pulled gently on Nat's young neck, tipping her head back to inhale deeply, taking large gulps of him. As it did, her body was pulled to a standing position, stretching its neck like a delicate bird, energy coursing through its new body.

Nat took in the flushed cheeks and realized her youthful

face was happy. A contented sigh escaped her lips. The sound of an appetite quenched.

Recharged.

Gavin's gaze faded not long after it did whatever this was, and all she could do was hope he didn't feel it. As it dropped him to the ground to rest in a pile of carrot peels and coffee grounds, he forced out one last wheeze. Only the shell of a kid gone too soon remained. His eyes stared ahead, expectant, like they were waiting for someone, anyone.

I tried, a tiny voice inside consoled her. Unwilling to let go of the failure, she pushed it aside. It didn't matter if she tried; Gavin still died alone. Biting her lip, she thought back to what Gavin told her about the day he died.

The whole time, I swear there were people there, watching me die.

What kind of person just stands around and doesn't help?

Not-her sighed in contentment, spinning and walking back to the idling car, running the tip of her index finger along the chipped paint job as she moved toward the passenger side. The car belonged to Chris, really. Dad's attempt to stick it to Mom.

It backfired when Mom accused him of being a sexist prick, creating a weird double standard because he didn't offer to chip in for a car for Nat when she got her license the year before. To keep the peace, they ended up sharing. They would go to a drive-thru and share some fries, go to the movies, and hang out at a park.

Anywhere that wasn't home, just for a little while, was fine with them.

She could hardly stand to look at it now, but at one time the car was a sanctuary, a place where they could pretend everything was fine when they needed to. Their grown-up version of a treehouse; it was the safe space they needed now and then.

The demonic puppet glanced down at her, scrunching its face into an odd expression, one eye held tightly shut.

It was winking at her, as if it had learned from step-by-step instructions.

"Leave him alone!" Nat shouted, still kneeling beside Gavin.

It ignored her, setting its sights on her brother. Chris hadn't stopped babbling, a stream of thought that didn't stop running in his panic.

"Oh my god, oh my god, what did we do?! The radio...oh my god! We didn't see him...we have to call someone! Help him..."

"Brother," it said, calling him by title rather than his name. *"You need to shut. The. Fuck. Up."*

The stilted speech was sharp, hitting its mark as surely as an arrow slamming into a bullseye.

Nat glimpsed Chris' face through the cracked windshield, trusting her implicitly to know what to do.

Chris was breathing heavily, sweating and shaking, gulping as it opened the passenger door and leaned over him to reach into the backseat, grabbing an old ratty shirt. Nat recognized it as her gym strip. It formed its new mouth, *my mouth,* into a frown as it concentrated, holding it to her face and searching inside itself for the right word.

"Soft," it said, laughing in delight.

Nat's half full water bottle was in the cupholder between the seats in the front, and it grabbed it, going to work and dumping the water over the dented hood. The monster silently wiped off the blood, tossing the shirt back in the car before getting back in the driver's seat.

One sleeve, wet with rose-tinted water, landed in Chris's lap, soaking into his khaki-coloured cargo shorts, and he leaned sideways out of his still open door.

The demon moved with a swiftness that Nat had never

possessed and grabbed the collar of her brother's green t-shirt, pulling him back in the car just in time for him to spew vomit onto the dash. Dripping lazily, it pooled onto the floor mat and molded itself around the soles of his shoes.

"Jesus! What is wrong *with* you?" The words were right, but the inflection was off.

It's learning.

"M-m-m-eeee? What is wrong with *you*, Nat?! We can't just leave this kid here!" The words were hoarse, his face still green, and he spat onto the floor.

There was blood on Chris' forehead that had sluggishly emerged from his hairline around what would be a nasty bruise, a smudge of it marring the dusty dash. His eyes looked unfocused as he struggled to make sense of the situation.

The police said he hit his head, but what she was looking at wasn't just the side effects of a concussion. That would be easier than this.

She was watching his heart break.

"Accidents happen, brother. Do you want to go to the place? The place where they put bad people?" She paused for a moment, searching.

"Crim...inals?" she said, victory seeping through the mispronunciation.

Chris looked concerned now, reaching over to push her hair back, to look at her eyes.

"You mean jail? Are you okay? I think we need to go to the hospital."

"Yes, jail. Prison. The house for the bad people. Do you?" she asked again, oblivious to his worry.

"*Chris?*" It hissed, urging him to reply.

Chris couldn't stop staring at Gavin's legs peeking out from the garbage cans, unable to believe this was happening. Regarding him with annoyance, it took another approach.

"Maybe you were driving, Chris. No one is here. You...put some liquids into your body today, yes?"

His head snapped upward at that, impatient, like he thought she was deliberately fucking with him.

"I had some drinks. Yes...but..."

Her eyes brimming with crocodile tears, voice suddenly distressed and pained, she babbled, clenching her hair in a fist, pushing her bangs back off her forehead.

"Officer, he was so drunk. I tried to take his keys, but he wouldn't let me. I just couldn't stop him. Oh, my god! I yelled for him to stop but it was too late..."

The words followed each other out without a fumble this time, and Nat's youthful features twisted into an expression of pride. This thing was learning from her, learning to *become* her.

"We're not calling anyone."

She reached down to turn the key in the ignition, the car roaring to life once more.

"But he's...." Chris fumbled for words. He stared at the shoe on the ground.

The quiet seemed to stretch into eternity before he finally whispered, "He looks younger than me."

"Did you know him?" It purred, full of deliberate malice. *"Oh no, you weren't...friends, were you?"*

The pauses between words were getting shorter with every sentence as it plucked more and more data from her mind.

Chris shook his head. "That's not the point, Nat."

"Get in the car, Chris," it growled.

Tears streamed down his face as he complied, head down, resigned as he re-buckled his seatbelt.

The car pulled away, and she stood still, wondering how she got out of here. She had to find Gavin and make this right.

Where do I even start?

In the rearview mirror, she met her own eyes. As the driver

tossed her head, trying to keep her hair out of her face, she was pulled to the vehicle, still tied to the thing that had ruined her.

Pulled through the rear window, she found herself in the backseat, an invisible travel companion behind her shaking little brother. The car moved slowly as it pulled into the bright, cheerful cul-de-sac, trying not to draw any attention to itself as they drove past Gavin's body, baking in the sun.

She scrambled for the door locks.

Enough.

The thought was futile. This wasn't where her story ended.

Not even close.

Not remembering had allowed her to believe that everything was fast for Chris, like a light going out. She scrambled for the door handle out of habit, knowing full well it wouldn't do any good.

No more. I want to get off this ride.

"Nat, where are we going?" Chris' voice sounded so small, but resigned to the drive.

The driver didn't answer.

She barely saw her young self through the dark fog hovering around her neck and shoulders, curling in on itself to fit into the confined space. She held up a shaking hand and tried to touch it. It grew stronger, and as she made contact, it felt like something bit her, a jellyfish sting in the dark. Her finger burned, and she yelped, putting it into her mouth.

"Nat, please," Chris tried one last time. "We have to..."

"We don't *have to*. I don't *have to* do anything. I can do what I please."

The car pulled up at a red light, the dented hood rattling away. Without looking, Nat knew where they were going. They would turn off at Exit 52, the road winding upward, headed toward the end of the story.

It turned, smiling at her, a horrifying facial movement

appearing like it was trying to sort out how it was done and why humans did it. It was an imitation of a smile, not quite reaching its dead eyes. This thing was trying to hurt her. To break her. She narrowed her eyes.

The car accelerated, for better or worse, heading toward the moment her life ended and she became someone brand new.

48

GAVIN REMEMBERED HIS DEATH ALL TOO WELL. THE pain in his chest, someone standing over him, his vision narrowing as he struggled to breathe. The layer of betrayal made it infinitely worse, and he didn't think that was possible.

It was just an accident, he always told himself. Hands shaking, he tried to rein himself in. It was over. There was no point in being angry. Maybe he could just ignore it. He didn't have to talk to her again, could pretend he never seen Nat standing over him, the pleasure of power in her eyes as she watched him go.

He was tired of sticking his neck out for people. It was just like it was with his dad.

People just let you down.

I hate her! I hate her! I hate her! I hate her! I hate him! I hate him! I hate him!

He wasn't sure why he kept coming back to the basement. Memories of his dad and how badly it all ended should have made him want to avoid it, but it didn't. As soon as he was at the bottom of the steps, he felt safe, and he wasn't sure why.

The clock ticked on and on and on, time folding over on

itself as Gavin slipped away. He spent hours and days staring at the concrete walls. Occasionally, his attention wandered to the model planes on a small ledge near the door. He couldn't bring himself to throw them away, wondering what his dad would have thought if he came back and they were gone. That would never happen; every fibre of his being *screamed* it, but still the tiny ember of squashed hope burned.

The basement was always their hangout spot.

"No girls allowed," his dad would say, and his mom would tip her head back and pretend to be upset. They would share a kiss, he would swat her playfully and tell her she had to go. She didn't know the password. There was a sort of thrill at being just the two of them. Sometimes he felt bad about kicking out his mom, but later he came to understand she went upstairs and had a bubble bath with a book, a brief break from him needing her. Dad was the toys, and Mom was the books.

The dim, cool room was full of endless weekends spent building model airplanes, conducting science experiments, and constructing intricate building sets. Maybe if he were the dad that plopped him down in front of some Saturday cartoons, it wouldn't have sucked so much after he left.

After the divorce, Dad moved into an apartment, telling Gavin it could be just like the basement, a new hangout spot. That lasted a few weeks, until a woman moved in with him, big and round, and they told Gavin he was going to be a big brother.

Sherry wasn't the problem, not really. When Gavin came over, she was always nice. They would play for a while, and then she would try to give Gavin and his dad some time, but his dad never let her go. Distracted and distant while Gavin played, his hand remained possessively on Sherry's mysteriously expanding belly. After the baby was born, things only got worse, and by the time Sherry got pregnant again, Gavin was only there every couple of weeks.

The day he sat in Sex Ed, his face was white as a sheet, tightly gripping the seat of his chair as he mentally counted backwards, was the day it all came crashing down. His dad made a fool of him.

Gavin knew now it was all doomed from that moment, a powder keg ready to explode. On his last visit, they got into a fight about something stupid—putting away the laundry.

"You've got to lose this attitude, Gavin," Dad shook his head. "What's your problem, anyway?"

Before he could stop it, the words bubbled up to the surface—the thing he was thinking but promised himself he would never ever say out loud.

"I don't know. Maybe the fact that my dad is a cheating, lying asshole?"

Frozen completely, his dad's mouth hung open as if he wanted to say something, but he didn't know what. Gavin waited and waited and waited. He waited for anger, for excuses, for an apology, for something, for anything.

What he said surprised Gavin, but didn't surprise him, all at the same time.

"Look, it's nothing. Just please don't tell Sherry, okay?"

Gavin stared at him, dumbfounded.

"No problem," he said, knowing it would be the last time he set foot in his father's house.

He blew into the hallway, shaking with rage. Sherry stood quietly, eyes wide and dry, a hand over her mouth.

"I'm sorry," he said as he slammed his door. A quiet knock interrupted, and then his dad's voice boomed from the living room each time.

"Jesus, Sherry. Just leave him be."

A short phone call later, he left to meet his mom outside. Sherry trailed behind. "Wait..."

Barely waiting for the car to stop, he crawled inside, refusing to look back.

I'll never be him.

It used to be an everyday thought, something in passing, a guideline for how to do the right thing. Now it was eating him up, on constant repeat.

The only way not to become someone who abandoned was to have no one.

He remembered his little brother, who loved to toddle over and grab his thumb. His baby sister, so tiny, who smiled at him first.

Do they even remember me? He wondered now; the slime entering his mouth and nose, cold and dripping down his throat. He was disgusted, but also couldn't seem to care.

It is what it is.

Once in a while, the phone would ring while he was watching TV in the living room, and he would find the phone cord stretched down the hall and into the bathroom. Behind the bathroom door, his mom spoke in a hushed voice, and he knew it was his dad.

"Do you want to talk to him?" she would ask.

Holding his breath in the hallway, he pressed his ear to the door, waiting for her to call his name.

All he ever heard was the soft sound of the phone being placed back in its cradle.

He left you, Gavin. Just like she did. The voice whispered, over and over, faint and far away.

He was so angry at his dad, for not wanting him, for not being willing to admit it when Gavin saw him for what he was. What Nat did felt worse, somehow. His dad's actions felt less personal, less about him.

It was pretty hard not to take your own murder personally.

He would disappear for a while, lost in his swirling thoughts, and catch himself staring at the door, hoping she would come.

It was dawning on him that he hoped she would follow. More than that, he *wanted* her to. Maybe if he brought himself to forgive her, this would all stop. Mad as he was, maybe she was right. Maybe they were each other's ticket out of here.

The doorway remained empty.

She's not coming. The whispers were getting louder, a hissing that spoke from inside and outside all at once.

Who said that? He would wonder, but no one replied.

He muttered to himself as he turned the perfect glossy pages of one magazine on the coffee table. It was brand new, but he read it a hundred times. He was oblivious of the tiny thread snaking out of his ears.

Gavin's subconscious continued to steer the weather. The summer days shortened, and the night air grew cooler, whole seasons revolving in a day.

The days passed, an eternity, or an hour, and still Gavin flipped, the slime drawing tracks along his face like tears. Inching its way through his dark hairline, it crawled along his collar and down over his chest, covering him in the same numbness he felt back then.

At first, it was tiny droplets, but soon it ran non-stop, forming oozing pools gathering on the chocolate brown carpet, reds and blues and greens forming a topographical map at his feet.

She made you like her, and she lied.

The colours blended and weaved and tore in and out of him until he lost track of it happening. It was just one long sensation, an endless cresting of pain that never broke. It covered his eyes, and he let the blanket enfold him completely, weighing him to the couch.

How could she do that, Gavin?

The voice was so close now, and it was a voice he recognized. It was her voice and his voice blending together, the liars forced to tell the truth. All that mattered now was finding Nat, making her feel like this.

Making her pay.

Blurry through the constant mask that coated his face, it finally appeared, its dripping teeth obscured. Reaching to hold him lovingly in its arms, it whispered to him.

"I can give you what you want."

No further promises needed, he leaned into its embrace and let it take him away.

49

Chris sat in the passenger seat, staring out the window. The growing darkness outside seemed meant for him. His face was red and blotchy, tears falling silently down his pale cheeks. Glimpsing his face in the side mirror, he looked like a ghost of himself.

The afternoon ran through his head, over and over and over, the sickening crunch of the kid hitting the ground getting louder and louder in his ears.

We killed someone.

His sister changed, becoming cold and unfeeling. Nat only got stranger as they drove. Largely ignoring Chris, she muttered to herself, repeating random words, then nodding once the pronunciation was perfect.

Stopping at a red light, she fixed her eyes on the rearview mirror, tossing her hair and assessing herself. The motion was stiff-necked at first, becoming more and more fluid with practice. His body rocked forward against the seatbelt as she accelerated abruptly, running the light at the abandoned intersection.

"Can we go home, Nat? *Please.*"

"I am home," Nat grinned, and he shuddered as she glanced at him, a cannibalistic glint in her eye he had never seen before.

The dead boy's face appeared in Chris' mind, fading in the alley as Nat stood taller, so sure of herself, languishing in the scene's chaos, grabbing him so roughly.

Without looking over to the driver's seat, he whispered, "You're not Nat, are you?"

"Shut up," it muttered, looking pissed off.

Apparently, it wasn't passing as well as it thought. He felt a brief twinge of pride in that.

"What are you?"

"I'm Nat!!" it screeched.

His sister's face flashed in and out of focus, the mask slipping as its true face appeared just below hers. A piercing scream crawled up its throat, and Chris covered his ears against his sister's agonized struggle inside. Fangs emerged and transformed back to Nat's recently straightened teeth so fast he could almost believe he imagined it.

But I know better.

They bypassed the downtown core with all its cheerful shops. He longed for the single-lane traffic crawling at a snail's pace, searching for a place to park. Instead, they avoided the many people who could have helped or noticed a dented hood on a car driven by two teens by driving through on the frontage road that wove through the industrial district.

Employees already escaped home at the end of the workday, leaving dusty lots containing plenty of construction equipment but mostly devoid of cars and trucks. The small scattering of people who remained were too busy, too far from the main road. Their heads were down, marking their paperwork on clipboards and emptying their trucks of their deliveries for the day, too busy to notice one car.

The billboards on the outskirts of the farmland gave way

to trees by the time they hit the highway, dark clouds rolling in overhead. The cheerful sun disappeared, dipping low in the sky and overcome by the dense forest lining either side of the road. A few drops of rain tapped the windows, the gentle patter putting him on edge, making the thing that remained silent beside him a ticking time-bomb. The temperature dropped slightly in the shade, and Chris shivered.

Nat turned sharply to the right, nearly missing the turnoff. His shoulder jammed uncomfortably into the door, and his head swam, dizziness making the darkening road ahead of him waver like a desert mirage. As the sun dipped even further, the headlights illuminated an endless sea of trees on either side. Chris reached down slowly and undid his seatbelt as the car made its way past the sign for the Plank Cliffs.

The winding, bumpy roads were steep and mosquito-ridden by day. At night, rattlesnakes emerged from the high, dry grass to hunt mice and other tiny creatures.

It was a tempting spot for jumping, the dense trees giving way to a perfect view, the shimmering water appearing jewel green on the warmest summer days. Picnic tables and benches were scattered unevenly to form a makeshift park, with longer wild grass and flowers growing unchecked farther back. If you were there by yourself, it was easy to feel you were the last person on the face of a wild earth.

As beautiful as it was, as calm as the view was, Plank Cliffs was named ironically. The water below was shallow and rocky near the cliff edge, and a steep drop-off led to the deeper water a little farther out. The trick was, you needed to carefully time your leap, ensuring you propelled yourself off far enough to avoid the rocks in the shallows.

Without fail, every year, people jumped the cliffs despite the warning signs. Hell, Chris did it himself. Everyone hooted and clapped when he emerged from the water below, a small gathering of daredevils meeting on a nearby stretch of beach.

He took the high fives, playing it cool, but in truth, it scared him shitless.

The water was a freezing slap, choppier than it looked from so high up. Weeds tickled his ankles from the depths, and he kicked away frantically, terrified that something would pull him under.

Just last summer, a kid from their school jumped, timing it just wrong, a milligram too little force sending him to the shallows. He was pulled into the deeper water, unconscious, and never came up again. There was an article in the paper with a photo of him in it—floppy hair, a goofy grin, not a clue it was all coming crashing down so soon.

Looking into the boy's newspaper-inked eyes, Chris had thought of the tickle on his ankle, wondering if it held the boy there, whispering as it pulled that he belonged below. The incident had everyone worked up, parents reminding their kids of the dark local history that the cliffs were named because jumping was akin to walking the plank.

The car rolled to a stop, pulling him out of his thoughts. In the dark, the effect of coming up to the park was completely different. Instead of the promise of a beautiful view, the grassy ground led to a wall of blackness in front of them, the absolute end of the world.

Nat got out of the car, slamming the driver's side door shut with a rusty bang and walking over to Chris' side, slowly relishing the dented hood, the cracked windshield. The crack was much smaller than he thought it would be. The car took a whole human being and erased them from the face of the earth. At a glance, it didn't look any worse than what a decent-sized rock could do.

Chris locked his door and launched across the seat to lock the driver's side as well. Reaching for the ignition, he wilted as he found only empty space.

A yellow-tipped nail rapped against the glass. He bit his lip as a muffled jangle cut through the air; the keys dangling off of one finger by the window, taunting him.

"Get out."

His lower lip trembled, and the thing raised Nat's knuckle and knocked harder in annoyance.

It's okay, bud. It's going to be okay.

The message was fading from his memory as quickly as he heard it. Twisting around to see what terror was waiting for him in the backseat, he half expected the monstrous face he saw on his sister outside to be leering at him. The monster remained outside, his sister's eyes that were no longer her own staring him down from outside. A light pressure clamped down on his shoulder from behind as he fell back in his seat, leaning into the reassuring squeeze.

He should have been terrified, but he surprised himself by responding, fingers splayed across his chest, seeking a hand to hold.

50

Nat gasped as her brother reached for her hand. His fingers moved through her invisible flesh to scratch absently at his shoulder, oblivious of what was causing the feeling.

In its haste to beat her down, it left a door unlocked and she reached through. With no idea how long it would last, she shoved her excitement down, focusing her energy on not playing her hand too early.

The thing inside was making itself more and more comfortable. Her body backed away from the car, shoulders slumped, arms loose, dancing and spinning in the headlights to a tune only it could hear. The dark fog divided into smaller, delicate tendrils, twirling in a braid around her youthful body, a passionate partner.

It was a poisonous fruit, beautiful to look at but slowly eating away at her as it took control. Face to the sky, it relished in the now humid air, tinged with just a little preview of the cool night breeze to come.

Something glinted in one of her hands, dangling by her thigh. A bottle. *Vodka.*

Nat remembered bringing it to the beach, purchased by a random stranger in the liquor store parking lot, who winked at her as he handed it over. People at the party saw her with it, and she swore up and down she didn't drink it.

Of course, there were stupid things she did at that age, things she shook her head at now. Maybe they were bids for a little attention, or maybe it was the rush of being just a little reckless, but she never would have gambled with Chris.

Not with Chris in the car, she insisted. *Never. Please. Please listen to me.*

No one believed her, of course. Meg was in her corner, telling the police Nat wasn't drinking, that all she saw her with was a bottle of water. The relief and gratitude at being believed was overwhelming, reassurance covering her like a warm blanket when Meg squared her shoulders and said she would tell everyone the truth.

When the blood test came back, showing Nat's blood alcohol was off the charts when they found her, the bit of doubt that crept into Meg's eyes was a fist around Nat's heart. Even when they told her what they found after, a piece of her always hung onto the hope that it wasn't her, it couldn't have been.

The uncertainty whispered to her, questioning her, every day of her life. It framed the first thought that came to her mind every morning, before she even opened her eyes.

How could I? Slowly drowning out the fading scream of, *I wouldn't.*

The constant yo-yo took its toll, and as her guilt won out, she erupted at those around her with increasing regularity, longing for them to mirror her anger.

How could they love her after what she did?

As she watched the thing polish off the bottle in less than two minutes, that rage rebuilt.

Had it ever left?

Panting and weaving on her feet, her teenage self relaxed as the alcohol coursed through the newfound host.

"Wow. This feels...wow."

It tossed the empty bottle toward the cliff's edge, glass exploding as it pounded into the rocky ground there. It fell onto her backside, laughing breathlessly.

"C'mon, Chris. Let's hang out." Wrist flopping in a friendly wave, it called to him. *"The stars are coming out. This view is going to be amazing."*

The foggy aura was thinning as it entered her ears, nostrils, mouth. There was no trace of the strange, stilted speech it had exhibited this afternoon. Despite the alcohol, her arms moved fluidly through the air, none of the disjointed movements from earlier on display.

It was becoming *her.*

Nat shuddered, unable to do anything but watch the violation of her own body. The last of its essence entered her with a dull slurp, smothering whatever was left inside. It was over.

It is me. I am it.

"No," he said, shaking his head.

"What?" It raised a hand to her ear quizzically, pretending it didn't hear correctly.

"No!" Chris yelled to be heard through the cracked windshield.

Pushing itself up from the ground, it approached the passenger side once again, slapping pieces of tall dry grass from its hands onto her sweats.

Head cocked to the side, watching Chris as it considered its next move. The rain picked up speed, with tiny rivers running down and obscuring her view from the backseat. It could break through that window without hesitating, drag him out kicking and screaming, but it didn't.

Hair wet, plastered to the sides of her face, it turned its

attention from Chris, staring into the eyes of the stowaway in the backseat. A look of supreme satisfaction was written across her young features, taunting Nat's future. Standing on its tiptoes, it stared down at her, teetered, and then took a stumbling step backward.

"You were right, you know," she circled slowly back to the grassy area, absently flicking away some dirt that water had slicked to her leg. "I'm not her."

"Yeah, no shit," Chris called out.

He was still looking around the car, opening the glove compartment, the centre console, anything that might give him something to defend himself.

Anger flared inside it, an inhuman red glow was visible for a brief moment, as startling as a flashlight in the dark before it composed itself again.

"She's in here with me. Did you know that? Squirming. And you know what?" It leaned forward at the hips conspiratorially, ready to share a secret. Its mouth spread slowly open in a winner's grin as she spoke. *"I like it."*

Chris said nothing, not wanting to let a bully get to him. From the backseat, Nat could see him shaking as he snorted through his nostrils, keeping his mouth firmly shut.

Without breaking eye contact, it took a determined step back, moving toward the ledge.

"Don't you want to help her, Chris?"

Another exaggerated stride carried her back toward the water.

"Your sister is special, yes?"

Chris held his chin high in defiant silence. A thrill of big-sister pride ran through Nat, and she held onto that feeling.

Fuck you.

"Hey, *I mean it,*" its mouth drawled, suddenly agreeable. *"I was drawn to her for a reason. I knew she was meant to be the one."*

"The one?"

Her body was succumbing to the effects of the alcohol, stumbling as her feet lifted in a steady backward march. Her tall, thin frame looked like a marionette with a couple of loose strings, the puppeteer losing a bit of control with every tug.

A stalemate, it seemed. Still the demon grinned, taking another slow, exaggerated step back toward the abyss. The broken glass crunched under her brand-new sneakers.

"Are you coming, Chris?" Its eyes narrowed, testing him, making sure he understood.

"We can only survive in this world by being stealthy, Chris. We hide in plain sight. So if I'm revealing myself to you? You're smart enough. I'm trying to frighten you. You should know what that means."

Chris' voice trembled slightly as he said, "Why should I get out if you're just going to kill me?"

Understanding washed over Nat, and she gripped the seatback as she realized what it intended.

Her body was its bargaining chip.

51

"Get out of the car, Chris. *Now.*" Standing dangerously close to the edge, it wobbled on her feet as the alcohol coursed through Nat's body.

"Or what?" Chris shouted.

It swung a foot in the air lazily, the icy waves below the only thing to catch her fall.

"Or I'll throw her right off this goddamn cliff."

Chris lowered a resigned hand to the manual push-button lock on the door, sweaty fingers slipping once, twice, before they gained purchase and pulled it up.

"*That's right,*" it hissed, crooking a finger to beckon him to approach the abyss.

The door creaked and gaped open as he swung his feet out onto the newly green grass. Walking toward his sister, he approached the sound of the water lapping against the rocks below. Rain pelted down on him, soaking through his shirt almost instantly.

"*That's it,*" it smirked. "*Come closer.*"

Feet shuffling slowly, his eyes flitted around in panic, looking for any way he could escape without endangering her.

333

"*Now,*" it said. "*I was telling you about how special she is, right?*"

Walking along the edge like a balance beam, it held its arms out to the sides, tracing relaxed circles in the night sky.

"*She has the honour of bringing me to life, of building my form. And the boy? He was the first innocent life your very special sister took. That we took together.*"

Lost in thought, it dug deep, trying to understand how Nat felt about everything that was happening around her.

"*A piece of her anxious little soul weakened then, you know. She watched herself do it, unable to stop it. It broke her.*"

Reaching up, it roughly pinched her cheeks, and they bloomed red on her pale face as it cherished her misery.

"*Just that tiny little scrap was all that I needed from her to take over.*"

A light glowed from within, and it vibrated with pleasure as the tiny piece of Nat embedded itself further into its being.

"*She and the boy together inside me, they form my foundations. A....*" It searched Nat's mind for the word and crowed triumphantly as it came.

"*...a BATTERY! That's it!*"

Nat thought of the energy that pulsed between herself and Gavin, how he said it never happened before. Whatever the monster was, whatever it wanted, there was only one thing she was sure of now.

It needs us.

The car behind them rocked ever so slightly as the wind picked up and battered the door, driving the rain sideways into the windows.

"*Bet you're wondering why I'm telling you this, aren't you?*"

Chris said nothing.

"*Of course you are. Humans are curious, after all. It's perfectly natural. As natural as me.*" It giggled, snorting as it breathed heavily, trying to keep its balance. "*It's simple. Fear makes your souls last in here. It makes them potent. Perfectly seasoned, and oh, so filling."*

Its tongue flitted out from between her teeth, rotting and slimy, licking her lips obscenely.

"So satisfying."

It glanced back out over the water. Chris was almost there now, his steps slowing as he began running out of rocky ground.

Nat swallowed. The moment her world imploded was approaching; she sensed it.

"She loves this view, doesn't she?" The water stretched out below them, inky black in the dark, whitecaps appearing as the wind picked up even more. *"This is one of your favourite places to go. When your parents are fighting?"*

"Yes," he answered carefully, his voice hitching.

"She loves you, you know."

"Yes," he said again, unwavering this time.

"Nat would never let anything happen to you, would she?"

"No."

It turned slowly to face him, blinking rapidly, confusion spilling out across Nat's features. Goosebumps broke out across her skin, and she shook in the rain.

"Chris?" Nat asked, her tiny voice bubbling up from somewhere deep inside.

It reached out a hand to him, palm up, and Chris tentatively placed his hand on hers. His sister's features remained still, impassive.

"Nat?" he asked cautiously. "Is that you?"

Her eyes didn't change as she crushed Chris's fingers in her powerful grip. He barely reacted to the unexpected pain before it jerked, flicking his arm forward. Kicking his feet across the mottled grey and brown rocks, she dragged him as if she didn't feel his weight, as if he were nothing. She spun suddenly; the momentum pushing him off the edge.

Chris dangled over the side. Nat's hand opened to drop him, but he still had a grip on her wrist. His feet kicked wildly, with nothing but open air below him. A gleeful grin split her face open above him, the comforting look in Nat's eyes remaining, a jarring contradiction.

"Please! Please, Nat! Please, don't!"

"Stop!" The shrill, desperate command emanated from Nat's throat, a shocked silence following as the monster reeled backward, choking on it. It was her again, just for a moment.

Grabbing his wrist with both hands, she fell to her knees, his weight too much for the real Nat.

Chris' fingers slipped, sliding over her wet skin, and he toppled into the night. His scream evaporated into a grunt as his body swung and slammed against the rocks, his hands tangled up in the weeds rooted at the top of the cliff.

Above him, Nat wailed, struggling to maintain control.

52

The horrible silence of the fall expanded until it burst into relief at the sound of Chris' feet scraping against the rock face just below the ledge.

The monster rose to its feet, wild-eyed with rage. It grunted as teenage Nat rose again, doubling over as if she punched it from inside. Possessor and possessed remained locked in battle, Nat fighting to stay at the surface, trying to get to him before it was too late.

"Chris, *push*!" The order erupted in the still air, her youthful face red and sweaty with the effort of suppressing the monster. Her mouth still hung slack, as if surprised the words escaped.

Both Nats lay on the edge, watching Chris.

"Push!" they screamed in unison.

He stilled his upper body, walking his legs up the side and tucking them between himself and the rock face

The sound of the splash seemed to take an eternity, the rush of the waves after they swallowed him worse than silence as she waited. The stillness drew out, and she held her breath until faint splashing followed by an even fainter cough punctuated the rhythmic lapping of the waves.

It screeched and rolled over, clutching at the hard ground as it tried to crawl. Her fingertips scraped across the rocky ground, the yellow nails snapping. The beast was gaining control, snarling and stumbling as it dragged its sharp joints toward the car.

Her body was covered in sweat despite the chilly wind. It howled with painful exertion, its actual face exposed once more. It flickered in and out of focus, her own face contorted when it appeared, the agony of trying to force her way back out escaping in a gurgling scream.

Her future self followed, feet lifted from the ground as her tether was hauled toward the car, pulled involuntarily into the backseat once more.

It jammed the car in drive, and hit the gas. From her position behind the driver's seat, she grabbed at her youthful body ineffectually, trying to stop it. It glared at her in the rearview mirror as her hands slipped through it.

The car picked up speed as they careened down the winding road. With one last impressive feat of will, her sweaty, determined hands turned the steering wheel with all her might. The car seemed suspended for a moment, the thick greenery of the treetops held it before plummeting down, plowing through the bushes growing out of the sandy embankment.

As the front end crumpled into the shallow creek bed below, the monster inside her lost its grip. Her unconscious body slumped forward, her face striking the wheel. It poured out of her, filling the car with its essence. Icy fear surrounded her, plunging her into darkness as if she were in the depths of a cave.

A tiny pinprick of light floated in front of her and slowly expanded. It built and built until she needed to shield her face;

the light obscured everything as surely as the darkness had. Her soul hovered above her battered body, spinning, gathering all the light to it.

As it returned to her, Nat noticed the blank spot, a missing piece, tiny as a chip in a piece of fine china. The darkness of the woods filled the car once again, the regular chirp of crickets and rustling of leaves returning. Her younger self stirred, moaning against the steering wheel.

She closed her eyes and waited for the connection to yank her, bracing to be pulled to her next destination. The sound of her body's steady breathing grew, combining with the rushing creek. Counting silently, focusing on the surrounding woods, she wondered how long she would be here, how much she would be forced to watch.

The girl's eyelids fluttered, the dried blood on her cheeks now gummy with tears and sweat. What she experienced that night was already gone from the girl's memory, a secret that would haunt her until this very moment. Tears streamed down Nat's face as she watched the girl, knowing what was coming for her when she woke up.

When she finally stirred, awakened by something dripping steadily onto her forehead, she would be in pain, enough that she couldn't really identify where it was coming from. Her head would throb, and she would wrench the car door open to throw up on the damp earth, a strange metallic burn coating her dry tongue.

Exhausted, the rushing of water and the dripping of gasoline would lull her back to awareness, and she would look over at the passenger seat to find it empty. There was blood on the dashboard, and somewhat dried vomit splattered on the floor below it, chunks of it suspended in a growing pool as the creek water flowed in and saturated the floor mat.

"Chris!" she would scream into the dark, the world

spinning, one sneaker filling slowly with cold water, the sock a withered and clammy second skin.

Nothing makes sense, nothing, nothing, it's time to wake up, I'm back at the park, back in the sun, waiting with the A/C up and I have a headache, that's all, just a little headache and none of this is happening.

She would wander alongside the flowing creek until she came across a small footbridge and a path. A couple walking their dog slowed as they came around the corner, proceeding with caution as the girl fell to her knees.

"Oh, my god!" the man said, reaching into his pocket, pulling out a phone.

He walked slightly backward, murmuring into it as the woman grabbed her by the shoulders to steady her. She took off her sweater and draped it over Nat's shoulder. Nat called out to the man, her voice hoarse.

"My brother...tell them I can't find him."

All of this was yet to happen and had already happened. She reached down and brushed her bangs out of her eyes, fingers blazing with the contact that she had been trying so hard to achieve. There were so many things she would have liked to hear afterwards, so many things she never got to say.

The car shifted slightly, groaning as something heavy landed on the trunk. She closed her eyes.

Giant hands burst through the back window, pebbles of glass imploding inward and surrounding her as she shrieked and lifted her hand to her face. The clawed hands once again latched onto her tightly, the searing burn tearing her inside out. The woods evaporated around her, melting away as she was stolen into the night.

The side of her face and the back of her neck still burned where it grabbed her. Lifting her hand to her cheek, a slippery flap of skin closed in on itself as it healed around a gaping tear.

It was dark, but the forest was gone. Her feet were on pavement once again, and she turned to orient herself as her eyes adjusted.

A bank of trees with a chain-link fence closed her in on one side, smooth concrete beneath her feet. In the distance behind her, the trickle of water wove its way through the night. She walked a little farther down the path and realized why it was familiar.

She hadn't recognized it right off the bat. She had always used the other side on her way to and from work.

Ahead of her, the overpass presided over her fate. The lamppost stood near the stairs, keeping its silent and useless sentry over the stairwell as someone approached in the dark. The footsteps stopped to reveal a woman standing at the bottom, hand on the dirty railing, staring right back.

It's me.

"Wait! WAIT!" she shouted as the harried footsteps echoed up the steps and she moved out of sight.

She thought back to meeting Gavin, the confusion that flickered across his face when she had accused him of following her.

It was always me.

She was drained; her efforts to escape taking their toll. Suddenly dizzy, she sat down to rest. She closed her eyes experimentally, hoping that she could catch up before it was too late. When she opened them, she breathed a sigh of relief as she sat on the neighbour's lawn.

Keys jangled in the still air, and she remembered nervously moving them between her fingers. She slipped on the wet grass as she tried to stand.

"Don't! Don't go in there!"

Her past self turned, and Nat reached out an arm, one last time. "Please."

Helpless, she watched as she ran up the steps and into the arms of another monster waiting inside. Her name hung in the air, someone calling to her from down the street. The inevitable overcame her, and she screamed at the unfairness.

It wanted me to see that night. It let me see.

She crawled toward the house, hearing a thud as her body hit the living room floor. In the ominous silence that followed, the front door cracked open, the tiniest sliver.

Motion and a flicker of light across the street caught her eye. Barb stood on her balcony, her cry of Nat's name lingering in the air. Instead of looking at Nat's front door, she was staring across the street, looking at Nat with such a sad expression that it made her ache.

Pulling herself over to the house, she heard the back door open and shut, saw someone enter the backyard from the side of the house. The rustling of bushes near the alley caught her attention, and she moved to the opening of the alley.

Brian's brother Darryl was crawling through a partition in the fence. As he stood, he pulled off a bloody t-shirt and placed it inside a plastic bag he pulled from his pocket.

Barb was coming down the street, and Nat followed her inside. Whether the brothers worked together or it was all Darryl, Nat didn't know, and it no longer mattered. Barb couldn't see Nat this time.

As she stood beside Barb and took in the bodies in her living room, she understood now what the creature was trying to show her. She knew it would keep her hopeless.

It will always happen this way.

53

HE BROKE THE SURFACE OF THE DARK WATER, sputtering and gasping for air. The cliff above him was a dark and jagged outline, jutting out through the sky as if it were cackling at him down below. Taking a moment to rest, he floated, trying to gather his strength. Every instinct in him told him to swim.

Where?

He could barely see and did not know what would await him wherever he reached the shore.

He was exposed, helpless in the water. Muscles burning from holding himself up on the rock face, his breath came in short, panicked gasps. Floating on his back to steady himself, gazing at the stars. The stars tethered him to reality after all of the unreal things he saw.

The water lapped gently at his face before growing stronger, more insistent.

Move.

The faint sound of a motor grew steadily louder, the most beautiful sound Chris ever heard. Maybe a late-night fisherman, or someone taking the boat for a spin before the summer months got too busy.

"Help!" he waved his arms wildly, spitting water as it swelled into his mouth, hoping their light would catch him.

He splashed his way toward the dark shape ahead of him as the boat cut its motor.

"*Help!*" he cried again, his voice shrill, his mouth filling up with water as the waves rose to flow over his face.

"Hello?" came the gruff reply in the dark.

Something touched his ankles, tenderly, feeling his skin, deciding if it would pull him down to join it.

Stop it. Kicking at the weeds, he focused on the boat, ignoring the tickle climbing from his ankle up his legs to his neck. *It's not real.*

"*Here!*" he tried again as the beam of a flashlight began a slow arc around the front of the boat.

Fingers grabbed his neck, and Chris spluttered as his head went under. He tried to scream again, but this time it burned, and he coughed as cold, black water filled his lungs. He scrambled for the surface, feeling it crawling inside him, reaching for something.

Chris raised his arms, hands splashing frantically above the gentle waves as his lungs burned with the torture of being so close to taking a breath. A light glowed from inside him, illuminating the watery blackness around him. Teeth and limbs held him there effortlessly as it fed, its face emerging in front of him, fully exposing itself to him for the first time. The inky water overpowered his screams, bubbles dwindling as he spent the last of the air in his lungs.

You can't come in.

The big, bad wolf didn't listen, though. Huffing and puffing relentlessly, it was gaining ground. As the light in the water dimmed, the brightness was stolen, sliding inside the monster. A glowing trail slid down its translucent throat to rest in its belly.

Chris could feel how many pieces were chipped away. He was trying to hold on to them, to himself, but he couldn't. The light was fading, a tiny glow remaining with him as the monster swam away.

Vision fading, he imagined himself being pulled away, down, down, down, overpowered by the peaceful blackness he floated in.

Hands pulled him up, yanking him from the water. He was laid on his side and coughed, a reflex. Water flowed from his nose and mouth, a stream he didn't think would ever stop. A firm hand slapped his back, and he took a surprised breath in.

Two men in flannel coats sat in the boat, grabbing him under the armpits to sit him up as his head lolled forward. A can of beer rolled around by Chris' feet, sloshing in the puddle that was growing around him as his sopping clothes drained, clinging uncomfortably to his skin.

"Oh, my god! Is he okay?"

"Does he fucking *look* okay?"

Chris tried to tell them he would be fine, to thank them for saving him. Panicking, he found he couldn't speak, couldn't move.

"What's wrong with his eyes?" One of them whispered, transfixed.

Chris thought of the piece that it left him with, throbbing painfully and stubbornly within, preventing him from letting go. There was so little of him remaining that he wondered what was left for the man to see.

"Jesus, just gun it, will you? The marina's just around the bend. We're almost there. We can dock there and call an ambulance."

"Kid. Hey, kid. Can you hear me?"

Yes.

"You're going to be fine, alright? Can you squeeze my hand?"

Yes.

He thrashed inside himself, kicking and screaming.

Let me the fuck OOOUUUUTTTTTTTTT!

A gurgle inched up his throat, drool mixed with lake water dribbling from his lips to coat his chin.

"Jesus. Hurry, man. He's breathing, but...I don't know."

His friend gave a low whistle. "Look at that bruise. He must have hit his head."

"Don't worry, okay, kid? We've got you. We're almost there."

No hurry. It didn't matter. The damage was done. Too much was missing, scraped out of him like leftovers into the trash. No one could help him now.

It left just enough to trap him here forever, flailing just below the surface.

54

Less than a year later, her dad moved back in. They were already talking about getting remarried next month.

We've been through the worst, Nat. All those things before, they just seem so trivial now.

She should be over the moon, a childhood fantasy come true, but she couldn't bring herself to be excited about this. A deep chasm opened between her and her parents, painful in a way that she couldn't explain.

Part of her was resentful of the anxiety, the pain, the guilt, the fighting, everything they had put her and Chris through. All of it was for nothing. It *was* nothing compared to how they suffered since, but it was something to Nat, was something to Chris.

That wasn't all it was. The feeling that they were united against her grew stronger every day; them versus their son's killer.

What her mom could never accept was that he *was* dead, in every way that mattered. Complete brain damage; a bunch of medical jargon, didn't amount to *anything* but that.

When the decision was made and they finally gathered together around his hospital bed, she was more than a little relieved, and even more ashamed. The evidence of her sins would soon be gone, and maybe they could move on, move forward together.

The thought held so much hope that every defence mechanism inside her was determined to crush it. Maybe she didn't deserve to be forgiven. Maybe this was the easy way out.

Chris was always staring at the ceiling, which usually unnerved her. Today, she was glad he wasn't looking at her, so she wouldn't have to imagine his eyes accusing her of what he couldn't say out loud.

On that day, they taped his eyes closed, and she was glad. Without those staring eyes, she could tell herself she was forgiven for all of this.

The doctor pushed some buttons, made some notes, looked at the time, and held Chris' pale wrist.

The clock ticked on, the doctor frowned, and Chris' raspy breath filled the room.

It doesn't always happen right away. It can take some time.

Time marched on. Nothing changed that day, or the day after, or the week after that.

A miracle, Mom said.

The doctor grunted, a noncommittal sound, but he couldn't explain it.

Breathing in, breathing out, the clock endlessly marching on, Chris stayed. Periodically the conversation turned to ways to make him comfortable, an option that her mother never wanted to think about.

He'll suffer, Nat.

He already is! This is torture for him. It's torture for US.

Her dad sat with his arms folded across his chest. She saw the glimmer in his eyes, a spark, a hint that he knew what she was saying was true. A deep pit opened inside her, dread crawling out and filling her. What was happening to Chris was wrong; she sensed it.

Dad. Please. This is the last thing we can do for him. Please. He isn't there. Not anymore.

He looked away, but didn't speak. Mom jutted out her chin. *He's gone right now. I know that, but this is a sign. Maybe he'll come back. We won't know unless we try.*

For how long? A year? Two? Ten? Nat narrowed her eyes. *What's the expiry date on miracles, Mom?*

Mom burst into tears, Dad rushing to console her. She stood in front of them, that newly formed little unit against the cause of all their family's pain. Her tears flowed freely, but it didn't matter. That tiny hope of moving on was snuffed out by the first rattling breath after the ventilator was removed.

Months went by, and nothing changed. She woke up every day in the same reality. The fight with Meg gave her clarity; she knew what she needed now.

I can't stay here and watch.

She already found an apartment and a job. All that was left was to say goodbye.

Just like always, he was staring straight up. His pupils were unnaturally large, and the whites were red with the drops they placed to help keep them lubricated.

"Meg and I had a huge fight. She said I was being an asshole. In a nutshell. She wasn't wrong."

"This is hard to say, Chris, but I think...I think she's right. I know if I stay here and watch this happen, I'll never pull myself out." Her eyes prickled but remained dry, as if she ran out of tears through all of this. She watched for any sign that he might hear her.

The vacant eyes gave no hint of acknowledgement, the life behind them lost forever. Straining in the oppressive silence of the hospital room, she longed to hear his voice, to hear him forgive her, her constant comforter. The quiet sounds of the hospital, squeaky shoes, ringing phones, murmured conversations, and quiet sobbing remained unbroken.

"I found a place. A couple of girls are renting out one of their bedrooms. Maybe I'll save up, go to school?"

Why am I telling him this?

She supposed it was because she needed to tell someone, but she didn't want anyone to talk her out of it. A suitcase of her essentials was all she needed. A single box of carefully packed mementos sat in the back of her newly purchased car, a beater of her own with no memories attached, purchased from the classifieds with the money she'd saved for college fun.

She wondered if the day would come that she could bring herself to unpack them.

There was a note folded into a tent on her bed, and she idly wondered how long it would take them to find it. The note promised she was safe, that she would call them when she got there.

She wasn't so sure they would care.

"I'm sorry," she said. There was nothing else to say.

"Goddamn it," she sighed, her face hot with unshed tears.

The ticking clock grew louder, pulling them into its hypnotic orbit as the silence pressed down on them.

His hand shot up, violently grabbing her chin and drawing her face towards his, her lips squeezed into an expression of surprise. Dry fingertips dug into her cheeks, forcing her to look deep into those dark eyes, to take in the nothingness in his enlarged pupils. His eyes grew shiny and yellow, the black orbs slimming down into slits.

Opening his mouth wide as the monstrous eyes fixed their gaze on her, sharp teeth pried their way out of his shiny, opaque gums to gnash in her face. Time froze, her open mouth a dark chasm that her screams couldn't escape from as she pulled back in terror. Spittle splashed against her face as it roared. Pulling herself free, she fell backward into the chair at his bedside.

Her eyes blinked away from sleep to find nothing had changed; Chris' hand sat still in hers, the skin coarse and thin. The clock ticked on, his breathing even and unchanging.

Just a dream, she thought as she pushed herself up from her slumped position in the chair.

A chill spread across her face, and she was surprised to find it wet. *When did I start crying?*

"Chris?" she asked, afraid to blink and miss it.

She sat there for another ten minutes, waiting for a sign. Shaking, she gave his hand a last squeeze and kissed his forehead.

She stood in the hallway, rubbing her face as she pulled on her sweater. The elevator dinged its cheery arrival, and Meg stepped off.

Pivoting on her heel, Nat walked the opposite way down the hall toward the stairs. Meg's eyes drilled into her, and she knew this was it. Now or never.

Talk to her!!!!!

Nat wiped the last of the tears from her face and kept walking, never once looking back.

July 2014
Things Unseen

55

It was resting, watching through Darryl's eyes. They both needed to be careful. It was a relationship, and a delicate one at that. Darryl gave it a home, a life, and it gave Darryl what he always wanted.

Darryl came into the house on his own, letting himself in with the key that Brian always hid. Annoyed that Brian wasn't there yet, it nudged him inside. A petty, mortal worry, it was beneath them, and they just wanted to get this over with.

They were supposed to be here to clean it out, to keep mementos. Remembering attachments is such a pedestrian activity, and neither of them really cared to take part. The only reason they were here was out of concern for some things it saw in Brian lately, a sort of calm heroism beneath the surface that might prove dangerous.

Brian proved very useful to them. He was a pawn, someone they could blame it all on if the situation called for it. Darryl voted to get rid of him years ago, but in truth, it silently thanked Brian for his ability to talk Darryl out of getting carried away at the wrong time.

Darryl proved to be a valuable host, one that required less

force to help it gain what it needed to survive, but he could never pick the right time or place. He was a master manipulator when it came to Brian, but he was an overactive puppy, always making a mess. Even now, Darryl was foaming at the mouth inside, itching for a chance to stretch his legs.

It sighed. Darryl was eager to please, but could be so impulsive. It spent so much time and energy just feeding itself, and keeping Darryl in check was exhausting these days. Keeping Darryl satiated was not high on its list of priorities.

Calm down, Darryl. It will happen soon enough.

Gently guiding Darryl to the basement, a sense of peace washed over them. It liked it down there, could put Darryl's hand to the wall and sense the squirming, screaming pieces of soul entangled in the roots that grew in the dirt outside. It knew it was smart to stock up for winter, but releasing them just before it finished was taking its toll.

It sighed, longing for just one full meal.

There was mail piled up on the little table inside the door, with a business card on top. Squinting in the low light of the room, the name printed on it came into focus. *Ricky Johnson.*

Brian's friend. Darryl supplied helpfully. *He was at the funeral. He's in real estate.*

Digging through the pile of papers, they discovered more. Brochures, pamphlets. *Preparing to Sell Your House. Tips for a Great Open House. What Your Agent Can Do for You!*

Darryl laughed, relieved to be unburdened by Brian's whining. *Great! Let's throw everything out, just burn it down! I'm getting tired of Brian dragging us down.*

It slapped Darryl.

Hard.

He retreated to a dark corner inside, remained silent.

We can't leave this house, Darryl.

Why not?

It balled Darryl's hands into fists, cranky at being disturbed from its rest to deal with this.

We need the backyard, Darryl. Don't make me say it again.

Warmth rushed to their cheeks, Darryl flushing at the shame of being inattentive to its needs. What was below the ground in the backyard was inconsequential to Darryl, simply leftovers, rotting garbage, but to his guest, they were a lifeline, an anchor.

It explained to Darryl what happened with the girl who left it for dead, how it was stuck with the boy it killed, right beside this very house. That it took the boy completely before the girl escaped was the only reason it was still here. Without the host that killed the boy, it needed to eat so much more frequently.

It talked about the girl as if it loved her, the same way it loved him. Darryl thought she was an idiot, a stupid, spoiled little girl who was ungrateful for such an incredible gift. It had spent some time in the early years gathering its strength inside of Darryl, visiting nursing homes and retirement communities.

Darryl signed them up for some community volunteering opportunities with seniors in case they were ever caught. Greedy in those early days, it gulped down sometimes three or four a night. It often left them there, still alive; couldn't afford to arouse suspicion with too many deaths in one place. Age and disease easily explained their confusion and memory loss the next day.

Once it was strong enough, it tipped the scales with Eva. Darryl's mother was droning on about how she hated the Halloween fireworks and wouldn't shut up about it.

"Do you see?" It hissed in Darryl's ear as she chattered incessantly; the plan materialized between them without him saying another word.

After they devoured Eva, they felt wonderful, strong and

pleasantly powerful. It grinned and danced inside of Darryl, basking in the blood like a fine wine, feeling Eva's soul twist inside.

By the next morning, the feeling was already fading.

It continued on with scavenging, topping it off with sips from Darryl's mother here or there. The neighbours on the street could also provide a light snack in a pinch. He stalked through the neighbourhood like a vampire at night, all the while the monster inside cringing at the thought that it needed to stoop so low. Darryl loved it, the creeping, the power he held over others. He couldn't understand what made it so upset.

I might as well be eating rats, it snarled.

One night while Darryl slept, a feeling crept over the monster, Eva nearing the end of her usefulness inside of them. It crept into the yard, to where it buried Eva under the tree. As it grew, the limbs spread, the trunk becoming stronger, with the slightest tint of blood red in its dark bark. It placed its hands over the grass, feeling the pulsing roots below.

Eva's luminosity emerged, scorching the grass. Eva wailed, futilely clawing at the earth that suffocated her. The small piece of her it scavenged returned to her remains, the skeletal ribs surrounding it as it glowed, trapped there. Her sole purpose now was to sustain it, becoming part of a growing stockpile it needed, just in case. It savoured it, feeling the power surging as it fluttered weakly, slowly fading until it was next to nothing.

Don't worry, it reassured Darryl. *That won't be for centuries.*

Darryl breathed a sigh of relief, but it wasn't satisfied. Centuries of this, of lowly scavenging, it wasn't what it was built for. Darryl knew if he wanted this to keep going, this ride they were on together, there was only one answer. One that would satisfy them both.

We'll add more.

Over the years, many souls joined Eva in the backyard. The hunger abated with each one, the gap between meals growing, but it always came back. Stalking senior citizens became an activity of the past. They were both happy about that, Darryl wanting more of a challenge, the old people sleeping helpless in their beds an affront to both of their abilities.

Just a bit of the mother's soul here and there when there wasn't a full meal available was enough in between.

It thought Darryl might show signs of dissent and push back a bit at that, at least question it, if it was his own family. To its delight, it found it underestimated the depths of Darryl's curiosity, his fascination. He would have been right at home with the first surgeons, poking and prodding without regard for the person housed inside the flesh.

Darryl thought of his mother's eyes, begging by the time it slurped out the last of her essence. It could practically hear the air in the straw when it had done so.

It tasted sweet, like a berry. It brought Darryl to the foreground, wondering if this was the moment that Darryl would turn on him, any familial loyalty realized, and struggle.

Darryl simply licked his lips inside as he observed her dead and vacant eyes. He touched her papery skin and hair, pocketed a button from her nightshirt.

"You can't let him sell this house, Darryl." It broke them both out of the walk down memory lane, as intimate as two lovers replaying their home movies on an important anniversary.

Brian was weak and pitiful, and had caved so easily. *A personal best*, Darryl bragged, cocky as always.

56

"Darryl?" Brain called as he came in through the front door.

His voice boomed through the house, highlighting its emptiness. Darryl wasn't there. He sighed.

Why am I not surprised?

Brian always hated the main entrance. There was a short dividing wall to separate the dining room from the entryway. With the pony wall on the other side, it basically formed a tunnel.

One at a time, his mom used to yell, and he lost count of how many times he accidentally tracked mud on the rug because Darryl had gotten impatient and shoved him forward into the living room to get in.

Kicking his shoes off, he dropped his keys on the rickety, ash-covered coffee table and slouched down on the couch. He leaned back into the cigarette smoke-infused fabric, sneezing a little at the smell. He hated they could never convince their mother to quit smoking, but as she got sicker, he thought it was kinder to leave her with something that made her happy.

It was hard to be in this house alone; the silence talked to him whenever he shut his eyes. His mother's presence was there. The horribleness of her last weeks as she finally wasted away was a stain that he didn't think any amount of washing could get out.

After another twenty minutes, he stretched and got started without his brother. It was bright and cheery upstairs, the summer sun that filled the room sitting high in a cloudless blue sky. As he trudged down the stairs to retrieve some boxes, the gloom grew, wrapping him in shadow. He flipped the light switch as he entered the basement suite, but the room remained in darkness. He frowned, trying a few more times as an experiment. Sighing, he felt his way across the room to his desk to see if his lamp worked.

The darkness grew, and he rubbed his arms as the temperature seemed to drop. He made a note to turn up the thermostat when he went back up. Now that she was gone, he could crank it up a little more. He caught his foot on his desk chair and cursed, hands feeling for the lamp.

The tiniest of movements caught his eye, something shifting in his oversized armchair in the corner. The subtle glint of eyes hovered there, and he held his gaze, afraid that he would blink and it would take that tiny fraction of a second to lunge.

As he watched, more and more came into focus. The shining eyes were bright but sunken against the pale high cheekbones below it. Teeth appeared to protrude from the flesh that was retreating away from its mouth. It was a walking skeleton, someone barely clinging to this life.

A breath hissed quietly but powerfully from the corner, like the air out of a punctured tire.

A death rattle.

He was spurred into action then, looking away to turn on the light.

"Darryl?" His brother came into view, and he breathed a sigh of relief, chalking it up to a trick of the light.

As he appraised his brother, his initial relief fell away, and he frowned. He saw the basic facial structure underneath, the spacing between the eyes identical, the prominent jawline now covered with soft and healthy flesh. Darryl's eyes, his flinty gaze, were the same as always.

"Jesus," Darryl eyed him skeptically. "What the hell is wrong with you?"

"Nothing," Brian shook his head. "I didn't know you were here. I thought I saw..."

"Saw what?" Darryl snapped, cutting him off.

"Forget it," Brian mumbled, turning away from his brother to take off his coat.

Brian didn't like when Darryl got this way. The next one was never far behind when he got impatient.

"Got any plans this weekend, Bri?" No one but Darryl ever called him Bri, always Brian.

It should be a term of endearment, but not the way his brother said it, like he had a surprise and couldn't wait to show him.

"Like what?"

"Like maybe seeing a nosy friend?"

Brian's hand paused on the edge of the closet door. Most people wouldn't even have noticed his reluctance.

Darryl wasn't most people.

Careful, Brian thought, steadying his hand and hanging his coat before he spoke. The cold metal hangers clanged softly, a nearly imperceptible warning to him to tread carefully. He composed his facial expression before he turned to look at Darryl.

"What..."

Darryl held up Ricky's card, the brochures, his thumb

indenting the bottom of the pile of shiny paper as he struggled not to lose his temper.

"You thinking of buying a place, Bri? Or maybe," Darryl leaned forward, the conversational grin on his face hiding the satisfaction at catching Brian in a lie. "Maybe you're thinking of selling."

Darryl's face froze in that special calm, the one Brian knew masked a viper underneath. The brochures began crumpling under the pressure of Darryl's controlled fist; the sound of crackling across the room as loud as a campfire.

"Just some information. What can that hurt? Ricky thinks we can get a lot of money for the house."

"*Ricky* thinks?"

"Yes."

That slow, villainous smile climbed Darryl's face again. "Are you insane, Bri?"

"What?"

"Have you forgotten about the little surprises in the backyard? Our little..." he leered, "vegetable garden?"

Brian lifted his head to meet Darryl's eyes. "How could I?"

"We can't exactly have someone deciding that they want to dig it up and put in a pool, can we?" Darryl was so smug, probably wondering how Brian got this far; he was just so stupid.

Brian floundered, trying to come up with a rationale that would make any kind of sense.

"I swear to God, Brian..." Darryl sighed impatiently, a parent with a toddler who just knocked over the garbage can for the fiftieth time.

If you think we're going to Heaven, you've got another thing coming.

The thought laced its way through Brian's head, just another that he kept at bay for so long. They were coming more and more these days. Flashes of rebellion left him feeling warm and reassured him he still knew right from wrong. Before he could stop himself, a barking laugh escaped from his mouth, and he tried unsuccessfully to turn it into a cough.

A dangerous flush crept up Darryl's cheekbones. He looked at Brian, those eyes still gleaming.

"What's so funny, Briiiiiiii?" He dragged out the name, mouth frozen and slack, tongue protruding slightly as if his video was buffering. "You think you're gonna start telling me what to do?"

"No, of course not," Brian backpedalled, stammering as he tried to put the pin back in the grenade. "I just...we could really use the money, Darryl."

"I'm sure you'll come up with something." Darryl waved dismissively, once again leaving the management of those insignificant little things like food and shelter to Brian. "You'll take care of your brother as long as I need you to."

Brian's blood ran cold.

"What do you mean? You *are* my brother. I *do* take care of you."

"Do you?" Darryl's eyes looked up again, less feral this time, cold and calculating.

Bristling that it was even a question after everything, Brian forgot himself.

"When's the last time you worked, Darryl? Do you even know how much your rent is anymore?" He didn't want to talk about the other help he was providing, not right now.

"Huh," Darryl seemed to consider it, thinking back to when he last received a paycheque. "Well, maybe you should walk away. Maybe you don't want to help me anymore. Is that what you're saying, Brian?"

Brian didn't know a lot of things in this world, but he knew that until he figured out a way out of this mess, he needed to stay useful to Darryl. He knew what happened to people when they outgrew his needs, when the cat got tired of the mouse.

Darryl's face melted into sadness, but it was an exaggeration, an imitation of what a sad person looks like.

"I'm soooooorrrrrrry, Brian," he drawled, jutting out his bottom lip in an exaggerated pout. "I am. It's just too soon after Mom, that's all. I'm just not ready to let this house go. All the memories, you know? Maybe there's another way. Maybe we could get a tenant, or something?"

Brian eyed him skeptically, not wanting to pick a fight, but he didn't like the eagerness that spread across his brothers features, the way he was jiggling his knees up and down with excitement at the idea of a captive prey living right upstairs if he ever got itchy.

"Sure, I guess we could maybe think about that. I'll tell Ricky I won't sell."

Darryl narrowed his eyes. "I think you mean *we* won't sell. Don't you, Brian?"

Brian's stomach flopped. Darryl didn't know that their mother had left the house solely to Brian, and for now, it was his only ammunition.

"Yeah, of course."

Brian's gaze moved down the arm of the chair, and for the first time, he wondered if something was medically, physically wrong with his brother. His hands seemed like talons, fingers digging into the nubby old fabric so hard that his knuckles were white. Periodically losing control, his chin would list to the side in an odd, stony expression.

With any luck, he'll have a stroke.

Guilt and fear warred within him, and his fingers trembled as he reached for the phone inside his jacket pocket.

"Come on, Brian! Can we at least talk about this?" Ricky's voice boomed through the phone, far too loud.

Brian kept his eyes trained on Darryl, trying to keep a poker face.

"Okay, sounds good. You're right. No point in meeting this weekend."

"What? Brian…"

"No, I'm fine. Just a lot going on lately, you know? With mom and everything. Lots of paperwork."

Confused static made its way through the phone, but he and Ricky were old friends. Ricky knew Brian, but, even more importantly, he knew Darryl. A long pause stretched over the line before Ricky replied, his voice lowered nearly to a whisper.

"Okay. We'll talk at Flanagan's like we said. Saturday at 8, okay?"

"Sure. Yeah, it's too bad I won't see you. Next time, maybe. Mmm hmmm. Okay. Bye."

He hung up before Ricky could say any more. Darryl continued to stare, and this time, Brian knew he wasn't imagining things when he looked at his face and saw the beast underneath.

"Happy?" Brian asked, looking at his shoes.

Darryl smirked. Of course he was. He was always happy when Brian was miserable.

Brian had a shot here. He had no ties. Hell, he didn't even own a credit card. He could change his name. Get the hell out of here.

He felt good for the first time in a long time. Great, in fact. Hopeful.

57

THEY WENT BACK UPSTAIRS AND PACKED BOXES, Brian watching Darryl stealthily as they moved around the house.

Darryl's companion was not so convinced Brian was the same pushover as when they had started.

When Brian casually mentioned that he was going to call it a night, Darryl didn't argue. He went to his car and drove off like nothing was wrong. Pulling around the corner, he parked partway down the block. He cut his headlights, watching the mouth of the cul-de-sac in his rearview.

Fewer than ten minutes went by before Brian's car pulled out and turned in the opposite direction to the main road. It leaned forward, whispering about deception to Darryl, not about to be fooled.

He must think I'm stupid. Darryl's fingers squeezed and popped on the steering wheel as he slowly pulled away from the curb to follow, staying a few car lengths behind. When he turned down Greenview, he figured he knew where his brother was going. That idiot and his watering hole.

So predictable.

He circled around the building to park around back so that Brian wouldn't see his car. Grabbing a heavy flashlight from his glove compartment, he walked down the side street, past a filthy dumpster, and across the street. He took a seat on a bus stop bench slightly down the block.

He waited, and when the pub's door closed behind Ricky, and Darryl squeezed his hands into fists.

He froze there, rage building and throbbing over the next few hours as they ate and drank inside. Ricky was likely filling Brian's head with all kinds of nonsense. It returned to the surface, feeling Darryl's control slipping away, minute after minute.

"Let me handle this one, Darryl."

He considered, not liking the tone of the voice that hissed inside his head. It lacked confidence in him, and he so badly wanted it to believe in him.

"Don't you trust me?" His voice sounded so tiny and weak, and he hated himself for that.

A barely perceptible pause cut through Darryl, piercing him like a violent knife.

"I know you want to, Darryl, but I also know how humans feel about..." hesitation again, this time because of the disgust of rolling a word around its tongue *"...friendship."*

He was locked in place, unable to move his limbs. It was getting harder in the last few years to take back control, but he didn't complain.

It knows best.

This time, something changed. He felt small. He sensed he had something to prove, but he didn't know how if it didn't let him.

"He's not my friend. Not for years." Darryl trembled at its doubt of him.

"Let me stay," he whispered. "Please."

A woman at the bus stop gratefully stood as the lights of

the bus roared through the night toward him, casting a glance in his direction as it pulled up.

It didn't answer, keeping its grip tight. Darryl waited, and then beamed as it let him stay, fingers tightly wrapped around him but not dragging him under.

58

RICKY SCOURED THE WALL OF BOOTHS AS HE walked into O'Flanagan's. It was crowded as usual on a Saturday. As the crowd parted, he spotted Brian hunched over, seated in the far corner.

They fell out of touch here and there over the years, but Brian was like an overeager puppy, waiting patiently day after day and running to the door as soon as it opened even a crack. Brian was way too trusting, and it screwed him time and time again.

This time, Ricky wasn't about to let that happen.

Whenever he saw Brian, Ricky always contemplated how his life could have turned out if he followed the path he was on back then. He considered himself successful enough. Not a millionaire or anything, but comfortable by his own standards. He made all the right choices, did everything he was supposed to, never rocked the boat. Sometimes it worked for him, sometimes it didn't, but it kept him out of trouble.

Whenever he say Brian, Ricky remembered that everything he had could be taken away in an instant. Poor decisions, bad investments, bad mortgage rates…all of it could lead to one moment that turned everything you knew upside down.

That's why when Brian shied away from selling the house, Ricky pushed.

Taking in Brian's posture at the table, Ricky's heart sank. He seemed beaten down, and Ricky knew from experience that when Brian got like this, he let himself get bullied.

Maybe this time, Ricky could use that.

It was a good time to sell. The neighbourhood went to shit in the last fifteen years, and investors were looking for homes they could flip at a profit or rent out to tourists over the summer. Ricky thought back to when Brian called and told him he wasn't leaving town after all, that his mom was sick. The economic poison that ate its way through the area began around then, Brian's helplessness infesting the house and working its way outward.

Ricky didn't know exactly what the problem was, but based on the phone call they had the other night, he guaranteed it had something to do with that deadbeat brother of his. There was a sharpness in Brian's voice over the phone, a warning, pleading not to make things messy.

Brian's brother was always an asshole. The three of them knew each other since they were kids, and whenever there was trouble, Darryl was right there on the periphery, always too smart to be right in the middle of it.

Ricky knew he was part of the problem, never speaking up, always too scared of getting in trouble himself. Whenever Brian confessed to some misdeed or other, Mrs. Edwards would look surprised and disappointed, simply shaking her head and walking away.

His adult eyes looked back on it differently now, seeing she was relieved she didn't have to dig too far to find out what happened. Maybe she could chalk it up to Brian being a troublemaker, just boys being boys, and it meant she didn't have to think about how there was something wrong with Darryl. She was a single mom, struggling to make ends meet, but sometimes Ricky thought they would have all been better off if she kicked his ass off to military school.

On the surface, it was the good-natured shit gone wrong kind of stuff that guys did. It wasn't anything that harmed anyone, not until the incident involving a few too many beers, some firecrackers, and Ricky's left pinky.

But then there were those times Ricky knew were on the verge of *Something Else*. He wasn't sure even now how to describe the feeling, other than some primitive instinct telling him there was no turning back once the can of worms was opened.

Darryl's eyes would go hooded and dark, the wheels turning on some part of the plan that Brian and Ricky weren't privy to.

The thing was, Darryl always *observed* people, looking at them like you would a bug under a microscope, as if he was gathering data for some grand experiment. Personally, Ricky didn't want to be anywhere near Darryl when the experiment was performed. Watching the fascination on Darryl's face as the blood gushed from his hand, losing his pinky was as close as he ever wanted to get.

The day he decided he didn't want to hang out with them anymore was etched in his mind, a permanent part of who he was. Brian and Ricky were about fifteen, Darryl just about to get his driver's license. A neighbour came by. It was just them alone, Darryl away with their mom at a dentist appointment or something. The neighbour, Mrs. Biddle, the very definition of the sweet old lady next door, had come by and asked about her cat.

"I haven't seen Whiskers in a couple of days. I'm a little worried since he usually comes back every night. I know he sometimes wanders over here. Have you seen him, Brian?"

The hope in her eyes, the trust she had in Brian, put Ricky on edge.

Brian said no, but there was something in his eyes that told Ricky he knew more than he was saying.

"What was that about?" Ricky asked after she left.

Brian avoided eye contact and shrugged.

"Dumb old ladies lose track of their shit sometimes, I guess."

Ricky heard Brian's mom on more than one occasion raging about how the "goddamned devil was crapping in the snapdragons again!"

It wasn't unreasonable for Mrs. Biddle to assume Whiskers was there.

Looking at Brian's face, Ricky knew without a doubt that he was. There was only one reason Brian would lie, and Ricky was pretty goddamn sure whatever happened to the cat, Brian wasn't the culprit.

The thing with the fireworks happened a few weeks later, and it was a good excuse to say his mom didn't want him there any more. Brian came over occasionally by himself, but Ricky never set foot in their house again. He didn't have any meaningful interaction with Darryl for years. He saw him at the funeral, head held high, a small, peaceful smile on his face that gave Ricky the creeps. Avoiding Darryl until the end, he politely shook his icy hand on the way out. Darryl barely recognized Ricky, giving a stiff thank you before leaning into him.

"How are ya, Ricky?! Gosh, it's been ages!"

Tightly gripping Ricky's hand, Darryl leered as his fingers moved to touch the stub where his pinky had been. Ricky ripped his hand away, unable to stop himself from recoiling in disgust.

He shuddered as a table shifted and grunted on the floor by the bar, bringing him back to the conversation at hand. A glass fell from a tabletop and shattered on the floor, and a couple broke out into a loud argument over whose fault it was. The server in their section bolted over, murmuring as he plied them with some free food. Ricky glanced down at his hands, self-consciously covering the remaining stump of his finger with his opposite hand. He could still feel Darryl's skin snaking across his, as if claiming the missing pinky as his own.

"Come on, Brian! You don't have to do what he says anymore! He'll be fine. He's smart, he'll land on his feet." The thought hovered there between them, unsaid. *He always got what he wanted.*

Maybe not this time, though. This time, they knew something that Darryl didn't, and was a rare step ahead of him. That house belonged 100 percent to Brian, free and clear. The last thing his mother did in this world was try to make it all up to him. Her lawyer called him, saying he had explicit instructions to tell him the contents of the will in person.

Without Darryl.

Brian called Ricky almost immediately afterwards, asking what he thought he could get for the house, and if he could help him find something farther north.

Brian still didn't say a word, barely grunting hello when Ricky arrived. He looked like he would stay glued to that seat all night if you let him. Loneliness was a dangerous thing. It ate at people, made them desperate. Ricky wondered if he was about to cause more trouble for Brian than he meant to. Desperate people fit right into Darryl's wheelhouse.

Ricky didn't think that he ever wanted to be caught in that guy's comfort zone.

A server came by, placing plastic-covered menus in front of

them. They were still damp, the bottom one suctioning slightly to the table as Ricky picked it up.

O'Flanagan's was one of his favourite spots, had been since college. People bitched a lot about there not being anything healthy on the menu. In Ricky's opinion, if you were going to a pub and wanted to order something without the word 'fry' right there in the name, what were you even doing on your night out?

"Look, you called *me*, man! What was the point of sneaking around like this if you were just going to say no?"

Brian looked uncertain, staring at the table as he slowly twisted his beer bottle back and forth. Beads of condensation slid off of it, methodically drenching the cardboard coaster below. He picked at it, soggy brown flakes sticking under his thumbnail. He flicked them onto the table as they built up.

"Brian. This is your chance. Take the money and make a fresh start somewhere. Just leave and never look back."

"I can't do that," Brian murmured, looking at Ricky with an innocent expression that made him want to cry.

He grew up with this man, seen him systematically broken down by the shadow of a dad that wasn't around, a mom who expected too much, and a brother who kept him down at every turn. Brian was trapped, a prisoner in a hellhole everyone knew was escapable.

Everyone except for Brian.

It was now or never. Ricky knew beyond any doubt this was his last shot at saving Brian. He took a deep breath and forged ahead.

"Brian. I know this hasn't been easy for you. What happened to your mom? It was awful. I can't even imagine how that must have felt. Watching someone...watching *her* just waste away like that. But she left it to you! That means something, okay? It means she didn't want Darryl to have it."

His own mother's death was mercifully quick, a heart

attack. It was easier in some ways. No pain, no worry, just here and then...gone.

Not like Mrs. Edwards.

The woman clawed and fought for every free minute. She seemed convinced that if they didn't know what was wrong, nothing was, and she just had to wait out the bad patch.

In the end, she was completely unresponsive, but Brian refused to put her in hospice. There was nothing anyone could do, so they hired a nurse, who did little other than watch and wait. It drained Brian dry, financially and emotionally. The funeral was almost a month ago, and even now he was still checking his watch, his phone, as if expecting a call about a past due bill or getting ready to run off to an appointment. It was like she was still here, lingering just out of view.

Brian remained silent, fidgety. He finished destroying the coaster and was now carefully scratching his fingernail across the label on his beer bottle, grating it one little strip at a time. The pile of scrapings on the tabletop grew, a little brown mountain from the coaster with a small scattering of snow on top courtesy of the bottle's white label. Ricky desperately wanted to reach across the table, but Brian didn't like to be touched; it just wasn't his style.

He didn't even shake a single person's hand at the funeral, for Christ's sake. Don't scare him off.

"Brian, honestly. How the hell can you even think about staying in that house after that? It's all you'll think about every day. I know you think you don't have anywhere else to go, but you can sell. Take the money and find somewhere new. This is your chance, Brian. You need to take it."

He gambled then, sliding across the round booth. Brian looked up as Ricky clapped him on the shoulder encouragingly, a skittish deer in the headlights.

"What are you so afraid of?"

Brian trembled under his arm. Ricky slowly removed his

hand, taking a deep breath. *Christ, he really is an abused animal.* It was like being at the pound picking a dog to take home. They're all so defeated, resigned.

"I'm trying to help you, man." He paused, unsure he was getting through. "*Hear* me this time, okay?"

Brian gave him a wavering smile. Eyes brimming with tears, he wiped his hand on the sleeve of his grubby denim jacket, trying to dislodge the cardboard bits that had gotten stuck on the cuffs. A deep, jagged breath burst from his lips, breaking his silence.

"Okay, Ricky. Okay. I'll sell."

Ricky was stunned.

"Really? Oh man, that is fantastic. Really. I'm so happy for you! I'll help you, okay? I bet we can get you an amazing price on it. We might just need to fix up a few things."

"A few things?"

"Well, maybe more than a few things." Ricky laughed.

They had a pleasant time after the elephant in the room left the building. A few rounds led to a few more, way more than Ricky was planning on. Hell, it was way more than he did in years.

Ricky inhaled his food while Brian only picked at his, running the same fry through a pile of ketchup until it looked like it had met an unpleasant end.

"You gonna eat that or drown it, Bri?"

Brian forced a laugh. He stood up, averting Ricky's eyes.

"Let's have one last round. On me, okay?"

Beaming, Ricky saluted him with his half-empty drink.

"Done. Man, Brian. This is going to be huge for you. A fresh start."

Brian headed to the bar, shuffling in that mild-mannered way that he had. Pausing, he turned back to really look at Ricky, even more introspective than usual.

"Hey, Ricky?"

"Yeah, Brian?" His friends' eyes were clear and focused, a weight lifted off of him at a decision made.

Ricky took a sip of his beer as he waited for a response. It was a little unnerving, to be honest, but he wasn't complaining. This was an enormous step for his friend. Maybe Brian could step out of his family's shadow, pull himself out from under Darryl's thumb.

"You're my best friend. You know that, right?"

Ricky was taken aback. Sure, they had a history, but they only talked maybe once every couple of years, tops. *That is the saddest fucking thing I have ever heard in my life.*

"Sure, Brian. I know."

Brian held Ricky's gaze a moment longer, nodded, then headed to the bar. As always, he kept his eyes on the floor, mumbling apologies to people's feet as he slid by.

BRIAN RETURNED WITH THE BEERS, AND THEY clinked their bottles merrily, listening to their favourite golden oldies on the juke box. Ricky would not deny him a little revelry, but boy, was he going to feel this in the morning.

"Woooo! Guess we aren't kids anymore, huh, Brian?" He heard the slur in his words, slightly embarrassed. *Guesssss weer nah kiddzzzz no more, huuuh Brian?*

The conversation wound down, and they sat in companionable silence. He was flushed, his forehead sweaty, all signs of a good night in a warm bar. Ricky knew this must feel great right now, but it was also a vast change for Brian, and a lot to process. *I should let him off the hook.*

"Hey, man. Great catching up, but I have some stuff to take care of in the morning. I should probably head out." He stood and stumbled a little, grabbing onto the table. "Damn, had a couple too many. Let's grab a cab." *Lesssss grab a cab.*

"Wanna share?" Brian asked. "We could both just crash at your place, if that's cool?"

The calm smile left his face, a fleeting sober realization taking hold. Brian never took him up on the offer of crashing at his place. Several times over the years, he tried to get him to move in.

"Come on, man. Cheap rent, and you can keep me company!"

Between girlfriends, Ricky got sentimental, falling back on the camaraderie of friendship and 'bro out' as the younger guys at work liked to say.

He was kicking himself for missing it. All the extra rounds of beers, the insistence on paying. He didn't see Brian was avoiding leaving.

I wouldn't want to be in that place either.

"Sure, man. Whatever you want."

They left the pub, the night air slapping their faces, a chilly respite from the close air inside. Ricky lost his footing on the curb, taking him back to his college days. He laughed, wobbling slightly.

"Damn, those beers went right through me. I've gotta take a piss." Ricky looked back at the pub.

Now that they were outside, it seemed a long way back, the tiny, crowded bar bathrooms too much of a hassle to navigate.

Ricky jerked his head toward the gap between the buildings, away from the door.

"It's crazy in there, man. I'm just gonna go in the alley."

Brian tilted his head back and laughed, the first honest to goodness laugh Ricky thought he'd heard from him in a long, long time. *Glad I could entertain.*

"Wow, I haven't pissed in an alley since I was twenty." Pulling a battered flip phone from his pocket, he gestured to the entrance to the alley, waving his friend along. "You go ahead. I'll call for a cab."

Ricky hoped Brian's mood would stick, that the visit did him some good.

I really shouldn't have waited so long.

He whistled as he made his way down the backstreet, the sound ping-ponging off the brick walls above him until it escaped into the sky above.

59

By the time Ricky and Brian came out of the pub, Darryl was seething.

Rage came off him with such strength, the monster was amazed they couldn't feel it from here. Brian was smiling, his hands deep in his pockets as he rocked back and forth, shoulders hunched against the chill in the air. Ten years were shaved from his features, as if he didn't have a worry in the world.

Disrespectful liar, the accuser inside him hissed.

The words were venom, matching the intensity of his own feelings. Vision darkening, he saw red as Brian's smile grew.

Brian pulled out his phone and frowned, tapping at the power button. Ricky said something, shrugged, then headed down the alley beside the pub. After a moment, Brian turned back inside.

The battery. It was draining way too fast for months. Darryl asked him why he was such an idiot, just to get a new phone. Brian mumbled something about not having the cash, all while eyeing Darryl's own smartphone.

Darryl grinned. This was the universe again, telling him this was his path, this was all meant to be.

As the heavy pub door heaved slowly and groaned shut behind his brother, Darryl crossed the street and made his way down the alley. Thunder roared somewhere in the distance, and tiny patters of rain bounced off his jacket. Another sign of the natural world washing them clean, allowing them to keep going.

Ricky was mumbling to himself, the sound of a steady stream of water hitting the bricks. As Darryl drew closer, he realized what he was doing.

Disgusting, it said, and Darryl felt his hands twisting around the flashlight. *Hold on tight.*

In his haste, Darryl tripped over a tin can, trash that hadn't made it into the bin. Darryl turned, but it was too late. The savagery of his hand was quick, brutal, with a strength he knew he wouldn't be able to muster on his own. The flashlight hit Ricky's head with a hollow *thunck*, sinking into the bone as if it was soft as butter.

Fascinating, really, how very little force it took to do so much damage to a human being. Blood streamed down past Ricky's cloudy eyes, and he lifted a hand weakly, as if it would convince his assailant not to land a second blow. It was like watching a movie or playing a very realistic video game. It was fun; it was entertaining, but he wanted more.

When will I get my turn?

They returned to the car parked just down the alleyway, watching his hands fumbling in the trunk for the tarp. He asked this often, never knowing when it would let him play too, and hated how he sounded like a whiny child.

It grinned, a drooling sneer, and gestured to the tire iron in the trunk. Salivating at the opportunity, Darryl returned to stand over Ricky. He grabbed Ricky's wallet, snorting that so many of his killings could be so easily explained away. The police would say it was a random robbery, senseless. Wrong place, wrong time, like so many of the others.

He didn't even keep the money, burning their wallets, their purses, their IDs, as soon as he got the chance. The rewards of this plane weren't what they were trying to achieve.

Shhhhhhhhhhhh, it comforted him. *We have all the time in the world.*

Tipping their head back to feed, Darryl enjoyed the ride, the feeling of euphoria that it shared with him, so much more than any average serial killer could ask for. He was above those childish games; they were above all that.

As it sat back to relax, full, Darryl brought the tire iron down again and again, each wet splatter against Ricky's face and grinning teeth solidifying its trust in him.

60

THE VOICE OF THE OPERATOR CAME THROUGH THE ancient, grimy payphone, one of the last he knew of in the whole town.

"That'll be about forty-five minutes, sir." Her trepidation came through the phone.

She expected him to rip her a new one any second now. The air in the pub was too close and sweaty. Juggling the receiver from hand to hand, he unzipped his jacket.

"No worries!" he smiled, shouting over the din of last call to be heard. "We can walk."

Her relief that she finally came across a happy-go-lucky drunk was palpable.

"Thank you, sir. Have a good night."

Walking suddenly felt like an adventure, and he looked forward to getting back out there, breathing in the damp air. Everything felt new, more possible, somehow. Not standing up to Darryl sooner was going to cost him if there was any kind of afterlife, he knew that.

In the meantime, maybe he could enjoy this one, just for a second?

Reaching into his pocket for the thousandth time that night, he thumbed the note in his pocket. The pills had come from his mother's medicine cabinet, crushed them up on her good china platter and folded into the paper before he left, a makeshift envelope.

Getting up from the table to order the beers, he felt guilty for lying to Ricky, knowing he would never sell the house.

Why not make him happy? Why bother disappointing him one more time?

He dumped the powder into his bottle, planning on one last toast, a quick nightcap he would chug at the last minute as he was saying goodbye to Ricky. Just park somewhere quiet by the water, turn on the radio, fall asleep and never wake up. The note took Darryl down with him.

Simple.

He never believed in signs before, but when the beer bottle broke, his plan went out the window. It was a second chance, and he clung to it.

Shame flared in him as he thought about how little it took for him to let himself off the hook. Doing up his jacket once again, he braced himself against the night, expecting to see Ricky waiting on the sidewalk, maybe sitting on the curb, grinning up at him through the hazy, pleasant spell of one too many beers.

Instead, he found his brother's car idling by the sidewalk, Ricky nowhere to be found.

"Hiya, Brian!" Darryl leaned over and yelled through the open passenger side window. He was soaked with rain, water from his wet hair running down into his eyes and over his lips. "Need a ride?"

Brian peered in through the rainy windshield, watching a slow smile creep to Darryl's dangerous eyes. The first time he saw this expression on his brother's face, Darryl was telling their mom he didn't have any idea where the neighbour's cat was.

Haven't seen it in weeks.

Darryl ducked back in and pulled directly in front of Brian, stopping short. Something shifted, thudding loudly against the trunk.

Something heavy.

Brian's heart cracked.

"It's your mess. You clean it up."

Darryl sputtered, unsure how to handle this act of mutiny. He walked away and the car peeled away from the curb, as angry as its driver.

This was it. The final sign. He needed to plan while he still had time.

The only way out now was to burn it all down.

<h1 style="text-align:center">61</h1>

Ricky tried pulling himself off the wet, cold pavement and lost his balance, his feet slipping on the damp grass of someone's lawn instead.

What the hell?

He didn't remember leaving O'Flanagan's. Thinking back, the last thing he could bring to mind was a vague memory of the worst headache of his life and a car coming toward him.

Did I pass out? Christ, my head is pounding. He lifted his hands to his temples, trying uselessly to rub away his hangover.

I need a greasy burger.

He wrenched his eyes open, his eyelashes cemented to his skin. Everything was spinning, and he shut them fast, resting his head between his knees to avoid throwing up.

A kid stood across the way, looking as if he was also in the last place that he expected to be.

"Are ya 'ven olll ennnufff ta be inna bar, kid?" Ricky slurred as he staggered. "Jussss had a li'l too much. Nah, drivin tho...ma frennns grabbin a cab."

The boy looked around, as if surprised he'd even noticed him in his state. "Oh. Well...that's good, I guess."

"I'll go fine, immm. Roun' front."

"Ummmm, okay."

What happened to him in the alleyway was already nothing more than a fleeting concern. Getting home was his priority; anything else could wait.

Brian's house came into focus down the street. *I could use his phone. And his bathroom.* He pulled himself up, feet barely moving at a shuffle.

When he reached Brian's front lawn, he turned to find that he was alone on the street. The kid *disappeared*.

What was that kid's problem, anyway?

Acting like he never saw a guy trying to take a leak before.

62

SLICK AND TWISTING IN ON ITSELF, IT WAS ANTSY, squirming inside of Darryl.

Brian outlasted his usefulness; that was why it suggested renting the little house in the first place. A semi-observant tenant coming across something that Darryl planted would be all it would take.

Nevertheless, Darryl was extremely uninterested in the labour of finding a tenant. The beast inside agreed, shying away from the pedestrian work of mortals.

Let Brian pick his own hangman.

Sitting out on the deck he'd built with his own two hands, sun resting in a clear blue sky as he looked out over the grass, Darryl definitely wasn't complaining. To the average person, it looked normal.

Tiny droplets of water clung to the smooth, lush blades in the rays of morning sunshine like a closeup on a goddamn nature channel. To Darryl, the true beauty of the yard remained of the people below his feet. Some were skeletal by now, whereas some, like Ricky, were fresh, a squishy feast for maggots.

He cultivated all of it and cared for it, loved it as he would a child.

There were a few Brian didn't even know about. Those were his prizes, his best work. When Brian wasn't around, he could really be himself.

Darryl considered himself a visionary, the pair of them destined to be legends, icons. What happened when they killed together was a work of art, the way the glow emanated from the body, splintering before entering his mouth and nose. The first time he hesitated, and the thing inside pushed, annoyed.

Darryl scrambled to explain he just wanted to savour it, to remember the moment for the rest of their lives together.

I want this, he assured the doubter inside himself. *Show me what comes next.*

Invisible hands wrenched his head backward, and his mouth fell open to accept the offering. The pieces of her fractured soul had entered him, feeding his new partner and leaving Darryl with a euphoric glow, a high that he knew he could never replicate with anything in the uninspired life he led.

Light poured through his throat, and he half-expected to choke. Instead, it was like he *was* in the air; he was everything to her and she to him. Her wants, needs, fears, hopes, regrets, everything she ever felt or heard or saw all flowed through him, more intimate than sex. He was taking everything from her, not just her body. It was like reading someone's diary with zero fear of being caught.

There was no fear at all. Nothing could ever hurt him now that they were together.

It held Darryl's head patiently, operating its muscles as it swallowed.

Like a ventriloquist dummy.

The unwanted thought intruded on the fond memory, and he batted it away. Every once in a while, poisonous thoughts would course through him, fear that they weren't a team making his limbs numb, making him want to pull the covers over his head and sleep for decades.

There were times it seemed to disregard him, considering him a passive participant, but that couldn't be true. He was important, it told him so. When they first came together, it praised him, complimenting his fantasies and darkest thoughts.

You have a special quality, Darryl. Just what I am looking for.

He had never looked back since that day, repeating the compliment to himself over and over. He had courage now, courage to do what he was meant to do, what he *wanted*, but could never have done alone.

I know you want to get your hands dirty, Darryl. No one will understand you like I do.

I am a god. After all, it wouldn't be here without his body. He felt a warning rumble, and he backed down. It was getting harder to stay in his lane, to know his place.

Kicking up his feet, he crossed his ankles and rested them on the low railing, sighing contentedly. A bottle of beer sat beside him, sweating in the sun. Condensation sliding down in rivulets to pool on the rustic wooden table next to him.

Paradise, he thought. The day stretched on as potential tenants came and went.

"Hey, Darryl?"

Opening his eyes, he squinted against the sun, suddenly so much higher in the sky. The bottle in his hand was warm; the damp glass long dry. *How long have I been out here?*

He had to pay attention, not about to let his brother pull a fast one. He wanted Brian to know that he was watching, especially after the Ricky fiasco.

Whenever they took Brian down, Darryl wanted him to know that he lived so long because he willed it.

"There's just one more person, okay? You can go home if you want."

"I'm fine here. Thanks," Darryl replied.

His tone was clipped, welcoming no arguments. Pushing his sunglasses higher on his nose, he kept his eyes trained on the yard, the tree just another monument to his greatness. Brian nodded, tight-lipped, and went back inside.

A few minutes later, a car pulled up out front. The engine stopped, and he heard something in the stillness—a scratching—coming from under the deck. Sitting up in his chair, he stood still, waiting for the sound to repeat.

Nothing but the sound of a bird overhead remained, and he tried to relax once more, pulling his hat back over his eyes and making a note to check later to see if some stupid squirrel had gotten itself stuck in there.

Another scraping, long and drawn out, interrupted him as he was about to doze off. He pulled his hat off, staring around the yard as a moan reverberated through his brain. Looking out over the once tranquil expanse of green, the grass appeared to be shifting in a wave, as if a billion worms were making their way across the lawn, just under the surface. The moans became wails as the earth boiled over and an endless plea escaped.

"Please!" the voices cried in unison. "Please, please, please, please, *please, please, please...*"

The noise reached a fever pitch, threatening to pierce his eardrums. Slinking toward the house, his feet were suddenly frozen, telling him to hold still. A hot flush of shame spiralled through him as he realized the thing inside him was delighted.

Shut UP, Darryl. LISTEN!

He took a deep breath in, closing his eyes and trying to pinpoint what the voice was talking about.

A low, steady hum, was hidden below all the noise. The trapped voices whispered, coming to the surface as he concentrated. Whatever it was called out to him, but he couldn't make out what it was saying.

A fluttering deep inside himself was awakened, and he staggered back to his chair. It was a hunger pang to his partner, but to Darryl, it was love, tugging at him, pulling him closer, even stronger than Eva, his first.

She's here, she's here, she's here...

Whatever was causing it, he wanted to harness it, to break it.

Find her.

Darryl torpedoed through the doors and down the hallway to stand behind Brian as he sat sipping at a cup of coffee and looking at some kind of paperwork on the dining room table.

He could feel...

"*Her,*" he whispered, the euphoria of this moment threatening to overwhelm them.

This was something they both wanted, that they would do anything to have. Whoever it was, he knew beyond any doubt she was his chance to prove himself.

Brian jumped, pushing his chair back and sending papers swirling down to the floor as he caught sight of Darryl behind him.

"Jesus! What?" he asked, a wary expression creeping into his eyes.

People can never hide what they're feeling. Those eyes told Darryl everything he needed to know, that his partner was right. Brian was up to something.

"Beat it," Darryl said, his own eyes fixed on the door.

The thing inside of him twisted in excitement, could barely contain itself. Brian seemed happy to get away from Darryl, backing quietly down to the basement.

With those lessons in mind, he took a stabilizing breath, hand on the doorknob. The second the knock broke through their reverie, he whipped it open, a sunny expression plastered across his face to balance out his eagerness. Surprised at the speed at which the door opened, she took a step back.

"Hi!" he said, extending his hand. "I'm Darryl. My brother is busy right now, said I could show you around, if that works?"

"Oh," she said, tentatively reaching out to grip his hand, shifting her bag on her shoulder. "Well, that's fine with me."

Emotions swelled inside him. A symphony. A crescendo.

The one that got away.

Darryl was intrigued, but her loss was his gain. Why anyone would want to get rid of this feeling, this being, this *power* was beyond him. His eyes narrowed for a moment, wondering just who she thought she was.

Jealousy is ugly on you, Darryl.

"I'm Nat."

He took it, determined not to let his envy of her get in the way. The hand was soft, and remarkably small, too small for the feelings it aroused in him. *In us.*

"Darryl," he said, shaking her hand vigorously. "C'mon in. It's not much, but I think you'll like it."

She smiled shyly, her hand awkward and limp in his as he continued to shake, mesmerized. He could tell his smile was charming today, and he swelled with pride at his success when it really counted. He wasn't always able to retract his shark teeth fast enough. Dropping her hand, he stepped aside, gesturing inward with a flourish.

"After you."

An unmistakable purr rose within him, overpowering the cries of anguish floating to him from the yard.

Welcome home, Nat.

MARCH 2015

MEMORIES

63

Brian sat in the basement, cloaked in the room's gloominess with its tiny windows.

Normally, he turned on every light down here, didn't like the way the shadows crawled in the shifting sun, the dampness seeping into his pores amplified as it thrived in the dark. Tonight, the darkness was necessary.

Darryl was here nearly every day for the last month, watching him as he moved around the house, getting it ready for the new tenant. A stream of sudden helpfulness came as endless visits to bring new tools, fresh paint, a friend's lawnmower, an extra truck to take trips to the dump.

Maybe he was being paranoid, but Brian parked his car downtown, prepared to walk after he made the call. The only times Darryl did things for other people, unprompted, resulted from covering his tracks or getting what he wanted.

Darryl wants me isolated, alone.

With nothing but time to think lately, Brian was forced to come to terms with everything since that first time, the stupidest decision he ever made. The memory of that night on the mountain came rushing back to him, their first time, as vivid as if he was reliving it all over again.

***

I REALLY LIKE HER, MAN. I WANT TO ASK HER OUT. She's not like other girls I've dated. She's way too good for me. I need a reason to talk to her. Tell her you lost your dog. She'll go look for it, and I'll come down holding him. I'll be a hero, man!

Brian had never seen Darryl like this before, blushing and excited. From the day he picked him up from the bank and pointed her out through the glass, there was something in his eyes Brian never saw before. Maybe this girl could turn him around.

Still, there was something that made him hesitate.

"Are you sure about this?" he asked as they pulled into the parking lot. "Isn't it going to be kind of weird when you tell her about it later?"

Darryl scoffed. "No way! She'll love it. She'll think it's super romantic. You just don't know what girls like. You know," he smiled cruelly, "because you've never had a girlfriend."

Brian couldn't argue with that.

The lot just a few minutes up the hill was empty, the tourist season done for the year, any class trips all done for the day. Everyone was busy tonight, with friends and parties. He left the truck, Darryl planning on waiting a bit before following with Jinx in tow.

"Why not just come with me? You can hide a little further up."

Darryl looked at him as if he had two heads. "Because what if the dog barks, idiot?"

Brian nodded, then wandered down the road leading to the falls, watching out for Eva.

Everything seemed to work as planned. The pity in her eyes told him his nervousness put her at ease, and it wasn't even pretend. She moved awkwardly down the hill, crouched down to coax a dog that wasn't there. She must be a really nice person if she was willing to help out a stranger. As she worked her way down the hillside, clicking her tongue occasionally, he waved Darryl over.

"Good luck," he whispered.

Darryl grinned, his usual bravado back, the assumption that the plan worked, and she was already his written across his face.

Same old Darryl, and Brian knew in that moment he would never change. Why should he? Things always worked out for Darryl.

There was a bend in the road just past the trail to the falls, a tree stump off the beaten path. He came here a lot when they were kids, a place Darryl didn't know about. A secret place, a place to hide. It was where Ricky told him that Darryl really freaked him out, and he didn't want to come over anymore.

Sudden exhaustion overwhelmed him as he thought of how close he was to leaving that all behind him. He got the courage and told Darryl a couple of weeks ago that he found a new job.

"It's just one town over. I'm leaving next month."

The confession erupted from him in a whoosh.

"Are you?" Darryl asked thoughtfully, the small amount of joy telling him that Darryl had a secret.

Brian didn't know what to say to that, and decided nothing was the safest route.

He was going to tell their mom next, but didn't know how. At this point, he wasn't sure why *Darryl* hadn't. Always looking for easy ways to make Brian look like the asshole was just another bad habit his brother never grew out of, but for whatever reason, he'd said nothing.

Mom made dinner for them, inviting them over for a family evening. This was his night, his chance before Darryl could say anything.

That plan promptly went out the window as their mom told them she was sick while passing the butter. They weren't entirely sure what it was yet, but she was going to need some help. Probably nothing major, getting to and from appointments. Brian knew it was bullshit, that she was minimizing like she always did to protect them.

Looking across the table, there was the same smirk painted across Darryl's face that he always had when he won and Brian lost. He already knew; she already told him.

Darryl knew Brian wasn't going anywhere.

"Sure, Mom," he volunteered, Darryl's gaze unwavering as he spoke. "How about I stay here for a little while and we see how it goes?"

Perking up in relief, she maintained her composure, still holding up the front that this was no big deal.

"Okay, then. Thank you, Brian. Why don't you stay in the basement for a while? Then you have your own space."

Darryl said nothing, just continued to chew. The awkward silence grew until Brian cleared his throat, picked up his fork, and choked down a mouthful of dry potatoes.

He scrubbed his rough hands down his cheek to swipe away the tears before he returned. A crack sounded behind him, and he spun, searching for the source of the sound. Wings flapped and a large black crow cawed above, but otherwise the woods were still. It was getting dark, and he was surprised at how he'd lost track of time.

Wandering back down the path, he took his time, expecting to find two people in conversation, Jinx nipping at their heels.

The path was empty.

He walked over to the side, eyes adjusting to the dark leaves in the rapidly growing darkness.

Eva was lying in a heap on the ground, Darryl nowhere to be seen.

Skidding to a halt by Eva's crumpled body, he could see she was still breathing. The side of her face was a bloody mess, and his trembling hands flapped over the blood, unsure whether he should touch her.

She groaned, eyelids fluttering before drifting shut again.

A sound erupted underneath him, a small shuffling in the dirt. He froze and looked at his feet. The ground seemed to shift, as if someone were walking through it.

The wind picked up, leaves and dirt pummeling him like bits of shrapnel. It was violent, unexpected, and he lifted his arm to cover his face with his coat. As quickly as it came, it was gone. The woods were silent again, though the dark made its peacefulness seem much more ominous. The last of the sun disappeared over the lake, and he shivered, as if whatever happened here made it so.

The crackle of wood underfoot got his attention, the sound of someone shuffling toward him.

"Darryl?" he called, and his brother wandered out of some nearby brush.

The skeletal limbs of some felled trees hid him from view, the dark between their dead branches sheltering him.

Darryl looked detached from his surroundings, like he only just gotten there. "Hmmm?"

"What the *fuck*, Darryl?"

Darryl brought his attention to Brian slowly, unwilling to tear his eyes away from the girl. He didn't seem overly concerned that the girl he wanted to be with so badly was lying unconscious at his feet.

He's in shock.

"She slipped. I startled her, and she fell, hit her head," Darryl responded, his speech sluggish but monotone.

Rehearsed, Brian thought, shivering slightly in the dark.

"On what?"

Darryl looked around, gesturing to a rock with a shaking arm. The hard, flinty grey of the stone sat above the soft leaves, shiny with blood.

"Jesus! We have to..."

Darryl interrupted him, seeming to snap to attention. "Look, I'm stronger than you. I'll lift her and take her to the truck. Give me the keys."

Brian handed them over blindly. "Are you crazy? We shouldn't move..."

"Look, she's already waking up."

He was right. Eva moaned again, moving slightly this time.

"What...?" she murmured.

Brian leaned over her. "Hey! Are you okay? Can you move?"

Disoriented, she squinted in the dark. "Who are you?"

"Do you remember? You were helping me look for my dog?"

Recognition filled her eyes as she sat up slowly. "Do you know what day it is?"

"Halloween."

Brian nodded, satisfied.

Darryl helped support her from behind.

"I'm going to take you to the hospital, okay?" Eva's eyes fluttered in pain as she tried to nod, and Darryl lifted her.

Brian moved back up the hill, adrenaline pumping as he ran. It was getting dark, and it was cold. He noticed no one on his way back.

When they made it to the parking area, Jinx was barking in frantic welcome from the backseat. Brian paced outside of the truck, supporting Eva's feet as Darryl lifted her in.

Darryl got in the driver's side and shut the door. The truck roared to life.

"I'll take care of it," Darryl yelled, leaving Brian in the parking lot, open-mouthed and abandoned.

It wasn't until later that he wondered why the dog, the adorable part of the hero plan, was still in the truck.

By the time he wondered how Darryl knew Eva would be there, it was already too late.

Brian walked home in the dark, taking about half an hour to get the rest of the way down the mountain, nearly an hour to get home.

His truck was parked in the driveway.

Alarm bells were going off in his head. *This isn't right.*

"Brian?" Their mother opened the door as he reached the driveway, the television blaring behind her. "Why are you so late? I thought you were going to help me hand out candy."

Brian was sweating, dizzy, as the events of the evening came crashing down on him. "Sorry. Is Darryl here?"

She gave him an odd look. "No. He just unloaded some supplies out to the shed. Said to give you back the keys and thanks for lending him the truck."

Brian trembled. "Well, come in, honey. Have some candy. There's lots left, most of the kids came earlier." She picked up the remote to mute the television, passing him the large bowl of bite-sized treats.

He unwrapped a cheap chocolate coin and crammed it into his mouth. The waxy lump was sickly sweet, refusing to melt on his tongue. Swallowing before he gagged, he moved past her to the basement door.

"Well, thanks, Mom. I'm going to head downstairs."

Both their heads snapped back toward the yard as a crack

rang out. All sound was suspended for a moment, sucked from the air. After a moment, more and more pops and bangs erupted while the sky lit up with white and orange.

"Fireworks," his mom tutted. "This city. Do we have to have them for every occasion? It used to be a special thing, now it's all the time. Takes some of the magic out, you know?"

"Sure, Mom. Goodnight."

"Brian..."

"Yeah, Mom?"

"Everything okay?" Sweat plastered his cap to his forehead, and he rubbed his damp hands against his jeans.

"Yeah, Mom. Everything's fine. Just tired, I promise. Long day."

Jinx emerged from the hallway, whimpering.

"C'mon, boy," Brian called, patting his leg. Jinx moved closer to his mother, refusing to go down.

She chuckled.

"Guess I'll have some company up here tonight, if you don't mind?" Leaning forward, she gave Brian a hug. "Love you, sweetie. Sleep well."

He banged down the stairs, flipping on the light and half expecting Darryl to be hiding in the shadows. The basement was empty, but Brian knew Darryl was here. He knew it because the first boom didn't sound like the others.

The television turned back on upstairs, at a volume that would cover a plane crash. He sighed, hearing aids just one more thing he was going to have to pay for, one more appointment to manage. A sudden twinge of guilt moved through him as he pictured her on her recliner up there, probably already fast asleep, waiting up for her sons having taken its toll. Dread mounted within him as he moved up the stairs. Opening the side door below the kitchen, he slipped into the backyard.

Darryl sat on the ground, next to the body. Brian

shuddered at how quickly she had gone from a person to a corpse in his mind. Glazed blue eyes stared up from her face, fixed at a point beyond Darryl.

Darryl was grinning, staring through Brian as if he were of no consequence. That look told Brian all he needed to know. This wasn't an accident, or some sort of blind, selfish panic Darryl would snap out of in the morning.

This was Darryl knowing that the fireworks would begin at exactly 8 o'clock.

A shovel was already being pushed into Brian's hands, and a finger directed him toward the rickety shed in the corner.

"If you don't, Brian, who knows what will happen? Do you want to go to jail? Your DNA is all over her, just as much as mine."

Brian's mouth hung open, not even sure what to say. Darryl grinned wider at his discomfort, looking up at the house, the lights dim and the TV blaring, flickering eerily in the darkness.

"She's dying, Brian. You want her to die with her sons in prison? No one to take care of her? She'll rot here. No one will find her for days. Do you really want that for her?"

Of course he hadn't. *What kind of monster would?*

By the time the sun came up the day after Eva's death, a patch of dirt had appeared next to the shed, a tree planted in the poisoned ground.

"For you!" Darryl said with a flourish when mom got up for the day. "Something to give you a bit of shade when it's hot."

Darryl removed the shed when Brian took their mom to a doctor's appointment a few days later, saying it was an old hazard, ready to blow over and hurt someone. Instead, he built the patio high, putting in French doors so that she could walk out of her bedroom onto a chaise once spring began.

"For you!" he'd beamed once again. "This way, you can

relax with a cold drink in the summer. Nice and close to your bed for when you're not feeling well."

Darryl had built up that backyard, and he was a great caretaker to the cemetery he had built.

A tight lattice surrounded the space, making a small door with a padlock to store their gardening tools. Brian remained cautious, but a part of him wanted to believe that maybe it was a show of remorse, that he could relax the tiniest bit. He hung onto that wish until he heard Darryl creeping around under the deck late at night.

Sometimes it was the sound of a shovel being dragged to the lawn, or Darryl talking to himself. On the worst nights, muffled, weak cries permeated his window. Brian would roll over and go back to sleep, a pillow clamped tightly over his ear as he squeezed his eyes shut. He would pretend it hadn't happened, that the freshly laid squares of grass the next day were just another nice surprise from Darryl.

The mornings after he heard the telltale scratching and scraping, he would come upstairs for breakfast, pouring cereal for them and trying to catch her gaze. Brian had looked for signs that their mother had known for years. She had to have seen that it was unlike Darryl to be spontaneous or thoughtful, or at the very least that Brian was drowning.

After he moved back in to help out, she was unable to hide the severity of her decline. She was more than just a little tired, sometimes sleeping up to fourteen hours at a clip. She would lie down for a nap and he'd come home from work hours later to wake her up on the couch, stiff-limbed from not moving all day. How long that had been going on, he didn't know. She would shrug him off whenever he asked, stifling yet another yawn. The doctors had run every test they could think of but never did figure out exactly what was wrong. Every specialist they had seen was still guessing and poking and prodding until the day she died. Eventually, her immune system weakened to the point that she was mostly confined to the house, a walking textbook of symptoms with no diagnosed disease.

Darryl had manipulated him, to be sure. Over and over again he told himself he was thinking of her, but the deep and nasty root of it all was that he'd been scared to be punished for something Darryl had done yet again.

Resentment simmered in him when he moved back in, not just for that, but for all the years she had seen things when they were younger and chosen to look the other way. There was something missing inside of Darryl, something beyond simple narcissism. There was no way Mom had been blind to that all these years.

Brian led a lonely life, but she never questioned it. Darryl always had a million friends, dates, all of the things that Brian longed for. Brian kept to himself, unable to bring himself to lure anyone into this circle of hell with him. The only thing he could do was protect their mother from the truth, telling himself for years that's what he was doing. Now she was gone, and he still hadn't done what he knew was right. Blaming her had been easy, and he'd used his mother as an excuse for too long.

In her last years, after the disease had spread but before it had taken her ability to form a coherent thought, he sometimes caught her looking at him. They would be sitting as they did most nights, in companionable silence, watching endless game shows on the satellite channels that Brian paid for.

"What?" he'd asked, alarmed, the first time it happened. "You need something, Mom?"

Shaking her head, she reached out to touch his face, an unusual act of affection.

"Are you happy, Brian?"

"Sure, Mom. I've got everything I need."

They both knew that wasn't an answer, but the moment

was gone, and she never pushed it. The resentful piece of him whispered that she didn't really want to know, that it was too late to fix it. To the end, she had hung on tight, and he sometimes wondered if seeing him happy in some way would have let her go in peace. After she was gone, the most he could hope for was that she had died never knowing the full extent of what Darryl had become. Over the years he built up this idea in his mind, that once she was gone, it would be over, that he could escape, but he had been so naïve.

He could never escape himself.

THE POLICE HAD OF COURSE COME TO ASK HIM about Ricky. They had figured out that he was the one that Ricky had met with the day he had, as they said, gone missing. He told them they had gone their separate ways, that Ricky had said he was going to walk home.

"He was really drunk, wanted to get some fresh air. The cab companies were all backed up. I called Yellow Taxis, around 2 in the morning." Darryl had watched him from across the kitchen table, nodding along, a director as Brian played the role of innocence to perfection.

The art of a good lie was something they both mastered long ago, and Brian knew that they worked best when the truth was sprinkled in as much as possible. Because he'd been working out of town a lot, telling Darryl that he was going to be away this weekend was easy. He'd spent the day getting his small number of affairs in order, papers gathered in neat piles on his desk. The phone was in his hand, fingers ready to dial.

Running his thumb over the digits, tracing their path, he wondered what he would say when he called. This was it, now or never. No more excuses. He would make the call then sneak around back and down the alley if he needed to.

The compassion in his friend's eyes when they'd sat down for that friendly beer clawed at him, the stabbing pain of realizing that Ricky was dead because of him burning freshly again. The guilt had kept him up that night, winding its way up from his guts to his brain, whispering away between his ears ever since. The phone remained in his hand, quiet, his thumb hovering over the 9.

He's gone now. Gone because of you. Because you waited so long. Gone gone gone. Dead dead dead. Never. Coming. Back. Your fault your fault your fault.

He dropped the phone, sending it clattering into the corner. *Coward.*

"Shut UP!" Brian screamed, overcome with sudden fury as he hurled the lamp that had once sat at his mother's bedside against the wall. The porcelain base exploded against the wall, pulverized bits clinging to the wall as shards scattered around the room. Dropping to his knees, he wept in the dark.

A door slammed into the stopper spring upstairs and footsteps trudged inside, heavy boots making their way up to stairs and across the kitchen floor Their passage stopped right above him, waiting in the quiet.

A tiny creak on the basement landing made him jump, unexpected after the heavy thudding steps upstairs. Light, fast steps began padding down the stairs, stopping in the dark doorway.

"Darryl?" he called, snapping the switch to illuminate the stairwell. The light blinded him, and he moved back as a shadow flickered on the stairs, someone moving by the adjoining door to the kitchen.

He closed his eyes, and when he opened them again, the shadow under the door was gone. He shook his head, trying to clear it as an empty feeling spread through him. Sometimes he forgot to eat, lost in his own world.

"Darryl?" he asked again, mouth dry, a little less sure this time. The door at the top of the stairs clicked open, beckoning him to join the party. He grabbed the baseball bat propped up at the bottom of the stairs and began a slow assent.

"You there?" He called out as he neared the top. Placing a flat palm on the door, he shoved it to swing open.

He leaned into the dark kitchen, listening.

"Nat?" he whispered, unable to believe that it hadn't occurred to him that the most likely person to have slammed their way into the house at this hour was the person who lived here. He shut the door, suddenly conscious that this would look very unsavoury if she happened to see him standing at her open kitchen door. As it latched behind him, the light in the stairwell flickered and then plunged him back into darkness.

A hand fell onto his shoulder, accompanied by a familiar voice. "Hiya, Brian!"

Memories began pouring out from a secret room at the back of his mind. The door had been quadruple-bolted, police tape on the outside, chained from the inside, several pieces of furniture shoved against it. Brian saw that the door was ajar, and there were things moving around in there, hulking horrors backlit in shadows.

This voice couldn't be here, had been taken from the world not that long ago. He whirled to see Ricky standing behind him.

Backing slowly down the stairs, afraid to take his eyes of his dead friend, Brian debated meekly. "You're not real."

Ricky grinned, his face pulling tightly on one side where his cheek was caved in. Above it was nothing but a swollen lump, a glistening substance smeared all over his skin all that remained of the eyeball. The muscles didn't seem to be co-operating any more, his eyelids drooping and his jaw slack. He seemed somewhat offended by Brian's reaction. "Sure, I am!"

Brian reached the bottom of the stairs and spun away, facing the wall, willing everything to stop. More forcefully, with a confidence that he didn't feel, he raised his voice once more.

"Not. REAL!"

Ricky attempted a smile with his ruined face again, pops and cracks travelling softly through the air as the bones in Ricky's face shifted and ground against each other. Drool tipped out of the corner of his mouth as he spoke. "Then who you talkin' too, Brian?"

Brian's mouth flopped open, unable to accept that this was what became of a good person when he'd died.

"Why are you here?" Brian asked.

"To say goodbye," Ricky said. "I can't go yet. Not until it's stopped." Ricky looked worried then, as if his next thought had never occurred to him before. "IF it's stopped."

"What do you mean? What Darryl did? "

"I'm sorry for what's going to happen, Brian. I really am. But you chose," Ricky whispered. "None of us should be in this mess." As the words left his lips. he vanished from the doorway. The light flickered back on, humming slightly at the top of the steps.

I'm losing my mind. It wasn't the first time the thought had occurred to him, and he knew that it wouldn't be the last. Slamming the door with hands clammy with sweat, he began to methodically pace the room, checking into corners and closets as if Ricky might be there, ready to pop out and yell "Boo!"

Another thump rang out, above him again. He raised his eyes to the unfinished ceiling, standing stock still as the floor above him began to squeak as someone...*something*...moved across it.

There was no doubt this time that someone was upstairs. *Nat?*

Overall, she was a quiet tenant, but damn, when she came in, she made no attempt to hide it. She would drop her shoes on the floor as she pulled them off, slamming the door shut behind her. Vibrations would jiggle his television and rattle the pens in the cup on his desk, the signal that she'd made it home.

The thumping upstairs stopped. He stood perfectly still, neck tipped back as if watching the ceiling would make a difference. A sporadic jangling in the corner drew his attention, causing him to draw a sharp breath in as he swept the dark corners of the room for movement. The ringing got louder, the merry song moving closer to him, and he tripped over his own feet backing up to the door. It was so out of place that it took him a moment to understand what it was.

A bell.

With shaking hands, Brian grasped the handle, pulling the door inward and letting the light from the stairwell flood into the room.

At the foot of Brian's bed sat a small orange cat with a tiny collar, the light bouncing off the golden bell that stood darkly against the white patch on its chest. The cat cocked its head, sizing him up, and then leaped to the floor, bolting across his feet and up the stairs.

Whiskers, an unwanted voice reminded him. *You know his name was Whiskers. It was a he, remember?*

Brian flinched as the memory struck him. It was safer when everything was hazy. The only way he made it through year after year was pretending that these things were happening to someone else, like he was watching them on the news. As long as he kept the details fuzzy, it was just a terrible dream, something he could snap in and out of.

Forgetting was survival.

The cat remained at the top of the stairs, staring at him. As Brian lifted his foot to climb the first step, it slunk around the corner and up the last few stairs leading to the house above. The dividing door resting on its latch made him pause; he was sure he'd pulled it shut. Before he could grab it, the cat (*Whiskers Whiskers Whiskers*) pushed against the door, disappearing through the crack that appeared pitch black against the stark white paint. The tinny sound of the bell swaying on the bright red collar faded down Nat's hall and then stopped abruptly, mid-jingle, as if it had vanished into another dimension.

Raising his knuckles, he rapped them against the slightly open door.

"Nat?" he whispered. *Why was he whispering?* "Nat?" he called again more forcefully.

The unoccupied quiet of the house pushed back at him as he opened the door wider. His nerves exploded as the light in the stairwell behind him clicked off once more, immersing him in the darkness punctuated only by the dim streetlight that made its way through the curtains.

Time was standing still, as if what he decided next was a defining moment. If he stood in this darkness forever, he wouldn't have to worry about anything.

Tap. Tap. Tap.

Feeling along the wall for the light switch, he moved deeper into the kitchen, heading toward the sound.

"Nat?" he tried again, his mouth and throat dry. It was as if all life had been sucked out of the world. He swore that even the crickets outside were gone, their song cut short by whatever was happening in the pitch-black night. The floor whimpered softly under his cautious step, giving him away, and he froze, planting himself, heart pounding as the sound pierced the still air.

He gasped in the dark as a chair moved across the floor, just ahead of him. It hadn't been dragged, but forced backward. As his eyes adjusted in the low light, he saw a form, stringy hair hanging off of a head tilting downward toward its lap.

There was someone sitting at the table. A scream crawled up his throat, cut short as he choked on it.

Like Ricky, like the cat, she shouldn't be here. *Couldn't be here.*

Sitting in the left-most kitchen chair, the same spot his mom had usually occupied, was the bank teller.

64

Eva, you know her name was Eva...

His hands flew instinctively to his ears, trying as always to drown out the truth.

Stop, stop, stop!

Her hands lay flat on the table, forming a triangle around a mug that Nat left there, dirt caked in the fine lines of her hands and under her fingernails.

Patches of skin were missing, mottled flesh peeking in and out underneath her tattered clothes. Blood, rusty and long dried, was splattered across every inch that wasn't covered in grime.

He took an experimental step forward to see if she would turn to him, but she didn't seem to care. Her hair dangled in her face in grungy, matted pieces, coated completely in dirt and mud.

Grave dirt.

The hairs on the back of his neck stood on end, an expression he always thought was so stupid. To feel it now, while he was wrapped in such intense fear, nearly made him burst out into inappropriate, maniacal laughter.

Crossing the kitchen, one leaden step at a time, his breath quickened as he got closer, his clammy hands balled into fists at his side. Three people crammed into it always felt like they couldn't get a moment's peace, and he always thought of the space as tiny.

The distance seemed interminable now, miles instead of the half-dozen steps it would take. His heart hummed in his chest, each beat barely distinguishable from the one before it.

Eva stood abruptly, ears ringing as the dead silence of the room broke. The chair skittered backwards across the floor. She turned toward him, and he jumped backwards, preparing for the spectre to come for him.

Anticipating the sensation of cold, dead fingers on his throat, Brian cringed, cowering in fear.

Brian wondered if Eva was here to hurt him. *She's the fucking ghost of a woman you helped murder, of course she's going to hurt you.* Maybe it was because he was planning on turning them both in that night, and didn't go through with it. She was here to correct that, to make sure he got his just desserts.

Eva glanced up at his eyes, and he braced himself, expecting to shrivel at the anger in her gaze.

65

L ost in the shuffle of time, Eva whirled through so many places she lost track. When she finally stood still again, she was in a kitchen at night, a room she didn't recognize.

There was a mug on the table, the first thing that came into focus for her. How long was she away, travelling mindlessly?

The heavy kitchen table rough beneath her hands, she steadied herself to stand, not sure how long she would be herself.

Spinal column cracking as she creaked her neck upward, she locked eyes with a man standing across from her. He stared back, his mouth open in a perfect expression of confusion and terror.

He can see me.

The difference between people sensing her with them and really seeing her, as she was, was such a strange feeling. There was a niggling of something there, something that was so ancient in her vocabulary that it took her several minutes to dredge it up.

Embarrassment.

Something about the man was familiar to her. She couldn't quite place him, but she was repulsed by him just the same. Losing her memories was maddening. She had no touchpoints to the world and simply observed, from the sidelines. The trail blazed in from her vision, and she had it, just for a second.

"Jinx," she rasped, touching the man's shoulder, and he stepped backward, stumbling into the dark living room.

Her fingers tingled, contact with another's skin such a foreign feeling to her. Bones poked through her flesh in parts, the nerve endings deadened. Like so many other things, this experience was muted, lessened, as if she were half asleep.

She came across other spirits, people who were trapped. Some were like her, rotting away, shuffling along, going through the motions. Eva was spit out, used for parts. The undigested scraps were keeping her here, tied to the earth.

This man, he was bright and whole, not like her, but just as stuck. She saw others like him, paralyzed, trapped in an endless hell of their own making.

There was something here she was meant to see, something important. Stopping at the front door, she turned to glance at the man in the living room. *Blink and you'll miss it.*

The door opened behind her, light from the street lamp spilled into the room, slow as molasses. The things revealed behind the man were so normal, so average, an everyday living room.

Bookcases lined the wall behind a sofa with a knit blanket thrown across it, splashes of bright flowers shaped from wool. She had a memory of puzzles she used to do as a child, finding the items in a picture that didn't belong. What didn't match was sprawled on the carpet behind the man, and for one flashing, lucid moment, she understood what she had in common with him, how trapped he truly was.

She mouthed the word; she tried to warn him, but her voice was gone, the door opening forever. The floor gave slightly under her feet, wilting and emitting an obscenely loud moan, and she wondered idly how old this house was.

Is this it? There's supposed to be a light when you go, isn't there?

Suddenly exhausted and excited at the prospect that all this could finally stop, she closed her eyes, willing it to happen

Let me off.

The beam was extinguished as the door slammed shut, taking her wishful thinking with it. A deadbolt hastily clicked shut behind her, the soundtrack to yet another disappointment.

Still here.

She sensed herself beginning to wander from this place, and then the living room was gone, and she was sitting in some shiny leaves above a darkened walking path.

Poison ivy, she idly thought, rubbing at the waxy leaves with her palms, knowing it would never matter.

She tried to stand, and it was midday, the lunch rush downtown. People rushed by, jostling her, and then another blink and it was a summer morning, kids running around a park looking for treats, some kind of scavenger hunt and then she was on a diving board, looking down at the sparking blue water of a swimming pool and on and on and on.

How many days passed? How much time?

She felt herself fading from existence, and even as she clawed to stay, the world around her was rejecting her, an abomination that didn't belong. Unable to stand still, she danced and spun through time, through memories, through things that were both important and insignificant.

It might take an hour, or days, or years, but she knew she would return to the house with the lonely kitchen when it finally all stopped.

66

Light washed through the sheer curtains, yellowed with age and countless cigarettes.

I've been meaning to replace those, Brian thought, staring dumbly at the door that Eva watched so intently. The light behind the curtain grew more and more intense, spilling into the entryway underneath the poorly sealed front door. The peephole became a glowing eye that drilled into him relentlessly.

Methodical thumping echoed outside, the sound of someone running toward the house. The clock in the kitchen was ticking, growing louder with each movement of the second hand until it was hammering into his skull. He covered his ears, curling into himself as the final tick vibrated in his chest.

The ticking stopped. The hands of the clock in the kitchen stuck at 10:31.

What is this?

Maybe she wanted to make him as scared as she was on her last day on earth. He wished he could tell her she needn't have bothered, that he lived every day like this.

The steps he heard were now right outside, accompanied by the sound of keys being lifted to the lock. Brian heard the scratching it made as it came into contact with the cheap, weathered deadbolt.

Scrape, scrape, scrape...

Click.

The lock engaged, the sound of the tumblers ridiculously loud in Brian's ears. He heard each individual one snap into place, as if it were minutes and not milliseconds.

The door began an agonizing arc, millimetre by millimetre, and Eva turned toward Brian. The door swung open, illuminating the room. She walked toward him, and he backed up, losing his footing as his calf hit something unyielding.

Her eyes were focused on the room behind him and then travelled slowly to the floor, a moment of clarity filling the cloudy orbs that roamed in her exposed skull. A bony finger pointed to the floor behind him, a worm inching its way out from under her sleeve to crawl over her palm and fall to the floor with a wet plop. Her mouth moved, but he couldn't make out the words.

A beetle burrowed its way out of her left ear. He tracked its progress down her cheek, frozen in horrified disgust. A look of annoyance crossed her face, so out of place it was almost comical. Making no move to brush it away, her eyes simply flicked downward at the prickle of its legs, then came back up to rest on him, a jarring reminder she looked like this because of him.

He dropped to his knees, wanting so badly to apologize, but with no idea what he could say. It was forever too late for *I'm sorry.*

There weren't enough words.

The door slammed shut behind her, and Eva disappeared. The room was plunged into the darkness.

Leaning against the door, knees raised to her chin, was Nat. She was sweating, red-cheeked and wild-eyed as she gasped for air.

As Brian's eyes adjusted, he sank to his knees, trying to get down to her level and get her attention. A squelching sound emanated from the carpet.

Why is the rug wet?

"Nat," he whispered.

Announcing himself seemed like the safest thing to do, though he didn't know how he would explain what he was doing up here. When she didn't respond, he tried again, slightly louder.

"Nat?"

Pitching herself forward, hands hit the floor hard and she pushed herself up onto shaky legs. She couldn't see him in the shadows of the living room and didn't acknowledge she heard anything.

She held her weight against the doorknob, checking the lock and slowly leaning toward the peephole. As she rested her face against the door, Brian thought about how flimsy it was, how little it would take for whatever monster was outside trying to get in.

The tension in the air was thick, the anticipation of attack potent, and he held his breath with her. When she finally huffed a sigh of relief, her body physically wilted with it. She broke down as her crying turned into a maniacal sound dissolving into a short fit of giggles.

Brian wanted to laugh with her, the adrenaline rush spreading a wave of warmth throughout his entire body, and he joined her, sagging onto the floor.

The floor beneath him vibrated through his arms, and he wobbled uselessly as a turtle as he tried to sit up. The second footstep passed right through his body, a booted foot landing on the floor between his legs. It was stealthy, slow and deliberate, avoiding the creaky places on the floor.

Nat was facing away as she reached for the light switch, oblivious to the stealthy steps approaching her.

Brian went hoarse with silent screams, helpless to stop Darryl as he advanced. Trying to grab his leg as he stepped methodically toward her was useless, as if his hands went right through him.

How can that be?

He had to be imagining things, Darryl's power overwhelming him.

In a panic, Brian tried furniture, books, anything he could throw to get her attention. Fumbling clumsily, he found himself unable to grab a single object, as if his depth perception was off. He screamed one last time as his brother grabbed her from behind, the biggest knife he had ever seen sliding into her back, cutting through muscle like butter.

She grunted and kicked wildly, trying to make it stop as Darryl held her close and punched her repeatedly with the blade. Nat's blood soaked the carpet, spraying with each slice of the knife.

Revelling in the blood that covered him, Darryl sighed in pleasure, the same way that Brian had heard him suck on a cigarette after trying to quit for months. Tears ran down Brian's face, and he crouched between the sofa and the armchair, biting into his own hand, trying to keep Darryl's eyes from fixing on him in the dark.

The deed completed, she was a husk to him now, not even a trophy, and he let her go, pulling her backwards by her hair to drop her heavily on the living room rug.

With the deed done, Darryl turned to him, grinning.

Brian clambered toward Nat, catching his foot on something as he crawled. As he looked behind him, the shadows moved to reveal the obstacle. He blinked, unable to make sense of it.

Brian was always there when Darryl got...carried away. Always.

The glint in Nat's eyes penetrated the dark to seek him out, glimmering with shocked recognition for a few seconds. As the light left her eyes, it wasn't peace he saw there, but accusation.

I'm sorry, he tried to say before she went empty, just like all the apologies he failed to make tonight.

Darryl had disappeared, and the room had a strange quality to it, as if it was fading from his vision even as he sat there. There was nothing more he could do for Nat, and he brought his attention back to the mound on the floor behind him. Eva died all those years ago, and he never saw her, or any of the others, until now. This was it; his reckoning was finally here.

He thought about Darryl's legs, all the objects in the room he tried to throw but couldn't. He thought they felt slippery, but were they? It was as if...

As if I'd never touched them at all.

Darryl was soaked in so much blood, but was it there even before he stabbed Nat?

Eva's mouth moved in his mind, no sound escaping. Her decaying lips formed a single word, and he knew now what she was trying to tell him.

Remember...

As he glanced down at his own corpse, blood soaking into the rug and mingling with Nat's, it all came back.

RECKONING

67

Darryl's shadow stretched long and dark along the alleyway; memories that weren't his flooded him as he walked.

The sound of a car folding into a body, of flesh slapping against the pavement. He felt his way to the hidden gate he had cut in the fence. The dense shrubs pulled him into the yard, swallowing him from the alley as if he was never there at all.

Stalking quietly through the dark backyard, he made his way to the side of the house. Brian had changed the locks when Nat moved in, giving him some line about her asking for it, that it was the law.

There was always an excuse when Brian asked for a new one. Too bad for Brian, he'd forgotten himself and lent his truck to Darryl one day, and getting a new one cut was a ten-minute detour Brian didn't even notice. The key clicked in so smoothly, effortlessly, and Darryl grinned at how easy this was going to be.

Latching the door behind him, he crept up the few steps to the adjoining door. He opened it, and her fat cat bolted past him hissing. Cursing, he did his best to quench the itch he had to kill it, to wring its fat neck, but the beast inside him balked at the impulsive thought.

Keep it simple, Darryl, it warned. *She'll be home soon.*

Opening the door a crack, he let the creature escape into the yard. He left the lights off, adjusting to the darkness as he shut the adjoining door behind him. Pacing the kitchen slowly, he waited for her return.

Nat kept her work schedule on the fridge; it was so easy to take a peek when she let him in to repair the kitchen sink.

"Nat?"

Brian's voice carried up the stairs. The hallway light clicked on, spilling through the crack under the dividing door. The click of the switch downstairs was a thunderclap on a sunny day, unexpected and definitely unwelcome.

What is he doing here? Darryl shrank from its anger as it raged in his head.

"I'm sorry," he whimpered, hanging his head. "He said he was working a job out of town this weekend."

"It doesn't matter," it growled. It didn't like when things didn't go according to plan. *"Two for the price of one."*

Shoving Darryl down, it grabbed the biggest knife from the knife block on the counter as Brian climbed the stairs.

68

"Nat?" Brian called, tapping his knuckles lightly as he pushed the door open. Clearing his dry throat, he tried again. "Nat?"

Two hands reached out and grabbed him by the collar, pulling him into the kitchen and shoving him against the refrigerator. Magnets scattered across the floor and the appliance rumbled and hummed against his back.

"What the hell are you doing here, Brian?" The voice oozed entitlement, as if being in his own home should have been something he asked permission to do.

Darryl. The corded muscles in his brother's arm were rock hard as he gripped Brian's shirt in his fists, tongue protruding slightly in concentration.

"Job got cancelled for the week. Supplies didn't come on time, so they told us to stay put."

The lie flowed off his tongue, the endless practice since Ricky's death for just this scenario.

"What are you doing up here, Darryl?" Brian wriggled against the hands that held him firm. "Let *go.*"

Unblinking, Darryl pressed his elbow against Brian's

throat, holding him tight. The pressure made him cough, and he stretched his neck to ease it. Brian's eyes flicked downward, registering the latex covering Darryl's hands.

"I won't help you anymore, Darryl. I'm done, okay? What you did to Ricky..." Sputtering, he surprised himself as defiance took over. "He was my friend."

Darryl said nothing, his stony face impassive, as if daring Brian to continue.

"The fuck do you think is going to happen if you kill a tenant, Darryl? You think the cops aren't going to come looking for you next?"

Darryl's jaundiced irises flickering as his brother's pupils flattened into reptilian slits.

"You're not Darryl," Brian whispered.

Darryl's head cocked to the side, contemplating the philosophical nature of the statement.

"I am today."

Brian strained harder against the arm, trying to maintain his weight on his toes as he choked.

"Let my brother go."

"*Let him go?*" It laughed in Darryl's voice. "*You think your brother doesn't want this? Don't beg for it? He was always on this path, and it was only a matter of time before he did something stupid. Without me to hold him back, he would have been caught a long time ago.*"

Showing off its teeth, it leaned closer.

"*You think I'm bad? I just need to eat. Darryl is the real threat.*"

Brian's eyes shifted slightly, and it saw that the truth hurt. Hot breath pressed against his cheek as it sneered in his face.

"*He won't stop me, Brian. He doesn't want to stop me. This has always been him. And you know what?*" It brought its lips to Brian's ear. "*He'd do anything for me.*"

"Bullshit."

Enjoying toying with the little worm on its hook, it cackled. Brian felt the pressure of the knife, cold at his throat.

"Oh, you think so? Let's ask him, shall we?"

"What do you mean?" Brian asked warily.

The reptile's eyes smiled playfully as the colour bled and changed, replaced with Darryl's steely blue ones.

69

"Your turn," Darryl heard in the dark.

Elated, he resurfaced, the feeling of warm skin pressed up against his forearm the first thing he was aware of. Brian strained under the pressure Darryl was putting on his neck, and the power he felt in his arm excited him. This wasn't what he was expecting when it let him up. He was napping peacefully, waiting for when he would wake, soaked in blood. If he were lucky, it would let him feel the things it did to her.

Nat's face flickered across his mind, longing hitting him in waves. She would be home soon. Whatever was going to happen had to happen fast.

"Darryl?"

A familiar weight held his other hand down at his side. Looking down at the flash of silver that hung by his side, he gripped the knife tighter.

It was quaking with excitement and Darryl understood it was testing him, giving him an ultimatum.

Him or me?

70

Confusion flooded Darryl's features as Brian watched. Despite recognition flooding his cold eyes as he took in Brian's features, he was unwilling to loosen the arm shoved up against his brother's neck.

"Darryl?"

Darryl seemed to debate, listening to a voice that only he heard. Hesitating, he leaned into Brian harder, hedging his bets until he could confirm what was happening.

"Darryl?" Brian wheezed slightly. "Is it you?"

Darryl lowered his arms and loosened his hold. As Brian's feet gently touched down on the linoleum, a shaky breath escaped his lips.

"We'll figure this out, Darryl. You and..."

His relief was cut short as Darryl sliced the blade across his throat.

71

Brian's eyes were enormous, but not all that surprised, as if this was an inevitable conclusion.

Accepting.

Darryl rolled his head on his shoulders, cracking his neck as he waited for nature to take its course.

Hands flailing behind him, Brian grabbed a dish towel that was hanging off the refrigerator handle. He reeled into the living room, choking as he tried in vain to put pressure on the blood flowing from his neck in waves. The effort was wasted, as ineffectual as using a bucket to catch a tsunami, and he slid to the floor.

Darryl stood above him, watching dispassionately, stepping backward to avoid the growing puddle. Comforted by his accomplice's hands on his shoulders, he slunk back into the shadows.

Well done, it purred, watching with him as Brian's spastic movements slowed, then stopped.

The kitchen clock read 10:31PM. It ticked on inanely, the rest of the night continuing on its way, the death of his brother just one tiny moment in the potential of so many others like this. He had his future to look forward to now.

I never doubted you, Darryl. Brian made a mistake. Thinking that brotherly love might mean something in the end.

Darryl was simply adjusting his grip on the knife, an extension of his own arm. Peering down into his brother's dead eyes, he felt nothing but the execution of an inevitable conclusion.

They came here to feast on the girl together, to lay it all on Brian, the last way he could still be useful. His death changed little. In fact, it was even better. Darryl could just fade out of public view soon enough, leave town at the shame of what poor old Brian did. No one would blame him, and no one would blink an eye. He pictured them together, riding off into the sunset.

Stick with the plan, it hissed in Darryl's ear.

Brian's face in that last moment pled with his brother to see him, to join him, to love him more than what they were doing together. The thought rankled him. He didn't need fixing, and he certainly didn't need a brother. Brian proved tonight he was only so much meat standing in the way of his work.

Our work, it corrected, an edge to its gentle voice.

There was still so much work to do.

What gave him the right?

Anger flared in him, and it warned him to hold it together. He didn't listen, couldn't, and grabbed a standing lamp from beside the couch. The heavy anchor slammed into the face that saw him through his best and worst, over and over. The silence was thick with his partner's disapproval; he tasted it at the back of its throat. In a rare treat, it retreated, letting Darryl finish, a carrot on the stick.

When he was finished, he examined the aftermath, finally

understanding what being beaten to a pulp looked like. Pieces of broken teeth dribbled out from between the gash that had once been Brian's mouth.

Darryl was covered in blood, probably not a smart move for a crime scene, but he didn't care. The knife wasn't his; it was from Nat's set on the counter in the kitchen. The gloves were a precaution, but he was always around quite a bit for maintenance, so it made sense for his fingerprints or hair to be around the house.

He made sure of that before tonight. If it came to it, he needed to explain any prints in her bathroom, in her bedroom, in all those places he crept when she wasn't home. Last week, he got bold, standing in her doorway for hours as she slept, listening to the breath he would soon take from her body

A random act of violence, or a robbery gone wrong—it didn't matter. He would leave the door open a crack when they were done, to make it appear as if someone left in haste. Maybe take her laptop, some jewellery, and dump them in the lake. Smash and grab gone so tragically, terribly sideways.

So simple.

As the gore slid down his face and onto the body's legs in a static tattoo, all his stress and worries left him.

The road ahead was clear, and he knew now what he needed to do.

The door opened behind him, and he tiptoed daintily ahead of the slash of light as it expanded on the carpet.

We can't miss this chance, Darryl, it cautioned him, still nestled away to let him finish with Brian. Politely waiting, it wanted to be sure it could be front and centre for what came next.

Darryl appreciated it gave him this opportunity; he really did.

But he wanted more.

What are you doing? It demanded, moving its way further,

picking up speed as the thought formed in his brain. The tables turned. He knew he needed to hold it at bay for as long as possible. He wouldn't need long; just long enough.

He wasn't stupid. He felt the change as soon as Nat knocked at that door. It wanted her, body and soul, and Darryl couldn't let that happen. There was no way he was letting this ride end, and once it had her, it didn't need him anymore. The door slammed shut, and he slid through the darkness, pulling the knife back with his elbow as he got closer.

It breached the surface as Darryl let go, plunging the knife into Nat one last time. Howling in rage, it flicked its wrist and sent Darryl flying.

"Please," he whispered, begging it to see he was the one it wanted. "I can't lose this."

Darryl screamed as it crushed him within, parasitic hooks sinking deep to pin him down inside. He saw Brian on the floor, his glow all but gone. It was too late, a waste of food. Moving over to Nat, touching her with his own hands, holding her head to look into her dead eyes, it felt her inside, becoming a part of its being, its strength growing even as it mourned the loss of its true host.

Darryl's world began to kaleidoscope as it took over, the sheer power of it shaking him in a way he didn't know was possible. The rage reached a peak, and it stepped on Brian, with the sinking sensation of his ribs cracking under Darryl's boots. It glanced down briefly, as if checking the bottom of its shoe.

Darryl sensed it giving up on restraining itself, to savour her. It lost control, gulping greedily, and just like that, she was whole inside of Darryl's body. He felt them meet, felt how affection surged through it.

With every sip it took of her, Darryl felt himself shrivel a little more, devoured by his more aggressive twin. He would figure this out, but for now, it needed him, its free ride. His body was breaking down already, the parasite overwhelming the body. Chastened, Darryl shrank into a tiny pinprick inside, the carnage in the room fading away until it was nearly nothing.

She would betray his friend again, he could tell. He just needed to be ready for when she did. There wasn't much of him left. Determined to prove himself a worthy host, he stopped struggling, quiet, determined to behave.

The door, Darryl suggested feebly.

It reached for the cheap knob, worn and desperately needing replacement. A smear of her blood remained, the door open the tiniest crack, a sloppy and cowardly burglar leaving from the scene.

Just like they planned.

He breathed a shaky sigh of relief in cave's blackness he was trapped in. As long as it was still listening to him, he had a chance. It needed a body; he just needed to show that he was the one it needed.

The door moved inward slightly, and her cat appeared, growling and hissing as it took in the scene, Darryl's body sitting amongst the carnage. The beast stared at it as it peeled them off of the floor, revelling in a feeling Darryl never knew in their time together.

It was finally full.

72

The loop reset, and Brian was fifteen, helping to bury the cat, tears and snot streaking his face as he blubbered. The shovel in his hands pierced the soil, and he was digging a hole to bury Eva in, nudging her over with his foot, not wanting her to look at him.

He was pulling out sheeting to wrap a body, the crinkle in the night air making Darryl tell him to shut the fuck up.

As the corpses piled, the dirt blackened the inside of his fingernails, embedding itself in the lines in his calluses.

The cat with its merrily jingling bell made its way to him in the basement, the thud coming from above.

Eva came again with her cryptic message, her ruined body stiffly moving to the doorway.

Darryl killed him, killed Nat. The blood covered his hands, covered his clothes, covered the floor.

He was on a carousel, faces and voices cresting as he came back to the basement, to the noises upstairs.

Remember...forever...

The basement door slammed as Darryl made his way out, and Brian sat with the quiet of the latest corpses, his last failure. A wail of despair built in him, a scream he didn't know was capable of.

As it all began again, the thin glass in the windows vibrated nearly imperceptibly, and the house remained dark. Chaos scratched half-heartedly on the door outside, not convinced he wanted back in.

April 2015

Escape

73

THE SCREAMS OF HER YOUNGER SELF FADED IN THE surrounding wind, and as the air stilled and grew stuffy, she opened her eyes.

A tidy house, silent in the aftermath of tragedy, surrounded her, everyone grieving in their separate rooms. The once-warm brown walls of her childhood home were dark with pain and stress. She grew up here, staying here most of the time with her mother after the divorce. The plush carpet on the gloomy wooden staircase sank beneath her feet as she climbed. After everything happened, the house seemed to lose all its brightness. It ceased to be home, just a place that kept her dry.

She hadn't set foot in this house since the day she left.

Reaching the top of the stairs, she opened the first door on the right. It swung open, and as her old bedroom came into view, she felt like she was taking it in for the first time. She crossed to her dresser, finding her jewellery box, the one that even as an adult she reserved for special things. It carried fewer scratches than she remembered, less faded and yellow with fewer years exposed to sunlight streaming through windows.

The sun outside the streaked glass moved behind a cloud, and the room darkened even further as if on cue, everything tainted with that post-loss hue. She idly wondered if it was really like this, or if she made it this way in her memories.

Does it matter?

Sitting cross-legged on her bed, the familiar creaks of the frame gave her a sense of nostalgia, if not comfort. She ran her hand over the lid of the box in her hands, opened it, and took out one of the friendship bracelets Meg made her all those years ago.

Even here, years later, it was already soft from wear. She pulled them out from time to time, rubbing each one like a talisman. Meg said once they were cut, the magic was gone. That's why they made new ones every year.

Nevertheless, Nat couldn't bring herself to get rid of them. Convinced there was so much power in them, she stashed them away in her jewelry box to make sure they would be friends forever. It would be bad luck to throw them away.

The quilt her grandmother made her when she was ten rubbed against her legs, the softness muted, and numbness spread through her. She slowly rubbed her fingers on the soft threads of the bracelet woven around her fingers, trying to think.

What passed through her head was the same thought she always had as a kid when something went wrong, when there was only one person in the world that she wanted to talk to.

I wish Meg were here.

The crackle of a connection kissed her hand gently, an energy she carried with her all this time.

THE MATTRESS GAVE WAY TO A THIN, NUBBY CARPET.

A stack of books sat on the floor beside her, dust motes floating lazily to settle on them under muted yellow lighting.

Thin metal shelves, flimsy alone but strong together, towered on either side of her, more book spines reaching to fluorescent lights that hung from an institutional white ceiling.

Sneezing slightly, she pushed herself to her feet. *The library.*

She didn't know *when or where* she was, but maybe she could use this to her advantage. She moved down the aisles, farther and farther from the front, until she spotted her.

Meg.

She was young here, wearing overalls ripped wide at both knees. The bracelet on her wrist was a different colour but the same pattern as the one she was still clutching.

Nat's smile faded when she saw the troubled look on her friend's face.

Shifting so that her legs stretched out in front of her with a resigned thud, Meg rummaged in her backpack, pulling out a folded piece of paper. The fold lines were worn, interrupting the ink, as if it was opened and closed many times. Nat moved to sit next to her friend, reading the note. There was no answer to the question, but she recognized the doodles. The style was unmistakable, and she was sure she would see it in print someday. Two boxes at the bottom posed a question; neither one was ticked.

At the bottom, in Meg's neat handwriting, was a two-word answer. *Sorry. Can't.*

How didn't I see it?

Memories from her youth flashed in front of her, all the things she was too stubborn or unwilling to admit in picture-perfect clarity. Meg was desperate to go tree climbing and Nat convincing her to go swimming instead. She wanted to get a dollhouse for a friend's birthday, and Nat told her it was for babies.

Nat told Meg a dress didn't suit her so they could wear the same colour to a dance. It was so different now, laughing with Meg in her kitchen. Their time together since they made up felt more open, more even, give and take. Did she really change, or was she being careful during a honeymoon period? She honestly couldn't say.

Eva, scrabbling away from her touch on the rope, terrified, flashed through her mind.

Maybe more subtle this time.

Nat reached down and tentatively prodded the paper with her finger. It crinkled slightly at the pressure, but Meg didn't notice. Reaching for the top, Nat focused on the edge until it was the only thing in her world. When she was ready, she pulled gently.

The note fluttered to the ground, Meg letting it go in surprise. Her backpack tipped over from where it leaned against the shelves. A pen slipped out and rolled across the floor.

"Chris?" Meg whispered, barely audible, in fragile hope. Her back was straight, flat against the wall in surprise, her expression full of so much longing that it hurt.

Nat's heart sank at the hurt she caused. The paper lay on the floor between them, and she saw her chance, reaching for the pen.

As her fingers grazed it, a squelching footstep clunked behind her, and then another. She turned her head slowly, not wanting to know what she would see.

A figure stood near the end of the aisle, staring in.

"Eva?" Nat asked, scrambling to her feet.

The sludge covering it reminded her so much of what she witnessed in Gavin's basement. The film over its face receded, the shimmering sea of emotions separated as the colours bled into one.

A sob escaped her lips as his anger-filled eyes found hers, devoid of anything else. Lifting his arm straight in front of him, he extended his pointer finger like a judge delivering a verdict.

Gavin.

The floor under her feet shook, something else was approaching from the other side of the shelves. It flickered in and out of her vision as it filled the gaps between the stacks.

Meg was still behind her, against the wall. She seemed oblivious of the horror standing at the end of the aisle.

"Chris?" Meg said hopefully again, a little louder this time. Nat barely heard her over the roar of blood in her ears.

The shadow turned the corner, and another Meg emerged, walking past Gavin to stand in front of her. She was older, exactly as she was when Nat last saw her.

"What are you doing here?" Nat cried. Meg smiled at her, holding out her arms, welcoming her into her embrace.

Nat slowed a few feet from her friend. Meg's grin stayed pinned to her face as she coughed, blood sputtering over her lips and pouring down her chin. One of her eyes was shiny and purple, swollen shut and pulsing with the force of the blood trapped underneath.

Nat couldn't tell where the red sweatshirt she was wearing ended, and the blood began. Her clothes were soaked in it, splattered down her dark leggings to her pristine white shoelaces, drenching them until they dripped. One was undone, and the shoelace left a crimson trail on the floor as Meg stepped toward Nat.

"Please," Meg choked, reaching out to Nat, the grin on her face not reaching her eyes. Her white teeth were shiny with blood, more gushing down her chin as she spoke.

"Nat, please." Something about the way she moved toward her was theatrical.

Gavin didn't move, observing the women with detached curiosity. The slime poured off him with increased force. The faucet turned on in his excitement at Nat's terror. The colour darkened, a pure red pouring off him. It was no longer the angry, fearful, crayon colour of her mood ring but the darker colour of cinnamon hearts at Valentine's Day. It was the colour of passion, of love.

Satisfaction.

As the sludge grew, the fountain of it now streaked with pitch black rivers. It overtook him again, closing in around his face, a putrid mask. His open-mouthed grin disappeared underneath the putrid sea as it invaded his mouth, and she gagged at the thought of how it must taste.

Revenge, she thought. *This is how he gets justice.*

"Meg? What happened to you?"

The lurid projection of Meg froze, a glitch in the system. Her glassy eyes and wide smile remained fixed on Nat, unflinching.

"Meg?" Nat asked again, and as she took a step forward, the monster burst through the projection of her friend.

As her fear spiked, it grew taller, towering over the shelves. Its spindly limbs strengthened, muscles expanding beneath the skin as she watched. She noticed its ribs were far less pronounced, as if it were eating well, and she shuddered as she thought of what a productive season might look like for this animal.

"Why are you fighting this so hard, Nat? You need to stop."

Gavin and the wrecked Meg were both mouthing the words. She couldn't see Gavin's lips, but the area where his mouth would be was moving up and down in time with Meg's. The voice was inhuman, gravelly, containing the sound of multiple voices, all roaring to be heard from within the beast.

"This is what will happen to her if you don't, Nat. You don't want that, do you? More destruction on your hands? Haven't you already done enough?" It appeared as though something were holding Meg's chin, moving her jaw along with the words, her expressionless eyes still above her slack, bloody mouth.

Gavin moved aside as it crouched lower, following her into the aisle. Its foot lifted high and barrelled down toward the Meg puppet, Nat's screams echoing to the ceiling. Booming laughter filled the air, taking pleasure in her distress as the claws on its toes swiped through the projection of Meg, her visage disappearing like so much smoke, those haunted eyes never leaving her.

A magician never tells.

Its skin was the rainbow sheen of gleaming fish scales, bouncing spots of colour off the surrounding shelves, a beautiful but deadly prism. It grabbed for her and lit up as she touched it, just like when she had trailed her fingers through the barrier.

We're inside, she reminded herself.

Meg wasn't dead. She was still alive out there. It had projected her, convinced her it was real, that her friend was here. The faces on its endless carousel flashed back to her, the souls in its body fuelling it. Herself, Chris, Gavin, Eva and so many more, but not Meg.

If they were inside it, it couldn't be in here with them.

You're not real.

Nat backed up, trapped in the aisle between the shelves and its body. Giant clawed hands gripped her shoulders, shoving her roughly up against the shelves, face first.

Damp, reeking breath moved past her cheek as it slammed her against the shelves again. Books jostled loose above her and fell to the floor in a heap in front of Meg. Nat patted herself, searching for something, *anything* she could use.

As quickly as the thought came to mind, her keys appeared in her hand.

Below her, Meg stood, looking up in confusion at the swinging lights, the swaying shelves. Nat gripped her keys, protruding from between her fingers, and swung as hard as she could. Two wide streaks opened across its cheek, and it lost its grip on her, more from surprise than pain. She slid against its slimy skin, dropping to the ground as it loosened its hold, keys clattering to the floor.

She flinched at the sight of Gavin as she leapt out of the aisle. He was covered in the soup that was everything he was feeling right now. A smirk emerged from the mess around his face. She couldn't really call it a smile, more like his face stretched.

Bracing herself, she barrelled into him as hard as she could.

Her hands slipped on the slime that covered him and continued to flow. His head lolled backward, jaw wrenching open to project the creature's cry of frustration as she tried to shake him. He was lost, like Eva, trapped in her betrayal. More colours appeared, running together again, that nightmare sheen that had overwhelmed him.

She dug her fingers through the hot, steaming mess, searching to reach him through the coating. He felt boneless, limp as a rag. His eyes were vacant, unseeing.

The charge flowed through them, instantaneous as they touched. The coating all over Gavin was lit up as the electric current flowed over it. It moved like a wave, a greenish line of light illuminating the sea underneath. She felt the hair on her arms rise. The ectoplasm covering Gavin seemed to solidify once the charge was introduced, slippery like silk.

She closed her eyes and thought of Meg: Meg in her living

room, Meg giving a tour, Meg writing her book, Meg having tea, Meg laughing, Meg living her life NOW.

A whoosh of air ran past her cheek, the tip of a claw dragging itself across her shoulder. She pushed Gavin as hard as she could, and they slammed into the slippery mass that contained them.

Holding his slack body by one shoulder, she grabbed the pen from the back pocket of her jeans and stabbed it into the barrier with all her might, bringing her weapon down again and again. Light spilled from the cracks she ripped in their universe. Sticking her fingers into the gap, she pulled, widening the hole. Shoving both hands in, she pulled as hard as she could in opposite directions. Viscera covered her up to her elbows, and still she pushed her way through.

It howled in anger and pain as she ripped at it from the inside. She took the power it had here and shredded it like paper. The library was shaking, books falling from shelves, their titles blurry as it tried to grasp her memory in its agony. Her hand was slick with blood and chunks of what she assumed was intestine, sliding along its flesh.

A groaning sound took over the world, as if giant gears covered in rust were crushing whatever locked them into place. Everything stopped, and then the machinery broke free. A hot, wet stench enveloped them as they slickly burst out, freed from the bowels of the beast.

74

DARRYL WAILED AT AN AGONY UNLIKE ANYTHING HE ever felt before; a hot, searing wall of pain trailed across his belly. Bile and saliva dripped from his tongue in the aftermath, a metallic taste lingering in his mouth. Normally a pleasant sensation, the taste this time was sour, and he realized he was tasting his own soul.

The stabbing pain of betrayal was almost worse than being devoured. The girl didn't deserve to be the vessel. Snapping and lapping at Darryl inside of it, all Darryl could feel was how angry his mentor was with him. Despite the fear that grew in him, Darryl welcomed his punishment.

Nourishment was what it needed, and he could provide.

Maybe it would let him stay. The two of them would be one, the host incidental in their quest.

It showed him what it saw, the girl in the aisle picking up a book. Nat's friend. He saw this book before, at Nat's house when she moved in. Touching her things helped them learn about the woman she became over the years, and he saw it when he snuck up one day after she left for work. The book seemed to have a place of honour, separate from the others, featured proudly on the coffee table.

"Chris?" Meg whispered, clutching the book to her chest as she peered up to the swinging lights in wonder.

Bits of Nat informed their rituals over the years, things she deemed important coming out as it fed, as it killed. Some of them surprised him, but he loved the innocence of her. The contrast was stark but beautiful against their brutality. The bracelets were his favourite, his fingers weaving them without ever learning how.

This book could be useful, it whispered. Eager to please, he stirred weakly.

His body crumpled as it let him up for air. The pain in his gut doubled him over, but it wasn't just there. His joints felt swollen and sore, and his vision was blurry. Tongue aching as if he didn't have a sip of water in years, his entire mouth throbbed as he coughed. In one crystal-clear moment, he realized he went too far. The creature planned to leave him, to start from scratch with Meg.

All he could do was show his worth, remind it of why he was worthy. With its host body nearly depleted, it was running out of time. If he could find a new host, it would be forever grateful.

Come back, he whined.

After a while he heard it within, buried deeply as it conserved its strength. In a calm and calculated voice, it gave him his orders.

Find it.

This was his last chance to prove his worth, and he planned to make the most of it. Dragging his stiffening body around the house, he began searching for the book.

He tore apart the living room, dropping books on the floor methodically as he looked at the cover of each, comparing it to the mental image the beast had shown him.

Meg's car was still parked in view in front of Barb's. When she left, he had watched her get in her car and saw her stop there.

He dragged himself down the street to the car. The door was unlocked, which he thought was foolish, but fortuitous. There was the book mixed with some other junk spread across the backseat. He opened the door and leaned over the centre console to reach for it. His muscles screamed.

As he leaned backward, he saw a glint in the cupholder. A ring. It would make the perfect souvenir when they were done. His fist clenched at the promise of more violence, so soon.

He continued to the porch, ring in one hand and book in the other. He heard people talking inside. There was a box on the welcome mat. He placed the book on top, smiling at how glaringly obvious it was. Meg would see it.

He gasped as a wave of nausea rolled over him, and he crouched down on the porch to ride it out.

There was movement inside now, and he crept down the stairs to return home. Her car door remained open, and he left it that way. He needed to get her attention.

He went back inside, turned out the lights, and then went out the back door to go through the alleyway to move his car. Returning to rest, he sat alone in the dark, watching and waiting.

The instructions were clear; he needed to have patience, and let her come.

They wanted her to feel safe.

Darryl sat back and let himself fall into the memory of how they met, trying to remind it that they were perfect for each other.

Nearly sixteen years ago, Darryl was walking on the side of the road when he felt an itch on the back of his neck. He swatted at it out of instinct, thinking it nothing more than a pesky mosquito. It was only June and already the air was rife with the bloodsuckers.

His car broke down, and he was hot, sweaty and pissed off. Irritation swelled in his chest, making him feel antsy as he thought of his last girlfriend lecturing him for not getting a cell phone.

"What if there's an emergency?"

There was no point in paying all the extra costs for something he was hardly ever going to use, in his opinion. Plus, who said he wanted to give her another method to nag him? He was glad they weren't together anymore; wouldn't want to give the bitch the satisfaction.

There are pay phones everywhere, so who gives a shit?

Except in this area, apparently.

Not having a cell phone wasn't his only problem. He forgot his wallet but could picture it jammed in the pocket of the jeans he was wearing yesterday. Fat lot of good it did him *right fucking now.* Despite several attempts to flag someone down, no one stopped to offer a ride. *Assholes,* he thought, his face reddening.

The mosquitoes were relentless. This stretch was still being developed, and it was mostly empty field, left to grow wild with tall dry grass. The chaotic cackling of grasshoppers was overwhelming, and he tried to step on one that hooked onto his sock. The crunching and popping of it beneath his shoe put a smug smile on his face.

The insistent insects persisted, the itch getting stronger and stronger each time he pawed at his neck to slap them away, the high-pitched whine of their buzzing growing louder.

Christ, what is it, my aftershave?

A painful pinch burned the back of his neck, spreading

rapidly into clusters, expanding until a swarm was upon him and he roared, a primal scream, spinning as he slapped. The ember of frustration within him burned at a fever pitch, ready to ignite.

The buzzing stopped; the surrounding air was silent once more.

A soothing sensation touched the area that was raw with bites, gentle, like a lover's arms wrapped around their partner's neck while dancing.

I am not in the mood to be fucked with. He whipped around, convinced someone was messing with him.

There was no one there.

He stood still, trying to identify where the feeling was coming from. It felt...nice. Accepting. Craving more, he leaned unconsciously into the touch. A couple of people approached him from the other direction, their conversation ceasing as they split apart to pass on either side of him. They wanted to give him a wide berth, obviously.

Who would want to be walking next to him? He imagined what he looked like to an outsider, his face pressed against the invisible hand coming from nowhere, moving up his neck, through his hair, and across his cheek.

A giggle reached his ears once they were out of range of his fists, still balled at his sides as if they were just waiting for an excuse to swing.

He reached the shopping centre, a strip mall with the standard anchor grocery, a bank, a craft store, and a post office. In his opinion, he didn't know why anyone would call it a shopping centre. It was more a place you went to run errands. Since they added the theatre across the street, though, he saw a lot more signs proclaiming COMING SOON in this area.

The bay of pay phones at the main entrance was covered with 'out of order' signs and no good without a quarter, anyway. *Always keep one in your sock for an emergency,* his mother always said.

By the time he hit the doors to the bank, the feeling of being caressed grew so he couldn't break away from it if he wanted to.

The feeling was delicious, and he wanted to taste it forever.

Let me in, it said, pleading ever so slightly. *I'm so tired.*

That it wasn't a question, but a statement, excited him, promising so much with so few words. Like him, it just needed a ride, but it had so much more to offer, could repay him in ways he couldn't even imagine.

Let me in, it whispered seductively. *Please. There's so much we can do together.*

Blood, so much blood, blurred his vision. Trailing his fingers over his face, he followed its path as it dripped down until he was bathing in it, taking as much as he wanted, when he wanted, and that was all it took for him to let go.

Surrender crept through his body, total trust as his transformation strengthened his limbs. Deep inside, he was the same old Darryl, but there was something else now, a host to something great and powerful. Unlike Darryl, it feared nothing. He flushed in shame, hoping it wouldn't see he was weak, that he wasn't living up to his full potential.

When he arrived at the counter, his eyes were glazed, a man who was struck by Cupid's arrow, united with his other half.

His soulmate.

"Can I help you?" an uncertain voice asked, annoyance frosted over with a thin layer of phony baloney friendliness. The hard shell would crack with the lightest tap of a spoon.

He glanced up and locked eyes with his destiny. His eyes travelled to her chest, searching for a name tag.

Eva, it read. *Teller.*

The swell in Darryl's heart, his quickening pulse, intrigued his passenger.

"Yes, can I trouble you to use your phone?"

Skepticism creased her face. "We don't usually…"

"Please. My car broke down, and I left my wallet at home."

"Well…"

"Miss…Eva," he glanced at her name tag, pretending he didn't allow her name to run through his mind a million times over in the time it took them to have the conversation.

"I am having the worst day. Worse than worst." He smiled his winning, charming smile. "Haven't you ever had a day like that?"

The human being underneath that customer service smile revealed itself with the ever so slight quirk of her lip.

"It's local?"

"Scout's honour, cross my heart!" he said, holding his fingers over his chest.

"Well, alright. It can't hurt, I suppose."

The cord just made it across the counter as she held the receiver out to him with one hand, dialling the number he gave her with the other.

"Thanks, miss."

"Don't mention it. Hope your day gets better."

He smiled at her, his first, the one to welcome him to his new world order.

"Things are definitely looking up."

SHOWDOWN

75

THE AIR WAS SUCKED OUT OF BARB'S LUNGS. THE cup in her hands slipped, and she miraculously cupped it before it spilt more than a few drops down her shirt.

"The car crashed down an embankment below the Plank Cliffs, by the rock face," Meg explained. "There was blood on the passenger-side dash, and he had a head injury. They think he hit his head in the accident, got disoriented, and wandered off on a footpath leading up. He slipped and fell from there."

Looking down at her tea, Meg continued. "When Nat came to, some guys out night fishing already found him. They swear he called for help, but he couldn't have. The doctors said he was under for too long. He's still here, but he's long gone."

As a nurse, Barb knew there was more than one kind of death.

"I haven't seen him in probably five years. Nat didn't handle it well, and then we had a falling out. We were still so young, you know? She ran and left town, but I kept going to see him for a while." Meg let out a wry laugh. "I think I went for so long because I was hoping she'd show up sometime, and maybe we'd be forced into talking. A real talk, you know?"

Barb knew the feeling, the powerful desire for closure, the intense frustration when it stayed out of reach.

"After that, it just got too hard to be around him."

Wiping a shaky hand down her face, Meg laughed.

"Sorry," she sniffed. "I don't know why I said all of that."

Still, Barb sat silent, knowing from experience it was better for her to come to it herself. Sure enough, Meg kept talking, unleashed.

"I don't really blame her for not coming back to see him. I feel guilty sometimes about not going to see Chris more, but no amount of me being there is going to bring him back."

Intertwining her fingers over her lap, Barb sat back on the couch, a poor substitute for the therapist Meg probably needed.

The teacup clattered against the saucer as Meg stood up suddenly, breaking the tension in the room.

"It's just all been hitting me hard lately. Memories, and regrets, you know?"

Barb stood to meet her, wrapping her hands around the cup as Meg's hands shook harder. "Do you mind if I use your washroom? Clean myself up a bit? Then I'll get going, okay? I'm so, so sorry for all of this. I shouldn't be dumping all of this on you."

Meg's face was blotchy and flushed, embarrassment and shame leaving a crimson trail up her chest and neck to her cheeks. The bathroom door shut quietly behind her, and Barb tried to process everything she just learned.

Those first days without Gavin, Barb was the same. Figuring out how to even process the loss was something her brain couldn't compute; it was such an unfathomable task. What she wouldn't give to see Gavin just one more time. A spike of resentment hit Barb's heart, and she shook it away.

Enough.

Barb thought back to the day Sherry came knocking at her

door, willing to talk. Until that moment, she didn't understand how badly she needed someone to listen.

Meg returned to the living room, her face raw where she must have wiped it on one of Barb's nubby old washcloths. Moving into the foyer, Barb stood awkwardly in the foyer while Meg put her shoes on.

Barb embraced Meg. She was surprised, stiff at first, then formed herself to Barb, melting into her arms like her life depended on it.

Maybe it does.

"People make mistakes," Barb said into Meg's shoulder. "They're not perfect. It's why we love them or hate them. Even both sometimes. Just remember you don't owe her your forgiveness, Meg. You don't owe anyone that."

The slight dip of Meg's chin told Barb she heard it, but it didn't mean she was ready to accept it. The honeymoon-funeral phase didn't allow her to admit Nat's flaws without guilt. Those rose-coloured glasses in the months after a loss were something else.

No one wants to speak ill of the dead, Barb thought as she let go of Meg.

Meg put her hand on the doorknob, opening it a crack. Light from the dim bulb on the porch seeped into the darkening foyer.

"Hey, Meg?"

"Yeah?"

"You live in town?"

"Yes. I do," Meg replied. "Not far from here, actually."

Barb smiled, small but genuine. "Come and visit, okay? Really."

Meg smiled back. "Okay."

Barb didn't know her well enough to tell if she meant it, but she hoped she did.

"Hey, when I said you don't have to forgive her?"

With shoulders stiff again, Meg remained facing the door. *Go on.*

"You don't, but you have to let her go eventually."

Meg smiled again, sadly this time, shooting Barb a knowing look.

"That's good advice, you know?"

Barb's eyes brimmed. "I do."

There was nothing more to say, and they could both feel it. As Meg opened the door and stepped out, Barb was surprised to hear her voice from the porch once again.

"Oh! The box is still out here. I can help bring it in, it's pretty hea..."

Barb came up behind her as she trailed off.

"It's fine, Meg. I can handle them."

Meg swivelled. "How did you...?"

"What?" Barb asked, looking down at the box.

On top of it, a black square paperback sat slightly off-kilter. A library barcode stood out starkly against the dark cover, greyed slightly with age.

"I've never seen that before. I don't think it was Gavin's."

"I know," Meg said, staring toward the house at the end of the road as if she were searching for someone.

Clutching the book to her chest, she ran to her car, staring into the rearview mirror as she whipped her seatbelt over her shoulder.

"It's mine."

"Meg, what...?" Before she could finish, Meg was already peeling out, accelerating quickly, leaving Barb to stare at the darkened windows down the street and wonder what it was she hoped to see.

76

As Meg drove off, vibrating with excitement, she thought back to that day at the library. That book was a sign; she knew it. It was enough to make her believe there was something else out there, another side to things. She learned to listen that day.

If Nat was going to reach her with anything, it was going to be the book. Meg changed the second she touched it; it made her who she is today, helped her deal. To Nat, it was Meg rubbing Chris' absence in her face.

Meg's parents worried when she started switching some of her courses from the sciences to history, literature, and the occult. They were puzzled, but she was an excellent student, so they entertained it.

After all, she was still getting an education, wasn't doing drugs, and came home to visit. In the absence of any massive changes in attitude or behaviour, they let it go, chalking it up to expanding horizons in her college years rather than a breakdown of some sort.

After a couple of years, the book was dog-eared. Meg was convinced Chris led her to it to show her something, convinced he was trying to talk to her, to give her a sign that he was okay.

Over and over, they had the argument. Meg tried to explain herself, and Nat snapped at her. Meg sighed for what felt like the thousandth time.

"Look, I can't explain it. It just fell into my lap. Literally."

"So you think what?" Nat laughed, a bitterness to it that developed with her newfound anger. "That Chris' aura reached out to start a book club?"

Meg sighed. "Just forget it, okay?"

Carrying it with her wherever she went, it was a reminder nothing was final, that it was never too late.

She never told Nat she noticed the book was gone when she got home, that she left it there like someone sadly clinging to the hope of a second date. She hoped Nat would call her to come get it and they could talk.

But the call never came, and she didn't see the book again until the day Nat invited her over. It was a gracious gesture for Nat to return it, but in truth, Meg got what she needed from the book a long time ago. It gave her closure, and it opened her up to possibilities beyond what she could see.

Idling at a red light, she rested her hands on the wheel. The tiny red eye glared at her from the cupholder, and she pulled out the mood ring once again, placing it on her finger.

"If you wanted to get my attention, Nat," she whispered, looking down the street, "you have it."

THE DESIRE TO KNOW MORE, TO UNDERSTAND, WAS in direct conflict with the tiny voice she always, *always* listened to. After many close calls over the years, she swore she would never be that person, the one people shook their heads about, murmuring, "She was such a smart girl." After her interaction with Darryl that afternoon, she had no desire to go back.

"Goddammit," she muttered, turning the car around to swing down the block and around the back, where Darryl mentioned parking to avoid the reporters. The street was eerily empty, with no cars in sight.

No Darryl, no problem, she reasoned, pulling the car back down the alley and in front of a neighbour's house. If something happened, she needed her car to be close, and hopefully he wouldn't notice it there. The voice screamed back that she was being stupid, reckless.

Listen, listen, listen, listen, LISTEN!

The plea rang through her entire body, throbbing in time with her heart.

Poking her head out from the end of the alleyway, the setting sun illuminated the empty driveway. The windows were still dark, no light coming through Darryl's entrance to the basement at the side of the house. Hopping up with steps, she felt oddly exposed. A quick, nervous rap with her knuckles on the front door echoed inside.

"Hello?"

The lights remained off, and no footsteps came clunking up the stairs. Digging in the mailbox, she found the key Darryl promised to leave for them the next day.

The sun was going down behind her, the light low but the room still visible as she poked her head inside.

"Hello?" she tried again, louder this time.

The door shut quietly behind her, and she moved slowly, footsteps soundless on the rug. The shelves were ransacked, Nat's belongings flung everywhere.

Heart pounding, Meg felt a flurry of excitement. She was here; she had to be.

What is it, Nat?

The adjoining door slammed shut, and she jumped. A shadow stood in the kitchen doorway, the silhouette crouching to fill the space in the doorway, long arms tapering down to claws that would finish her in just one swipe, watching her with the satisfaction of a predator that had cornered its prey.

"What are you?" she whispered, unsure why she expected the animal to answer.

It was something straight out of Nat's favourite movies, every horrifying element combined into one beast. It didn't answer. The shadow shrunk until it was the same frail frame she saw earlier. Darryl held himself weakly against the countertop, leaning heavily on his wrist.

"I'm sorry," she stammered. "I didn't think anyone was home."

A heavy paperweight sat on the shelf behind her. Bending her knees slightly, she picked it up and held it at her back. The smooth glass cool against her palm.

"I forgot something. I thought you were gone, so I let myself in. Hope you don't mind. I'll be going now."

He closed the gap between them in the darkening room, strategically placing himself so she would have a hard time beating him to either entrance. The voice inside that was screaming before became a roar in her blood.

"What did you forget?" Eyes gleaming, it wasn't really a question; he was daring her to answer. He knew she wasn't here for a memento.

Keep him talking.

"What are you doing back? I thought you weren't feeling well, that maybe you'd gone home."

Licking his flaking lips, he grinned at her, possibly the most menacing thing she had ever seen. "I AM home."

"Home? You mean you're moving back in?"

He nodded, irritated.

"Won't it be weird living here? After so much..." *Death.* "...history."

He snorted.

"Why should it be? It's perfectly natural. Besides," he said in a conspiratorial whisper, licking his dry lips. "I couldn't leave. So much of my...history is here."

The paperweight shifted slightly in her clammy hand behind her back. He was trying to be charming, reassuring, but his smile slipped a millimetre at a time as he looked behind her out the front window. Following his gaze, she saw nothing.

"Natural? Death might be sure, but not what happened to them here." The twin swords of anger and sorrow pierced her sharply. "I'd hardly call that natural."

He sighed again, his impatience becoming clearer with every passing minute.

"I'm sorry," she said.

Sweat was seeping through the gray collar of his t-shirt, his chest moving up and down rapidly with each heavy breath. He moved toward her, and she took a step back.

"I didn't mean anything by it."

She watched him, looking for any changes in behaviour like she saw earlier. Tears welled over her eyelashes, threatening to spill over. He seemed to soften, taking it as weakness. He sagged slightly, something falling delicately from his shirt pocket to the floor.

Is he buying it?

He relaxed, seeing her back where she belonged. Emotional. Malleable.

Hysterical.

A pungent scent wafted toward her as he drew even closer, and she wrinkled her nose. It wasn't the sweaty scent of body odour, someone who spent a day hauling boxes in a freshly scrubbed house.

The sickly-sweet smell emanating from the emaciated man in front of her belonged in a graveyard.

77

THE SIDEWALK BURNED, STINGING NAT'S LEGS AS she slid across it. She slapped her hands on her jeans as she stood, flecks of dust dancing away from the rough denim.

This was *real*. Not like she imagined it, projected it, wished it, but how it *was*.

Turning to orient herself, she wasn't surprised to see her house at the end of the street, the setting sun gleaming off the front windows.

If she never saw this house again, it would be too soon.

Voices increased in volume inside, and she moved toward it, curious and more than a little excited as she peeked inside.

Meg.

Her excitement was short-lived, her mouth falling open in fear as she saw who Meg was talking to. At first, she didn't recognize him.

Her skin crawled as she recalled hoping to rent this place, something feeling right in a way she couldn't explain, as if she was drawn here by fate.

Darryl answered the door, almost before she could knock. He was tall and had a stature screaming that he was a jock in high school. The blue golf shirt completed the look. This was a man used to getting what he wanted.

Still, she couldn't shake the feeling that this was it, where she was supposed to be. By the time he uttered the words "pet friendly," it was a lock.

Then he told her how much it cost, and her heart sank. The neighbourhood was awful, with tons of 'For Sale' signs up in the yards. The optimistic side of her brain whirred at calculating ways she could make it work, even as the realist in her screamed there was no way it was going to happen on her single income.

He rubbed his smooth-shaven cheeks thoughtfully, his salesman's mouth opening wide to expose smooth white teeth. Inside the friendly crinkles of skin around his eyes, the blue irises were marbles, deep but expressionless.

"Look, our mom passed away, and we really just want to get this over with. How about we knock it down a bit?"

She'd fallen for his snake oil, hook, line and sinker.

No sign of his former charm existed now. Meg looked the same, but Darryl was practically a mummy. She took in his hollow cheeks, those flinty blue eyes beady and calculating in their sunken cavities. His body was worn and withered, and he stood bowed and sweating as if he were in terrible pain. Skin stretched over his bones as if they were independent from each other, sagging with hardly any muscle to support, his joints pointed and knobby.

The monster's features became his own as it took the wheel, teeth protruding, muscles flexing and shrinking. Darryl's face was frozen in agonized ecstasy, his smile genuine despite the enormous pain he must be in.

He wants this, she thought, shivering in disgust. She recalled being pushed deeper inside herself while it took what it wanted, and she wanted to vomit.

Darryl's true face under his unnaturally serene expression

was that of a corpse. His skin was dry and wan. A tiny fleck shone out below his forehead, and she realized with horror that it was what was left of his one remaining eye. The skin on his arms was all but gone, strips of it missing where it had peeled away. What was left was flaking off, dry dandruff hailing all over the ground as he chatted with Meg.

Catching her face in the window, it was distracted from Meg for a moment. The skeleton seemed to leer a bit less, awareness settling in as its bones jangled, eager with the opportunity to make her watch.

This was the last stop. The future was now the present, and it couldn't know what lay ahead.

Darryl was glowering at Meg, ready to pounce. Nat saw Meg's cautious stance, recognizing that predatory look that women for centuries learned to avoid, the one that said the damage would be irreparable. The face underneath though, the one pulling the strings, only had eyes for Nat.

Exhaustion weighed down on her, and she fought the desire to sit down. *What is happening to me?*

"Nat?" A small voice quavered behind her.

Gavin stood behind her, disoriented, looking about ready to faint.

"Nat?" he looked surprised, as if he didn't remember where the name came from, like it slipped from his mouth without him saying it.

There was something on his face. She was tempted to reach for it, brush it away, until she realized it was a flap of dead skin. As she watched, it flopped downward, exposing the inside of his cheek before it shrivelled and fell to the ground heavily, like a piece of overripe fruit. She glanced down at her own skin and saw it pinching as it dehydrated, turning first blue and then an array of colours she didn't know was possible. A fingernail fell off, a sight that should alarm her, but didn't.

"Run," she pointed down the street, to Barb's.

She felt herself rotting away, but she knew that wasn't the worst of it. Pieces were disappearing, bit by bit. The feeling wasn't physical, but something deeper, like she was being drained of what made her Nat. The look was in his eyes, too. She already forgotten his name, but she hoped he would think of home, that he could make peace with whatever he needed to while he still could.

We aren't supposed to be here.

Walking backward, his lips moved, and she strained to hear. He still seemed hurt. She didn't blame him. She couldn't ever make it right, but revenge wouldn't change anything. Stopping in front of his house, he smiled. Something was coming; she sensed it.

Thank you.

The world shook.

She turned her attention back to Meg, inside. The demon circled Meg, trying to move her toward the hallway, away from the front door. Darryl with that grin, the monster with its fangs—they maneuvered Meg's feet with the confidence of a ballroom dancer leading a partner.

Part of it looked morbidly curious, like it wondered what Nat was going to do.

Good question.

She didn't know, but she was always taught to be polite, so she did the polite thing.

She knocked on the door.

78

A KNOCK INTERRUPTED THEIR STALEMATE, diffusing the tension. As Darryl turned away from her to look at the door, she bent to scoop up what he lost, tucking its prickly length into her palm.

"Can I use your washroom?"

The tension in the room thickened, and she found it difficult to regulate her breathing as her heart raced. Deciding the deal with whoever was at the door, he waved her back, his aggravation growing more palpable every minute.

Head high, she walked down the hall, willing herself not to look back, not to give herself away. The item she picked up from the new, stiff rug was clutched tightly in her palm, nails digging into her sweaty palms.

She ducked into the bedroom on the right, slamming the door behind her. The cheap lock was just enough to provide the illusion of privacy, but she knew it wouldn't hold forever. She ran toward the French doors, only to find them jammed shut, a rake looped through the handles on the outside.

"Help!" she cried, hoping to catch the attention of a passerby or whoever had knocked at the door.

She opened her shaking hand to reveal the friendship bracelet resting there, a devious twin to the ones she and Nat made for each other. The consistency of the thread length was off, and it poked outward sharply in places.

The bracelet was made entirely of layer upon layer of hair.

She recalled her hair scattered across the bedspread after she fell asleep in Nat's bedroom, outraged at the violation, the bastardization of this symbol of their friendship.

Screaming, she slammed the paperweight against the glass panels of the patio door. The glass shattered, and she wrapped her sweatshirt around her wrist to reach for the rake. The panels were tiny, the door suddenly resembling a prison cell. She couldn't get her hand through far enough to get the leverage she needed to pull it out.

Loud bangs shook the flimsy door just below its hinges, as if he was kicking it. The room was mostly storage, with a ledge around the room containing paperback copies of Nat's guilty pleasures, her TV tie-ins.

She opened the small closet, rifling through piles of craft supplies, her hand coming to rest on a large plastic bin labelled *Sewing*.

Behind her, he roared as he pounded on the door. A sickening crunch filled the room—the sound of the cheap material, hollow inside, giving way.

79

Darryl poked his head out the door.

"What?!"

Furious at the interruption, his features exploded with rage at seeing no one there.

She slipped in behind him as he slammed the door. He staggered slightly, raising his hand to his temple as if overcome by dizziness. The beast inside was showing intermittently, Darryl's forehead bulging as it struggled to keep itself inside, to stay nice and safe and warm as long as it could.

Now that she and Gavin were expelled, it was weak; the energy they had provided quickly depleted. Its strength peaked when it savoured them together, the steak dinner it was waiting for after surviving on the appetizers all this time. It needed a new host, a new perfect pairing for the menu.

Killer and killed, the perfect complement.

Darryl's living flesh rippled, trying to abandon ship as the monster jittered inside. His elbows elongated, arms nearly to the floor one moment, then limply at his side the next. His eyes were dull and glassy, blue competing with yellow, changing so quickly they were becoming an emerald green. The body couldn't decide which side it was on.

The parasite's dry tongue lolled from his mouth, moving over his cheeks and up through his sweaty hairline, seeking the tiniest drop to refresh it.

If it got that thirst quencher, there would be no stopping it. There was only one living target in the Darryl-thing's way, and there was no way she was going to let it happen.

The door down the hallway slammed shut, and he flew toward it in a rage.

"Let me *in*!" he shouted, kicking furiously at the door.

She grabbed Darryl's arms from behind, slipping as the flesh of his body melded into the slimy skin of the demon raging inside him. Darryl's eyes were full of confused betrayal.

This thing was his forever match, his long-term plan. It had made all his dreams come true. Now, midnight arrived, and it was all about to come crashing down, the coach about to turn back into an ordinary pumpkin.

It sustained itself until she found it again, drawn to the piece of her soul she thought was forever lost. It knew she would come back for it.

Unable to hold on to the oily arm, she stumbled backward, the heavy thud of her body reverberating through the hallway.

Darryl turned, wild, searching the floor but unable to find her. His face morphed into the beast again, and she froze as the monster sniffed the air, trying to pinpoint her.

She hoped she was buried in the now overwhelming stench that was Darryl's decaying body, but after a moment, it stretched Darryl's mouth into a grin.

It stepped down onto her stomach as she tried to roll over. The wind was knocked out of her with a grunt, her ribs creaking against the weight.

Its talons appeared, pushing out of Darryl's socks. The

largest one pierced her torso above her belly button. The pain burned through her, firing all of her synapses at once, and she screeched as she pushed up feebly against the leg holding her there, as immovable as a tree trunk. She tipped her chin down to survey the damage. Without a living heart to pump it out of the wound, there was less blood than she expected.

"Did you think," it hissed at her, *"that you would get out of this?"*

Not a question. A statement.

Writhing underneath the ball of its foot only ripped the hole in her flesh wider and deeper. Dark blood oozed from Darryl's stomach, a tear appearing across it as it crowed in delight at the sweet revenge of inflicted pain.

"How do you like it?" Darryl's clenched teeth barely let the seething words escape, and he rested his hands on her throat, the look in his eyes telling her he hoped he would be able to end her today.

The claw wormed its way completely through her. It leaned forward, further crushing her. The wooden floor ground against her shoulder blades as she arched her back in agony. The talon continued through her insides, a screw anchoring her to the floor.

What was left of Darryl was coming in and out of focus more frequently, features constantly flickering as if both of them were disappearing. It was enraged, but weakening as she watched.

All I have to do is buy some time. Forcing her shrivelling lips into a smile, she laughed.

"Optimism," it sneered. *"I like it. It's what made me pick you. Breaking someone who thinks they can get through anything is my favourite game."*

Exhausted and sweaty underneath its immense weight, she let her head fall backward.

"The worst is yet to come," it sneered, drool inching through its gaping lips toward her face.

The spittle sizzled as it hit her sinking cheeks, and she lifted her chin, pinching her lips together to avoid it getting in her withering eyes, her mouth.

The smell of Darryl's decaying teeth intermingling with the steam emanating from its mouth flooded her senses as it drew closer.

"Your ride isn't looking so good," she said.

Darryl's eyes flickered darkly, the prospect of the beast leaving him clearly a touchy subject.

"You should consider it a compliment I even wanted you. If you'd just let it happen, we wouldn't be in this mess."

The impaling claw twitched inside her belly, and the memory struck as cleanly as if it hit a confident middle C on a piano, erasing everything in its intensity, eliminating time itself. It could have been a second, or an hour, or forever.

Body coated in a slick sweat, she was shaking in the A/C as she waited for her brother. A projection of Chris was in her head, of what it would do to him, every inch of him torn and tattered until he was only an empty glove tossed bonelessly into the parking lot.

"I wanted him at first, but then I felt you....your feelings. How you held them to yourself, how you were a pretender, just like me."

Nat laughed, a rueful chuckle. "How's that choice working out for you?"

Its weight struck that painful chord again, bringing her back to the front seat of the car.

Don't take him, she cried in her head. *I'll do anything.*

"Hey," Chris said, hopping in the passenger side, leaning over to hand her some more water. The cold liquid slid down her throat but offered no relief. "You okay?"

Smiling, it hissed.

"Yeah," she forced the corners of her mouth up, wavering on the edge of hysteria. "Fine."

"You sure?" he asked skeptically. "You good to drive?"

"Yeah, of course," she said, turning the key and backing out of the parking lot.

As the car gained speed, the blast of air against her sweaty forehead brought her back to herself, and she concentrated on keeping them on the road. Chris warbled along to a song on the radio, turning up the volume. Nat bobbed her head in time to the music out of habit, but it found the chorus absolutely insipid. The pressure on the back of her neck built. *Be good.*

She turned to her brother, an enormous feat of will, and told him the only thing that she could muster. The only thing that mattered.

"Love you, idiot." Sweat poured off of her.

Chris elbowed her.

"What's your problem?" he grinned, but it was too late.

It was on her, *in* her, and then it *was* her.

The universe selected the first victim for its new body. As hard as she tried, she could do nothing but let the feel of the soul guide its new hands on the steering wheel, pulled by Gavin's energy.

Two peas, it said, laughing. *One afraid of being abandoned, the other afraid of being loved.*

It was wondering who it would be, what they would be like. Her soul would be drawn to others like those she cared about.

The thought made her sick, but she couldn't move, couldn't do anything to relieve herself of the sensation. Claustrophobia set in as she was pulled deeper, choking on her own screams.

"I know a shortcut," it made Nat's mouth say as it sped along the road. "We'll be home in no time."

A moment later, Chris' body leaned back, going stiff as he faced the road, his mouth forming words she couldn't hear but didn't need to.

It forced her foot down on the gas, and then everything went black.

"That word..." It observed from the future, overtop of the scene like the narrator in a movie. "*Anything*. A world full of promises. *Anything* was endless possibilities."

The image snapped away, and she flinched as its hot breath caressed her face once more.

"*But you lied.*" It was comical how forsaken this thing felt, how it whined as if she had broken a contract. "*I was so looking forward to the journey with you, but you ruined it.*"

"Well, you killed me, so I guess that one's on you," she panted, her voice barely a balloon leaking air as she struggled to gather enough oxygen to speak.

"*All I did was eat you,*" it shrugged. "*The skin sack was the one that killed you.*"

Potato potahto.

Darryl peered out, his eyes within its enormous face stung by the slight.

"*And now here you are, all that struggle for nothing. I hope you enjoy rotting for eternity, Nat. Stuck among all the people you once knew, unable to touch or feel, unable to remember yourself. You'll be gone, never fully finding who you are again. It was me you were running from when you left. All of that guilt and pain and self-loathing fed into that tiny little scrap that I kept. You could still be enjoying the ride, but you made your choice. I'll get a new snack, find a new special someone. You are going to wish that you had stayed inside me, safe and warm.*"

The time between flickers was shortening. Darryl's wild, blood-filled grin and sunken eyes appeared and disappeared, fingers on her throat one moment, claws the next.

"*A little illusion, Nat. Safety. Security. Relive your greatest hits, your favourite places. Never have to live with consequences, with regret. No decisions to be made. Just...more."*

Raising its head above her, it stretched its neck, a peacock so proud of the home it had made for her and Gavin. Another flash of pain ran through her, her bones beginning to shrink in her skin. Darryl's paper-thin flesh fell away under her grip, squishing through her fingers.

"Life is what you make it, Nat. Just like the death that I offered you." The utter disappointment in its eyes cut through her.

"A painless life for a bit of food? Living what feels like years however you want? You could have had whatever your heart desired, but look at you now." It cackled, but there was something almost sad in the way it held her down, disappointment flaring in each syllable as it spoke.

"You're joining the ones I spit out, doomed to wander and wander and wander, losing yourself until you writhe in agony and confusion. The last of what makes you you now belongs to me. You were elite, prized. Look at you now. Just so much rotting meat I'm going to throw in the trash." It chuckled, its hybrid face blurring as her vision swam.

"All because you couldn't just stay still."

She held her breath against the chokehold, not giving it any satisfaction.

"When then you showed up on my doorstep, asking to rent a room, Darryl felt my excitement. He was ready to help however I needed." An imitation of a whistle came struggling up Darryl's dry throat. *"There was a...creative streak in him I didn't expect. He was a pleasant surprise. It worked well until the little shit got greedy, refused to sacrifice himself for the greater good."*

A lock clicked, the door squeaking gently on its hinges as it swung open.

"Lucky me, I guess."

"Oh no. Not luck. Tell me. How many other places did you look at before you came to settle on this one?"

She was silent. It already knew the answer.

"There's a tiny piece of you at my center. You dictate what I've become. Over the years, your guilt, your fear, your regret, all of it has fuelled me, forming the little world inside. Why do you think failure to comply results in the damage you've seen? Why my guests need to keep their feelings to themselves?"

She ground her teeth together, not sure what it wanted her to say.

"Your... mismanagement of your feelings turned into such a beautiful way to keep people in check. Gavin picked up on that quickly." It leered at her.

"You've always fought against your desire to return home, and you know it. You were drawn here by the need to be whole again, to reclaim the piece of your soul that was missing, that I kept. No matter how broken you left it, how you allowed yourself to taint it, it was always calling out to be found. Eventually, you were going to return to do what you were told."

It leaned closer. *"You're here because I willed it."*

A hesitant step travelled through the floor, vibrating toward them. She lifted her chin, looking for any sign that it had noticed, but it was too wrapped up in its captured prey.

Darryl's face came forward for a moment, leering on top of her.

"So, be a good girl and hold still."

The monster returned. Although it seemed dissatisfied that she didn't make the sounds of fear it hoped for, she was surprised to see it seemed flat out disgusted with Darryl.

"Just. Stop. Squirming."

It said it as if she barely amounted to a fish flopping on a line.

"Do you know I didn't finish your brother off so he could be leverage if the time came? You are both useless to me now. This is

pure enjoyment. When I take your friend and make her my new host, you will watch and you will scream. And you and the brat will rot for eternity."

A second shadow filled the hallway, and she grinned up at its grotesque face, waiting for her moment. Its eyes flickered again, reptilian in what remained of Darryl's human face.

"What?"

"You can't have Meg. Just like you couldn't have Chris," she spat. "But you can keep choking on this asshole all you want."

Darryl's face flickered back into view.

Gotcha.

She lifted the flat of her hand and slammed it into Darryl's nose.

"You BITCH!" Darryl cried, rearing back a fist to punch her when a sickening slice sounded through the air.

His mouth opened wide, hands fluttering to the side of his neck.

Gasping like a fish out of water, he turned, hands gingerly touching the pair of scissors protruding from his neck, handles resting above the collarbone.

Meg stood behind him, with shiny, slick blood on her hands.

The thing squealed as it was forced out of Darryl, skittering across the floor. It was no more than a large, slimy cocoon. Something glowed inside of it, and it spat out a dark, cancerous mass.

The steaming ball of tar crawled toward Darryl, slithering hotly against his face. He moaned as it entered his nose and mouth, his soul rejoining his dying body now that the host was no longer needed.

"No," Darryl croaked, barely a whisper around the blades in his throat. "No, please let me stay."

The substance covered his face now, and Darryl choked as

it entered his mouth. Across the floor, Nat watched in horror as the mass transformed.

A slimy substance pumped from its pores to lubricate it. Tiny fingers grew from the cocoon-like body, mini versions of the ones that encircled and scorched her arm.

Knuckles popped into place and the digits stretched, hands growing to their full, terrifying size, followed by arms and spindly elbows. Its face developed in the centre, and the soft belly of the creature cracked open, sharp teeth gnashing as they pushed their way out. The rest of its head pushed forward, a rolling roster of familiar faces rolling across it as it tried desperately to take shape without a host.

Feet burst from under it, and it toppled on its side, kicking and thrashing in agony as they grew beneath it, the bones cracking as they developed and snapped into place.

Meg stood frozen, trapped in the hallway between it and the bathroom. She screamed in disbelief as it struggled to its feet, standing over her. Its feet slipped in its afterbirth and howled, reaching for its sole salvation.

More creaks filled the air, the floor moaning under the additional weight. Silence fell over them as it looked to its feet. As the screeching of the house stretched out, the world slowly closed in on itself.

Meg made a break to pass it and head for the door, but it was too late. The house screamed as the floor buckled under the monster's weight, plunging them down into the darkness of the basement.

80

MEG HIT THE BASEMENT FLOOR WITH A SICKENING crack, hitting her head on a dresser against one wall and gasping as she felt her ankle bend unnaturally underneath her.

The drywall debris from the ceiling rained down on her, shards of cracked wood pelting her hands as she lifted her arms to protect herself. As the dust settled around her, she coughed, trying to clear her head. Her temple throbbed where she connected with the hard corner of the dresser, and she reached up gingerly, wincing as blood smeared her fingertips.

Something hot and slimy dripped onto her hand and she snapped her neck upward, trying to spot where it was coming from.

The gunk from her hand oozed down her arm, squelching as it rolled from her skin onto the floor. Congealed and cold, it crawled away from her, searching for something. She recognized it as the stuff that covered that...*thing* that came out of Darryl.

It made its way through the rubble in the middle of the room. She watched it go, following its trail before looking slowly up at the hole that was once the floor she was standing on.

The multicoloured slime dripped from the ragged edge of the pit. Electrical wires sparked around it, the drips fleeing to reunite themselves with something. There were claw marks on the remaining ceiling over her head where something big scrambled to pull itself up.

"Help!" she yelled, squinting through the gloom, trying to determine if the stairs were still usable.

Several were twisted and caved in. All hope of crawling out left her as she twitched a toe experimentally, pain shooting up her leg to escape her mouth in a gasping scream. Her ankle felt tighter in her shoe with every pulse of blood through her veins.

There was movement to her right, a slight puff of dust rising as something moved.

"H...hello?" A little cat ran through the debris, unbothered, the bell around its neck tinkling as it made its way up the stairs.

A man was making his way across the wreckage, following the cat. Meg felt confident she would be saved, but the moment vanished, and her heart sank as the man walked away, seemingly not noticing her. He moved toward the still intact doorframe, intent on trailing the cat. The last time she saw him was in the middle of the photo array on the news.

He shouldn't be here.

"Darryl?" Brian inquired timidly, looking up toward the demolished kitchen door as he moved through the debris, disappearing before he could move through the doorway.

"HELP!!!" she tried again, louder this time.

Thud.

Her heart raced as she glanced at the ceiling again. Hanging wires swung gently as the lights flickered and popped. Meg heard nothing but her own breath and blood rushing in her ears as she scanned the basement. All she saw were the remnants of Nat's belongings from above, dust still settling, the sound of water splashing down from a burst pipe somewhere above.

Thud.

"Hello?" she said, now a whisper. *Someone must have heard the noise?*

The hope flowed through her for a single glorious moment until something creaked above her, close.

Something fell from the edge of the pit, and landed heavily across her legs. Fiery pain shot from her foot up her leg, her vision whitening as she squeezed her eyes shut to contain the agony flaring up and threatening to escape her in a piercing scream.

Red filled her vision, and she leaned forward to scrabble at the weight, instinctively shoving it over her feet. Bones ground together, shifting as bile bubbled into the back of her throat. When she caught a shaky breath, she opened her eyes again. Darryl's body lay just beyond her feet.

His eyes were open, staring blankly at her. The maliciousness she sensed in him was now exposed, unable to hide. Inspecting his skin more, it seemed *wrong*, sliding to the side to pool into his cheek.

It looked...loose. Stretched out. Like an old shirt.

He coughed, and she shrieked. He blinked slowly, reaching for her, the skin on his arms sagging toward the floor.

"Where is it?" his voice sounded disused, like he had an awful cold.

The scissors remained in his neck, blood bubbling as he breathed, barely trickling out as his heart continued to slow.

She pointed up with one hand, bringing a finger to her lips with the other. He lifted his hands as if in prayer.

"I can do it," he rasped. "I can. Please. Don't leave me."

The floor above groaned, steps approaching the side. The tip of a claw peeked over the rim of the hole.

"Quiet," Meg hissed.

Darryl felt around, his long, skinny fingers searching for something. He grinned as they connected with a metallic strip of T-bar holding the drywall ceiling tiles in place. It bent and snapped, forming a sharp edge. He ripped it from its burial place and pulled himself toward her; the point wielded like a stake.

The walls shook again as it leapt down from the top. Darryl hooted in maniacal glee, this last opportunity to please its master too good to pass up.

"Come on!" he said. "You can watch. I'll make you proud."

Meg didn't shrink away from him. The act of lifting his makeshift weapon weakened him, and his hands flapped uselessly, unable to muster enough energy to drag himself any closer.

As she watched, the monster grew, standing tall, towering over her as it considered them both. A vibrating shriek filled the room, the rubble behind it shaky as the mass of dark ooze amassed itself and slunk toward it. Oozing up its legs, it whimpered as if in pain before making its way back inside its flesh.

Giant feet took a shaky step forward, claws catching in the uneven rubble. The steps were shaky, and Meg saw how weakened it was. What she didn't want to find out was whether it mattered; the sheer size of it could easily overtake her.

She grunted and shoved herself backward until her back hit the wall behind her. More dust snowed down on her, settling lazily as she coughed. The creature ignored her for now, turning all of its attention on Darryl.

"Yes," Darryl whispered, opening his arms as it reached for him with outstretched hands.

His face was filled with relief and gratitude, and for a moment, two halves made whole.

Its expression hardened as it snapped Darryl's neck, tossing the wilted corpse aside like a broken toy it had no more use for.

Darryl's desperate screams echoed long after, permanently imprinted on the foundations of the house. It wasn't a scream of pain or rage.

It was sorrow.

"You want to see, don't you, Meg?"

The voice came from around her and within her, all at once. The back of her neck twitched. Scratching, gummy dirt dampened with sweat gathered under her fingernails.

"You've always wanted to see, haven't you? What could have been. What comes next?"

The weight on her neck pressed harder, and her temptation grew.

"I can show you, Meg. If you just Let. Me. IN!"

Her eyes clouded over as it showed her things. Things that made her feel wonder, curiosity.

Stop.

A voice she recognized cut through it all, grounding her.

"No!"

Her voice was muffled, animalistic cries coming from her mouth as it shoved its way inside, choking her. She felt a lifting of pressure, and it slithered out of her throat, the door slamming shut behind it. Leaning sideways, she vomited as her body rebelled against the slimy stew coating her teeth and tongue.

It growled as it rushed at her again, slipping to its knees as its legs buckled. Meg lifted herself onto her hands, searching for something she could grab to stop it. It came closer and she lifted her arms in a poor attempt at a shield.

As it leapt, she screamed. Breath hot on her arm, it shrieked as she felt the wall at her back reverberate. She waited for the pain, a foregone conclusion.

It never came, and she lowered her arms to find it drooling and panting as it gazed at a point above her head. A metal rod was embedded in the wall above her, coated in the substance, slime and blood mingling and stretching down to coat her hair, steaming in pools around her.

It roared and tried to free itself. Gradually, the visible pulsing beneath its skin stilled, spindly legs kicking slower and slower. Opening its mouth to catch a breath, she heard chaos, screams of excitement, the breaking of a dam.

It glanced over its shoulder one last time, and then its head fell forward. Its face hardened into a grotesque gargoyle, an ancient artifact that didn't belong. Tiny cracks appeared, and a glow came from within. Sparks of all colours burst out, hovering before moving lazily through the air up the ruin of the stairs, searching for something. As each piece of light escaped, it caused chunks of its stone face to chip away and fall to the ground.

As the last of the pieces of stone fell away, a horrible oozy ball emerged, floating in the air, melting slowly. It glowed bright and hot, and a howl wove through the air as its spindly body collapsed in on itself.

Meg shut her eyes as it exploded, the last of the sparks shooting into the air, a final dramatic show.

Exhausted, she fell back, listening to the house settle again. In the silence, something picked its way toward her.

She forced her eyes open and craned her neck, trying to see who stood above her.

"Nat?" she breathed, her friend's face blurry through her plain, but undeniably hers.

Nat locked eyes with Meg and smiled. She placed her hand on Meg's shoulder, and Meg covered it with her own.

Memories entwined and overwhelmed her as they touched, as if they were a living creature. At their first concert, screaming in the crowd, glow stick necklaces bouncing as they jumped. Toes in the sand, overloaded beach bags shoved under their heads as pillows. Passing notes to each other in the halls, several-page diatribes about nothing and everything all at once. Holding each other in a fierce embrace at the police station. Tying on the first friendship bracelets.

Forever, Nat said without moving her mouth.

"Forever," Meg agreed, tears spilling down her face.

A light enveloped them, and Nat gazed off in the distance, lifting her hand to shield her eyes.

RELEASE

81

WHAT THE HELL WAS THAT?! THE CRASH FILLED THE air, consuming the neighbourhood.

Barb grabbed her phone and her first aid kit from under the sink, fully expecting to come out to a pileup on the street. The street was filling up with confused neighbours coming out to see what was going on.

The world is ending. The dial tone shrilled in her ear, and she bit her nails at the hollow sound.

As she watched, the Edwards house seemed to sag, cracked windows shattering and spitting dust onto the street. The neighbours congregated across the street, all of them on their phones, some speaking animatedly to an operator, others filming stoically.

"Oh, my God..." she whispered, spotting Meg's car parked down the street.

Phones were out in force, everyone scrambling to call 911. The tiny office must be flooding with calls, the sound travelling for blocks. She looked at the small crowd, chest tightening as she realized Meg wasn't there.

Walking briskly toward the house, she pushed past a woman who was flagging her down.

"What are you doing? They're on the way."

Barb ignored her, the shrill voice protesting as she continued toward the house, another shouting at the woman to shut the hell up, she was a nurse, goddammit. The murmuring voices faded behind her as someone appeared on the front lawn.

Her eyes brimmed as she took in the boy standing there, wearing a white t-shirt, and missing a shoe. Looking down at his dirty sock against the pavement, he flexed his toes, smiling.

"Gavin?" She didn't trust her voice, but she croaked out his name, her voice catching as it was closely followed with a sob.

Both hands flew to her mouth as he glanced up at her, his eyes just as mischievous as ever.

A pinpoint of light expanded around Gavin, breaking through the shadows cloaking him. He was always here, but now he was finally going home.

"I love you," she whispered.

"Me, too," she heard him say as he knit fully back together, his face flushed and healthy, sweat from a long-ago spring day clinging to his hair. He held up a hand, waving as he walked into the light surrounding him.

"HELP!" The yell pierced the air, muffled and barely audible.

With one last backward glance, Barb rushed into the remains of the house.

"Meg?" she called, running through the crooked doorway, gasping at the level of destruction.

Nat's home was destroyed. Furniture lay on its side, books scattered everywhere. The ceiling fan impaled her TV to the linoleum floor in the kitchen.

"Meg?" she tried again, crawling to the edge of the abyss that was once Nat's home, terrified at what she would see.

82

As Gavin came out on the other side of the light, walking shadows emerged from all directions. The night was clear; the sun long set. Goosebumps arose on his skin, and he wished he was wearing a jacket. He didn't know where he was, only where he was going.

This is it.

He smiled, unburdened for the first time in so long. Now that he said a proper goodbye, it was okay. She would be okay.

As they came out of the glare to join him on his march down the dark street, he saw them for who they were. Eva moved across Nat's lawn, suspicious and uncertain of the surrounding beings, making her way to the door. Tripping over the top step, she fell through it, as if she couldn't control how she moved.

They popped up all over the cul-de-sac, looking as if they weren't sure why they were here. Most were making their way to the house at the end of the road. Some were familiar to him; he remembered seeing on his street throughout the years.

There was Thomas, looking barely in one piece, staring at the skeletal remains of his hand with a new awareness as fresh skin grew to cover it. Ricky followed close behind, scratching absently at his healing eye as he strolled confidently down the street. There was no sign of his stumble, no weaving as he moved.

Gavin stopped at the mouth of the alley where all of this started so long ago. Thomas moved toward the backyard, following the stranded ones reuniting with the last piece of their souls. Gavin lost count as more and more made their way to Nat's backyard.

Patches of colour lit up the sky, a matching glow grew and swelled in his chest. A tiny green speck of light floated toward him, down the alleyway where it all started what felt like forever ago.

He reached out to touch the tiny light, and it played with him, dancing in front of his face before it drifted down, touching his chest. His body was lit from within. The light grew, warming him as the pieces of his soul were reunited.

A red car was there in front of him, with the driver's door open, green fuzzy dice swaying as if someone just stepped out. He got in, pulling the door shut behind him. He sat for a moment, hand on the ignition, hesitating as he glanced around at the neighbourhood he lived in for what felt like centuries.

Above him, a single spark left on its own, moving away from the yard in search of its mate as he turned the key.

<h1 style="text-align:center">83</h1>

Everything swirled, the memories that made up her life painting a stop-motion movie spinning around her. She thought of her school notebooks, the stick figures she drew in the corners hopping dizzily with each flip of the page, fast and fleeting yet so much more intricate than you thought if you only looked at the first page.

The faster it moved, the more she felt herself coming back. Her hand itched, and she raised it to her face, aware of the sensation for the first time in ages, noting how it was blackened in places. She poked one spot experimentally, the skin sinking in and releasing a stench that made her stomach churn. An image came to mind—a moldering sponge on the side of her sink—and she gagged.

Everything stopped spinning, and she was still here.

She was at the end of a cul-de-sac, gazing up at a house. The windows up and down the block were dark, inhabitants sound asleep. A pull of longing for a bed tugged at her, a desire for all the worries to keep her awake. It all seemed so small now, so insignificant.

The street was cast in shadow, but she wasn't alone. She

saw them all, so many of them, in various states of decay and confusion. They walked or crawled across the pavement, clambering for space on the lovely green lawn at the end of the road. Some were barely more than a pile of bones, a shrunken face open in a soundless howl. Others appeared injured, but otherwise intact.

Fresh.

She recognized herself when she peered at them, and the thought terrified her. The corroded bone of her ankle was exposed, scratching along the road as she dragged her leg. The other leg was muscular enough to hold her weight, as long as she crept.

A maggot dripped out of her ear as she rotated her neck experimentally, and she shuddered, but was able to tilt her head again without further incident. She reached up and gently prodded her face, surprised to find one of her cheeks felt firm again. The numbness consuming her was fading, the sensation of her fingertips like a bruise on her own flesh.

A skeletal hand brushed against her leg as another fallen soul crawled its way toward the house. She ignored it and pressed forward, following what seemed like an endless parade of damaged souls flooding through the gate. She stopped in the middle of the yard to take in the surrounding scenery. The others groaned and writhed, many hovering by the patio, snuffling at the plain wood as if they were dogs on a hunt.

She felt the pull again, an urge she couldn't explain or resist. Moving to the large, twisted tree in the corner by the fence, she glanced up into the branches, trying to make sense of what she felt.

Standing here felt like fate but like she was in terrible danger all at the same time. Fate was cruel, she learned, and wasn't surprised at the mixed message.

More memories began flooding her, things that were just outside her reach until now. Sitting down against the rough and sturdy trunk, she drew her knees to her chest, crying out as they flooded her. Everything she remembered about that night pounded into her, snapping her head backward, her twisted spine crunching and grinding as it flexed and rebuilt. For one beautiful moment, she saw it all, knew it all.

She held her head in her hands and rocked. A pus-filled tear trickled down the still-rotting side of her face, and she felt it slither into the closing hole in her cheek and down her throat.

Lying down on the grass, she gazed up at the stars, forcing the fingers on her left hand to straighten to splay her hand across the grass. She knew what was under there, dumped facedown so he wouldn't have to look at her eyes, her skeletal mirror image entwined with the roots as if she died in a lover's embrace. Strength filled her, and she felt more like herself again.

As the last of the memories flowed through her, she remembered someone, the day she died. They tried to help her, whispering in her ear, pushing against her, encouraging her not to give up. On her worst days, she thought back to that moment, convincing herself that none of this was real, that her mind simply fractured in her terror when she saw no one was there in the shed with her.

A guardian angel?

Maybe not, she thought as the crack of the rifle echoed through her mind. Some sort of nightmarish reflex prompted her to finger the slowly closing bloody hole in her chest again, and she felt the exit wound on her back burn in tandem.

As suddenly as she thought of her guardian angel, she was back in the house. It was nothing special, just a plain living room with plain-coloured walls and a plain-coloured carpet. There was a large screen propped up on a low shelving unit on one side, and she suddenly understood it was a television, though it was the thinnest one she ever seen.

Bookcases lined the room, mostly empty. Movie posters she didn't recognize lay sandwiched in heavy-looking frames resting on the floor, propped up against the shelves. A pile of boxes stood nearby, ready to reveal its treasures.

The light was off in the kitchen, but the hallway was brightly lit. There was a dark bathroom at the end, but a warmer, more subdued glow came from the bedroom on the left.

As the minutes ticked by, she felt more and more whole, feeling things inside her moving and clicking into place. She stepped toward the friendly light in the bedroom when a ligament coiled and tightened in her leg. The sensation was sudden and unexpected, and she took a sideways tumble onto the floor like a newborn baby deer.

"Chaos?" came a timid voice from the bedroom. Eva felt bad; she didn't mean to scare anyone.

Eva tried to stand, grabbing for a shelf as she stood up. The books slid sideways as the shelf tipped under the weight of her fingers, coming to rest noisily in a slanted pile. Above her, the bookcase wobbled, dislodging a framed picture of three smiling teenagers. The glass broke and scattered across the floor.

This was all a lot of effort, more than Eva spent in a very long time. She felt herself fading.

A woman came around the corner, with some kind of device in hand. She seemed relieved to see a mess on the ground. Conflicting emotions spread across her face as she glanced at the photo, her eyes hiding nothing when she thought no one was watching.

After the woman finished cleaning up, the sound of the drawer slamming shut on the picture was a gunshot in the quiet night, speaking volumes to Eva.

The woman crawled back into bed, Eva watching curiously as she fell asleep with the light on, splayed out across the sheets. A cat stood against the windowsill, watching the outside world intently. Bright pieces rose from the earth in the backyard like embers from a bonfire, climbing into the night sky to blend with the stars.

Eva moved closer to the foot of the bed, stretching to look outside. Among the souls leaving the yard, there was her killer, wandering, as if he was looking for someone. He leaned against the tree, sobbing.

"Come back," he said. "Where did you go?"

They locked eyes for a moment through the glass, and her features hardened. She gave him the finger.

This journey wasn't for him.

It's not enough, she thought, her anger at what he put her through growing as her little light found her.

In a single moment for what seemed to her to stretch on for eternity, a warmth spread through her. Her fingertips tingled, and she became whole again, healed. She caught her reflection in the glass and almost didn't recognize herself.

Smooth skin, eyes bright and sad peered back at her, and for the first time in her life she thought she was beautiful. She pulled her hair tie out, letting the soft and healthy strands float around her face. She felt as if she just spent fifteen years packing for a trip that finally arrived.

Eva wasn't sure any of this was real until the woman in the bed stirred. Her eyes fluttered open, and she groaned, reaching instinctively for her cat. Catching Eva's reflection in the glass above her, she screamed.

Eva didn't have a clue what she was meant to learn. All she knew in the moment before she faded in a shower of sparks, gently rising to the night sky, was that for better or worse, she was where she was supposed to be.

Following the others, she joined the exodus.

Wherever she was going, the universe could fuck itself.

84

Nat thought a lot over the years about what home meant to her. She decided maybe it meant different things at different times.

Sometimes it was the person she was living with; sometimes it was an aspiration, a place she wanted to be. Other times, like right now, it was where she felt like second chances were really and truly possible.

She closed her eyes and thought of home.

Others joined her, pulled across time, drawn to the one who would set them free. They were gathered together, one place across time to say goodbye.

The house was back how she remembered it, floors intact. She watched herself unpacking boxes, rubbing her arm across her forehead, hair pulled back in a messy ponytail.

Stripping off her sweatshirt, she walked in her sports bra into the bathroom. She splashed water on her face, looking into the glass. A slow smile spread across her tired face, nervous energy radiating off her and filling the house with excitement.

Her warbly voice floated out over the sound of the shower

as she sang her favourite song. Clothing hit the floor in with a disorganized thump, tossed in whatever direction without care. The volume of her voice increased and decreased at strange intervals as she tested the waters, seeing how it would sound to her now that she was the only one to hear. She belted out the chorus, and it unlocked something, a kind of reckless abandon that wasn't like her.

In a day of ups and downs, she found a perfect moment, a moment telling her that no matter how she felt from minute to minute, this move was the right thing.

As her past self serenaded her solitude in the shower, she stepped over to the hall closet. The door was open; sheets, towels and all the other things she couldn't be bothered to fold were shoved in haphazardly.

Putting her hand inside the blanket her grandmother made, she dug around, fingers exploring the soft, open-weaved wool. She felt like ancient paper exposed to air, dry and crumbling.

Moving her fingers deeper, she felt it, the corner of a hard object buried there. Moving her fingers along the smooth wooden frame, she found her grip and pulled it out.

The singing continued from the bathroom, even louder now, more confident in itself.

She traced her fingertip across their smiles before reaching up to the top shelf and propping up the frame.

The time in the picture was over. *Her* time was up. She sensed it.

The spark found her, dabbing her forehead. She felt it slip inside her, growing and spreading, filling her with every feeling she ever had.

Every memory, good and bad, flipped through her, gaining speed and gathering together. It all made her who she was.

She looked down as a small orange cat rubbed against her

legs, its tiny collar jangling. She picked it up and held its purring body to her chest.

As the water fell in the washroom, she let go, destination unknown, the smiling faces of Meg and Chris printed on her eyelids, permanently etching them inside of her.

We were here.

New Beginnings

85

"Meg?"

Nat was gone, and Barb's face came into focus as she peeked cautiously over the rim of the hole.

"Oh, my God! Meg? Can you hear me?"

"Yeah," Meg winced, wiping away her tears. "There's something wrong with my leg. Pretty sure my ankle's broken. I can't move it."

"Hang on, just stay still, okay? We've called for help. I can hear the sirens."

Meg admired his calm, collected tone of someone used to dealing with emergencies, to not giving away how bad it could be.

"What the hell happened?" Barb asked, trying to keep her talking.

Meg shook her head. "Darryl. He tried to kill me."

"Wait, what?"

Meg laughed then, the laughter that couldn't stop once it started. Tears streamed down her face, leaving tracks through the white dust there.

"You didn't hit your head, did you?"

Meg shook her head.

"No. Well, yes," she admitted. "I saw something, Barb. Really."

Barb nodded. "So did I."

Meg glanced up, beaming through the sweat and grime on her face.

The surrounding air changed, that dank, oppressive sensation reminding her so much of a tomb was now gone.

An engine revved outside, breaking through her thoughts. She lifted her hand to shove her hair out of her face and glimpsed the ring on her finger.

The garish red was gone, replaced by a crystalline blue, like the ocean at a tranquil tropical beach. There was a palpable sense of something finished amidst the chaos of the surrounding wreckage.

It was done.

All of it.

"Hey, Meg? Keep talking to me, okay? They're coming in to get you out."

"Can you feel that?" Meg whispered, a smile ghosting the edges of her lips before the throbbing in her leg took her over.

86

The wing was mostly empty, with a receptionist reporting an incident to security and everyone else helping patients with dinner.

Chris' eyes snapped open as a small spark moved into the room and in between his dry lips. As the room filled with light, his eyes changed, now aware and alert. He coughed and tried to swallow, his throat uncomfortably dry.

"Hello?" he rasped, his voice no louder than a deflating balloon but practically a marching band in the room's silence.

A nurse holding his chart walked in, busy making some notes as she moved.

"Hello?" he tried again, a little stronger this time.

She cried out, clutching the clipboard to her chest and running from the room, yelling some words he didn't understand.

Soaked in cooling sweat, he listened to the sound of shoes moving away, some kind of alarm starting. The terrible dream lingered in his mind, and he tried his hardest to hang onto it. The maddening feeling he was supposed to remember something important coursed through his body. He closed his thin, icy fingers into a fist, frustrated.

He thought he remembered her saying goodbye. He wasn't sure, but he thought it was a long time ago. Closing his eyes, he calmed his mind, trying to bring it back into some semblance of order.

Another spark, dark and drooling, followed the first, hovering over his closed eyelids. It moved past his lips and down his weak throat, finding and consuming the other, latching tight to drag him down. This time, he was drowning with nothing but air around him.

It didn't take much to hold him under until he stopped struggling, too weak to fight it. The light dimmed, then disappeared completely inside its dark counterpart as it swallowed what was left of his soul.

By the time the squeaking shoes made their way back to him, it was already too late, and his smile was no longer his own.

***

THE WIND WHIPPED HIS FACE; THE SKY ABOVE HIM was bright and clear. No longer trapped, he laughed with relief, raising his arms to the sky. Arms stretched above his head, bouncing on the balls of his feet as he looked out over the beautiful water.

The path to the road was empty, eerily silent as he made his way down, encountering no one. With no cars, the highway was empty, and no birds flew overhead. The tree line around the highway was hauntingly still; the complete absence of sound in the wilderness unnerving.

It took him hours, but he made it home. His car was in the driveway, but no one was there. The clock in the living room ticked on, echoing through the empty house. Wandering through the house, he touched random surfaces, everything so much cleaner than he remembered. As he was leaving his bedroom, he caught his reflection in the mirror on his wall.

His eyes were the same except for the dark circles under them, but his face was so different. Tiny wrinkles creased his face, his skin pale underneath his freckles. Rubbing his cheeks as if he could wipe off his own features, he wondered when he had gotten old. A sudden memory grasped him, of not getting any air, his lungs burning, skin wrinkling and pruning as if he was in a long bath.

How long was I down there?

"Nat?" he called, increasingly panicked as he roamed the streets, nothing but empty homes, abandoned streets, and dark windows to greet him. "Nat? NAT?"

Chris was alone.

He waited and waited, hoping someone would find him.

And then one day, he found himself back at the cliffs. He was avoiding the place since he died. It was silly, he knew; it's not like a beautiful view was going to kill him.

A woman stood there, her brown hair blowing in the breeze, gravel crunching under her shoes.

"Hello?" he asked, taking a tentative step forward, hissing as her swollen ankle flexed.

She turned toward him, and her eyes grew wide with shock.

"Chris? What are you doing here?"

EPILOGUE
PARASITE

HIS FINGERS FLEXED, THE KNUCKLES CRACKING AS he settled into this new body. Short, choppy breaths smoothed out as it relished the feeling of being behind the wheel once more. This body was weak, easy enough to take over, but it would need to build its strength.

"Chris?"

The parents stood in the doorway, hesitating. It forced a smile.

"Come in," he forced out, his little-used voice barely squeaking out.

"Shhhh," the mother cried. "Don't try to talk. It's okay."

She leaned in to hold the boy tight, and it watched her pounding artery fluttering on her throat. Nothing would give it more pleasure than pulling her close and biting into her flesh, burying his teeth into her neck to taste her. The boy was fading, but still sobbed quietly inside.

Be quiet, it hissed. *Or I'll make you watch.*

What were a few more hours when it lived for years on rats?

"Mom?" it said, making its voice young, boyish, widening its eyes, tears manufactured to manipulate.

It would take practice, of course, but it learned so much during its time with Darryl.

"Oh, honey," she whispered, her tears wetting Chris' already sweat-soaked hair. "It's going to be okay."

Chris' head rested on her shoulder, and she reached up and stroked his hair. It would save up its energy, striking when the moment was right.

It zoned out now and then, thinking of how badly it needed to eat, weighing the benefit of choosing the perfect match over whoever came along. Darryl's downfall was impulsiveness, and impulsiveness was a reaction that was beneath it.

But god, it was starving.

Days passed where no one besides the parents were allowed in, nurses and doctors coming and going in a steady rotation. One was no-nonsense, cold and clinical. It preferred her to the one who was all smiles. It used these hands to kill that nurse, right here, right now, and be sated. If it wasn't careful, Chris would end up in jail, both of them withering into nothing as they starved, unable to stalk at night.

Behave if you want out.

Scavengers were survivors, after all.

"Chris?" the mother worried, touching his shoulder.

It flinched, but these interactions were necessary. He couldn't wait to eat her, and feast on that sniveling husband of hers for dessert. It would be so easy.

Patience is a virtue.

A hesitant knock at the door broke the emotional moment in the room, and she wiped away her tears. "Come in!"

Meg entered, also in a hospital gown, gingerly pulling herself along on crutches. Her skin had the tint of a person too early for the next round of painkillers. It cherished the sight of her pain, of knowing it inflicted it.

The first chance it got, it would do more.

"Meg?" the under-used voice cracked, weak but more confident than before.

Eyes brimming with tears, unaware that her wonder would be her downfall, she nodded.

"I can't believe I'm talking to you right now."

She moved over to the bed, leaning down to hug him. She was shaking as he lifted a hand to her shoulder.

"Can I get you anything?"

He was practicing inside, waiting for the moment he would need to turn on the crocodile tears.

"I'd really like some fresh air," his voice croaked as he looked over at a wheelchair by the door. "If you want to come with me?"

A doctor interrupted. "We should let him rest. But if everything looks good in the morning, I think sitting outside for a short while won't be a problem. With a few precautions, of course."

Patting the front of his lab coat, he frowned, searching for something.

The Parkers nodded, following the doctor into the hallway. Mike tapped Meg's shoulder on his way out of the room.

"Go ahead," he mumbled. "Take a minute. And come back in the morning if you want to spend some time with him outside."

Meg pulled away and sat beside Chris. The indistinct murmurs of his parents talking to the doctor cut short as the door clicked shut. He squeezed her arm.

They hadn't told him about Nat yet. He heard them in the hallway, snippets floating in through the crack in the door.

"...too much right now..."

"...to have him back..."

"...when he can handle it..."

"How do you feel?" Meg asked.

She broke through the strategizing and was looking at him with worry in her eyes.

She would come back in the morning, and it wouldn't be long before it could join these two. It was romantic, really. In the meantime, it needed to conserve its strength, and honesty would be so much less effort.

Patience is a virtue, it repeated to itself, lovingly fingering the pen in its hand.

"Hungry," it replied.

It licked its new lips, watching the soft flesh of her neck as it pulsed and quivered.

Acknowledgments

I couldn't have gotten here without support from so many people.

Colten, thank you for so many things, most of all for giving me the courage to try. Thanks for being able to tell when I needed a break, and when I needed a kick in the butt to get going. I couldn't have written this without your support and encouragement.

Jean, thank you for being my constant cheerleader, scary movie partner, one-line quoter and ride or die. From strutting in the bookstore to long distance TV obsessions to wearing shark outfits in public, twenty years of friendship has gone by too fast. I can't wait to see what the next twenty bring.

Michelle, thank you for years of conversations in the car long after we said the night was over. We have spent more hours than I can count talking over each other and meticulously dissecting world building, story and our favourite doomed characters, which undoubtedly helped me get here.

Thank you to my mom, who always called me weird, but never like it was a bad thing. You've always given me the best advice, and have always been there to listen.

Thank you to my little brother, who grew up but never changed. We don't get to see each other as often as I'd like, but I always know you're there to make a super strong margarita if I ever need it.

Thank you to my dad for my love of movies, even if our tastes aren't always the same.

For all the friends and family I have missed that have cheered me on this journey, you know who you are. I love you all!

Thank you to every horror author who has inspired me over the years, who are too numerous to name. I consider it a privilege to be anywhere even close to your orbit.

This book would not exist without Adam and Ray at Wicked Ink Publishing–thank you for your endless support and for pushing me to look at my work in ways I never had. You've made a lifelong dream come true and I am forever grateful.

And last but not least, thank you, reader, for taking a chance on this first time author.

About the Author

© Morrigan Ellis

Morrigan Ellis is a horror author from Western Canada with a lifelong passion for unsettling tales. Her writing defies genre conventions, blending elements from various subgenres to create innovative and thrilling narratives. Morrigan thrives on the unpredictability of her characters, allowing them to lead her stories to surprising and disturbing places. When not writing, she enjoys reading, discussing horror films, and playing board games. A fan of slasher movies, Morrigan has mastered the art of typing with cats draped across her arms and legs.

instagram.com/morriganellisbooks

threads.com/@morriganellisbooks

x.com/MorriganEllis